**BEN
SHA**

Christy sprinted for the trees off to the right. As their shadows closed around her, she caught a flicker of movement from the corner of her eye. With a hoarse sound she tried to fling herself aside, but it was too late.

A hard hand clamped across Christy's mouth, stifling her scream. A long arm went around her shoulders and jerked her back, holding her with a strength greater than her own. Christy fought anyway, until her feet were kicked out from under her and she went face down to the cold ground. Her captor followed her down, pinning her until she no longer struggled.

The world spun dizzily as her captor turned her onto her back with frightening ease. The man turned Christy's head toward the moonlight.

"Jackpot," he said softly.

His smile was a bleak flash of white against a face hidden by darkness, but Christy recognized the voice.

Aaron Cain.

Also by Ann Maxwell

The Diamond Tiger

Available from
HarperPaperbacks

ATTENTION: ORGANIZATIONS AND CORPORATIONS

Most HarperPaperbacks are available at special quantity discounts for bulk purchases for sales promotions, premiums, or fund-raising. For information, please call or write:
Special Markets Department, HarperCollins Publishers,
10 East 53rd Street, New York, N.Y. 10022.
Telephone: (212) 207-7528. Fax: (212) 207-7222.

the Secret Sisters

Ann Maxwell

HarperPaperbacks
A Division of HarperCollinsPublishers

If you purchased this book without a cover, you should be aware that this book is stolen property. It was reported as "unsold and destroyed" to the publisher and neither the author nor the publisher has received any payment for this "stripped book."

This is a work of fiction. The characters, incidents, and dialogues are products of the author's imagination and are not to be construed as real. Any resemblance to actual events or persons, living or dead, is entirely coincidental.

HarperPaperbacks *A Division of* HarperCollins*Publishers*
10 East 53rd Street, New York, N.Y. 10022

Copyright © 1993 by Two of a Kind, Inc.
All rights reserved. No part of this book may be used or reproduced in any manner whatsoever without written permission of the publisher, except in the case of brief quotations embodied in critical articles and reviews. For information address HarperCollins*Publishers,*
10 East 53rd Street, New York, N.Y. 10022.

Cover illustration by Jim Griffin

First printing: May 1993

Printed in the United States of America

HarperPaperbacks and colophon are trademarks of HarperCollins*Publishers*

❖ 10 9 8 7 6 5 4 3 2 1

1

Call Jo-Jo. Urgent.

The message on the call slip was three days old, just one of many notes that had built up during Christy McKenna's two-week vacation. But reading it made her stomach feel as though the bottom of the world had just fallen out.

Christy hadn't heard from her younger sister in twelve years. It had been bad news then.

Undoubtedly, it would be bad news now.

Even as the thought came, Christy felt the old familiar mixture of love and guilt snake through her. Jo-Jo couldn't help being born with the kind of beauty that literally made people stare. It wasn't Jo-Jo's fault that most people tripped over themselves in their rush to please her. Why should she be blamed for thinking she was the center of the universe?

You like people because of certain things, Christy reminded herself wryly. You love them *despite* certain things.

For better or for worse, Christy loved her beautiful younger sister.

The cool breath of the past chilled Christy's spine as she flipped through more messages. After more than a decade of silence, Jo-Jo had called five times in two weeks.

Christy had never entirely forgiven Jo-Jo for taking whatever caught her eye on her way through life—her sister's clothes, shoes, boyfriends, friends, Grandmother McKenna's gold nugget necklace.

Of all that Jo-Jo had taken, only the necklace still rankled. It was the only piece of the past that Christy wanted.

Jo-Jo had known it. That was why she took it.

Christy knew it too.

So what? she thought. Gramma is dead. I'm in New York. Jo-Jo is wherever Jo-Jo wants to be. I'm doing what I love. Right?

Frowning, Christy looked around her office. The shelves were still crammed with books on art, fashion, philosophy, and human adornment, from Stone Age body painting to Tiffany's most astonishing diamond necklaces. The lone window still needed washing and still had a view of another Manhattan high-rise an arm's length away. The nameplate on the door still said CHRISTA MCKENNA, CONTRIBUTING EDITOR.

Nothing had changed, yet Christy couldn't help

feeling that everything had changed. Maybe it was as simple as wanting a few more weeks of vacation. Maybe it was as complex as the restlessness that had overtaken her in the months since her thirty-second birthday.

And maybe it was the past, wounded but not healed.

Call Jo-Jo.

The past, and the hope that this time would be different. This time the old wounds would be healed because Jo-Jo was finally old enough to understand that other people hurt, other people cried, other people bled. Not just Jo-Jo. Everyone.

Even her sister.

Christy reached across her desk for the newest *Horizon* magazine and flipped to Peter Hutton's standing six-page ad package. The layout had been shot on the deck of a yacht off Martha's Vineyard and featured Hutton's signature model, a internationally famous beauty known to the world by only one name. Jo.

Leggy, blond, innocent and salacious in the same instant, Jo-Jo was dressed in a pastel silk pullover sweater and white silk slacks. The sea wind swept her straight hair to one side, letting her look up from under at the world with her wide green cat's eyes.

Christy stared at the ad as though it might give her a hint as to why Jo-Jo was calling after all these years. Nothing came but the sheer physical presence of the woman herself.

Jo-Jo was a departure from the fence-post standards that often prevail in American modeling. Her waist was as slender as a girl's, but she had a woman's hips and high, full breasts. The weave of the silk sweater was so loose and the yarn so fine that her nipples stood out clearly.

The silk of the slacks was equally thin, almost sheer. A brunette would have had to shave up to her navel to wear those slacks. On Jo-Jo, the clingy material was an "accidental" striptease frozen just before the moment of revelation.

Pure Hutton, pure Jo-Jo. Seemingly casual, sensually challenging, and manipulative as hell. Jo-Jo—and Hutton—skated breathtakingly close to being coarse yet always managed to escape that label. Sheer beauty had a lot to do with it.

"What's the matter?" Christy asked the ad. "Did Hutton finally discover you aren't his alone? Is he going to throw you out on your fantastic tush?"

Urgent.

Christy shivered and set aside the magazine. She could no more ignore her sister's needs now than she had been able to long ago, far away, in another part of the country.

Get it over with. Call and find out what's wrong. Because you know something is.

The call-back number had an area code of 505. Christy pulled out a phone book and flipped to the map in the front.

Colorado.

For a moment she was too surprised to do more

than stare. Jo-Jo had hated the West even more than Christy.

With clipped motions, Christy punched the number into the keypad. Somewhere in Colorado a phone rang. It was answered abruptly, with a single word.

"Yes."

But the clear, sexy alto was all the identification Christy needed. She could send her own ID along the line, too. She knew of no other person on earth who called Jody McKenna Jo-Jo.

"Hi, Jo-Jo. What's wrong?"

There was a starkly drawn breath followed by silence.

"Hold, please."

Jo-Jo's voice was neutral, the tone of someone talking to a phone solicitor.

Christy waited, puzzled and irritated. And guilty.

Where Jo-Jo was concerned, nothing much had changed in the twelve years since the sisters had last spoken. Christy still felt that the breach between them should have been fixed by her. She was the one who understood human nature. She should have been able to teach Jo-Jo more.

Through the phone came the sound of a chair being pushed back, a door closing, and Jo-Jo returning. When she spoke again, her voice was animated, teasing, faintly taunting. It was the old Jo-Jo, to the last full stop.

"Hi, Christmas. Bet my call shocked hell out of you."

Christmas.

Red hair and green eyes. It had been a long time since anyone had called Christy that.

It had been a lifetime.

"You shocked me," Christy agreed. "You were the one who told me never to bother you again. You were the one who never answered my letters. Now you're calling me. So what's wrong?"

"I read your stuff all the time," Jo-Jo said, ignoring the question. "Must be nice to be admired for your mind."

The uneasiness in Christy doubled.

"What's wrong, Jo-Jo?"

"What do you mean?"

"You need something from me or you wouldn't have called."

Jo-Jo's laugh was like her voice, smoky, alluring, subtly mocking. There was a pause followed by the quick intake of breath as Jo-Jo lit up a cigarette. She exhaled softly.

"Christmas?"

Jo-Jo sounded wistful—and something more. Something that made cold fingernails march down Christy's spine.

She leaned back in her chair, trying to relax, trying to tell herself that she hadn't heard a plea in Jo-Jo's husky voice. She hadn't heard loneliness. She certainly hadn't heard fear.

But Christy knew she had.

"I turned thirty this year," Jo-Jo said.

"Consider the alternative," Christy said dryly.

"Besides, most people don't have the consolation of your success at thirty."

"I've only had one success."

Huskiness had given way to bitterness.

"You only need one success if you're Peter Hutton's signature model," Christy said.

There was the quick sound of Jo-Jo taking a drag on a cigarette. The exhalation that followed was like a sigh.

"So tell me," Jo-Jo said. "You're the international style maven. What do you think of the new layout?"

The subtle current of defiance in Jo-Jo's question told Christy that her sister already knew. As a child, Jo-Jo's sporadic efforts to win her older sister's approval had torn out Christy's heart and filled the hole with guilt.

"Jo-Jo," Christy said gently, "if we have different tastes or see the world differently, it doesn't matter. That's what growing up is all about."

"Is it? You were the only person who could hurt me. You still are."

Even as Christy wondered if she were being manipulated, she was touched. Her throat ached around tears that had waited years to be shed.

"What about Gramma?" Christy asked. "Didn't you care about her approval?"

"You were always her pet."

"You were everyone else's."

"I wanted to be hers."

The sound of Jo-Jo drawing in smoke and exhaling

and drawing in more smoke came over the line, defining rather than filling the silence.

"You know why I left home, don't you?" Jo-Jo asked after a moment.

"To hurt Gramma."

"I wanted you to be free to go off to a fancy eastern school and be a big success," Jo-Jo said, "so I split."

Christy winced. She thought she had outgrown feeling guilty over taking the scholarship, her personal ticket out of the rural hell of Wyoming, but she hadn't.

Nor had she ever gone back. Not once.

"I was really proud of you winning that scholarship," Jo-Jo continued. "And what you're doing now, too. You're really tough, you know?"

"I have to be. People wouldn't pay much attention to a pansy writer."

Jo-Jo laughed. The huskiness of her voice was edged with malice and cigarette smoke.

"Peter swears you're the best in the business, even if you've cut him to ribbons a couple of times. Was that because of me?"

The incoming-call light blinked on Christy's phone, distracting her.

"Was what?" Christy asked.

"Would you like Peter's designs better if I wasn't his model?" Jo-Jo asked.

"No."

The intercom buzzed, summoning Christy.

"Hutton doesn't care what I think," Christy said, ignoring the intercom. "He doesn't need me. He's a household name of five continents. So are you."

"I'd rather be twenty-one again."

"Time only runs one way, kid. Where are you?"

"A place called Xanadu."

"Where and what is Xanadu?" Christy asked.

"It's a nifty ranch in southwest Colorado. Peter bought it last year."

"We must have a bad connection," Christy said. "I thought I heard you say 'ranch' and 'nifty' in the same breath."

"The West has changed," Jo-Jo said. "People are much more aware of the primal forces of the land than they were when we were growing up."

Christy grimaced. Jo-Jo's words had the cadence of a publicity release, something memorized and then repeated often enough to remove the natural rhythms.

"You'll see when you get here," Jo-Jo said.

The intercom stopped buzzing.

"What are you talking about?" Christy asked.

"You're coming to Xanadu."

"What?"

"Hasn't your boss told you?" Jo-Jo asked. "I figured it was all set up by now. That's why I tried to get hold of you before you left."

"I left, but not for Colorado. I've spent the last two weeks on vacation."

The intercom buzzed again. Christy wondered if it was her boss, trying to tell her what Jo-Jo already had.

"When you come," Jo-Jo said in a rush, "you might hear some things about me that aren't true."

Christy became very still. Her instincts told her that Jo-Jo was finally getting down to the reason she had called.

"I've made some enemies," Jo-Jo said. "Men. You know . . ."

"No. I thought men were crazy for you."

"Yeah. Well, that can be a problem. Some don't like it when you say yes *or* no. Some get really pissed. Like Cain."

"Who?"

"Aaron Cain. So stay away from Cain when you come here. Do you hear me? He hates me now. He's *not* safe."

"Jo-Jo. You're not making any sense. What's wrong!"

This time there was no question in Christy's voice. It was a flat demand, big sister to little.

"I'll give you Gramma's necklace if you get here in three days," Jo-Jo said. "I need you!"

The line went dead.

For a few instants Christy stared uneasily at the phone, wondering how much of what Jo-Jo had said was truth and how much was lies. As a teenager, Jo-Jo had had a taste for psychodrama and a flair for involving others in her adrenaline head trips.

Yet the undercurrent of fear in her sister's voice had seemed very real.

It couldn't have been, Christy thought. I must be mistaken. It's been twelve years. I don't know her anymore.

Yet even as the thoughts came, Christy knew she

was lying to herself. She had held Jo-Jo through too many long hours while nightmares shook the beautiful golden-haired child. Christy knew what her sister sounded like when she was frightened.

Jo-Jo was afraid now.

2

The buzzer shrilled, dragging Christy back into the world of *Horizon* magazine. She punched in the button and spoke automatically.

"McKenna here."

"About time," said Amy, the editorial secretary. "Myra is on me every three seconds. She wants you in her office."

"Now?" Christy asked. "Technically, I'm still on vacation."

"You should have left word where you'd be while you were gone."

"The point of a vacation is to take time off."

"Tell it to Myra."

Christy hung up and gathered herself for the showdown to come.

Myra was no friend. She represented a certain stratum of Manhattan—smooth and polished as a marble sphere, and just as warm.

The fundamental differences between Christy and Myra were reflected in everything from their politics to their clothes. Myra followed trends. Christy analyzed them. Myra wouldn't wear anything that hadn't been approved by the very fashion world *Horizon* covered. Christy had long since realized that what models wore wasn't necessarily what looked good on her.

The intercom buzzed again, a strident reminder that Myra was waiting.

With a silent curse at office politics, Christy headed for the managing editor's suite. She hesitated outside Myra's door, then opened it and stuck her head in.

"You called?" Christy asked.

Startled, Myra looked up from the stack of color prints on her desk. She scowled and snatched a pair of tortoiseshell glasses from her nose, as though annoyed at having been caught using them.

"I didn't hear your knock," Myra said.

"Sorry. I gave it up after Howard threatened to fire me on grounds of formality."

Myra smiled rather grimly as she straightened her pastel jacket over her dainty print skirt. Both were Peter Hutton designs. She lifted her manicured hand to the single strand of pearls she wore, letting the silence build while she counted the beads of her WASP rosary. Then she glanced at the gleaming brass clock on her desk.

"Were you out on the pistol range playing Annie Oakley again?" Myra asked coolly.

"We can't all be brave and wealthy enough to choke muggers with a rope of pearls."

"Staff is expected to be in the office by nine unless other arrangements have been made in advance," Myra snapped.

Silently Christy prayed for Howard's rapid recovery.

"Of course," Christy said aloud. "I was counting this as a vacation day. I still have more than a month coming to me."

Myra's smile was as cool and perfect as her pearls. "Would you shut the door and sit down, dear?"

Christy shut the door, sat down, and waited.

"Howard died yesterday," Myra said.

Pain twisted through Christy, surprising her with its intensity. Three times in the past twenty months, Howard Kessler had been hospitalized with complications from AIDS. Each time he had recovered and returned to work, thinner and more frail, yet with renewed wit and sharpened sensibility. As a result, the staff had come to believe that Howard would beat the odds and survive until a cure was found.

Christy tried to speak but knew her voice would break. She closed her eyes for a few seconds, fighting for self-control.

"Tomorrow," Myra continued, "I will be named editor in chief."

"Congratulations," Christy managed.

Myra looked at her for a long moment, then nodded.

"Thank you," Myra said calmly. "Although we've had our—ah, differences in the past, I'm certain things will run smoothly in the future."

Christy nodded and said no more. She was still caught in the painful moment of discovering the depth of her feeling for Howard. She had been very different from him, but they had been bound together by a shared fascination with the ways human beings use clothing, jewelry, and objets d'art to express their own unique and individual selves.

"We will be doing things a bit differently now," Myra said. "I'm rethinking your piece on diamonds. I feel it was a bit too gushy when it came to the *nouveau* . . ."

She paused, looking for the right French word.

It didn't come.

Christy didn't offer to fill up the silence.

"Your provincial prejudice against tradition and continental sophistication was just too obvious," Myra said finally.

Christy felt her temper gnawing at her self-control. First Myra quietly gloated over Howard's death, then she attacked a piece of writing that Howard had regarded as one of Christy's best.

"The article was designed to showcase some of the exciting new Pacific Rim jewelry designers," Christy said evenly. "Was I too kind to the new kids, or was I too hard on some of the high-priced hacks who advertise with us?"

"Are you suggesting that an advertiser could pressure me?" Myra demanded.

"They wouldn't have to. As Howard so often pointed out in staff meetings, you have a gift for celebrating the costly mundane."

Myra ignored her.

"Your unnecessarily hostile piece on the makers, buyers, and sellers of important jewelry will go on the hook for the time being," Myra said. "I have something much more meaningful for you to work on."

She straightened and folded her small hands on the desk, waiting for a reaction.

Christy did her best not to show what she felt. Most of the anger she felt was at herself. She had been naive. She had assumed that good work and an enviable reputation for intelligence and integrity would assure her editorial freedom.

She had been wrong. Her decade of hard work at *Horizon* was as fragile as a giant, shimmering soap bubble.

And Myra Best was sitting with a needle in her hand.

"Sounds irresistible," Christy said. "What is it?"

"*Horizon* has become too unpredictable, too undisciplined, too tangential," Myra said promptly. "Our readers aren't interested in bizarre little trends and no-name Japanese designers who might or might not be in business tomorrow."

She looked at Christy, who made a noncommittal noise.

"We must pay closer attention to the best-known people in fashion and design," Myra concluded. "Those are the names the public recognizes, because they are the names on the labels the public buys."

"And those are the labels that advertise most heavily in our pages. Friends helping friends," Christy said quietly, remembering Jo-Jo's blunt summary of how business was done.

"Advertiser influence has nothing to do with it," Myra shot back. "If you even hint at such a thing again inside or outside this office, you will be fired. And then you will never work again in fashion in this city."

Christy had no doubt of it. Myra had connections that went back farther than the *Mayflower*. Christy had none. All she had was a flair for style and the discipline to put it to work.

"Do we understand each other?" Myra asked angrily.

"Completely."

There was a taut silence. Then Myra nodded slightly and went back to her carefully prepared presentation.

"*Horizon* is one of the great fashion magazines of the world. Naturally the greatest designers advertise in our pages. Inevitably those same designers will create new styles that will take the international fashion community by storm. Peter Hutton is a case in point."

Myra paused and looked narrowly at Christy.

"You don't approve," Myra said.

"I haven't seen his new designs. How can I approve or disapprove?"

Spots of color appeared on Myra's pale cheeks.

"Christa, why don't you put that shrewd little Irish brain to work on pulling *with* me instead of against me?"

"Scots," Christy said evenly.

"What?"

"I have a shrewd little Scots brain."

"Irrelevant," Myra said impatiently, waving her hand. "My entire point is that *Horizon* must move in a new direction, and I am telling you what that direction will be.

"We will record megatrends, not obscure Japanese or South American metalsmiths. We will showcase the design studios and designers whose work is sold in every world capital and whose fashions are worn on the most exclusive streets in Paris, New York, London, Rome, and even—God forbid— Los Angeles and Tokyo."

Christy had told herself she wouldn't argue, but she found it impossible to hold her tongue.

"Peter Hutton isn't the first name most people would have chosen for a piece on the best of international design," she said calmly. "He's hardly at the top of his game anymore."

"Nonsense."

"Is it? Sales are down in his own stores, retail chains are reluctant to feature his lines, and there have been rumors that—"

"Nonsense," Myra interrupted forcefully. "This industry is always full of groundless rumors. Peter Hutton is the most recognized name in contemporary American fashion. You see his logo everywhere."

"Yes. Everywhere."

Myra frowned delicately, not liking the reminder that a designer couldn't be exclusive and at the same time be sold in shopping malls across America.

"Peter is on the verge of announcing an exciting, entirely new line," Myra said firmly.

Christy made a noncommittal sound.

"I've previewed some of the materials and motifs," Myra said. "I'm convinced this will be his biggest success yet. It will also be a *Horizon* exclusive."

As Christy listened, she felt her whole life slipping out of control. Myra had already decided what *Horizon*'s position on Hutton's new collection would be. She was expecting praise for a designer whose work had become increasingly marginal, mundane, and predictable.

"I know you'll do a wonderful job of capturing the spirit of Peter's bold new venture and delivering its excitement to our readers," Myra concluded.

Her triumphant smile dared Christy to object. Christy wanted to, but the memory of Jo-Jo's plea was too fresh.

Jo-Jo, what have you gotten me into? Christy asked in silent bitterness. I should tell this smug-faced piece of Brie to lie down in traffic on Fifth Avenue.

But I can't. All I can do is pray that I find a new job before she gets around to ruining my old reputation.

Or I could pray that Peter Hutton has rediscovered his original vision.

No, that would be asking too much. A miracle.

"That's an interesting idea," Christy said aloud.

It was her all-purpose response to certain types of modern art and music.

Myra smiled with real relief.

"Thank you for signing on with the new program," she said. "Your reputation within the avant fashion elite will be a boon to *Horizon*."

"And Hutton?" Christy suggested.

Myra frowned. "Amy has your plane reservations on her desk."

"Isn't Hutton showing in Manhattan?"

"No, no. His preview showing will be in the same place where his vision first came. A place called Xanadu. Rather like the Native Americans and their vision quests."

"Did the Indians smoke opium?" Christy asked.

"What?"

"Coleridge did."

Myra gave Christy a blank look and returned to her own agenda.

"I expect you to generate copy and coordinate with photographers for a package that will be due here in Manhattan in thirteen—no, twelve and a half days."

"That's not much time to research a story of this magnitude," Christy said.

"You'll find a research file with your tickets. If you read quickly, you should be fully briefed by the time your plane leaves tomorrow. If not, there's always the plane trip itself. Coach class is so boring.

"Now, if you'll excuse me."

Myra picked up a stack of glossy color photos and began sorting through them.

Christy left the office without a word.

As soon as she closed the door behind her, Christy stood and tried to control the shaking of her hands. After several slow, deep breaths, she headed for her office, mentally revising her résumé and drawing up a list of job prospects.

The list was frighteningly short. Jobs like hers were made by an editor/mentor. Christy no longer had one. It would take time to find a new one.

If she could. People with Howard's rapier mind and unerring taste were rare.

First Jo-Jo and Xanadu, Christy thought. Then a new job.

Christy waited in the airport with her bag at her feet. Every few seconds she glanced at her watch.

"Come on, Nick," she muttered. "If you aren't through customs real soon, we'll barely have time to say hello before I have to run for my own plane."

It wouldn't be the first time. Nick Warren was an international investment banker whose one real passion was making deals. He had spent the past three weeks in London, negotiating yet another addition to his bank account.

A glance at her watch told Christy that there

were eleven minutes to go. The window of opportunity between Nick's arrival and her departure was closing. There wouldn't be time to say hello, much less to talk about something as personal as a secret sister.

The first-class passengers filed slowly in from customs. Nick was among them. Normally a stylish man, at the moment he resembled a street person. His pima cotton shirt was rumpled from neck to tail. His trouser legs looked like a pair of broken accordions.

His face broke into a weary smile as he approached.

"You look as tired as I feel, Christa," he said. "Don't tell me you were awake all night too?"

Christy forced herself to smile. Nick's greeting was so like him, civilized and dispassionate. She gave him a quick, light kiss. Nick brushed a kiss over her forehead in return.

"Hi," she said. "Other than that, how was your trip?"

"Worth every bit of your temper when I missed your vacation," he said with satisfaction.

Christy's smile slipped, but she said nothing about Nick's broken promise to spend a few quiet weeks with her. It had been her hope that the time would lead to a breakthrough in their relationship.

In a way, it had. It just hadn't been in the direction she had hoped.

"I heard about Howard in London," Nick said. "I'm sorry."

"Myra isn't. She's the boss now."

"Too bad. This isn't a good time to be looking

for another job. Everyone is cutting back and playing safe."

"I've noticed. Come on, I'll walk you as far as the security checkpoint."

For the first time Nick saw the carry-on bag at Christy's feet.

"Going somewhere?" he asked.

"New assignment. Colorado."

Nick frowned. "But I haven't seen you for weeks."

Christy managed not to remind Nick that it had been his choice, not hers. She looked at her watch.

"In eleven—no, now it's ten minutes," she said, "I'm off to preview Peter Hutton's new line. With any luck I'll be back in three days."

"More likely three weeks," Nick said irritably.

"Whatever it takes. Just like your job."

Nick sighed. "Oh, well, it's only temporary."

"What?"

"Your job. We both know it will be a race to see whether you quit before Myra fires you."

Christy wanted to argue but knew Nick was right. She picked up her bag and headed for another gate.

"Don't worry," Nick said, catching up. "I've got a better job offer for you. Have you given any thought to what we talked about last month?"

She glanced sideways at him and tried to head off the inevitable.

"Home, hearth, and heathens?" she asked lightly.

Nick looked pained. "I'm serious, Christa."

"If I'm not on that plane Myra *will* fire me. That's as serious as it gets."

"No." There was a hard edge to Nick's voice. "I've been doing a lot of thinking."

Christy kept walking, hoping to avoid the discussion, but Nick persisted.

"I have no wife, no children, no real home," Nick said. "In a week I'll be forty. That's serious, Christa. The rest of it is crap."

"Then why did you fly off to London after promising me—"

"I told you," he interrupted impatiently. "This deal couldn't wait."

"And we could?"

"Bloody hell, are we going around this track again? I make a hundred times as much as you. Quit and we'll spend more time together."

"You're right. Let's not go around this track again."

"I can support you," Nick said tightly. "Hell, I can support twelve like you out of petty cash."

"Well, hurry along, darling. You've got a week to find twelve like me to support. But if they're really like me, they'll support themselves!"

"Oh, shit. You're so damned touchy about your work."

Nick pulled Christy's stiff body closer and kissed her ungiving lips.

"I'm tired and jet-lagged and I want a home to go home to," he said. "Make me a home, Christa."

Guilt snaked through Christy. She liked Nick,

but she no longer believed they had a future together. He just wasn't . . . passionate.

The realization startled her. Nick's cool, unruffled style had been much of his attraction for her. But the weeks alone on Fire Island had given her a lot of time to think.

Nick was the wrong man for her. She was the wrong woman for him.

She stopped and faced him, frustrated that there was never time to do anything properly with Nick.

Even break up.

"I can't pass up this assignment," Christy said. "It involves my sister."

"I didn't know you had one."

His expression was one of mild surprise and total lack of interest.

"I haven't seen her in twelve years," Christy added.

"So what's the rush? A few weeks more won't matter."

"Apparently she's on a tight schedule."

"Another career girl?"

"She's Peter Hutton's signature model."

Nick's jaw literally dropped. "Jo? *The* Jo?"

"Yes."

"Incredible! Fantastic! I can't wait to meet her!"

"Jo-Jo and I haven't spoken since before I left Wyoming for New York."

Nick stared at Christy, but she knew he wasn't really seeing her. He was comparing her to Jo-Jo.

Christy's temper flared. Suddenly she knew why

she had never mentioned her relationship to the sensuous model in the Peter Hutton ads.

"She takes after our mother," Christy said grimly. "I favor the McKenna side of the family."

"Your mother must have been gorgeous."

"She was. Like Jo-Jo, she was a user."

"Jo could use me any time," Nick said, grinning.

Christy looked at her watch.

"What did you do to make Jo angry?" he asked.

"I got a scholarship. When she found out I wasn't going to stay in Wyoming, she seduced her boyfriend's father, got pregnant, and talked him into running off with her. On the way out of town, she stole Gramma's gold necklace. The scandal broke my grandmother's health. She died of a stroke."

"Was the necklace valuable?"

Christy grimaced. Trust Nick to be curious about the money rather than the emotions.

"At most, the necklace was worth a few hundred dollars."

"So how did Jo end up in the big time?"

"I don't know. She refused to talk to me and never answered my letters. All I know is she had an abortion, traded up in men, and was a cover model before she was twenty-one."

"No surprise there. A face and a body like hers come along once in a century. Did you call her while you were on vacation?"

"No. She called me."

"Why?"

"Good question. I don't have an answer yet."

Christy suddenly glanced at her watch.

"I've got to run," she said.

She moved away quickly, joining the flow of hurrying passengers headed for the domestic terminal.

3

"Christa McKenna?" the hotel clerk muttered. "No, there aren't any messages."

"Thank you," Christy said automatically, hanging up the phone.

Well, I made it here in less than three days, but there's no gold necklace waiting for me, she thought. Not even a "Hi, Christmas, got you again, huh?"

Irritated at losing the old game, Christy checked her watch. Too much time.

She wasn't due at Hutton's private prepress showing for several hours. Plenty of time to bathe. Plenty of time to change. Plenty of time to wonder why she was such a sucker for Jo-Jo's games.

Suddenly Christy knew she couldn't bear waiting around the phone like the carrot-topped teenager she'd been, praying for a date. She grabbed her faded black blazer and clattered down the hotel stairs.

When she hit the sidewalk, the sun poured hot and clean through the cloudless sky.

Leaving her rental car in the hotel lot, Christy headed on foot for the art gallery she had seen advertised in the guest literature stacked by the phone in her room. She wondered if the gallery would be as pleasant a surprise as the hotel had been. She had been expecting linoleum floors, knotty pine furniture, and wallpaper covered with fake western brands. What she got was elegant pseudo-Victorian decor.

Halfway to the gallery, Christy realized that Remington itself was rather like an old frame home that was being made over one room at a time into an expensive bed and breakfast. Some of the storefronts were expensively refurbished, with beveled or stained glass insets in the doors and hand-carved wooden trim freshly painted. And some of the stores hadn't been painted for longer than Christy had lived.

The gallery wasn't far away because Remington wasn't a very big place. There was only one stoplight and one paved road. The side streets were dusty, but the merchandise in the Main Street shops was both expensive and unexpectedly cosmopolitan.

Christy stopped in front of a boutique whose windows offered French lingerie, Italian sunglasses, Ecuadoran weaving, and modern Navajo jewelry. The cultural mixture was subtly electrifying, a reminder of how small the world had become.

Maybe Hutton's line will be good after all. The most exciting styles have come from cultural collisions.

The thought loosened some of the tension in Christy. She looked around Remington with renewed interest, measuring both the old and the new. Like the Tru-Value hardware store down the street, most of the people who walked up to the town's sole stoplight were childhood memories come back to life.

There was a woman who moved with the unmistakable sore-footed walk of a tired waitress. Three schoolgirls shrieked and giggled because they were still young enough to believe they wouldn't end up like their mothers. Two working cowboys wore faded jeans, down-at-the-heel boots, and an arrogant tilt to their hats. There was a slight stiffness to their gait and a complete disregard for traffic as they crossed against the light.

There also were several tourists, flatlanders, outsiders who were dressed more like California or New York than Colorado. There were some young men who affected the western look. But their clothes were new and their bodies hadn't been broken by bad horses, worse weather, and rotgut whiskey.

Drugstore cowboys, Christy thought. Imitation may be a high compliment, but it's a sad excuse for individual style.

The vehicles parked diagonally along the street were a mixture of visitors from the outer world and Christy's memories of an insular West. A few exotics such as BMWs, Range Rovers, and Japanese baby pickups were sprinkled among the inevitable full-sized American pickup trucks with gun racks—and often guns—hung across the back window. The local vehicles were dirty and carried the dents and scars of ranch use. The exotics had out-of-state license plates and the sheen of good wax beneath recent road dust.

In front of the Two-Tier West gallery was a vehicle that didn't quite fit in either the exotic or the local category. Intrigued as always by anything different, Christy studied it.

It was a one-ton truck and it was American, but there were four doors instead of two. The truck bed was enclosed, giving it the appearance of an oversized, muscular station wagon with cargo doors instead of a tailgate. *Suburban* was written in chrome letters on the black body.

Oversize tires and high-lift suspension hinted at off-road use. Dings, dents, and parallel horizontal scratches confirmed it. Everything was caked with dirt except the front windshield and side mirrors. They were spotless. The paint beneath the dirt had the gloss of good care. The license plate was local.

Now there's someone who doesn't fit in either tier of the West, old or upscale.

After a second glance, Christy turned her attention toward the gallery. The Two-Tier West had genteel alarm wires around its plate glass windows and a generic cardboard placard announcing that the gallery was open. A bell pealed sweetly at the

top of the door when Christy pulled it open. Two
people were inside. One was an Indian woman
with the broad, serene features and solid build of
an R. C. Gorman model. She dressed the part with
a floor-length dark green velveteen skirt and a
heavy maroon satin blouse. Her smile lit up the
white-walled gallery space like a floodlight.

The man at the counter was no drugstore cowboy. Nor did he look quite like a ranch hand. He
wore a heavy, closely cut beard and a slate-gray
Stetson with a low crown, medium brim, and an
aura of hard use. There were no pheasant feathers,
conchos, or other decorations on the hatband.

The hat was right for a local cowboy, but the
beard wasn't. The shirt was just right, blue chambray with steel snaps instead of buttons, and faded
from long use. A gallery case hid his feet, so
Christy couldn't tell whether he was wearing cowboy boots or something more comfortable.

If the man smiled in return at the Indian clerk, it
didn't show in his profile. Hawk-featured with
hooded eyes, he looked proud and rather grim. He
was somewhere in his thirties, dark-haired, tall,
and long-boned. There was both strength and stillness in him.

"Can I help you?" called the woman to Christy.

"Just browsing," Christy said automatically.

"If you need me, my name is Veronica."

"Thanks."

Veronica turned back to the man who didn't fit.
He was carrying a cardboard carton, which he set
carefully on the counter.

Christy sensed the restrained excitement in the Indian woman and wondered whether the man or the carton was the source. Curious, Christy drifted closer to the two while she catalogued the contents of the gallery with eyes that had seen the best and the worst of many cultures and styles.

" . . . long time," Veronica said.

The man's reply was a low rumble of sound that could have meant anything.

Quite shamelessly, Christy strained to overhear.

"Danner said you weren't coming back ever."

"Danner is a horse's butt."

The man's voice was baritone, clear and faintly drawling. Either a native or someone with a good ear who picked up local accents.

Covertly Christy watched as he handed Veronica an envelope before turning and going back out the front door. He moved with the easy gait of an athlete or a hiker rather than a cowboy. Despite the hat, jeans, and shirt, he was wearing scuffed hiking boots rather than cowboy boots.

Christy watched the man the whole way, conscious of staring but not able to look away. She had seen more handsome men—Nick, for instance—but she had never seen a man who appealed to her senses more. Now she was trying to figure out why.

He went straight to the black Suburban parked out front. The man who didn't fit owned the truck that didn't fit.

A decent contemporary painting on the wall behind the counter caught Christy's eye. The

painting was a stylized neon-blue cowboy against
a glaring crimson and black backdrop that could
have been Times Square or the Las Vegas Strip.
The cowboy radiated a masculine intensity and
lean power than was much older and more endur-
ing than the twentieth-century techniques of the
artist.

Stepping back, Christy studied the painting,
compelled by it in a way she couldn't name.

The front bell rang again, announcing the man's
return. He was carrying another carton. He set it
down on the counter across from Veronica and
went to work on the fastenings. When he pulled
something out of the carton, Veronica set aside
the papers she had been reading and gave a low
whistle.

"Did you take photographs in situ?" Veronica
asked.

"What do you think?"

Veronica laughed. "I think you have a batch of
them."

For a moment there was quiet while they
admired the bowl cupped in the man's long fingers.

Christy watched from the corner of her eyes,
intrigued both by the obvious excitement of the
gallery owner and the way the man was holding
the bowl. She had never seen a man touch anything so carefully, as though it were a butterfly or a
woman's breast rather than pottery.

"Have you shown it to anyone else?" Veronica asked.

"For sale? No. I had Mike over from Mesa Verde
to look at it, though."

"What did he say?" she asked.

"That he wished he'd found it."

The front door opened with another cheerful peal and closed with a bang.

A big, hard-shouldered man in white shirt and light straw stockman's hat strode in. He wore a tooled gun belt with a white-handled revolver in the holster. Silver gleamed in his hair, and a five-pointed silver star glinted on his pearl-buttoned shirt. He was perhaps fifty and physically fit in the manner of a man accustomed to hunting game and riding rough trails on horseback.

Christy had seen smaller bulls.

"Afternoon, Sheriff Danner," Veronica said. "What can I do for you?"

"You can stop buying pots from that Moki-poaching, high-grading son of a bitch."

Christy was close enough to overhear Veronica's unhappy hiss. "Shit."

Danner wasn't.

Nor could the sheriff see the change that went over the man who held the pot. In the space of a breath, he went from relaxation to predatory alertness.

Christy instinctively stepped back.

The only move the man made was to return the pot to its carton with great gentleness. Yet when he turned to face the sheriff, there was nothing gentle about his expression or his stance. His eyes were wolf's eyes, pale amber, unemotional, unflinching, revealing nothing.

"Danner," said the man.

"I want to see papers on those pots," the sheriff said curtly.

"I'm sure you do."

Silence grew until Danner realized that nothing more was going to be said unless he said it.

"Get them."

The man didn't move.

Veronica did. She scooped up the papers she had been reading and handed them across the counter to Danner.

"All in order," she said. "Landowner's notarized signature, in situ photos, USGS map coordinates, the works."

The sheriff scanned the papers so quickly that Christy was certain he either didn't know what he was looking at or didn't care. The way Danner threw the papers back on the counter suggested he didn't give a damn.

"All in order, right?" Veronica said with forced lightness.

"This time," the sheriff retorted.

"Every time," she said, "and you know it as well as I do. Everything in my gallery is aboveboard and top quality."

Danner didn't answer. He had already dismissed Veronica. He was focused on the younger man, who was watching him with cool disdain.

"You disappoint me, boy," Danner said.

The man's smile said he knew he wasn't anybody's boy.

"Because I'm still alive?" the man drawled.

"Because you don't have enough sense to stay out of places you aren't wanted."

"Last time I checked, it was a free country."

"Seems to me," Danner said, "a kid who had a bullet in his lung a few months back would have better sense than to try the high country again."

Christy flinched at the sheriff's casual words: "a bullet in his lung."

She looked at the younger man, seeing for the first time that his clothes were a bit loose, as though he had lost weight recently. Brackets of pain or anger cut into either side of his mouth so deeply that even the thick, closely trimmed beard couldn't conceal them.

"Don't worry about me," the man said. "I'm a survivor."

Danner grimaced. "What do you want here?"

"Same thing I always did. To be left alone like every other law-abiding citizen."

"You better move on, boy. I'm going to ride you like a green pony."

"Why?"

Danner seemed surprised by the cool question.

"We don't take to murderers around here," the sheriff said bluntly.

"Then why aren't you looking for the man who tried to murder me?"

Danner straightened up fully and dropped his hands to his sides. His right hand brushed against the holster as though to reassure himself that the gun was still in place.

"I've only been in office a few months," the

sheriff said. "That's hardly enough time to draw up a list of your enemies, much less talk to them. Anyway, it was just someone after spring venison, and you know it."

The younger man's teeth showed in a quick, cold smile. "I don't know anything of the sort. As for your busy schedule, you might have more time for investigations if you spent less time playing security guard out at Xanadu."

"Look here, you—"

"But, I can see how Hutton's campaign contributions—"

"—son of a bitch! You have no—"

"—might be more important than solving a shooting."

"—right to question me!" Danner finished angrily.

"Ten thousand dollars is a lot of money in a county like this."

"What's that supposed to mean?" Danner demanded.

"You tell me, *sheriff*. You're the one cashing Hutton's checks."

"And not Larry Moore, is that it? You're pissed off that your buddy didn't get elected sheriff."

"Larry couldn't be bought."

Danner turned his head a little and squinted, as though he wasn't sure he had heard correctly. He hooked his thumb into the gun belt just ahead of the holster, and his palm curled back over the hammer of the gun.

The other man faced the sheriff and hooked his

right thumb into his own belt, a clear and conscious mimicking.

Christy blinked. She had never seen an unarmed man face the threat of a gun so calmly. The closest thing the "Moki-poaching son of a bitch" had to a weapon was his sterling belt buckle, which was mounted with a disk of fine turquoise the size of a silver dollar.

"I wasn't bought," Danner said. "I got *elected* to keep bad actors like you from getting in the way of good citizens."

"I did my time," the man said flatly. "I don't owe you anything. I don't owe the state of Colorado anything. The only person I owe is the son of a bitch who shot me and left me to die.

"And I always pay my debts, Danner. Ask anyone."

"You better watch that mouth, boy. Might make a man nervous enough to cause another hunting accident."

The man with the beard became very still.

Instinctively the sheriff started to back up, then stopped himself. His hand closed over his gun.

Christy's breath wedged in her throat. This can't be happening, she thought. This is an art gallery in the twentieth century, not some saloon in the Wild West.

"Are you trying to tell me something, Danner?" asked the man.

"I'm only telling you the same thing your doctor told you. Remington isn't a healthy place for a lung-shot ex-con. Everyone would be better off, including you, if you'd just drift."

The man's laugh was even harder than his smile. "Every western town needs an outlaw to keep the tourists happy. Looks like I've just been elected."

Deliberately he turned his back on Danner and spoke to Veronica.

"I'll be by tomorrow to talk about these pots."

Christy watched the man walk out of the gallery and get in the Suburban.

The sheriff swore under his breath and left without a word.

When the bell over the door shivered into silence, Christy forced herself to draw a deep breath.

"A decade doesn't seem to have changed the average western male very much," she said.

Veronica gave a hoot of laughter. "Yeah, that's one hell of a man, isn't it? Six foot two of trouble on the hoof."

"He looked taller than that. Must have been the gun."

"Gun? Oh, you mean Danner. Yeah, he's six four. But I was talking about Cain."

"Cain?" Christy asked faintly.

"Aaron Cain."

Christy shook her head, feeling disoriented. The man with the dark beard was the man Jo-Jo had warned her against.

"If I were a betting woman—and I am—I'd back Cain in a brawl against anyone."

Christy hardly heard. She was staring out the

window at the man her sister had warned her against.

"What's a Moki poacher?" Christy asked faintly.

"A thief."

"Is that why he was shot? Was he stealing something?"

"Cain? He's no Moki poacher, no matter what the university types say."

Christy looked as bewildered as she felt.

Veronica smiled and began carrying one of the cartons Cain had left into a back room, talking all the while.

"People around here take their Anasazi sites seriously," she said. "If you have a degree from a fancy school and dig up pots, you're an archaeologist. If you don't have a degree, you're a grave robber."

Veronica vanished into a back room but kept talking.

"And if you dig on public lands without a degree, you're a pothunter and a Moki poacher."

"And a son of a bitch?" Christy offered dryly.

Veronica's laughter rang again.

"Well, Danner and Cain never had much good to say for each other," Veronica admitted, grabbing the second carton. "Danner liked giving orders even before he was elected sheriff."

"Cain doesn't look like he takes orders worth a damn."

"Not that boy. Then there was their little disagreement over Hutton's model, that fancy blonde."

Christy was glad Veronica couldn't see her reaction. She was certain her shock would have shown on her face. By the time the gallery owner came back out, Christy had her expression under control.

"The one they call Jo?" Christy asked carefully.

"That's the one."

Veronica disappeared into the back room again.

"What happened?" Christy asked.

"Danner wanted her. He didn't get her. But I saw Cain and the blonde over in Montrose one night, working the honky-tonk trapline."

Jo-Jo and Cain? Christy thought blankly. But she said he hated her.

"She was all over him like a rash. It was the only time I saw them together, but . . ."

Veronica's voice faded.

Had Cain been able to teach Jo-Jo that there were some things beauty couldn't buy?

The thought went through Christy like a shock wave, unsettling everything in its wake.

Maybe that was why Jo-Jo had called and offered the gold necklace. Maybe she had finally grown up and wanted to mend her fences. Maybe Aaron Cain had accomplished a miracle in Jo-Jo's relentlessly self-centered life.

He didn't look like a walking miracle, but stranger things had happened between men and women.

Maybe Jo-Jo had changed. Maybe she finally was able to love and laugh and share. Maybe she had become the person Christy always hoped and prayed lay beneath that beautiful, selfish exterior.

Is there a softer Jo-Jo who can be reached with enough patience, enough understanding, enough love?

That was the ultimate lure, the irresistible one, the shining promise of a childhood healed.

Suddenly Christy couldn't wait to see her sister.

4

Empty cattle vans rocketed past Christy,
heading for the high country to bring cattle back
down to the valleys for the winter. The slipstream
of the big trucks made her little rental car shake.

One more thing that hasn't changed, Christy
thought wryly. Big trucks and narrow roads.

On either side of the two-lane highway, small
dirt tracks led off between barb-wire fences to
ranch houses that were more than a hundred years
old. Despite the brightness and warmth of the sun,
there was the feel of winter's depths in the run-
down brick and turn-of-the-century frame houses.

Christy knew the way those houses smelled,
how they felt, how they creaked when the wind
blew in the middle of the night and tree branches
scratched against the glass. She knew what it was
like to be a teenager staring through tears at a

cheap dresser mirror and asking herself why God had given her a brain instead of a face and body that brought men to heel like hound dogs with long tongues hanging out.

Slowly the timeless beauty of the land itself drew Christy's thoughts away from her sister. The last weeks of September were serene in the long meadows and lofty divides of the Rockies. On the hard shoulders of the mountains, the highest aspen groves had already turned a pure, burning gold. Above timberline the wild mountain peaks varied from dark red to steel gray and ebony. The sky was a blue so vivid it hurt unshielded eyes.

There was a compelling, muscular grace to Remington County. Christy was drawn to the land even as it revived unhappy childhood memories. A stubborn, unchanging part of her still loved being amid the grandeur of untamed mountains rising against the vast sky.

She turned off the road onto a narrow paved lane that led to Xanadu. Ahead, a lush stand of spruce grew right up to the road. A new snake-back fence zigzagged alongside the pavement on both sides. The fence was picturesque, but it also carried a message.

Keep out.

The message was reinforced by a guard in a self-consciously rustic shack at the edge of a spruce grove.

When Christy stopped in front of the shack, she quickly realized that the folksy appearance was barely skin deep. Underneath the shack's cedar shingles was a gleaming steel security center with high-tech connections to the rest of the world. Peter Hutton had erected an efficient armed barrier between Xanadu and the rest of the world.

The guard stepped out of the shack. He wore blue jeans whose crisp look came from being ironed, and probably starched as well. His white western shirt was equally crisp and definitely starched. He wore a pistol and a five-pointed star like Sheriff Danner's. The name plate beneath it said SANDERS.

Christy remembered Cain's remark about the sheriff playing security guard for Xanadu. She wondered if the people of Remington County cared that their money was being spent to guard a world-famous designer's privacy.

"What can I do for you, ma'am," the guard said.

No question in his voice. Sanders was polite, but just barely. His tone and his body language said that his job wasn't to help.

"I'm Christy McKenna from *Horizon* magazine in New York."

Sanders pointed back the way she had just come.

"All reporters are supposed to check in at the press center in the hotel in town," he said. "The media party isn't until tomorrow night."

Christy took off her dark glasses and looked at him with eyes that were more gray than green. When she spoke, her voice was every bit as cool as his.

"I'm not here for the press party. I'm here at Mr. Hutton's personal invitation."

The guard looked skeptical, checked a clip-
board, and shook his head. "McKenna?"

"Yes."

"I've got a list of special guests, ma'am. Your
name isn't on it."

Christy smiled without warmth. "Please check
with your supervisor."

Sanders reached for a phone just inside the door
of the shack, punched in a number, and waited.

Christy waited too, wondering why such aggressive security was necessary in Remington County.
The West of her childhood was one of unlocked
doors and unchained gates.

"This is the front gate," the deputy said into the
phone. "I've got a Miss McKenna here from some
New York magazine, says she's supposed to see the
Man."

Christy couldn't hear the reply. She didn't have
to. She saw the effect immediately.

The deputy glanced quickly at Christy.

"Yeah," Sanders said to the phone. "Okay."

He listened some more.

"Yes. Yes, sir. Right away."

Sanders hung up and whistled shrilly through
his teeth. "Yo! Hammond! Front and center!"

A younger deputy emerged into the sunlight.

"Sorry about that, Miss McKenna," Sanders said
to her. "Nobody ever tells us anything down here.
You're to go right on up."

"Thank you."

"Deputy Hammond will show you the way. If
you have any luggage, Hammond will take care of

it. Mr. Hutton has one of the guest suites ready for you."

"That won't be necessary. I have a room in town."

"But Mr. Hutton—"

"Thank you for your help," Christy said over the deputy's objections. "Mr. Hutton knows—or should know—that I'm a reporter, not his personal guest."

"Uh, yeah. Sure."

Shaking his head, Sanders stepped back into the guard shack.

The deputy named Hammond slid into the front seat beside Christy. He looked barely twenty. He wore a badge and carried a pistol but lacked the confidence to be comfortable with them. He glanced sideways at her quickly, almost shyly.

"Right through the gate, ma'am."

The heavy wooden gate slid open as Christy's car approached.

For the first half mile, the road was lined with spruce trees and the snake-back fence. Through gaps in the trees came the green gleam of pastures. Christy frowned, bothered by something she couldn't name. Despite the land's beauty, something about it was not quite right.

"I don't get an armed escort very often," Christy said casually. "Is the West really that wild?"

Hammond touched the gun on his hip self-consciously and shook his head. "No, ma'am."

The road climbed up a long grade to the top of a sandstone mesa that was studded with dwarf cedar and juniper.

"Mr. Hutton just likes to treat his really special guests well," the young deputy said as they crested the mesa.

"So I'm a really special guest?"

"Yes, ma'am."

"Do you have many?"

"I don't know. I'm new to the deputy trade."

New but trained well enough to keep your mouth shut around reporters, Christy told herself wryly.

With a stifled sigh she concentrated on the scenery, letting impressions sink into her.

After two miles the hardtop gave way to a broad, graveled ranch road that had been graded recently. The road crossed the mesa, dropped into a narrow meadow, and wound upward into scattered, tall pine trees.

The afternoon air was like polished crystal. Christy rolled the window down and inhaled old familiar scents, meadow grass and pine, sunlight and clean, silky air.

The shadow of a hawk riding the wind caught Christy's eye. She watched the bird's graceful, predatory ease and wished she could ride the winds of change half as well.

The fan of the hawk's tail was a startling russet, the color of fire burning just beyond reach.

"What a gorgeous color," Christy said.

The deputy glanced at her, then at her hair.

"You and that bird related?" Hammond asked with a wide grin.

It took a moment for Christy to understand.

When she did, she smiled spontaneously, totally unaware of the change the smile made in her.

Hammond wasn't. His eyes narrowed with sudden male calculations that were much older than his smooth face.

The road brought them to the far edge of the mesa. Reflexively Christy braked to a stop and stared at the beauty that was Xanadu.

The valley lay between two red-gold sandstone mesas. A mile wide and three miles long, Xanadu was mostly meadow and pasture. The grass was a green so deep and rich it was almost black. Watercourses were marked with graceful cottonwood and willow.

At the head of the valley, on the steep slopes that led up to the San Juan Wall, stands of aspen had fully turned. They stood out a bright yellow against the cobalt sky and starkly white afternoon clouds.

Like the mountains, the ranch house was made of uneven levels and surprising angles, a redwood and glass mansion with soaring windows that faced the wall of mountains on one side and the western sky on another. The huge house was set on a knoll at one edge of the valley. Below, on the flats, a huge barn with outbuildings and corrals spread out in balanced asymmetry, as though arranged by a Japanese landscape designer.

Somehow the buildings blended rather than clashed with the uncluttered landscape, becoming part of it in the way gemstones become part of a well-designed setting.

"Gorgeous," Christy said simply. "How far does the ranch go?"

"Way up into the mountains and clear across both mesas. Boundaries are kind of hard to pin down, when you're talking about this much land. Darn shame it's all going to waste."

Puzzled, Christy looked at the deputy.

"Not one head of real stock," Hammond said.

Abruptly she understood why Xanadu's beautiful meadows and pastures had seemed wrong to her.

"The only cows on this place are the ones they'll be barbecuing for tonight and tomorrow," Hammond said. "Some of the best pastureland in the state, too. Put a lot of ranch hands out of work."

Christy suspected the young deputy was one of them.

"An idle ranch for the idle rich?" she suggested.

Hammond shrugged and let the empty land speak for itself.

"What happened to the stock?" she asked.

"Sold. I guess Mr. Hutton didn't like cow flop on his pretty grass. Or maybe he was afraid they'd wander onto his target range and stop a few bullets."

Hammond's contempt was strong enough to override his caution. He was drawing Hutton's wages but he was still frankly offended by the changes the wealthy outsider had brought to Remington.

Christy tried to imagine the impact of Hutton's many millions on a community like this one. There was bound to be envy and resentment, as well as a general rush to rake in any crumbs falling from the rich man's table.

In Manhattan, Peter Hutton was one among many members of the megarich. Here he was the cash cow for an entire county.

Frowning, Christy released the brake and drove through the city man's dream of a well-designed West.

The meadow with its landing strip and apron for small planes spoke eloquently of quick, expensive transit across the wide open spaces.

A shooting range lay on the opposite side of the meadow, well away from the landing strip. The bold targets were set at distances that suggested both pistol and rifle.

"Six-guns at twenty paces?" Christy suggested ironically.

Hammond smiled slightly. "Hutton's not bad with a pistol for a city sli—uh, man. One or two of his boys are pretty good with a rifle, too."

"Especially for city slickers?" she asked innocently.

The deputy looked uncomfortable. "Uh, yeah."

"Don't worry. I was raised in Wyoming."

"You were?"

Christy nodded.

"It sure don't show," Hammond said.

"Thanks. I think."

The young deputy laughed.

"What are they doing over there?" Christy asked.

She pointed to an area in front of the barn where a dozen carpenters were working hard.

"Making a dance floor out of rough lumber," Hammond said. "The barbecue pits are over there. Going to be a big party tomorrow night."

Off to one side another work crew was sweating over a fire that was slowly turning a side of beef into a feast for the smaller private party tonight. Four damp mounds of earth marked the locations of fire pits big enough to contain whole pigs.

As the outbuildings fell away on either side, the road passed through an elegant wrought-iron arch and wound up the hill to the big house.

As soon as Christy parked and opened the car door, a white-haired man dressed like a drugstore cowboy came out to meet her. The white boots, dark pegged pants, and pearl-buttoned white shirt were expensive and amusing.

"Miss McKenna, I'm Ted Autry, Peter's administrative vice president," he said.

Christy got out before Autry could help her. She gave him a professional smile and a handshake to match.

"You're just in time for a glass of wine," Autry said. "Peter's giving a few friends an unscheduled look at the Sisters Collection."

Christy glanced at Autry and asked sharply, "The Sisters?"

"Sorry, I forgot. You haven't been briefed about the background of the collection. Myra Best wanted you to see the designs cold."

"Here I am." Christy smiled. "Cold as ice."

Autry was a good vice president. He caught the edge in her voice immediately.

"The designs are drawn from a stunning archaeological find Peter made right here on Xanadu," Autry said.

His smile invited Christy to share the excitement. She resisted.

"He actually unearthed an old Anasazi site," Autry said. "It was dedicated to two sisters. Princesses."

"Royal sisters?"

Christy's voice invited Autry to keep talking.

He resisted.

"I'll let Peter have the fun of filling in the details," Autry said. "He loves to tell the story."

Standoff.

Autry escorted Christy across a manicured lawn, onto a smooth redwood deck, and into a huge room that took up one entire end of the ranch house. The cathedral ceiling rose almost three stories above the floor, giving a sense of vast space within a sacred enclosure.

Two of the three exterior walls were entirely of glass. The third wall was an extraordinary mosaic of hand-crafted wood. A freestanding stone fireplace went from the floor to the full height of the ceiling in the center of the room, like an altar.

Beyond the glass was a panoramic mountain view from deck to roof. Mellow afternoon light filled the room, making everything glow with a special beauty. The floor was wood with a warm reddish cast and a superb grain. Glass display cases were scattered artfully about. Western art and artifacts lay within them, waiting to be admired.

Christy spotted a Remington bronze she was quite sure was genuine. There were a dozen paintings on the walls, including a Catlin, a Bierstadt, and a Moran. There was a small O'Keeffe, some very good watercolors, and a Charlie Russell with the trademark vivid colors.

That explains the guards and guns, Christy thought wryly. This secular church has several million dollars in art gracing its various altars.

Gradually Christy focused on the people in the room. They were gathered around a huge glass case in the most prominent display area. She recognized several of the other guests immediately: Tim Carroll, a dark-haired Hollywood actor who made $10 million a picture; Shannon Prell, his girlfriend, whose ditzy-blond roles made her as much money as Carroll; Frank Rohrlick, a New York author with a string of blood-drenched bestsellers to his credit.

The rest of the guests were strangers, but they all had the look of well-dressed confidence that Christy associated with the wealthy at play. They were a cross section of the Beautiful People, the jet set, the top tier of the two-tier West that had grown when nobody east of the Rocky Mountains was looking.

And at the moment, all of these people were gathered around the display case. No one even looked up when she walked in.

Christy glanced at Autry. He put a finger to his lips, smiled, and gestured her toward the others.

" . . . so all the evidence suggests that the two

women were members of an aristocracy. They had magnificent jewelry: several kilos of turquoise and six thousand pieces of jet.

"The body of the tortoise is solid argillite of a kind not found anywhere but the Queen Charlotte Islands of British Columbia. The mother-of-pearl inlay is from California abalone shell.

"My archaeologists tell me that there should be another tortoise somewhere in the dig, because the sisters were probably priestesses. I can't tell you how wildly impatient I am to find that other tortoise!"

When the lecturer straightened up from his position over the case, Christy recognized Peter Hutton. Tall, spare, curly-haired, he had the sculpted features of a male model, the lazy smile of a sybarite, and the supple voice of the Broadway actor he had wanted to be until he realized how much more money there was in dressing rich women.

"What you're seeing is mother-of-pearl," he explained. "Abalone shell, to be precise. The nearest abalone beds are in Malibu."

Murmurings rose from the people as they leaned closer, trying to see better.

"In other words, this tortoise proves that the people of the Chaco empire had the power to reach out a thousand miles for materials and the artistic vision to create a piece of grave goods that is every bit as elegantly stylized as anything from an Egyptian tomb."

Hutton paused and smiled his trademark smile.

The women who were watching smiled back.

Christy watched, wondering if Jo-Jo enjoyed looking at her sexual opposite in Peter Hutton, or if the competition made her uneasy.

"That's why I'm so enthusiastic about this find," Hutton said. "Not only is it an inspiration for me artistically, it's also a real breakthrough in our understanding of ancient Mesoamerican cultures.

"Until this find, the Anasazi were dismissed as backwater clods. Now people will be forced to admit that one thousand years ago an important imperial culture existed from the New Mexican desert to the the Colorado Plateau."

Hutton glanced around, measuring the enthusiasm of his audience. When he saw Christy, his expression changed.

"Excuse me for a moment," he said to the people gathered around the case.

Hutton crossed the huge room toward Christy with the odd, flowing grace of a runway model. While his chiseled Grecian beauty wasn't to her taste, it was compelling in the way that all good art is compelling.

Jo-Jo had the same effect on the senses. People stared because they couldn't believe such physical perfection existed anywhere short of heaven or a movie screen.

"Christa? We've almost met so many times, and now I find out you're Jo's sister. I'm still in shock."

Hutton took both Christy's hands and held them with every evidence of pleasure.

"Hello, Mr. Hutton."

"Never. For you I'm Peter and you're Christa for me." Then he smiled.

For the first time in her life, Christy was grateful that she had spent a childhood in Jo-Jo's glittering orbit. Otherwise, Hutton's sheer physical beauty might have left her speechless and scrambling for balance.

"Mr. Hutton—"

"Peter."

"Peter. You're everything people said you were."

But Christy smiled because it was impossible to see Hutton's smile and not return it.

"Oh, I hope not." He winked, sharing a secret with her. "People say some pretty awful things and forget to say the nice ones."

Christy laughed.

Hutton leaned down and said in a low voice, "For instance, Jo never mentioned that you were a beauty in your own right."

"Jo-Jo is beautiful. I'm merely well turned out."

Hutton laughed. Then he looked Christy over from the crown of her head to her feet.

"I beg to differ with you, darling," he said after a moment. "And I'm the acknowledged world expert on female beauty."

With a confident pressure of his hand over hers, Hutton drew Christy toward the case.

"I was just giving some friends a preview of the treasure of Xanadu," Hutton said. "You can't imagine the magic of these pieces."

As he approached the people grouped around the case, they looked up expectantly at him.

Christy didn't blame them. There was a vividness to Hutton that colored everything within reach.

"Mind your nasty tongues, children. The press has arrived," Hutton said.

Christy watched the predictable result with a mixture of resignation and amusement.

"Such shocked looks," Hutton chided. "Relax, Tim, she's not going to mug you for some sleazy tabloid."

The movie star grimaced. The rest of the group laughed.

"Christa McKenna is class all the way. She's the guru—or is it guress?—of taste and style in the U.S. If you don't believe me, ask *Horizon* magazine."

A wave of interest went through the people as they looked at Christy.

"Shannon," Hutton said, "you're blocking the case. I, personally, don't mind, but I'm sure Christa would rather look at the artifacts than your heart-shaped ass."

Laughing, the actress stepped to the side.

Christy saw instantly why the guests were so fascinated by the display. Every piece in the case was marvelously preserved. None showed the rude execution that she associated with Anasazi works.

The turquoise fetishes and strings of jet beads were tiny and immaculately polished. The pottery's painted designs were both irregular and artistically inevitable. The intricacy and elegance of the baskets were breathtaking. The arrowheads and the stone and bone implements were timeless in their balance and purpose and superb in their execution.

Most compelling of all, some of the artifacts transcended the limitations of form and function to become art.

"What do you think?" Hutton asked, watching Christy with shielded intensity.

"Elegant, elemental, and extraordinary," she said.

Hutton smile was genuine, relieved, and triumphant. "And you haven't even seen the best!"

He set a simple rosewood display box lined with soft green velvet on top of the case. When she hesitated, Hutton pushed it closer.

"Look," he urged.

Resting on the velvet was a tortoise effigy. The pendant was a big as a man's palm. The creature's shell was highly polished black argillite. The potent head and neck were mother-of-pearl inlay, as were the limbs. The collar at the base of the neck was turquoise inlay. The eyes were polished turquoise spheres.

Beyond the age of the object, beyond its superb craftsmanship, beyond its rarity, there was an aura about the tortoise that fairly shouted of longevity and reverence, wisdom and fertility. It was a god effigy from a sophisticated culture.

"Isn't he marvelous?" Hutton said.

"Yes," she said simply.

"I believe he's the highest expression of Anasazi art ever to be found," Hutton said, his voice rough with excitement. "For my money, this is one of the highest expressions of ancient art of any culture."

Christy let out a breath she hadn't been aware of holding. "This came from Xanadu?"

"Yes." His voice softened. "Everything in this case came out of a sandstone cave we found last year."

Christy bent closer, inspecting the icon intently. A tiny piece of abalone inlay was missing from one foot. Somehow the loss reassured her, made the piece more genuine, more human.

Imperfect, and therefore real.

"Go ahead," Hutton said, picking up the tortoise with heart-stopping casualness. "Touch it. Hold it."

Reverently Christy took the tortoise in her hand and touched the polished shell with her fingertips. The surface was smooth, cool, almost seamless. The inlays were so carefully done that she had to concentrate to feel where stone ended and mother-of-pearl began.

"My archaeological consultants tell me that the cave was a tomb for two royal sisters," Hutton said.

"When I studied the Anasazi in college," Christy said, "we were told they were simple farmers."

"Textbooks are being rewritten as we stand here," he said. "Hundreds of Anasazi sites are being uncovered every year, all across the Colorado Plateau and the Southwest."

Christy glanced up at the excitement in Hutton's voice. She was caught by the beauty of his eyes, as vivid as the mountain sky.

"The latest thinking is that the Anasazi were an

imperial people," Hutton explained. "Their capital was in Chaco Canyon, New Mexico. They maintained a system of roads that reached all the way into Colorado."

But even Hutton's excitement and mesmerizing male beauty couldn't keep Christy's attention from the icon for long. Both timeless and atavistic, the tortoise enthralled her.

"Our archaeologists believe Xanadu's cave is the northernmost reach of the Chaco empire," Hutton said. "Not far from where we're standing was the edge of one of the greatest ancient empires in the world."

"Why, it's like finding King Tut's tomb right here in Colorado!" Shannon Prell burst in.

"Anyone have the movie rights?" Tim demanded. "I think I could make a hell of a film out of it."

Hutton smiled, but he didn't look away from Christy. Gently she placed the ancient tortoise back in its modern rosewood box.

"It must have been thrilling to discover it," she said. "I can't wait to see the cave."

Hutton's disappointment was immediate and intense. "I'm sorry. It's not safe."

"It can't be more dangerous than midnight in Manhattan," Christy said dryly.

"It's so bad they're not digging, they're stabilizing walls."

Christy looked up, startled. "Sounds serious."

"It is. Besides," he added sheepishly, "the archaeologists would have my balls if I went back in there. They're still screaming about the stuff I already took out. But I couldn't leave everything there. What if the rest of the ceiling came down and buried the tortoise forever?"

"May I assume the tortoise is what inspired your new fashion collection?" Christy asked.

"Naughty, naughty," Hutton said, shaking his finger slowly at her. "You can't be a reporter until tomorrow tonight. Tonight is just for a few of my friends."

"Actually, I wasn't trying to steal a march on them. I really came to see Jo-Jo. Where is she?"

Hutton gave Christy a puzzled look.

"I haven't seen her since yesterday," he said. "I thought she flew off to New York to meet you."

5

Another dead end.

"Damn!"

Christy hung up the phone and leaned back against the headboard. Her shoulders were stiff and her neck muscles were in knots from seventy minutes on the telephone. She had checked every message center, every link, every point where she and Jo-Jo might have missed connections.

She might as well have saved herself the effort.

There were no messages at the *Horizon* office. Nick, groggy and grouchy from being awakened, said there had been no calls for her. Jo-Jo's modeling agency had heard nothing, and her favorite Manhattan hotels had not seen her. Nor had the Hutton office in New York.

Christy's mouth flattened into a grim line. With

clipped politeness she battled the telephone switchboard long enough to reach the private number Hutton had given her.

"Autry speaking. May I help you?"

"This is Christa McKenna. Is Mr. Hutton available for a moment? It's rather urgent."

"For you, Peter is available any time, anywhere. But he's up to his ass in party alligators, so don't keep him too long, okay?"

"Sure."

"Hang on."

A few moments latter Hutton answered the phone, sounding harried.

"What's up?" he asked.

"I can't find Jo-Jo."

"Did you try the Beverly Hills Hotel?"

"Yes. They haven't seen her for a month."

"How about—wait a minute."

Hutton's voice was muffled, as though he was holding the receiver aside while he resolved a petty crisis involving vegetarian guests who might be offended by barbecued meat.

"Did you try her agency?" he asked finally.

"She hasn't checked in for a week."

"Even with her personal agent?"

"Yes."

"Then maybe . . ."

Hutton's voice faded again into a muttered dialogue with Autry.

"Sorry," Hutton said into the phone a minute later. "It's a little crazy here."

"Aren't you worried about Jo-Jo?"

There was silence, then laughter. "That's a joke, right?"

"No."

"Babe, Jo is thirty years old. We are, as they say, an item, but not of the till-death-do-us-part variety. She comes and goes as she pleases. So do I."

"Without telling you?"

"If she wants me to know where she is, she'll be the first to tell me. Until then, you might as well whistle for the wind. It will come to heel sooner than Jo will."

The flat certainty in Hutton's voice told Christy that he had tangled with Jo-Jo on that subject.

And lost.

"Isn't she modeling tonight?" Christy asked.

"The regular runway girls can fill in for the private showing."

"What about the press showing tomorrow night?"

"If—hang on, Autry, I'd better talk to him myself—Christa, I've got to run. You're coming tonight, aren't you?"

"I don't know. Either way, I'll be at the formal press showing."

The last words were spoken into a dead line.

Christy hung up, stared at the phone for a few minutes, and felt tension tightening her nerve endings. She remembered all the other times Jo-Jo had manipulated the people around her with sulks and disappearing acts.

Come out, come out, wherever you are.

But Jo-Jo wouldn't. Not until she was good and ready.

Abruptly Christy stood up and began pacing. She wished she had a big swimming pool within reach. Twenty laps would have gone a long way toward working the tension out of her body.

She paced the length of her room three times but only felt more confined. She needed to be outside. A barbecue at Xanadu was preferable to waiting around her room for a call that most likely wouldn't come.

Christy showered and dressed in black silk slacks, a loose black silk pullover, and a pair of low black shoes. Swimming might be beyond her reach, but there was a lot of Xanadu to pace around in. In any case, she preferred being outdoors to being trapped in the pseudo-Victorian decor of her hotel room.

When Christy finished tying off her French braid, she checked her appearance in the mirror. With a grimace, she turned away from her reflection. Basic black went everywhere, but it required at least one piece of jewelry. She had brought this outfit expecting to showcase Gramma's necklace against the black silk.

But the necklace was still beyond Christy's reach, and she had brought no other suitable jewelry.

Impatiently Christy pulled on an unstructured black linen jacket and went to the hotel lobby. She considered driving herself, then decided it wasn't worth the hassle at the gate. She would ride the shuttle with the rest of the hotel guests who weren't staying at Xanadu.

She stepped outside into the cool evening air and took a deep breath. A full moon was just sliding up over the San Juan Wall, pouring silvery light over the land. A gleaming white van wheeled up to the entrance of the hotel. A driver in a cowboy hat leaned out.

"Xanadu?" the driver asked.

Three couples were waiting. They climbed into the rear seats of the van, leaving Christy to take the front seat next to the driver. She didn't feel like being sociable, so she simply turned her head and looked out the side window.

Even so, she learned a great deal about her fellow guests before they reached the top of the rocky mesa. The most vocal of the group was a wealthy Seattle brain surgeon and his wife who collected Anasazi artifacts. They were traveling with a primitive-art gallery owner from Houston and his wife.

Silently Christy listened to the boasting and shouldering she had come to associate with full-time, well-heeled collectors.

"At the Tucson show, he paid twenty-nine thousand for a pot I wouldn't have pissed in."

"That's nothing. Herman was bidding on a basket that went to fifty-three."

"Did he get it?"

"Shit, yes. He always gets what he wants."

Christy looked out at the moon-silvered land and tried to imagine what it would have been like to live and die within the same handful of square miles, having known nothing but the sun, the sky, and the land itself. The idea seemed a melancholy counterpoint to the avaricious conversation behind her.

" . . . grave goods from Springerville. Only these were special."

"Turquoise?"

"I should hope to shout. Buckets of the stuff."

"So?"

"So it was wrapped around seven skeletons like a winding sheet."

A soft whistle came out of the silence.

"Were they complete?"

"Except for a few toe bones, and those will probably turn up. Even had some hair."

"Male or female?"

"Female."

"Holy Christ. Why wasn't I called? I've got a standing order for female bones. Nobody pays more than I do."

"These aren't for sale."

"Bullshit. Everything is for sale. Look at the McElmo grayware that came on the market last month. We both know where we saw that last."

"Yeah, and we know where it is now. Damn Japanese are driving prices over the moon."

"The Germans are worse. They'll buy anything Anasazi, even a piece-of-shit potsherd I wouldn't step on. In fact—"

"Shelby, for chrissake, can you talk about something besides dead Indians and greedy foreigners for just two minutes?"

There was laughter at the woman's long-suffering complaint. The conversation shifted locale but not subject matter, from Colorado to a private showing in Sedona—pots, fetishes, and the skull of a baby inlaid with turquoise.

Christy watched the moonlight on the top of the mesa, grateful she had never been possessed by the urge to collect. The only object she had ever really wanted was Gramma's necklace.

I'll get it, too, and to hell with Jo-Jo's games. That necklace is mine.

The conversation shifted to real estate prices in Telluride, Aspen, Santa Fe, and Taos.

Christy began to get the feeling that the West was being overrun by looters of all kinds—those who sacked archaeological sites for artifacts and those who sacked old ranches for condominium sites.

She thought back to the young cowboy who had been crowded off the land and turned into a deputy sheriff when Peter Hutton's millions had changed the way his part of the West was run.

Shutting out the voices, Christy watched the land flow by in dreamlike shades of black and silver. When the light was just right, her window became a bottomless mirror reflecting both herself and the land in odd unity.

When the shuttle arrived, some thirty couples were already dancing on the rough-lumber floor she had seen being built earlier that day. Another hundred people—fashion groupies, Hutton executives, and art collectors—were gathered around tables laden with food, wine, and beer.

In what had once been a pasture and now was a

carefully groomed meadow, small planes were tied down near a moon-silvered runway. Other planes circled in the high, clear air, waiting for their turn in the landing pattern. A Range Rover waited off to the side, ready to whisk newcomers one thousand feet away to the party.

Peter Hutton appeared for a moment, framed in the doorway of the barn, talking to someone who was out of sight inside. When Christy reached the big, gambrel-roofed building, she discovered it had been turned into a makeshift dressing room.

In a quiet frenzy, seamstresses and dressers made last-minute adjustments for a dozen models. Jo-Jo wasn't among them. Lighting technicians went over the script with the narrator, who was a New York stage actor brought in for a one-night gig.

Christy caught glimpses of flowing fabric with lightning-stroke designs that reminded her of the Anasazi pots in Hutton's cases. She saw several pieces of jewelry in the turtle's turquoise, black, and mother-of-pearl motif. There was a breath-taking gown in white silk with a glittering black design that was like a curving variation of a child's stick figure. The design had extraordinary verve.

When Hutton spotted Christy he walked toward her, flashing his trademark smile.

"Glad you decided to come tonight," he said. "You class up the place."

"Thanks."

"I'd like to show you around, but—"

"No problem," Christy said quickly. "Just one quick question."

Hutton raised his pale, arching brows. "Sure, babe."

"Do you know a man named Aaron Cain?"

Hutton's eyes blazed. "That bastard! What about him? Last I heard he was in a hospital in Grand Junction."

"He's in Remington now."

With a grimace, Hutton controlled his temper. "He won't last."

"Would he know where Jo-Jo is?"

"Jo did lots of slumming around Remington and Montrose," Hutton said, shrugging. "I doubt if she kept in touch afterward."

Someone yelled Hutton's name.

"Sorry, babe." He brushed a fast kiss across Christy's cheek. "Catch you after the show."

Within seconds Hutton had disappeared into the whirl of fabric and female flesh that would miraculously become a fashion show.

The smell of food drifting from the barbecue pits reminded Christy that it was well past dinner hour, Manhattan time. She had eaten little on the plane or during the drive to Remington, and nothing since she had arrived. She had been too busy, too angry, or both.

But now the cool night air and the fragrance of cooking foods revived her appetite. She went to the place where buffet tables groaned beneath platters heaped with three kinds of meat. Pans of chili, salads, and vegetables filled in the spaces between mounds of fresh bread and tortillas. There was cold beer by the bucket, chilled white wine for the urbanites, and Dom Perignon for those foolish enough to think it would go well with chili.

Christy ate barbecued pork tenderloin, a square of tender buttered cornbread, and a casserole of red-and-white Anasazi beans with chiles and molasses. She washed it down with a pale Colorado ale.

The combination of Xanadu's seven-thousand-foot altitude, jet lag, and alcohol should have numbed Christy. Instead the food gave her new energy. But the tastes of the food and textures of the western night made memories rise.

Restlessly she set aside her plate and glass and strolled around the edge of the crowd, looking for the flash of Jo-Jo's pale blond hair, listening for the husky laughter that made everyone who heard it feel part of a delicious conspiracy.

When the band took a break, the workmen descended, carrying a runway into position for the fashion show. The separate knots of people slowly began to converge, anticipating a preview of the fashion event of the year.

Christy watched the setup long enough to see that it would take about half an hour to finish. Abruptly all the anger and disappointed hope flooded her, making her restless and irritable and ready to explode.

She didn't want to wait around like a staked goat for Jo-Jo to make her entrance. That game of hide-and-seek had grown old years ago.

Jamming her hands in her pockets, Christy strolled away from the strings of lights and groups of laughing people. A hundred feet from the perimeter of the barns, she was alone. It was a relief. She simply wasn't up to the demands of her professional role as a *Horizon* reporter or her social role as the plain sister of the gorgeous Jo-Jo.

Once, just once, I'd like to set my sister back on her perfectly shaped heels.

The thought was tantalizing.

Jo-Jo knows what the necklace means to me. That's why she dangled it in front of me when she thought I might not come.

All I have to do is take it and then enjoy the look on her face when she finally sweeps in—and sees Gramma's necklace around my throat.

The beautiful glass and wood house gleamed like a beacon on the knoll a quarter mile away. A road wound up to the front door.

Christy didn't follow the road because she wasn't sure whether Hutton's security troops would be on duty. In any case, her mission was too personal to explain to some stranger.

Sparse brush and grass covered the knoll. Christy stumbled a few times until her eyes adjusted to the darkness. The altitude and the small amount of alcohol she had drunk made her a bit light-headed. Moonlight added to the sense of unreality.

By the time Christy reached the edge of the lawn that wrapped around the house, she was breathing rapidly. Dew sparkled on the grass. Lights were on inside the house, but there was no sign of movement.

At the far end, away from the display room and its walls of glass, there was a kitchen big enough to service a restaurant. Pans hung from hooks on the wall. As Christy drew closer, she saw that the kitchen was empty. Apparently the caterers were all busy out at the barn.

Feeling a bit foolish and very determined, Christy looked around before she went up to the open kitchen window and listened. Somewhere inside a radio was playing country music. No one was singing along with Merle Haggard. No one was making any noise at all.

The kitchen door was locked.

Christy circled around behind the house, trying several more doors. She was about to give up when she found one open. She closed the door quietly behind her and looked around, trying to orient herself.

Her heart beat frantically. She hadn't felt this foolish and little-girl frightened since Jo-Jo had talked her into hiding spiders in the teacher's desk.

It took two tries, but Christy found the corridor leading off in the direction of the house's residential wing. The soles of her shoes were wet from the grass. They squeaked on the tile floor. To her adrenaline-heightened senses, the squeaks sounded like cymbals clashing.

The corridor opened into the huge room where Xanadu's treasures were on display. A fire burned cheerfully in a fireplace big enough to roast an ox, but the room itself was empty.

Christy retraced her steps and found another

hallway. This one led to what she hoped was Hutton's quarters. She went down the hall quietly, unsure whether Jo-Jo and Hutton shared a bedroom as well as a bed.

The hallway was lined with paintings. Each canvas had its own light. Automatically Christy stopped to look at one of the paintings. After a few moments, a chill swept over her.

The painting was a surrealistic drawing of a sunset storm sweeping across the red-rock mesa country. Inside the dark crimson storm cell, the artist had painted the faces of ghouls whose eyes and cruel smiles were human skulls. The squall itself was a vicious demon raking the land with talons of lightning.

Wherever the talons touched, wounds appeared. Within the wounds were headless skeletons. Their gleaming ivory arms were extended upward, fingers clawing toward the missing skulls that would be forever beyond their reach.

Technically, the painting was expert. The artist had a keen appreciation of force and energy, light and shadow, color and shading. That was part of the picture's horrifying impact. The rest came from the enjoyment of pain that was implicit in the demon's cruel smile.

With a repressed shudder, Christy turned away, feeling cold to the marrow of her own bones. She could no more have lived with that demon-ridden painting than she could have used a corpse as a coffee table.

She hurried away from the ghastly art. An open

door farther down the hall led to what was clearly a guest bedroom. The decor of the room was as expensive and impersonal as a suite in a five-star hotel. The room was so clean and orderly it felt as though it had never been used.

A second door opening off the hallway was locked. At the end of the hall, Christy tried a third door, found it open, and let herself into a large master suite. Expensive men's clothing hung in the walk-in closet. Hutton's, undoubtedly.

An odd, half-familiar scent tickled Christy's memories. She breathed in deeply, trying to place it.

Baby powder? No . . . it can't be.

She inhaled again.

Baby powder.

Even with the smell of baby powder in the air, there was a decidedly masculine feel to the bedroom. The decor was lean and sinewy, red and black with silver accents.

Another intense work by the artist who put ghouls in his rain clouds hung over the bed. The gleaming silver-white of skeletons and lightning from the painting were repeated as accents in small sculptures around the room. The effect was that of walking into the painting's demonic soul.

Lord, how could anyone sleep in this place?

To one side of the suite a door led into an adjoining room. The door was slightly ajar. Christy pushed it open a bit more and looked into another bedroom.

A full-size nude photo of Jo-Jo dominated the

wall of this room. The color combination of creamy skin, pink lips and nipples, golden hair, and emerald eyes was repeated in the off-white walls, the pink-and-gold fabric of the canopy bed, and the emerald accents supplied by carved crystal perfume bottles placed in artful disarray across the white-and-gilt dresser.

The effect of the room was rather like Jo-Jo herself—creamy, sensual, with gemlike flashes of temper.

Gotcha, sister mine.

Now what am I going to do with you?

6

Christy started to draw the door closed behind her, then thought better of it, afraid there might be an automatic locking system. Very carefully she left a finger's width of space between the edge of the door and the frame.

Then she took a deep breath and looked around quickly, remembering the French doors that led from Hutton's room onto the cantilevered deck that overlooked the grounds. There were no similar doors in Jo-Jo's room. The curtains were drawn over the windows.

Good, she thought. I won't be spotted from the outside.

Feeling both elated and foolish, Christy headed for the white lacquered jewelry box on top of the dresser.

She wasn't surprised or disappointed when she

found little of value inside. Jo-Jo had always known instinctively that her aura of primal sexuality was undermined rather than enhanced by flashy accessories.

But Christy was disappointed when she didn't find a delicate gold necklace that had been made from a man's watch chain.

You little liar! Did you hock it after all?

Stubbornly Christy refused to accept the possibility that Gramma's necklace was beyond her reach.

I've come this far, she told herself, I'll be damned if I'll tuck tail and run before I look in all the usual places.

And a few of the unusual ones while I'm at it.

It wouldn't be the first time Christy had searched her sister's room for forbidden fruit of one kind or another.

But, with luck, it would be the last.

The ornate, vaguely Louis XIV dresser held enough sexy lingerie to stock Frederick's of Hollywood. Christy ran her hands beneath the drawers, checking what had once been Jo-Jo's favorite hiding place for small things; there was nothing but surprisingly rough wood for such an obviously expensive dresser.

She made a quick run through the bedside tables, the bed, and between the mattress and springs before she turned toward the double doors that shielded the walk-in closet. A huge, knobby, old-fashioned brass key rested in a scrolled brass keyhole. A single turn opened the lock.

Inside, the closet was permeated with the sharp aroma of cedar. The faintly astringent odor was pleasing after the cloying room full of cream and gilt, perfume and lingerie. After a bit of fumbling, Christy located a light switch.

Lordy, lordy, as Gramma would have said. Unbelievable.

Jo-Jo had always loved clothes. Finally she had been able to indulge that passion. Rank after rank of costumes hung on padded hangers on all three sides of the large closet—sports outfits, cocktail dresses, winter sweaters, slacks, and skirts.

Shoes, boots, sandals, and slippers of every color were placed in rainbow array in an alcove made just for the purpose. A full set of Hartmann luggage was stacked at the back. The soft leather cases were scuffed, but the result was attractive. Even the most beautifully made tools are meant to be used.

The closet was orderly, which meant a maid had straightened it. No matter how great her passion for clothes, Jo-Jo had no patience for picking up after herself. That had always been left for Gramma or Christy to do.

Christy dismissed the clothes and went to the built-in chest. The top three drawers held socks of all colors and fabrics. She patted the carefully matched pairs. Nothing was hidden inside or beneath. She ran her hand beneath the drawers. Nothing.

The fourth drawer was full of starched and ironed Hutton dress shirts, man-styled but in the soft colors Jo-Jo preferred. No necklace. Nothing concealed underneath the shirts.

The fifth drawer held jeans, ironed, no starch. Nothing between the folds. Nothing on the bottom of the drawer.

Nothing.

Christy's flying fingers almost missed the key taped beneath the sixth drawer. She hesitated, caught between disappointment that it wasn't the necklace and triumph at finding anything at all.

It's not Gramma's necklace, but it must be important. Important enough to trade for the necklace, perhaps?

Gently Christy eased the drawer free of its tracks, turned it upside down, and peeled off the tape. The key had the blank anonymity of a public washroom. Plain steel, not a curlicue or flourish of gilt anywhere.

Hardly Jo-Jo's style.

The key showed signs of long casual use, as though it had passed through many hands. Clearly it didn't fit a lock in any of Jo-Jo's fancy boudoir furniture.

Frowning, Christy replaced the drawer, wondering where the lock that fit the key might be. She moved closer to the closet light and held the key up. The metal was so worn she couldn't decipher the words that had been stamped in it. No matter how hard she stared, a vague " . . . SP . . ." and a faint " . . . ot Dupl . . ." was all she could make out.

The sound of someone walking down the tiled

corridor from the main part of the house penetrated the closet's silence.

Without stopping to think, Christy flipped off the light switch and held her breath like a child sneaking through a graveyard on a dare.

The sounds came closer, then stopped.

Christy guessed that whoever had made them was still in the corridor. Perhaps it was just a bored guard walking a beat that included the display cases and the ghoulish but undoubtedly first-rate paintings on the walls.

Breathing very softly, Christy listened. No other sounds came from the hallway. Cautiously she opened the closet door and tiptoed across the bedroom to the hall door. Putting her ear against it, she held her breath.

She heard nothing except the roaring of her own blood in her ears.

Necklace or no necklace, it's time to go, Christy told herself.

She shoved the key she had found into the pocket of her black slacks and headed for the hall door, not wanting to face the demons in Hutton's bedroom again. As she reached for the doorknob, she noticed the rheostat on the wall. When she twisted it cautiously, the light in the room dimmed. She twisted a bit more and then even more until the room slowly slid into darkness.

With great care Christy turned the door handle, praying it wouldn't squeak. It didn't. Letting out her breath in a soundless rush, she eased the door open just enough to peek into the hall.

The man outside was huge.

He stood with his back to her and seemed to fill the hallway from floor to ceiling and wall to wall. His face was hidden by the straight brim of a big Stetson.

While Christy watched, frozen by shock, the man knelt in front of the locked door that lay between the display room and the entrance to Hutton's bedroom. When he moved his hand, small pieces of metal glinted and rang softly.

Christy had never seen a set of lock picks, but she was certain she was seeing them now.

The man was trying to open the locked door. He wasn't having much success. There was a metallic snap followed by a muttered curse. Metal gleamed and clicked as he tried a new probe.

Somewhere in the house a door closed and boot-steps rang like shots on a tile floor. The steps were confident, open, unconcerned about noise, and they were going from the kitchen area to the display room.

The huge burglar straightened, listened, and glanced down the hall in Christy's direction as though looking for a potential escape route.

The confident footsteps came closer, then became muffled when they went from tile to one of the Navajo rugs that were scattered around the display room's floor. The sound of the steps became clear again, then faded.

Obviously one of Hutton's guards was making a circuit of the display room. It took no great intelligence to figure out that the hallway paintings would be next on his rounds.

The burglar reached the same conclusion. He stood swiftly, glancing toward the display room.

The instant the man's attention shifted, Christy eased Jo-Jo's door shut. Heart pounding, she headed for Hutton's bedroom. The escape route through the French doors onto the deck was her only hope of avoiding a confrontation that now could be dangerous as well as embarrassing.

Christy was reaching for the knob of the connecting door when she heard one of the French doors open and shut. Someone else had just entered Hutton's bedroom. The burglar's escape route was cut off.

So was Christy's.

She spun around and felt her way through darkness back to Jo-Jo's closet. As she opened the door, her hand brushed against the oversized antique key in the lock. She pulled out the heavy brass key and shut the door quietly behind her.

In the darkness, she tried to insert the key quietly into the back side of the lock. Her hand was shaking too hard. By steadying one hand with the other, she managed to fit the key into the thumb-sized opening. As she turned the key, she prayed that the lock was as old-fashioned as the key itself.

It was. The key turned and the mechanism clicked. Anyone who tried the door from the outside would find it locked.

The heavy key fell to the carpet while Christy stood in the darkness and trembled, adrenaline racing through her body. She was certain that the sound of her heartbeat could be heard all the way to the barn.

The hall door into Jo-Jo's room opened and closed, followed by the sounds of someone blundering around in the dark. The burglar, no doubt.

Christy held her breath and wished she were a thousand miles away.

"Jack, where the hell are you?"

"Hutton's bedroom. Anything in the hall?"

"I thought I saw someone go into Jo's room."

"Check it out."

A light was switched on. A shaft of illumination poured through the closet's empty keyhole, piercing the darkness with light from the bedroom. Simultaneously there was a tangle of shouts and orders and curses.

By the time Christy dropped to one knee and peered through the keyhole, the brief struggle was over. Two of Hutton's security guards faced the big burglar. One guard had his gun drawn. Both guards wore the bright silver stars of Remington County deputies.

"Turn around, you son of a bitch. Hands on the wall. Do it!"

The orders were loaded with menace. The guard underlined the threat with a wave of his shiny chrome-plated revolver.

The prisoner shrugged, then turned and faced the wall.

"Frisk him, Jack."

The young man who had accompanied Christy up from the guardhouse earlier that day stepped forward and patted the burglar down for weapons.

"I'm just looking for the head," the burglar complained.

When the prisoner turned to speak, Christy saw that he was Indian, darkly handsome. A scar ran from beneath his eye to the point of his chin. The cut had been deep. The right side of his face didn't move when he spoke or smiled.

"Bullshit, Johnny," said the senior deputy, who was holding the pistol.

"Check it out, man," Johnny urged.

"Shit," Hammond said in disgust. "Hutton would never invite a no-account Moki poacher like you to his party. What are you doing up here?"

"Aw, c'mon, I was just—"

The big Indian started to turn away from the wall as he spoke, but Hammond stepped in close and delivered a quick, hard kidney punch.

"Don't move!" the deputy snarled.

"Aw, Jack, you know I'm not going to jump you."

"Face the wall," the senior deputy ordered with a wave of his gun. "What were you after?"

The Indian glanced over his shoulder, then spat in the direction of the two guards.

The senior deputy stepped forward and slammed his pistol across the right side of Johnny's face. Blood sprang from a new cut close to the scar on the Indian's face, but his expression didn't change. It was as though he had felt nothing.

Johnny spat blood carelessly. "Do that again and I'm gonna get pissed off."

"Cuff the big bastard," ordered the senior deputy.

He rested the muzzle of his pistol against Johnny's neck while Hammond fished a pair of handcuffs out of his hip pocket. The deputy's motions were awkward, for he was more used to pigging strings and calves than handcuffs and prisoners, but he got the job done. He snapped one cuff on Johnny's right wrist and dragged it down into the small of his back.

"Gimme the other hand," Hammond ordered.

When Johnny moved too slowly, the senior deputy rammed the muzzle of his gun into the Indian's throat.

"Do it!"

Unwillingly, Johnny dropped his left hand and let it be cuffed. Hammond closed the metal bracelet in place.

"Tighter," said the other deputy.

Hammond racheted down until the cuffs were hard against flesh. When he was certain Johnny was helpless, Hammond drew his fist back and delivered another kidney punch.

"That's for that bar over to Montrose," Hammond said, "when you busted Shorty's skull."

This time Johnny groaned softly and went to his knees.

"I'll get you for that, you—"

Johnny's words were cut off by a gun barrel raking across his mouth.

"What are you doing here?" demanded the senior deputy.

Johnny's response was a mumbled curse that could have been English or some older language.

Another raking pistol blow followed.

"What are you doing here?" the senior deputy asked again.

Silence answered him.

The senior looked at Hammond, who shrugged.

"I know this ol' boy," Hammond said. "You can hammer on him till your arm's sore and he won't say nothing he don't want to say."

"Autry isn't going to like this."

Hammond shrugged again.

The senior guard pulled a small portable two-way radio from his belt and spoke softly into it.

The Indian spat blood. "Yeah, call Autry. Tell that son of a bitch I want to talk to him."

The senior deputy ignored Johnny.

The Indian grinned, exposing bad teeth outlined in his own blood. "You better get Hutton up here, too."

"Mr. Hutton doesn't want to talk to your kind."

"Tell him it's about Kokopelli's sisters." Johnny spat again. "That'll bring him on the jump."

The two deputies exchanged puzzled glances.

"Kokopelli," growled the Indian. "Tell him."

The guards stepped back a few feet and conferred in whispers for a moment. The senior deputy shrugged, then looked at Johnny and frowned. Hammond went over and jerked the big Indian to his feet.

"Walk or git dragged," Jack said.

"I'll walk. But you gotta get Autry."

"Yeah. Sure," said the senior deputy. "Just as soon as we cool you off."

The two men shoved Johnny ahead of them in the direction of the hall.

Christy drew a deep breath and swallowed hard, fighting the beer and barbecue sauce that were trying to climb back up her throat. She had seen bar brawls in her Wyoming childhood, but she had never seen a bound man deliberately beaten. Even knowing that Johnny was a burglar didn't make it less sickening.

When Christy could no longer hear sounds from outside, she groped around on the closet floor until she found the big brass key. It took her three tries to unlock the door, and three more tries before the door locked again behind her.

The blood the big Indian had spat lay bright and red on the carpet. Christy's stomach clenched and threatened to rebel all over again. She swallowed.

Time to get the hell out of this horror show.

After a few moments Christy had herself under control again. She made a wide circuit around the blood, crept to the hall door, and listened.

Somewhere at the other end of the house, a heavy door closed. One of the guards came back into the hall from the kitchen. The men's voices carried clearly in the silent house.

"He ain't gonna die in that meat locker, is he?" asked Hammond.

"Not real quick. It's only about forty degrees. But when we drag him out in half an hour, he sure won't be running his mouth at us anymore."

The deputies came down the hall from the kitchen as far as the entrance to the display room.

Christy shrank back from the door. If she went out that way, she would be spotted and recognized instantly.

"Look here," said the senior deputy.

"Where?"

"There. See? He must of had someone with him."

"What?"

"Jesus, Jack, get some glasses. See those shoe prints on the tile? They're way too small to be ours, much less Johnny's."

"Oh, Christ. They're still damp. We'd better go through the place again."

"Yeah. And this time we'd better do it right, or Autry will kick our asses right out of Colorado."

Christy knew the closet would no longer be safe. She had to get out of the house, and she had to do it *now*.

She ran for the door that connected Jo-Jo's room with Hutton's. It was still ajar. She raced across the bedroom, headed for the French doors and the freedom beyond.

The door latch wouldn't work at first. Finally Christy twisted the lock until it opened. The doors seemed heavy to her frantic, fumbling hands, too heavy to push open. Then cool, clean evening air rushed over her.

Christy sprinted across the big deck. There was an eight-foot drop to the bushes below. She hesitated, heard a man's voice from Hutton's bedroom, and scrambled over the railing. Before she could change her mind, she was falling into the shrubbery below.

The ground had just been worked by the gardeners. It was soft and loose, cushioning Christy's fall. She pulled herself to her feet, tripped over a sprinkler head, fell, and rolled into the decorative shrubs. The low branches of an evergreen raked over her.

The prickly embrace was welcome. Christy curled beneath the branches, afraid she would hear the guards yelling after her or, worse, shooting. She prayed that the black of her clothes would blend seamlessly with the moon shadow of the thick shrubbery.

Christy held her breath when she heard a guard walk to the edge of the deck and stop.

"See anything, Jack?" called the other guard from the bedroom.

"Thought I did."

"Check out the front. I'll take the side."

Hammond cursed but did as his boss said.

Barely daring to breathe, Christy waited while steps overhead faded away into the house. She gathered her courage, scrambled to her feet, and fled down the back side of the knoll, intent only upon escaping the guards. A graceful stand of spruce marked the bottom of the slope off to the right.

Straight ahead, across the meadow, were the lights of the runway where graceful, leggy women glided like colored shadows through the night. Once Christy got to the barn, she could blend into the crowd. No one would know she had ever been inside the house.

But the meadow between Christy and the party was drenched in moonlight. If she went that way, the guards couldn't miss her.

She sprinted for the trees off to the right. As their shadows closed around her, she caught a flicker of movement from the corner of her eye. With a hoarse sound she tried to fling herself aside.

It was too late.

A hard hand clamped across her mouth, stifling her scream. A long arm went around her shoulders and jerked back, holding her with a strength hopelessly greater than her own.

Christy fought anyway, until her feet were kicked out from under her and she went face down to the cold ground. Her captor followed her down, pinning her until she no longer struggled.

She tried to scream then, but she had neither the breath nor the strength to throw off the man's hand covering her mouth. She forced herself to lie quietly, waiting for another opening.

The world spun dizzily as her captor turned her onto her back with frightening ease. Gently but irresistibly, the man turned her head toward the moonlight.

"Jackpot," he said softly.

His smile was a bleak flash of white against a face hidden by darkness, but Christy recognized the voice.

Aaron Cain.

7

"*Settle down, Red,*" Cain said in a low voice. "I'm not going to hurt you. Do you hear me?"

Christy heard. She just didn't believe him.

"I'm going to lift my hand," he said. "Before you scream, think about it. You listening?"

Slowly Christy nodded.

His white smile flashed briefly.

"Good. Hutton's guards are local boys—cowboys and hunters and miners. You run fast for a city girl, but they'll track you down real quick."

Cain's matter-of-fact tone cut through Christy's fear, as did the fact that he wasn't holding her any harder than he had to in order to make sure she didn't scream, giving away her position. And his.

Hesitantly, she nodded.

"I'm not going to hurt you," Cain repeated. "I'm

going to help you get out of here, if that's what you want. Is that what you want?"

Again Christy nodded.

After a long moment, the hand covering her mouth lifted slightly. She drew in quick, aching breaths, her body shifting against Cain's as she tried to get air into lungs starved by exertion and alarm.

He looked down into eyes darkened by fear, yet still watchful, still wary. Still thinking. Reluctantly he rolled aside and waited to see if she would try to flee.

The sudden freedom was as dizzying to Christy as being captured had been. After the heat and weight of Cain's body restraining her, the night felt cold and limitless.

"Ready to go?" he asked softly.

"Why are you helping me?" Christy whispered.

White teeth flashed. This time Christy had enough presence of mind to realize that the Cain's smile was cold rather than comforting.

"Good question, Red. When I have an answer, you'll be the second to know. Got your breath back yet?"

"I'm working on it."

"Don't take too long. The word has gone out."

Christy followed Cain's glance. On the hillside leading to the house, four flashlight beams swept the grass. Other flashlights flickered on the flats as more guards abandoned the dance floor and headed toward the house.

Sooner or later, someone was bound to notice

the trail Christy had left across the recently watered lawn.

"I'm ready," she said quickly.

Cain didn't waste any time talking. He came to his feet, pulling Christy with him.

His casual strength irritated Christy, reminding her how much of a disadvantage she was at when stacked against the average male, much less one with Cain's height and lean power. When he took her arm to lead her through the night, she pulled back.

Or tried to. Cain's hand tightened, chaining her as efficiently as the deputy's steel manacles had chained Johnny.

"Easy, Red. I know the way. You don't."

"I can walk without—"

"Quiet."

Though soft, there was no doubting the command in Cain's voice. As much as Christy wanted to argue, she knew this wasn't the time or the place to protest her ability to take care of herself. Silently she allowed herself to be drawn through the trees to a narrow game trail.

"Follow me," Cain said in a voice that carried no farther than Christy. "Try not to make too much noise."

His voice was like the night. Quiet. He blended into the darkness with no more fuss than a wolf. He moved like a wolf, too. Tireless, relentless, he pursued a trail only he could see.

Christy followed as silently as she could despite the quick pace. It bothered her that she wasn't nearly as quiet as Cain. It also bothered her that she was having more and more trouble muffling the rapid sound of her breathing.

When Cain came to a small, dry ravine cutting through the trees, he stopped. The sides of the ravine were four feet high and nearly vertical. He slid halfway down the bank until he found solid footing. Then he reached back up, caught Christy beneath her arms, and swung her lightly off her feet, setting her on the dry sand that covered the bottom of the ravine.

Being lifted like that was unexpected. The swiftness of the motion left Christy uncertain of her footing. Cain steadied her, then released her slowly.

She was certain she felt his palms brush the sides of her breasts as he let go.

Nothing in Cain's manner suggested that he had noticed the intimacy. He was already walking off through the lighter shade of darkness that was the bed of the ravine. His low voice floated back in the darkness.

"Move, Red. Or do you want to be carried?"

With a muffled word, Christy followed, feeling breathless, off balance, and thoroughly irritated with herself, with him, and with the night itself.

Moonlight turned the sand into a rumpled highway. When the dry watercourse deepened and widened, Cain waited until Christy came alongside.

"Real quiet, now," he said in a voice that barely carried to Christy's ears.

She nodded. Together they walked quietly, following the gently winding ravine.

Men's voices came from somewhere off to the right. Christy froze even as her heartbeat accelerated. When Cain's hand closed around her arm and pulled her toward deeper shadows, she didn't fight him.

Flashlight beams flickered through the woods, but no cry of discovery was raised. No one had found Christy's trail across the grass.

Standing in the chill clarity of the night, Christy was aware once more of the thin air at seven thousand feet. When Cain tugged at her hand, urging her forward once more, she concentrated on disciplining her breathing so she could keep up. After five minutes, he finally slowed.

Cain's breathing was easy but rapid. She wondered if the altitude was getting to him. Then she remembered that he had been shot not very long ago. He moved like a wolf still, and she had no doubt that he could run or walk her into the ground, but he was not a machine. He had to breathe too.

The realization somehow comforted her, making her feel more at ease with him. She let out a long breath.

Cain turned and looked at Christy in silent question. She smiled in equally silent reassurance. He squeezed her hand and turned back to the trail ahead.

After a few more minutes, a second dry wash came in from the left side. Cain pulled Christy into the shadow of a clump of willows. Then he pulled her right up against his body. Before she could protest, he was speaking against her ear. His mouth was so close she could sense the warmth of his breath.

"Quiet," he breathed.

Christy wanted to ask why but doubted Cain would answer. Silently she stood close to him in the black and silver darkness, feeling the heat of his body on one side and the chill of the night on the other. She heard nothing but the sound of breathing, her own and Cain's.

The sense of isolation and intimacy was both disturbing and oddly exhilarating. She had never been so completely alone with a man, any man, much less a stranger.

"All right," Cain murmured.

He tugged on Christy's hand and stepped forward again. Within fifty feet they turned a bend in the ravine. A low, open jeep loomed out of the darkness. The vehicle all but filled the narrow watercourse.

"Yours?" she whispered.

"Your fellow burglar's," Cain said.

"What?"

"That's his jeep."

"He's not *my* burglar," Christy said instantly.

"Shhhhh," Cain said.

"But—"

"Later," he interrupted ruthlessly.

He circled the jeep and kept walking quickly, pulling Christy along in his wake. A quarter mile farther down the dry wash, the black bulk of his truck loomed beside a clump of willows that had been silvered by moonlight.

Cain led Christy to the passenger side, unlocked the door, and opened it. No interior lights came on. She was just absorbing that—and the fact that it was a big step up into the truck—when Cain's hands closed around her waist. Before she could protest, she was dropped lightly into the passenger seat.

The door closed very quietly behind her. Cain circled around and got into the driver's seat. The truck's engine fired instantly. Smoothly Cain eased into gear and stared forward.

"Aren't you forgetting something?" Christy asked.

He looked at her. In the darkness inside the truck, his eyes were nearly invisible.

"What?" he asked.

"Headlights."

His smile gleamed coldly. "No, I'm not forgetting them. I'm just not using them."

Cain drove expertly in the moonlight. Despite the obstacles in the streambed and the lack of light, the truck made twice the pace a fast-walking man could have managed.

It was an effort for Christy not to stare at Cain's profile or his lean, long hands holding the wheel with such casual skill.

They drove for several miles in the bed of the creek before they came to a dirt road that led down through cuts in the bank. He turned onto the road and shifted out of four-wheel drive.

Little more than a dirt track, the road was almost as rough as the creek bed had been. Ruts led up a steep hill and then across a flat red-rock mesa. After more than a mile, the road dropped down through a slot into another canyon.

Cain still didn't turn on the headlights. Only once, when a deer started from the scrub and raced in front of the truck, did he slow. Then he hit the brakes hard.

Christy noted that the brake lights, like the interior lights, weren't working. The big truck would be almost invisible as it moved over the back country.

And this "Moki-poaching son of a bitch" accuses *me* of being a burglar? Christy thought. Talk about chutzpah!

Finally Cain snapped on the headlights and picked up speed. The black truck rattled and banged over the rough surface.

"Home free?" Christy suggested neutrally.

"We're getting there."

"How did you and Johnny get separated?" she asked. "Or were you the lookout?"

"What?"

"Oh, come on. I doubt that ravine is one of the usual parking spots for Peter's guests."

Cain grunted.

"You weren't in the house with Johnny," Christy continued, "but you were watching the house. You called him a burglar, so you knew he was inside with a handful of lock picks. It stands to reason you were the lookout."

"Got it all figured out, haven't you?"

"I'm working on it."

"Do you spend a lot of time with burglars and ex-cons?" he asked.

Cain's question was so calm that it took a moment for Christy to understand what she had heard.

"What?" she asked.

"You don't seem worried about being off alone in the ass end of nowhere in the middle of the night with a man you *think* is a burglar and you *know* is an ex-con."

That answered the question of whether Cain had noticed Christy eavesdropping in the Two-Tier West.

He had.

"So," Cain continued, "either you're used to crooks or you're the kind of woman who just can't wait to get in a murderer's jeans and see if he's different from the other men you've had."

Christy's breath came in audibly. Though spoken in a calm voice, Cain's words were so bitter she felt as though she had been slapped.

"Stop the truck and let me out," she said flatly. "Now."

Cain ignored her.

She reached for the door handle.

He flipped the master lock switch.

"Let me out!" Christy said.

The rising note of fear was clear in her voice, but there was nothing she could do about it. She was becoming frightened.

"Take it easy," he said. "The truck is going too fast for a flying exit. You'll break your neck. Besides, there's no need. Like I said back at Hutton's, I'm not going to hurt you."

Cain's tone was tired and disgusted, though whether it was with himself or with her Christy couldn't decide.

"Go to hell," she said distinctly.

"I've been there, honey."

Somehow she didn't doubt him. It didn't comfort her.

"What do you want from me?" Christy asked.

"I saved your ass. Don't you think you owe me something?"

"Forget it. I'm not going to crawl into bed with you, just—"

"I want answers," Cain interrupted ruthlessly. "Not sex. Jesus, why do women think that all a man wants is to get laid by any woman who's available?"

"Because it's true," Christy said in a clipped voice.

"Not always."

"Bullshit."

Surprisingly, Cain laughed.

"Come down off the adrenaline jag, honey. You're safe with me."

"How stupid do I look?" she retorted.

"If I were going to rape you, I would have done it back when I had you laid out beneath me on the ground. You felt damned good that way, especially when you breathed hard."

The matter-of-fact statement literally took away Christy's breath. She started laughing, only to stop abruptly when she heard echoes of hysteria in her own voice.

"You're not used to this, are you?" Cain asked after a time.

"To what? Being kidnapped? No, I'm not."

"The adrenaline," he said calmly. "You're not used to it. You don't know that it makes you irritable as hell after the first rush. Then, a while later, it lets go of you and you feel like you've been run over by a truck."

Christy let out an explosive breath. "I'm not at that point yet."

"Let go, Red. You'll get there."

The moonlit night turned cool, then cold, as the big truck descended from the last mesa into a broad canyon. The shape of the land seemed familiar to Christy. After a few minutes she realized that they were approaching Remington from a different direction. The lights of the little town danced in the far distance like a band of fireflies.

Cain drove toward the lights for a few miles. Without warning he turned off and headed up a graded gravel road. Ahead, the spruce forest fanned down from the dark peaks like a ragged slice of midnight. Then the truck was in the forest, growling happily and taking the road like a smooth black beast.

When Christy was certain her voice wouldn't show uneasiness, she asked, "Why aren't you taking me back to the hotel?"

"That's the first place Hutton's county mounties will look for you."

"County mounties—oh. The deputies. I don't think they saw me."

"How sure are you?"

Christy thought about it. There was no guarantee Hammond hadn't caught a glimpse of her as she went across the balcony.

Red hair could be a real pain in the ass.

"I'm not sure," she admitted. "Where are we going?"

"My place. No one will look for you there. Tomorrow I'll ask around. If it's safe, I'll take you back to the hotel."

"Won't the deputies be suspicious if I'm seen with you tomorrow morning when you drop me off?"

Teeth flashed coldly in the darkness of Cain's beard. "They'll assume the obvious."

"Love at first sight?" she asked ironically.

"Something like that, Red."

"I'll take your word for it."

For a time Christy said nothing, dividing her attention between the night whipping by and the reflection of Cain in the side window. With each moment she felt adrenaline sliding from her, stranding her in the midst of numbing fatigue.

Five minutes later, Cain turned off the main road onto a side road that led up into a stand of tall, elegant spruce. The headlights glinted on glass windows and picked out the shape of a small cabin with a pitched metal roof. A wood corral stood in front of a small hip-roofed barn.

"How about Johnny?" Cain asked as he turned off the engine. "Will you take my word for him too?"

"What do you mean?"

Without answering, Cain got out and walked around to Christy's door and opened it. He stood in the doorway, keeping her in the truck.

"I wasn't Johnny's lookout," Cain said. "I don't even know what he was after inside the house—assuming he was after anything."

"He was," Christy said flatly.

"How long have you known Johnny?"

"I don't know him. I never even saw him until tonight."

"Then how did you know it was Johnny up in the house?" Cain asked reasonably.

Christy tightened, remembering the instant she had first spotted the big Indian crouched over a door.

"Bigger than Sheriff Danner," she said rapidly, "no movement in the right side of his face, handsome despite that, a handful of metal rods that had to be lock picks."

"That's Johnny," Cain agreed. Then he asked casually, "Since you'd never met him, how did you know his name?"

"One of the guards called him Johnny."

Cain whistled through his teeth. "Guards, huh? Did they grab him?"

"Yes."

Something in Christy's tone caught Cain's attention. He looked up at her. In the moonlight, his eyes flashed with a feral light.

"What happened?" he asked.

"My turn," she said tightly.

"What?"

"If you weren't with Johnny," Christy said, "why were you following him?"

"To see where he was going," Cain said dryly.

"Whose side are you on?"

"My own. What happened when the county mounties found Johnny?"

"Why do you care?" Christy retorted.

"Because I think he's the back-shooting son of a bitch who tried to murder me four months ago."

8

Christy opened her mouth but nothing came out. She tried again with the same result.

Cain's hands slid underneath Christy's arms.

"The first step is a big one," he said. "Ready?"

"No. I just discovered how Alice felt on her way down the rabbit hole."

This time Cain's smile was genuine. "It's not that long a step. Hang on."

He lifted, swung, and lowered. The ground came up beneath Christy's feet, but her knees gave way. She hung onto Cain's forearms, bracing herself.

Despite the coolness of the night, his shirt-sleeves were rolled back to his elbows. The flesh beneath her palms was warm, hard, and roughened by hair. He smelled like woodsmoke and spruce forest. She was standing so close to him that she could see the pulse beating in his throat.

Into the quiet came the sound of running water. A light breeze teased the trees. Branches brushed over glass, whispering to Christy of childhood and a past whose pain refused to die.

Fatigue washed over her in a black wave, threatening to pull her under and drown her. She realized that she was holding onto Cain and trying to push him away at the same time.

Cain looked curiously at her. "Red?"

"Sorry," Christy said faintly. "I think I was just run over by that truck you mentioned."

An instant later the world tilted and then righted itself again. Christy looked up into Cain's face in disbelief as he started forward, carrying her as though she were a child.

"I can walk," she said.

"I can do it better. You're shaking."

"I'm not."

Cain smiled. "What do you call it, then?"

Christy realized he was right.

"I'm cold," she said. "But you're not. How did you get used to adrenaline?"

"Jail."

"What?"

"For killing a man, just like Danner said."

"My God."

"Too tired to panic?" Cain asked coolly. "Good. Hang on while I open the cabin door."

Numbly Christy waited while Cain opened the door and maneuvered through. Inside, he set her down carefully but didn't let go.

"I'm not going to faint," Christy said irritably.

"You look like you are. Your skin is white."

"I'm a redhead. And I'm a lot tougher than I look."

He smiled slightly. "What's your name, tough girl?"

"McKenna. Christy McKenna."

"Aaron Cain," he said.

"I know."

"The gallery," he agreed.

Holding on to Christy with one hand, Cain reached over with the other to a wall switch. Light welled up, revealing a large open living space that looked like a combination of museum and workshop.

The first thing to catch Christy's attention was a worktable littered with pottery and sherds. A large pot with geometric designs rested, half repaired, on a potter's wheel in the center of the table. Several dozen sherds of the same color and design lay next to the wheel, awaiting assembly like the pieces of a jigsaw puzzle.

At the other end of the worktable, a mud-crusted pottery bowl the size of a large frying pan stood waiting to be cleaned. The bowl was intact except for a crescent-shaped chip missing from the rim on one side. There was an intricate, sophisticated design of black diamonds and chevrons just beneath the layer of red clay, waiting to be brought to light for the first time in centuries.

"You have that Alice-down-the-hole look again," Cain said dryly.

"If you offer me a cup of tea, I'll hit you."

"Brandy?"

"Please," Christy said.

She spoke without looking away from the artifacts that were stacked in every part of the room.
There were pots and bowls and mugs, some black
on gray, some red on white, and some a clean
white with brown or black designs. All of them
were ancient. Most of them had a timeless beauty.

Many of them were clearly art.

Lured by a culture and an artistic style that were
both new and intensely pleasing to her, Christy
went from room to room in the cabin, forgetting
her fatigue in her growing excitement.

The cabin was much bigger than it had looked
from the outside. And it was filled with art and
artifacts of all sorts. In addition to the marvelous
Anasazi pottery, there was contemporary Indian
art and antiques that had once belonged to white
settlers and frontiersmen. There were stone axes,
hand-forged steel trade tomahawks, and a powerful
wooden bow from which eagle feathers hung.

A cast-iron Dutch oven that had been blackened
by the fires of a hundred years stood on a shelf
next to a lustrous old grandfather's clock. Nearby
was a cherrywood fiddle so old the varnish had
begun to crack. The varnish had already cracked
on several of the paintings on the wall. The paintings were landscapes of the West as it hadn't been
for two hundred years or more.

Throughout the rooms, like crystalline punctuation
marks, were mineral specimens whose like Christy

had not seen short of the Smithsonian Museum of Natural History. Spikes of quartz older than the oldest civilization on earth flashed and glittered from every corner. Some of the crystal spikes were smoky. Some were opaque. Many were as clear as spring water. All were of museum quality.

On a bookcase was a golden sunburst shooting through the heart of a cluster of crystals that were so clear they were nearly invisible.

Beneath the incredible specimen, the old wood gleamed with a once-living grain. The glass doors of the bookcase reflected back Christy's image and that of Cain, who was standing in the doorway with a brandy snifter in his hand, watching her.

"Is it—" she began.

"Yes," he said before she could finish. "The sunburst is pure gold."

Christy started to turn around, but the books themselves caught her eye. From their good condition she had assumed they were modern. Suddenly she wasn't sure. She lifted the glass shelf and selected a volume whose title was as familiar as her childhood, for the book had been required reading in the Wyoming school system.

The volume in Cain's bookcase was a great deal older than her school text had been. The title page told Christy she was holding a first edition of *Banditti of the Plains*. It had been published privately in Wyoming in 1893.

"It's an account of the Johnson County war," Cain said, coming up behind her. "The cattlemen lost the war but they tried to limit the damage by buying up every available copy of the book."

Christy nodded absently, enthralled to be holding a piece of history.

"Michael Cimino tried to turn it into a modern epic," Cain added. "The result was *Heaven's Gate*."

"Almost as big a fiasco as the original," Christy said dryly.

"Real people died in the Johnson County war. Only reputations died in Hollywood."

Something in Cain's voice reminded Christy that he knew very well how men died. Carefully she closed the old book and eased it back into place in the bookcase.

"If that book is what it says it is—a first edition—it must be worth a great deal," she said, changing the subject.

"It is."

Christy thought back to the avid collectors she had met on the ride to Xanadu a few hours earlier. A few hours and a lifetime ago. She felt as though she had crossed an invisible divide in her life.

"Are you a collector?" Christy asked.

Cain smiled coldly. "Do I look like a rich man?"

"Your clothes don't. Clothes can be changed. What can't be changed is the eye that selected all these things," Christy said, gesturing around the cabin. "You have an extraordinary eye, Cain. Are you a dealer?"

"Only when I can't afford to hang on to something any longer, or when I find something better."

Silently Christy wondered if Cain selected women on the same principle—keep them until something better came along. If he did, he was definitely Jo-Jo's hidden lover. When it came to physical perfection, Jo-Jo was definitely museum quality.

"Well-made things last longer than any of the people who own them," Cain said. "A good cooking pot, clay or cast iron, is like the land that way. It connects you with something that endures a hell of a lot more years than one human life."

"Yes," Christy agreed, surprised by Cain's matter-of-fact acceptance of death, his own included. "But most people don't like to think about that."

"Most people don't like to think, period."

Cain nudged Christy's fingers with the snifter he was holding.

"Drink this while I start a fire."

She took the fragile crystal glass and lifted it to her mouth. As she breathed in, tasting it, she made a surprised sound.

"Armagnac!" she murmured.

"What did you expect, wood alcohol with a twist of chewing tobacco for flavor?"

Christy ducked her head, hoping that Cain couldn't see the flush on her cheeks. Indeed, she hadn't been expecting much in the way of finesse from a Moki poacher's liquor cabinet.

"Sit down," Cain invited, gesturing to the furniture behind him. "I'll have the fire going in a minute."

The sofa was small, almost a loveseat. If two tried to sit on it at once, they would feel every breath the other took. Christy had been forced by circumstance to be that close to Cain more than once already tonight. The thought of any more intimacy was unsettling.

She passed up the couch and sat in the big easy chair near the fireplace. As soon as she settled in to its depths, she realized that it must be Cain's favorite chair—it smelled faintly of him, evergreen and woodsmoke, soap, and the elusive, indefinable scent that was the man himself.

I wonder if he scents me half so clearly?

The thought disturbed her. She wasn't accustomed to considering men and women in such primitive terms—scent, strength, danger, death, and life itself.

Rather grimly Christy took a drink of the Armagnac. The clean, complex, heady liquid spread through her like sunrise.

"You didn't get this at the state liquor store in Remington," Christy said.

"No," he agreed.

"As a matter of fact, I think they were pouring it at Hutton's party tonight."

Cain looked over his shoulder at Christy through narrowed eyes.

"Yes, they were," he said. "And yes, this probably came from Hutton's private stock."

"Are you friends with him?"

"No."

Cain turned back to tend the fire.

"Then it's the fabulous Jo who is your—ah, friend," Christy said.

"With Hutton's slut for a friend, a man wouldn't need any enemies."

The casual contempt in Cain's voice shocked Christy.

"Sounds like a man scorned to me," she said.

"Not as scorned as she was."

"What does that mean?"

"What do you care, Red?"

"I'm a reporter," Christy said quickly. "I ask all kinds of questions."

"A reporter. Jesus."

"You make it sound worse than being a burglar."

"Honey, I'd rather have an honest burglar any day. At least you know up front what he has in mind."

Cain stood and went to the liquor cabinet, which had been a icebox in the previous century. After a moment he pulled out a bottle shaped like a banjo and poured two fingers of Armagnac into a second snifter.

Then he leaned against the fireplace and cradled the snifter expertly against his palm, putting the stem between his long, surprisingly elegant third and fourth fingers. He held the snifter unself-consciously, the way a man would if he were alone and knew that Armagnac needed human warmth to be fully released.

And all the while he watched Christy with eyes the same golden color as the fire he had just kindled in the hearth. Unlike the flames, Cain's eyes were cool, a wolf's eyes studying something new, trying to decide whether it was dangerous, edible, or simply meaningless to a solitary predator's life.

"Is that what you were doing in Hutton's house tonight?" Cain asked finally. "Research?"

"After a fashion."

"What does that mean?"

"It's a pun," Christy said. "I write for *Horizon* magazine."

Cain said nothing.

"It's a magazine about international style," she added.

"I've seen it."

"Oh."

Christy started to take another sip.

"So you're doing another one of those fawning Hutton pieces," Cain said.

"I don't fawn in print or in person. I dissect style in the same way a critic dissects art."

Cain saluted her ironically with his snifter.

"So," he said, "you're doing another one of those pieces that tell women why they should buy Hutton's stuff even though it looks like dried flower arrangements from the five-and-dime."

Christy nearly choked on the potent liquor she was swallowing. Gasping, laughing, coughing, she wiped her eyes. When she could see again, Cain was watching her.

This time there was a smile in his eyes.

"I'm no advocate of floral arrangements, dried or otherwise," Christy said huskily. "I leave that to Myra."

"Who's she? Another model?"

"My boss. Until she fires me."

"Is that likely?"

Christy shrugged. As she did, she realized that Cain had diverted her questions about him and turned them into questions about her. It was a neat trick, one that few people could play successfully on her.

"Is that what you were doing tonight?" Cain asked. "Stealing a look ahead of the competition?"

"You'd probably like Hutton's new designs," Christy said obliquely. "Anasazi motifs all the way."

Cain bent over the snifter, swirled the liquid gently, and inhaled the aromatic fumes of the brandy. After a moment he tilted the crystal and let a bit of the tawny liquor slide down his throat.

"Anasazi?" he asked casually. "Are you sure?"

"Yes."

"How do you know?"

"The usual way," Christy retorted. "I saw the designs."

"When? In the house?"

"In the barn."

"Let me get this straight," Cain said. "You're here to cover Hutton's latest fashion twitch, but when the show began down by the barn you weren't there."

"I missed the formal show, but I saw some of the fabrics earlier. Grays, black, whites. Unusual geometries in the designs. Like that bowl on the worktable."

"Late Pueblo," Cain said.

But his eyes said he knew she was changing the subject.

"Very striking," Christy said. "There was an odd, curving stick figure too. Many of the designs revolved around it."

"Kokopelli."

The barely leashed intensity in Cain's voice and glance told Christy that there was more to the matter than a simple design. Then she remembered Johnny using that word to summon Autry.

And Peter Hutton.

Apparently Kokopelli was some kind of code word. Christy wondered if Jo-Jo knew it too.

Johnny used that word, she thought. Cain thinks Johnny shot him. Hutton is connected to Johnny. And to Jo-Jo.

Is that why Jo-Jo fears Cain? Is Cain why she's hiding?

"What does Kokopelli mean?" Christy asked.

"He's the Anasazi Pan. A hunchbacked, over-sexed flute player."

"A fertility symbol?"

Cain smiled thinly. "More like a symbol of unleashed sexuality."

"An odd choice for women's clothing designs."

"Not with his choice of model. Hutton knows what he's selling, and he knows just how to sell it."

The resonance of scorn and something deeper in Cain's voice made Christy feel chilled despite the brandy and the cheerful hearth fire.

Yet she wasn't afraid of Cain. Not really, not in any personal way. Wary, yes. Watchful, yes. Off balance, certainly. But she was certain at some primitive level that he wouldn't hurt her physically.

He was not the sort to take pleasure in giving pain.

Why did Cain kill whoever he killed?

And did someone really try to kill Cain?

Suddenly Christy became aware that the silence had gone on too long, that Cain was watching her with amber eyes that saw much too clearly. She started talking about the first thing that came to her mind that didn't have to do with death, near death, and Jo-Jo.

"Fabric isn't as rigid as clay," Christy said, "yet Hutton's designs work very well. They're mysterious, enigmatic, and primitive, yet sophisticated in the timeless way that balanced asymmetry often is."

Cain said nothing.

"After all the pastels and cloying designs he's been flogging these past few seasons," she said, "it's refreshing."

"You don't like Peter Hutton, do you?"

Christy was dismayed by Cain's insight. Usually people couldn't read her that well.

Usually she hid her reactions better, too.

"It's my job to write about Hutton, not to like him."

"Have you met him face to face?"

"Of course. Why?"

Cain's smile was thin and cold. "Most woman come into heat when they meet him."

"I'm not most women."

"No, you aren't," Cain agreed. "You're the woman I caught running flat out down the hill while Hutton's guards beat the underbrush."

Christy took a sip. She knew it was only a delaying

action. Soon she would have to stop fencing and either tell Cain the truth or tell him to go to hell.

Of the two, she would rather tell the truth. Not only was it her habit, she couldn't fight the growing certainty that she could trust Cain—up to a point.

That point was Jo-Jo.

The heady fumes bathing Christy's face were almost as intoxicating as the liquor itself. She took another sip and then another. The tawny Armagnac burst softly inside her, sending shock waves of warmth through her chilled flesh.

Distantly she realized that the top of her head felt light as thistledown, drifting, floating, flying . . .

Uh-oh. Altitude and alcohol are a potent mix.

Deliberately Christy set aside the snifter, but it was too late. The gleaming crystal was empty.

Cain leaned over, took the snifter, and poured another two fingers in.

"No, thanks," Christy said. "I've had enough."

"'In wine is truth,'" Cain said dryly. "I don't think you've had nearly enough."

Christy gave him a wary glance. "I've had as much as I'm going to."

"So give me as much truth as I'm going to get from you tonight."

She blinked, then smiled slowly. Not all the truth and no outright lies. The reporter's way.

"I was looking for Jo," Christy said.

The answer obviously surprised Cain. She smiled, pleased to have him off balance for once.

"Why?" he asked bluntly.

"Some people in New York told me she and

Hutton weren't as close as they had been," Christy said, choosing her half-truths carefully. "I thought she might be able to give me some—er, new insights into Hutton's character."

"Why were you looking for her in the house?"

"She wasn't in the barn with the rest of the models. Where else would she be?"

Cain said nothing.

"Some people hinted that she had a new lover," Christy offered.

Cain drank. Whatever he was thinking didn't show on his face.

"Do you know who it is?" Christy asked.

"Half the state of Colorado."

"Are you speaking from personal experience?"

"With Jo-Jo?" Cain asked sardonically. "No way. She doesn't have a personal bone in her body."

Jo-Jo!

Shock cut through the Armagnac's glow, shaking Christy. She thought she was the only person who had ever called Jo by that childhood name. No matter how much Cain might dislike Jo-Jo now, he had once been close to her, so close that he knew about her childhood.

He might even know about me, Christy thought. My God, what have I gotten myself into?

Without thinking, Christy reached for the snifter again. She took an incautious sip, swallowed, and blinked away the tears drawn by the powerful liquor.

"Jo-Jo?" Christy cleared her throat. "Is that what people call her?"

"It's what she called herself."

"Really? Any special reason?"

"Jo-Jo didn't need reasons," Cain said. "She thought just being sexy was a good enough excuse for everything she did."

"Did she tell you anything else about herself?"

"Why should she? She just wanted to see if making it with a murderer would feel any different."

Christy shuddered, relieved and horrified at the same time.

"You hate her," she said.

It was an accusation, not a question.

Cain sipped, swallowed, and lowered the snifter, revealing the grim lines of his face.

"Okay, Red. You didn't find the divine Jo-Jo in the house. What *did* you find that scared the hell out of you?"

"I saw—" Christy's voice caught as she remembered. "The guards. They beat Johnny."

The memory of the blows with pistol and fists, and the blood and the pain, made her feel cold all over again. She closed her eyes and took another sip of the fiery liquor.

"They beat Johnny in front of you?" Cain asked skeptically.

"They didn't know I was there."

"Where were you hiding?"

"Jo's closet."

"Why were they beating him?" Cain asked.

"He had been trying to break into a room down the hall. He spent several minutes working on the lock. Then he heard a guard and ran into Jo's bedroom to hide. I heard him coming and hid first."

"Must have been a hell of a lock."

"Why?" Christy asked.

"Johnny went to postgraduate burglary school—three years in jail."

As always, the mention of jail made Cain's expression even more forbidding.

"What did the guards want from Johnny?" Cain asked after a moment.

"They wanted to know what he was after."

"What was it?"

"I don't know," Christy said. "He didn't tell them."

"So they beat him."

"Yes. And . . . I think they were afraid of him. Physically."

"Smart men. Johnny's a famous brawler. He can take a lot of hammering. He can give even more."

"Tonight, he was taking it." Christy swallowed. "They hit him in the face with a pistol."

"Doesn't sound like Hammond."

"It was the other one. He liked hitting Johnny. I could see it. It . . . he . . ."

Christy took a quick sip, trying to take the taste of fear and nausea from her mouth.

"Then what?" Cain asked, but his voice was more sympathetic than his words.

"Johnny got scared," she said simply. "He wanted to talk with one of Hutton's aides."

"Anyone in particular?"

"Mr. Autry."

"Bringing Autry in would be like throwing a drowning man an anchor," Cain said.

"He seemed pleasant enough when I met him, despite his drugstore cowboy clothes."

"Autry is a retired FBI agent."

"I can see how a man in your position wouldn't think well of him."

"'A man in your position,'" Cain quoted coolly. "As in ex-con?"

Christy took refuge in another sip of brandy.

When she looked up again, Cain was watching the fire. She had never seen such raw intensity in any man as she did in him right now.

Automatically Christy lifted the brandy to her lips, trying to drive away the persistent sense of chill that had begun with Jo-Jo's call and had done nothing but increase since then.

"Red?" Cain asked softly.

She looked up.

"Why were you really up in Hutton's house?"

9

While Christy foundered for words, Cain watched her with a curious expression on his face. It was almost as though they were on a first date and he was trying to decide whether or not to kiss her good night.

But Cain's eyes were measuring rather than playful. They told Christy bluntly that he knew she had been lying to him. What he didn't know was why.

Christy closed her eyes. It was a mistake. Alcohol, altitude, and the aftermath of an adrenaline jag made her sway. Chills chased over her. She was cold. Shivering cold.

Instinctively she wrapped her arms around her body and held on tightly, trying to hold in her own body heat.

"Are you going to faint on me after all?" Cain asked.

"N-no," she said, her voice uneven. "Damn it, no! I've never fainted. Ever!"

Christy struggled to her feet and stood with her back to Cain, swaying slightly. Before she could take another breath, his hands were beneath her elbows, steadying her.

Cain was close, almost as close as he had been when he had grabbed her in the stand of trees. Christy remembered the strength of his grasp then. It was just as strong now. And just as careful of her softer flesh.

"What kind of trouble are you in, honey?" Cain asked gently.

"I'm cold," she said. "T-that's all."

And she was. All the way to the marrow of her bones. Cold.

Cain's fingers tightened for an instant before he let out a long breath and accepted Christy's refusal to confide in him.

"All right, Red. We'll play it your way for a while. Sure as hell my way isn't getting us anywhere."

"What does that mean?"

"It means if you're cold, I've got just the thing for you. Can you walk or do you want me to—"

"I can walk," Christy interrupted hastily.

"Damn. I was looking forward to carrying you."

Cain's lazy, teasing tone startled Christy. She gave him a swift look over her shoulder. His smile was as warm as the firelight reflected in his eyes.

"Don't look so worried," Cain said, amused. "I may be an ex-con and a Moki-poaching son of a bitch, but I'm a gentleman where good women are concerned."

Christy smiled uncertainly. "You forgot the bit about high-grading."

Cain laughed and shook his head at the same time. "You'd sass Satan himself, wouldn't you?"

Her smile widened.

"What is a high grader, anyway?" she asked.

"Someone who skims the best of a mine's ore and leaves the rest for the legal owners."

"Oh. The mineral specimens?" Christy asked, looking at the golden sunburst encased in pure crystal.

"Yeah. They were gotten legally, by the way. I have a permit to hunt specimens in a lot of the old mines around here."

"And the Moki poaching?" Christy asked casually.

"I have a permit for that, too. Digs on private land are perfectly legal. Ask Hutton."

"Why him?"

"My best stuff came from the old Donovan ranch before Hutton bought it, fenced it off, and started digging himself."

Christy remembered the fantastic artifacts she had seen that afternoon. The "stuff" must indeed have been good. She didn't blame Hutton for wanting to keep it to himself.

When Cain led Christy out into the night, the cold air bit through her silk blouse and jacket as though she were naked.

"This is going to warm me up?" she asked.

"Trust me, Red. On this, at least."

Christy looked up into the darkness but could see only the dense black silhouette of a tall man. The width of his shoulders blocked out part of the sky. His eyes were hidden. So was his expression.

But the hand beneath Christy's arm was patient, not demanding. He was waiting for her decision. She could go back into the house and the certainty of a fire in the hearth, or she could trust Cain and follow him into the cold night.

"All right," Christy said simply.

She sensed rather than heard the long breath Cain let out. His fingers curled caressingly around her arm for a moment, then relaxed.

"The moonlight should be bright enough," he said, "but if you want a flashlight, I'll get one."

Christy looked at the silvery light flooding the mountainside, making the world both beautiful and unreal. Far above the timberline, patches of white snow glistened like quicksilver against the darker peaks. Nearby, black groves of spruce whispered and sighed beneath the breeze.

"No flashlight," Christy said. Then she added in a tone of surprise, "I've missed the night."

"Too many city lights?"

"Yes."

Where the path entered a spruce grove, there was a sudden rustling in the underbrush.

"Are you afraid of dogs?" Cain asked quickly.

"No."

An instant later Christy wondered if she might not have spoken too soon. The animal that appeared in the moonlit path wasn't the sort to inspire confidence. Big, long-legged, rangy, the dog looked more like a wolf than man's best friend.

"Hello, Moki," Cain said as the dog trotted forward. "I hope you caught dinner, because I didn't bring any for you."

A long, bushy tail waved in response to Cain's casual ruffling of the animal's ears, but it Christy who was the center of the dog's attention.

"He won't bother you unless you ask," Cain said. "Maybe not even then. He's been on his own since I got shot."

"You left him to fend for himself?"

"Better hungry and half wild than locked in a pen," Cain said flatly. "Moki wouldn't have lasted more than a month at the end of a chain."

Cain's voice said more than his words. The time he had spent in jail had given him a hatred of being penned, locked up, chained.

In the moonlight, Moki looked lean and predatory. Yet there was something endearing about the set of his ears. Christy dropped to one knee and held out her hand.

"Hi, Moki," she said softly. "I don't blame you for being wary of strangers, but you're okay with me. I won't hurt you or tie you up. I'd even feed you if I had anything good to eat."

Drawn by Christy's low, calm voice, the dog came to her like a black wraith, sniffed her hand, and then nudged her palm with his nose in a frank invitation to be petted.

Christy laughed lightly and gave the dog his due.

"You sweet old fraud," she said. "You're not a big bad wolf after all, are you?"

Moki grinned, showing double rows of gleaming teeth. Christy laughed again.

Talking quietly to the dog, she scratched Moki's ears and down his muscular chest, enjoying the warmth and the sensation of lean, sinewy health the dog radiated. It had been years since she had touched anything but city dogs with fine pedigrees and the kinds of neuroses that come from living in tiny apartments and walking in Central Park.

"Come on, Red," Cain said after a time. "Moki will soak up that kind of loving until you go numb from the cold."

"He's warm."

"So am I. Want to scratch my ears?"

Smiling, shaking her head, Christy stood again. When she started forward into the brush, Moki fell in along her left side. Bracketed by male animals, she felt both amused and safe from whatever the darkness might offer.

From the path ahead came the sound of running water. As they approached, spruce trees gave way to a clearing where a small stream murmured and dreamed in shades of silver through the night. Water tumbled down the rock face of a little scarp, crossed one edge of the clearing, and disappeared again in the trees.

Cain guided Christy toward a small rock pool off to one side of the stream. At first the little pool seemed a part of the stream itself. Then Christy realized it was separate, although it was connected to the creek by a rock-lined channel that had been made by man rather than nature.

The pool was twenty feet across and so clear it looked like a condensation of moonlight. Wisps of steam rose gracefully from the surface.

"A hot spring?" Christy asked, hardly able to believe her luck.

"This country is volcanic. There are lots of hot springs around."

Cain dropped to one knee, tested the water, and made a pleased sound.

"I used to dream about this pool while I was in the hospital," he said. "Couldn't wait to soak out the aches. Better than any painkiller out of a bottle."

He went to the head of the pool and added rocks to the gate across the channel from the stream. The effect was to cut the flow of stream water into the pool. The surface of the hot spring became very still, with only lazy swirls at the center to mark the slow upwelling of water from far below.

"The stream is meltwater," Cain said. "Starts with snowfields at twelve thousand feet. Doesn't warm up much on the way here, but we'll be grateful for it once the pool starts heating up."

With that, Cain stood and undid his shirt in a ripple of steel snaps popping open. He was too far away for Christy to see anything more than the vague gleam of moonlight on naked skin.

There was a lot of it.

"Cain—"

"If you're too shy to strip, use this as a bathing suit," he said.

He tossed his chambray shirt to Christy. She caught it automatically. The cloth was warm with Cain's body heat. A shiver of sensation went through her that had nothing to do with the chilly air.

"What about you?" Christy asked.

"I'm about as shy around you as Moki is."

"He has a fur coat," she retorted.

"So do I."

White teeth flashed in a grin that vanished when Cain turned his back.

"Holler when you're in the pool," he said. "But hurry. It's damn cold with that wind off the snowfield."

Christy looked at the gently steaming water and then at Cain, remembering his words.

If I were going to rape you, I would have done it back when I had you laid out beneath me on the ground.

I'm a gentleman where good women are concerned.

"Cain?"

He made a rumbling, questioning sound.

"Am I a good woman as far as you're concerned?" Christy asked.

"Yes."

"Just like that? No qualifications, no questions about my past?"

"Just like that."

She took a deep breath. "Okay. I'll holler when I'm in the pool."

"Watch your step. It gets deep real fast. I built in

some high-backed wooden benches underwater along the left side."

Christy undressed quickly, shivering when the air bit into her unprotected body. She paused over her underthings but stripped them off too. Two wisps of black lace were more of a tease than a concealment.

Working quickly, she put on Cain's dark shirt. The cuffs came over her fingertips and the tails dragged well below her knees. When she reached for the last snap, she discovered she had fastened them crookedly in her haste to get into the warm pool.

"Tough," she muttered.

She hurried to the pool and stepped in. Cain had covered much of the pool's bottom in smooth river pebbles, all rounded and gentle on bare feet. The water was hot, but after the first shock it felt delicious rather than painful.

The benches Cain had warned her about were angular black shadows just beneath the silver surface of the water. The seats were set at different depths in the pool, where the rock shelved steeply down. She settled cautiously onto the closest bench. The water rose to her collarbones and stopped.

Cain's shirt billowed and floated around Christy like a tent. The sensation of liquid warmth against her naked skin made her feel weightless and free.

"Ahhhhhh," Christy groaned. "God, that feels good."

"Are you hollering, Red?"

"I'm whimpering with pleasure."

"I'd rather hear you holler so I can come in out of the cold."

"Holler holler holler!"

Cain's laughter rang in the night. "Keep your shirt on, Red. I'm coming."

"It's your shirt, remember? But I'm keeping it on just the same."

Still smiling, Cain sat down on a rock and started to unlace his boots. Christy watched him in the moonlight as he pulled off his shoes and socks with quick, efficient motions. The play of silver light and dense shadow on his shoulders both revealed and then concealed his lean power.

Like Moki, he was indeed furry. Unlike Moki, the hair was concentrated on Cain's chest before narrowing into a pencil width and vanishing below the waistband of his jeans.

Cain stood and undid his jeans with the same casual efficiency he had unlaced his hiking boots. As he started to peel off his pants, Christy realized she was staring.

He knew it too. It didn't seem to bother him a bit. Jeans and underwear together slid down his body far enough that the pencil line of fur flared suddenly into a wedge.

Hastily Christy looked away and muttered, "You worked as a male stripper, did you?"

"Several weeks in a hospital," he said. "Close enough."

The distinct sound of metal buttons hitting

stone came as Cain dumped his jeans on top of a boulder.

"Catheters and bedpans and hundreds of sponge baths given by lots of different nurses," he added. "After a while, modesty is just a word."

Christy studied the patterns of the current right under her nose. Soft splashing sounds told her Cain was wading into the pool. Then came a soft groan of pleasure and a swirling displacement of water as he slid onto the other end of the bench, an arm's length from her.

"Okay, Red. It's safe to look now. I've got my back to you."

The laughter in Cain's voice irritated Christy.

"I'm not a prude," she muttered.

"Who said you were?"

"You did."

"Not me," Cain said. "It's damned refreshing to find a female who can still blush."

"You've been chasing the wrong kind of women."

"More like vice versa. Ever since Hutton showed up, his high-priced whores have been going through the local men like grass through a goose. Especially Jo-Jo. She loves flat-backing with cowboys, Indians, and dangerous western trash like me. *Fighting* men."

The contempt in Cain's voice was enough to chill the pool. Christy turned toward him, but the protest on her lips died when she saw the ragged, barely healed scar that gleamed between his spine and his shoulder blade.

Then Cain eased down onto the next bench below, and the scar vanished beneath the blackly gleaming water.

"Ohhhh, Jesus," he said in a low voice.

"What's wrong?"

"Nothing," he said through clenched teeth. "That just feels better than it should."

"What are you, some kind of closet Puritan? It feels as good as it feels."

"God help me, a philosopher as well as a reporter."

With that, he slid all the way under the water and stayed there for what seemed like a long time. When he surfaced and drew a deep breath, he sounded to her like a great silky dolphin rising from a midnight sea.

Cain stretched, arching his back as though trying to make supple the muscles that had been ripped by the bullet and were still not fully restored.

"You shouldn't have been carrying me," Christy said.

Cain turned toward her.

"You weigh a lot less than the iron I pumped to rebuild my right side," he said. "More fun, too."

The lazy, teasing note was back in his voice. The white flash of his smile and the dense, water-slicked black of his beard were dangerously attractive.

And the clear, still waters of the hot spring didn't hide nearly enough of him. The moon was like a searchlight.

Christy closed her eyes and concentrated on the delicious heat of the pool rather than on more dangerous things.

"Chicken," Cain chided.

"Cluck cluck."

He laughed, took a breath, and slid beneath the healing water again.

Strangely, Christy sensed that Cain was more pleased by her reticence than put out.

"Cain?" she asked when he surfaced again.

He made a rumbling sound that said he was listening.

"Sheriff Danner said you weren't supposed to come back up to the mountains," Christy said. "Is that true?"

Cain took so long to answer that Christy thought he was going to ignore the question. She knew she should let it go, but even as the thought came, she knew she wasn't going to do it. She needed to know more about Cain, with an intensity that went beyond her customary curiosity as a reporter.

"Cain?"

"Whoever shot me was used to killing mule deer," Cain said after a time.

"I don't understand."

"He used a soft-nosed slug. I lost some of my right lung. It collapsed."

Christy made a low sound and wished she hadn't asked.

"The pulmonary specialist said I'd run the risk of collapsing the lung again for a while," Cain said.

"He said I'd probably do better down on the flats for a year or two."

"Then why did you come back?"

"I wanted to look around before the snows came."

"But—"

"I haven't had any problems so far," Cain said, talking over Christy's objection.

"You were breathing hard when we were running down the creek bed."

"So were you."

"I haven't been at this altitude since I left home," she said.

"A western girl, huh?"

"Why do you say that?"

"Land doesn't come this high back east."

Christy hesitated, then shrugged. "Yes, I was raised in high plains country."

"Wyoming?"

"Yes."

"Not a city miss after all," Cain said.

The satisfaction in his voice irritated her.

"I was born in Wyoming," she said. "I *chose* Manhattan. I'm city all the way."

"Bull."

"Not!"

Cain laughed quietly.

"Boyfriend waiting for you?" he asked after a moment.

Christy made a sound that could have been taken for agreement.

"A city man?" Cain persisted.

"Very much so. An investment banker. Manhattan, London, Tokyo, Cali, Los Angeles, Bonn."

"Sounds like he spends more time in jets than with you."

"And vice versa."

"A modern relationship," Cain summarized.

"I suppose."

Christy yawned deeply, unraveled by the heat of the pool.

Cain went underwater again. When he surfaced, both he and Christy sat quietly, letting the pool draw out the last of the adrenaline jag.

Knots of tension Christy hadn't even been aware of loosened. The hot spring was as comfortable as any European spa she had ever visited. The only thing lacking was the chlorine stink of water that has to be chemically treated in order to be safe.

Christy closed her eyes and lay against the back of the bench, listening to the quiet night sounds and the liquid murmurings of the stream. High above her, the ebony dome of the sky was strewn with sparkling diamond chips. Nearby the wind combed gently through the evergreens, making a long whispering sound, as though trees and stream were trading secrets.

Letting out a long sigh, Christy arched her back and spread her arms, letting them float just beneath the surface. She was as close to perfectly comfortable as she could remember being. Ever. Jo-Jo and Peter Hutton and all the rest of her worries seemed a million miles away.

And Cain was very close.

It should have worried Christy, but it didn't. She was too wonderfully unstrung to worry about Cain at the moment. Like Moki, his ferocity was more apparent than real.

At least, when it came to people. Cain had a very fierce love of the artifacts that filled his house. His words about *Banditti of the Plains* had been casual, but not his eyes. They had held a combination of leashed excitement and unleashed hunger that reminded her of nothing so much as Howard Kessler, the man who had taught her about the tangled relationships between human emotion and human style.

Cain understood what Howard had: there was a connection between an artifact and the human being who once had made it. That connection was elemental, compelling, and intangible.

But very real. It was the connection, not the price the artifact commanded in the marketplace, that mattered.

It's simple, Christa. Artifacts are reservoirs of human memory and emotion. Next to that, what is dollar value but something to amuse people who have no imagination? People who have money and no imagination follow fashion. People who have imagination and no money fashion styles.

Howard's words echoed in Christy's mind as though they had just been spoken. It occurred to her that Cain and Howard had more in common that either would have suspected.

For one thing, they both had been immune to Jo-Jo.

At least, Cain said he was.

Far above the hot spring, a jet tunneled with a faint roar through the night sky. Christy thought of Nick, a man who flew so frequently his body never knew when it was at home.

Nick was a modern man who never showed anger or passion or pain, who lived much of his life forty thousand feet above the rest of the world. No scars, no fears, nothing more real than a balance sheet at the end of the month.

Only now, amid the limitless western landscapes of her childhood, did Christy understand in just how many ways Nick was wrong for her, and she for him.

And, knowing it, there was no way of going back.

Wrong man. Wrong woman. Nothing personal. Just a case of mistaken identity.

Christy's thoughts drifted, wrapped in heat and chips of diamond stars. Slowly all thought drained away, leaving her utterly relaxed.

"Unwinding?" Cain asked in a lazy, rumbling voice.

"Unwound." She yawned. "My brain is guacamole dip."

There was silence, another yawn.

"What were you really doing in Hutton's house?" Cain asked.

The words were so casual that it took a few moments for Christy to realize what Cain had said. When she did, she felt as if she had been manipulated in a particularly unpleasant way.

"So that's what the kid-glove treatment was all about," she said angrily. "You were just softening me up for another round of questioning."

"Red—"

"My name is Christy," she interrupted, "and why the hell do you care what I was doing?"

"Because I think you know something that would help me figure the connection between Hutton, the Secret Sisters, Johnny Ten Hats, and the slut who set me up to die."

"*What?*"

"You heard me."

"Jo?" Christy whispered.

"The one and only."

"No. Never! She couldn't!"

"Yeah? How well do you know her?"

Christy shut her mouth and looked at the naked, powerful, and very intelligent predator who had neatly outmaneuvered her and was now watching her. The cold fires in his eyes had been rekindled. She felt his bleak intensity wash over her like a black wave.

"Sheriff Danner thinks it was an accident," Christy said.

"Sheriff Danner is full of shit."

"What about the rest of the town?" she demanded "What do they think?"

"They think someone was after a little spring venison, and I got in the way."

"But you don't believe that. You think Jo had something to do with it," Christy said.

"Yes."

"Why? What reason would she have?" Christy demanded. "It's preposterous!"

Cain looked at Christy and said nothing.

"That's one of the things I wanted to ask Johnny," Cain said finally.

"Johnny? What does he have to do with any of it?"

"I told you. I think he was the one who pulled the trigger."

"Why?" Christy asked starkly.

"I was going to ask Johnny the same thing, just as soon as I got my hands on him."

"Why not ask Jo, if you really believe she was part of it?"

"That lying bitch? I wouldn't piss on her if she was on fire. She knows it, too. She's made herself real scarce since I've been back."

Christy opened her mouth but could think of no words to say to the man who hated her sister with such breathtaking savagery.

A chill that no hot spring could banish sank into Christy's soul.

No wonder Jo-Jo fears Cain. And no wonder she's hiding somewhere. He blames her for a hunting accident that wasn't really anyone's fault.

Christy didn't believe for a second that Jo-Jo had any part in Cain's shooting. Jo-Jo was self-centered and spoiled and wild, but that didn't make her a murderer. Her thoughts raced.

Cain is wrong about Jo-Jo. All I have to do is prove it. The quickest way to do that is to tell him what I know.

Except for Jo-Jo being my sister.

If I tell Cain that, he won't listen to anything else I have to say.

And if Deputy Hammond recognized me jumping over the balcony, I'm going to need someone on my side. Someone who knows the territory. Someone who won't cringe at a little casual pistol whipping.

Someone like Cain.

What a mess. What a damned ugly mess!

"Kokopelli," Christy said.

"What?"

"He's more than one of Hutton's design motifs."

Cain waited.

"Johnny told the guards he wanted to talk to Autry about Kokopelli's sisters," Christy said.

Cain sat so silently that he seemed to have stopped breathing. Then he let out a sound that was both a laugh and a soft curse.

"Son of a bitch," he said. "I was right."

"About what?" Christy said, suddenly afraid that she might have hurt her sister rather than helped her.

There was no answer.

"About what?" she demanded.

Cain simply laughed again.

Anger shot through Christy.

"I see," she said in a clipped voice. "The usual old-fashioned relationship. The little woman gives and the big man takes."

She stood up abruptly and waded out of the pool.

"Red, what the—"

"Thanks for the lesson," Christy interrupted curtly. "I'd almost forgotten that western men are the biggest reason western women can't wait to go east!"

10

The gray light of dawn was split into four squares. A dormer window in a sleeping loft. A cover of clouds.

Christy awakened slowly, aware of a slight movement on the bed beside her. She felt the pressure of another body along her leg, and the warmth of something resting on her hip. It felt about the weight of a man's hand.

"You worthless son of a bitch. Enjoy it, because it will never happen again."

Cain's voice was soft and amused, despite his words.

The pressure along Christy's leg and hip shifted as Moki raised his head and stared toward the bedroom doorway. His tail beat once on top of the down cover, then again.

"Red, you awake yet?" Cain asked, flipping on the light.

He was standing in the doorway with a bundle of cloth under one arm and a cup of coffee in his right hand.

"Go to hell," she muttered.

"Still peeved that I wouldn't take you back down the mountain last night?"

Christy threw him a glance that would have frozen the hot spring.

"Whew," he muttered. "How about a truce?"

"How about jumping off a cliff."

"How about a cup of coffee?"

Christy looked at the steam gently rising from the mug in Cain's hand. The heady aroma told her the coffee was made the way Gramma had always done it—strong, thick, boiled. It would clear the cobwebs out of her brain and put the sun right up in the sky.

She tried to think of a way to get the coffee and still ignore Cain. She couldn't. A look at his gleaming eyes told her that he knew it.

"Coffee," she said in a clipped voice.

"You're welcome."

"Sorry, am I down on my etiquette? Are kidnappers expecting to be thanked these days?"

"Bullshit," Cain said without heat. "I haven't done one damn thing except refuse to drive down a mountain road after drinking brandy and soaking my brains out in a hot spring."

"Does that mean I dare to hope for my freedom this morning?"

"You can hope for whatever you want. Maybe you'd like me to call Danner and tell him you're coming in to talk about Johnny Ten Hats, Hutton's house, and Kokopelli?"

"You wouldn't!"

Cain's eyes narrowed. "Don't bet anything important on it, Red. Someone tried to kill me. I'm going to find out why."

Christy closed her eyes.

"Mexican standoff," he said casually. "You won't tell me why you were sneaking around in Hutton's house. I won't take you back to the hotel until you do."

Her eyes flew open. Cain was watching her, waiting for her decision.

"What's for breakfast?" she asked through her teeth.

"Oatmeal. Wear these. The slick city stuff you had on last night got shredded up pretty bad when you went over the railing."

Cain tossed the bundle under his arm to Christy. It came apart to reveal a pair of white denim jeans, a blue-and-white windbreaker, a fuzzy white silk pullover sweater, and a man-styled shirt in pale blue.

Jo-Jo's clothes.

"Where did you get these?" Christy demanded.

Cain's black eyebrows rose at the tone of her voice.

"Jo-Jo came prospecting here awhile back," he said ironically. "She left in such a hurry she forgot to pack."

With a hand that trembled slightly, Christy reached for the clothing. Though sturdier than the silk clothes she had slept in, the jeans and blouse were still lightweight.

Spring weight.

"Don't worry," Cain said sardonically. "I had them disinfected."

Christy let out a long breath. Whenever Jo-Jo had left the clothes in Cain's cabin, it hadn't been recently. Jo-Jo wouldn't have been caught dead in spring fashions after May first.

"They won't fit," Christy said.

"Honey, from what I saw last night, they'll fit just fine."

She turned toward Cain so quickly that her hair fanned out like wind-driven fire.

"What?" she demanded.

"When you stalked out of the pool, my shirt fit you like black paint. Anyone ever tell you that you have nice legs? And a really *fine* ass."

Christy's mouth dropped. "I don't believe this."

"Yeah, it set me back too. Spent a long time thinking about it before I got to sleep. You sure you're a good woman?"

"You're just doing this to . . . to . . . to keep me off balance!"

Cain's smile flashed against his black beard.

"Works both ways, honey. Breakfast in five minutes. Don't be late, or I'll feed yours to that no-good son of a bitch who slept where I wanted to."

Cain left, taking the cup of coffee with him.

Three minutes later Christy walked into the kitchen. To her amazement, Cain had been right about the fit of the clothes. She had left the waistband unbuttoned to make room for breakfast, and the pant legs were nearly two inches short, but the rest fit as though tailormade. Jo-Jo's key was in her left pocket.

"Shoes and socks by the chair," Cain said without turning away from a bubbling pot on the stove. "See if they fit. It's rough country where we're going."

"Where is that?"

"To see if we can't track down Kokopelli and his 'sisters.'"

Christy looked at the Gore-Tex walking boots and the white socks. She had no doubt they would fit. She and Jo-Jo had shared shoes since the eighth grade. Or, rather, Jo-Jo had regularly raided Christy's closet.

She went through a show of trying on the shoes anyway. They fit.

"Are prisoners allowed telephone calls?" Christy asked.

"Not if they keep harping about being prisoners when they know damn well they could leave any time."

Christy's teeth clicked together.

"May I use your phone?" she asked carefully.

"Sure."

Christy went to the phone on the kitchen counter and called the hotel.

"This is Christa McKenna in room eight. Any messages for me?"

"You have one from Mr. Hutton."

"Read it, please."

"Sorry I didn't have more time with you. What did you think of the show, or were you too busy looking around Xanadu to watch? Signed, Peter."

Christy's heart paused, then beat more quickly.

Is that a veiled hint that Hammond recognized me? Or is it just a polite way of letting me off the hook if I don't want to talk about my response to Hutton's designs yet?

"Thank you," Christy said tightly. "Any other messages?"

"Yes."

"Read them all, please."

"Staff librarian says no more material on Hutton or Xanadu. Call me when you've seen the designs. It's signed *Myra.* There's one more. No signature."

"Read that one too," Christy said impatiently.

"Thinking about you. Are you thinking about me?"

Goddamm it, Jo-Jo, you know I am!

"That's it?" Christy asked.

"Yes."

"Nothing else? No one asking about me?"

"No, ma'am. But the day is young."

The clerk's dry reminder that it was barely dawn made Christy flush. She had no doubt that the locals were being kept fully up to date on the immoral comings and goings of Hutton's guests.

"Thank you."

Christy hung up.

"If Sheriff Danner is after me, he's keeping it quiet," she said.

"Cops usually do."

"I'll bow to your superior knowledge of law and disorder."

"You do that, Red, and we'll both be better off."

With that, Cain pulled the pot off the stove and began dishing oatmeal into two soup bowls.

"No fried steak, fried eggs, fried potatoes, flapjacks, and toast?" Christy asked. "What's the West coming to?"

"At altitude, you need your blood for carrying oxygen, not for digesting a bellyful of heavy food. Later, you'll thank me for it."

"Hold your breath," she muttered.

Cain set a cup of coffee in front of Christy and sat down across from her.

They ate in a silence that slowly became companionable. Wryly she acknowledged that it was hard to be angry with a man who was eating mush across a small table from you.

Christy ate almost as much as Cain did before she remembered the top button of the jeans. After he finished his second bowl, Cain stood and began clearing the table with the easy motions of someone doing a familiar task.

"You cooked, I'll clean up," Christy said, falling into the childhood pattern of dividing chores.

Cain raised his eyebrows but said only, "I'll get a few things and warm up the truck."

"How long will we be gone?"

"However long it takes. All day, probably."

Christy started to object that she had to stick around in case Jo-Jo tried to get in touch. Then she thought of the taunting message.

Let her stew.

The kitchen took only a few minutes to straighten up. Christy was drying the soup bowls when she heard the truck rumble to life.

Outside, the morning was chilly and calm. The air carried a quiet promise of winter sometime soon. The sweater, blouse, and windbreaker Christy wore were just barely enough to keep her warm. Her breath hung like smoke in the still air.

Moki trotted past her and over to the idling truck. Its white exhaust plume was like a long exhalation from a great beast. The dog sat on his haunches beside the rear cargo doors. His rakish ears were held at an expectant, hopeful angle.

"Okay, boy," Cain said.

He opened a cargo door. Moki leaped aboard like a deer clearing a garden fence.

"Warm enough?" Cain asked, looking at Christy, frankly approving the fit of her jeans.

"So far."

"Let me know if that changes. There's an extra wool shirt in the back you can use as a coat." He smiled slightly. "If it's too big, we'll just wet it down and let it shrink to fit."

"Promises, promises," she retorted.

He laughed. "Glad to see you've got your sass back."

Cain dropped a full leather knapsack near the dog and closed the door. He was wearing a lightweight down vest and a long-sleeved wool shirt over his jeans and work boots. His Stetson had been traded for a black knit watch cap. He offered a similar cap to Christy.

"It'll be windy in places up on the mesa," he said. "If you keep your head warm—"

"—the rest of you will stay warm," she finished for him. "Followed by, 'It's easier to stay warm than to get warm.'"

"Your mama didn't raise any dumb ones."

"My mama didn't raise any, period, dumb or smart. But thanks for the cap. Cold ears were the curse of my childhood."

Cain headed the truck back in the direction they had come the night before. The light was just coming up in the east, behind the San Juan Wall. In the west, the stars were beginning to dissolve into a sky that was more indigo than black.

There were few other vehicles on the road. Cain tuned the radio to the local Remington station. The 6 A.M. local newscast was of the neighborhood bulletin board variety. Cattle prices, road repairs, bar brawls, and snow level in the passes.

"No bodies discovered in the ditch beside the road," Cain said. "No strange disappearances reported. No prowler caught in Hutton's house. No prowler *not* caught in Hutton's house."

Christy looked sideways at him.

"Either Johnny talked his way out of trouble or they haven't found the body yet," Cain summarized.

"But then, the day is young," she said dryly, quoting the desk clerk.

The weather forecast was more serious than the local news. Brisk northern winds and the expectation of snow flurries at higher elevations.

Cain shut off the radio when feed prices, hog futures, and the price of light sweet crude became the focus.

"How high are we going?" Christy asked.

"What we're looking for has never been found above eighty-one hundred feet."

"Just what are we looking for?"

"I'm not sure. A ruined house and a grave, most likely."

"Lovely," Christy muttered. "You're a real ray of sunshine this morning."

Wind outside buffeted the heavy truck. A chill passed through the steel doors into the interior.

Christy pulled the windbreaker more firmly around her. When a cold nose nudged her ear, she jumped.

"It's just Moki poaching a little affection," Cain said.

Turning, Christy saw what Cain meant. Moki had leaped out of the cargo area and onto the back seat. As she watched, he braced his hind feet on the cushion and his front feet on the console between Christy and Cain. She reached for the dog's shaggy neck and worked her fingers into his thick fur, enjoying his sheer animal warmth.

"What's a Moki?" she asked.

"Moki is what the local people called the Anasazi long before eastern professors arrived and started digging."

A dirt road came into the highway. Christy turned and looked at it quickly.

"Isn't that the road we were on last night?" she asked.

"Good guess."

"What makes you so sure I was guessing?"

"Most city folks can't find their way on any ground that isn't named, numbered, and nailed down by concrete."

Five miles farther south, Cain turned off the main road onto a dirt track that headed across the scrub flats toward a white sandstone mesa.

"Do you know where we are now?" he asked.

"We must be close to the south edge of Hutton's ranch."

"Dead on. You haven't been in the city long enough to lose your sense of direction and distance."

"I had the advantage of a detailed research package on Xanadu," Christy admitted.

"Good. From here on out, you can tell me if I'm on Hutton's land. That way we won't trespass any more than we already have."

"I thought he fenced all of it."

"He tried," Cain said dryly. "But along the back side, where the plateau unravels into a thousand nameless little canyons and gullies, Hutton sort of ran out of steam."

"How did the rancher who owned it before Hutton—"

"Donovan," Cain said.

"—keep his cattle from wandering?"

"The locals let God and the red-rock cliffs take

care of most of the fencing. The rest got sorted out at roundup."

Christy frowned. It had been a long time since she had been anywhere that wasn't laid out in a grid and measured down to the last inch.

"Where's your U.S. Geological Survey map?" she asked.

"Hip pocket. Want to get it?"

She gave him a sideways glance.

"We're maybe half a mile south of the technical boundary of Xanadu," Cain said, smiling slightly.

"Who owns the land on either side of the road?"

"We do."

"Yeah, right," Christy said.

"The Bureau of Land Management just administers it for us. Nice of them, huh?"

She laughed.

"So tell me when you figure we've crossed back onto Hutton's land," Cain said.

It wasn't as easy as it sounded. In the next mile, the gravel road deteriorated to a dirt road and then to a set of tracks that meandered across a heavily grazed meadow and started up a short chute canyon.

Cain slowed and reached over to pull the transfer case lever down into four-wheel drive.

"You do know how to drive, don't you?" he asked. "Just in case something happens to me out here."

"I drove a tractor before I wore my first pair of high heels. Actually, it's one of the few things about the West that I miss. Driving, that is. You can have tractors."

Cain's smile flashed against his beard.

"Four-wheel freedom," he said, "is something big-city folks just don't understand. Same way I'll never understand how two million people a day can march down piss-stained stairs into the underworld and commit their lives to a cadre of coked-out Puerto Rican subway jockeys."

"Let's hear it for the all-white West," she said sardonically.

"My mother's mother was born in Chihuahua. My father's mother was Sioux. Two of my great grandparents were Scots. The rest were garden-variety third-generation American mongrels."

Christy looked curiously at Cain.

"My only quarrel is with life choices, not bloodlines," he said. "Cities give me hives."

There was a finality in Cain's tone that struck Christy.

"Was it a city where you . . . ?" She hesitated, not sure quite how to ask. "Is that where you got in trouble?"

Cain's smile reminded her of Moki's toothy grin, more than a bit savage.

"Yes, a city was where I killed a man. Boy, actually."

"Why?"

"What makes you think it wasn't just for the hell of it?"

"Because you aren't a just-for-the-hell-of-it kind of man," Christy said impatiently.

"Thanks—I think."

Cain flexed his hands on the wheel and let out a harsh breath.

"I was a boy too," he said. "Rob was twenty. I was nineteen. It was a rowdy beer bar in Oakland."

Christy waited, holding her breath without realizing it.

"We were both students," Cain said evenly. "The judge called it 'mutual combat.'"

"Then why did you go to jail?"

"Mutual combat is good for a manslaughter conviction under California law."

There was a silence while Christy tried to think of a tactful way to ask her next question. In the end she simply asked it.

"How long were you in jail?"

"Two years, two months, and six and a half days."

Christy looked at Cain and tried to imagine him locked up. It was difficult. He was so fiercely independent.

"The second half of my sentence was spent in a forestry camp called Susanville, up near the Oregon border."

"At least . . ." Christy's voice died.

"I wasn't caged the whole time?" Cain finished bitterly. "Yeah, semi-freedom is better than none. But all of it is the only thing worth calling freedom."

The edge in his voice made Christy wish she had never raised the subject.

The little canyon narrowed to a slot, then suddenly widened out again into a mile-long valley. On both sides, white and rust-colored sandstone cliffs rose for at least five hundred feet.

Christy was amazed at how quickly and unexpectedly the terrain could change, and at how many nooks and crannies were carved in the edges of the mesas. The land was like Cain, full of surprises, rough yet compelling, in its own way and on its own terms.

"Well, Red? Are we on Hutton's ranch yet?"

Christy thought back over the twists and turns in the road and sighed.

"Without a compass and a map," she admitted, "I wouldn't even guess."

"Even with a compass, it's impossible to be certain. God didn't get around to painting geodesic survey lines on this land."

"That's why you like it," Christy said.

"A man can be as free as he wants to be here," Cain agreed.

"Look!" Christy said, pointing to the left.

A herd of eight dark, shaggy elk broke and scattered, startled by the truck's sudden appearance. The leader was a big bull with a rack of horns that spread like a wall trophy waiting to be claimed. He stood his ground on a little rise and bellowed a challenge.

"He won't feel so confident in a month," Cain said.

"Why?"

"Hunting season opens."

"Ah, yes. Blood sports. Welcome to the Wild West."

"You think the beef you ate at Hutton's party volunteered for the job?" Cain asked.

She sighed. "No. And yes, I loved each politically and medically incorrect bite."

Cain laughed. "Supermarkets and cellophane wrap insulates you from reality."

"Some of it," she agreed. "On the other hand, I don't think you would be able to walk past a psychotic or simply alcoholic human being in Manhattan with anything like the callousness I've been forced to learn."

"Is living in the city worth it?"

"It's better than what I came from."

"I didn't know farm life was so bad," Cain said.

"You were never a poor girl who was smart instead of pretty," Christy said in a clipped voice. "You were never raised in a rural hell where men looked you over like a pony they might want to ride or a heifer they might want to breed. Nothing personal. Just another farm animal."

"Pretty girls always—"

"I wasn't pretty," Christy said flatly. "My sister got the looks in the family. I got the brains."

The certainty in Christy's voice amazed Cain. He looked at her and saw she wasn't fishing for compliments. She believed every word she had said.

"Your sister must be drop-dead beautiful," Cain said after a moment.

"She is. What about you? Sisters? Brothers? Parents?"

"Yes. Parents in San Francisco. One sister in London, married to a diplomat. Another in Seattle running a coffee shop. A brother in Boston. Lawyer. I see them all when I make my rare book rounds."

"When is that?" Christy asked.

"Winter. Too damn cold to do much else, then. What about your sister?"

"What about her?" Christy retorted.

The buried emotion in Christy's voice made Cain glance sideways at her.

"Not close, huh?" he said sympathetically.

"Not the way you mean. But in other ways . . ."

Cain waited.

"Our parents died when I was eight," Christy said. "Not that I noticed. Dad was in and out of jail so often I barely knew him."

"So that's why you didn't run the other direction at the thought of an ex-con."

"Dad was a drinker. Mother drank right along with him. They had a high old time, right up until they drove into a train at eighty miles an hour."

"They missed a hell of a daughter."

Startled, Christy turned and looked into Cain's amber eyes.

"Who raised you?" he asked quietly.

"Gramma. Mother's mother. She died the year I left home."

"What about your sister?"

"She takes after Mother. Wild. But—"

"But?" he asked in a soft voice.

"She's all I have left," Christy said with barely leashed emotion, wanting Cain to understand. "In a whole world of strangers, she's the only one alive who shares the first half of my life, of my memories, of myself.

"There were times I wanted to throttle her, times

I wanted to scream at her to grow up, but . . . I love her."

Cain smiled crookedly. "Sounds like me and my brother. Don't get along worth a damn most of the time, but when it counts, we'll back each other right to the wall, no questions asked."

"Yes," Christy said, sighing. "And each time, you hope this time it will work. This time all the pain of the past be worth it."

Christy didn't notice Cain's look or the intensity of her own voice. She was caught up in a dream that was as old as her childhood and as deep as her need to love and be loved in return.

Right to the wall.

"This time," Christy said fiercely, "this time will be different."

11

"*How much do you know about the Anasazi?*" Cain asked.

Christy blinked and realized it was the second time Cain had asked the question. She shook her head as though throwing off the past, even though she understood that cutting free of the past wasn't possible.

"I know the Anasazi are called Moki by the locals," she said.

Cain smiled slightly.

"And Peter gave me the spiel yesterday afternoon," she added. "All about the new theories of the Anasazi empire in the San Juan Basin."

"What Hutton knows about the Anasazi empire could be put into a one-paragraph press release."

"So says the Moki poacher."

"This Moki poacher has a Ph.D. in archaeology."

She stared at Cain.

"Like I said, there's not much to do around here in the winter," he said dryly.

"Should I call you doctor?"

"I won't answer. I studied because I wanted to know, not because I wanted the world to know I knew."

Tilting her head, Christy studied Cain as though he were a new design of unknown origin and intriguing complexity.

"You're looking at me the way Moki looks at a rabbit," Cain said after a minute.

"Cultural synthesis."

"You do and you clean it up."

Smiling, Christy shook her head.

"Too late," she said. "You've already given the game away. You're not a tongue-tied cowboy. You're not a stump-dumb bar brawler. You're quite civilized under all the—"

"Don't count on it," Cain interrupted sharply. "A fancy degree doesn't make silk out of pigskin."

"No, but it makes some really intriguing patterns on even the toughest hide," she shot back. "The most elegant and powerful designs often come from cultural synthesis."

Cain steered the truck around a hole in the road.

"The story of humanity," he said. "Thesis, antithesis, synthesis. Repeat as necessary."

"You studied some philosophy along with pots and bones."

"Like I said. Winters are long."

"What did you specialize in?" she asked.

"Guess."

Christy smiled. "So, professor, according to your studies, what did the Anasazi do to amuse themselves during the long winters?"

"Beyond the obvious?" he asked dryly. "I've found small polished pieces of bone that could have been markers in various games."

"But no sign of written language?"

He shook his head.

"They almost certainly had a fine and complex oral tradition," Cain said after a time. "The Pueblo Indians still do. Much of it is secret, though."

"Medicine men?"

"Medicine *women.*"

Cain looked at the suddenly eager expression on Christy's face and smiled.

"Matriarchy," she said with satisfaction. "Those Mokis were no fools."

"I don't know about matriarchy. I suspect it was more a matter of women being given half of the cosmos to look after and men taking care of the other half."

"Good God. A nonabsolutist approach to the universe," Christy said ironically. "What makes you think the Anasazi were that unusual?"

"The Pueblo tribes today have a system rather like that. Each sex has vital work to do in ensuring the continuation of the clan and the universe."

"Yin and yang," Christy said softly, as though talking to herself. "The most subtle, elegant, and powerful symbol yet devised by human beings. Of course, because the Chinese created it, the women got the short end of the symbol."

Cain laughed outright. "Only in the written description. The symbol itself is neutral. Male in the heart of all that is most female. Female in the heart of all that is most male."

She gave him another surprised look.

"The Anasazi were sophisticated," Cain said. "Their empire spread all over the San Juan Basin, everywhere you can see from here."

Christy looked out over the rugged land, trying to imagine an empire spreading away on all sides. Wherever she looked, mountain peaks either distant or close rose like stone crowns from the Colorado Plateau. The vast plateau was itself a maze of piñon and cedar, big sage, and creeks lined by willow and alder.

The Anasazi had lived in all those places. But it was along the southern and western edges of the Colorado Plateau that they had left cliff houses built into the bones of the land itself, in places where the plateau eroded down to the desert in a series of mesas separated by finger canyons and joined by an endless sky.

"It's hard to believe there was ever an empire in the San Juan Basin," Christy said finally.

"There may not have been an empire in the way you mean," Cain said. "An empire suggests that somebody called the emperor was in charge. I don't think things worked that way."

Christy turned from the land to this man who was becoming more interesting the longer she was with him. It was an unusual sensation for her. Most people she met affected her in the opposite way, becoming less intriguing as they became more familiar.

"I think we're talking about informal domination," Cain said, "an integrated system of communities with its center in Chaco Canyon."

"Where's that?"

"Over in northwestern New Mexico. We're at the far northern reach of the Anasazi empire or sphere of direct influence or whatever right now."

Christy frowned, remembering something she had read years before.

"I thought Mesa Verde was the northern edge of the Anasazi range," she said.

"The academics used to think so too. The locals knew better. You can't walk out here without kicking up some shards."

Cain slowed the truck, letting it creep over a patch of deeply rutted road.

"Then how did we miss the signs of the Anasazi for so long?" Christy asked.

"You don't find what you're not looking for," Cain said dryly.

"Why are we looking now?"

"A few years back, Uncle Sam decided that a place couldn't be flooded, filled in, or paved over if there were signs that the area might have archaeological interest."

Christy frowned. "So?"

"So every time someone wants to put in a road to a distant site to wildcat for oil, or the Army Corps of Engineers pursues its mandate to dam up everything bigger than a stream of piss, potsherds and walls are found."

Christy made a startled sound. "What?"

"There are thousands of sites in the San Juan Basin. Hundreds of thousands, more likely. Hell, there were more people living in some parts of the basin seven hundred years ago than there are today."

"Good-bye dams and oil drilling."

Cain gave Christy a sidelong glance. "You really think so?"

She grimaced. "No. How do they get around the rules?"

"Other rules. The construction crews call in archaeologists, who go over the site."

The tires thumped and Moki's claws scrabbled for purchase as the truck "walked" over another rough patch of road. Christy braced the big dog, much to Cain's amusement.

"If the site looks special," he continued, "the archaeologists work like hell to save what they can before the bulldozers arrive or the dam is finished and the site is flooded."

"Does that happen often?" Christy asked.

"So often there's a name for it. Salvage archaeology."

"Sounds grim."

"It's better than no archaeology at all," he said. "There are probably five hundred professionals digging and exploring in the San Juan Basin right now, and the more work that's done, the more sites they find to explore."

The truck settled onto a less rugged course. Cain

accelerated but not much. The road was disintegrating into a track.

"They've discovered a network of roads that reaches all the way over into Utah and up into this part of Colorado," Cain said.

"Roads? Real roads like the Roman roads in Britain?"

"As real as it gets. Thirty feet wide and straight as a ruler, come hell or high ridges. When the terrain became too steep, they cut stairs."

"Must have been the male half of the Anasazi power structure that built the roads," Christy said. "Women are smart enough to go around an obstacle."

Cain's smile was white against his short black beard. Christy was discovering that the contrast fascinated her, making her want to see more of it.

"The Anasazi built those roads long before the Spaniards came," he said. "There were no wheels or four-footed beasts of burden to worry about on the stairs."

"How did they manage?"

"Probably it was slave labor," he said, "though a lot of the university folks would as soon lynch you as discuss the possibility. They prefer to think white men invented slavery."

Christy laughed. "I hope you got your degrees by correspondence course!"

Laughing quietly, Cain shook his head.

"But reality has a way of sneaking past ivory towers," he said after a time. "The Anasazi weren't simple, noble savages or New Age collectivists. Despite their lack of written language and metallurgy, they developed a unique, sophisticated civilization.

"In fact, astronomers have found evidence that Chaco Canyon could have been laid out as a giant solar and lunar observatory."

"Like Stonehenge?" she asked, startled.

"Same principle, different means. Same need."

"Religion?"

"Survival. When your growing season is dangerously short, planting at the best time is a matter of life and death."

Christy nodded, still watching the man rather than the land. The excitement buried in Cain's voice reminded her of herself on the trail of a new style, one that transcended simple fashion and became something very close to art.

Half closing her eyes, she settled more deeply in the seat, enjoying the intensity of Cain's deep voice as he talked about something he obviously loved.

"Lots of new information is turning up every day," Cain continued. "So much that the universities can't keep a lock on it. Hell, they can hardly keep a handle on it!

"Even Moki poachers have been invited to attend some of the university conferences and talk about what we've found. But we have to translate it into professor-ese and document it their way. No oral traditions for university types."

"If they tolerate you, they must be desperate

for your information," Christy said blandly.

He gave a crack of laughter. "That they are. We've found trade goods in Anasazi sites that could only have come from thousands of miles away."

"Argillite and abalone shells from the Pacific," Christy said.

Cain threw her an approving look.

"And copper bells and parrot feathers from the interior of Mexico," he added. "Trade routes almost two thousand miles long."

"Quite an empire. What happened? Where did it all go?"

"No one knows."

Christy blinked. "Why not?"

"No written language. All we know is that the empire began to collapse in the twelfth century, just about the time the Chaco community was reaching its zenith.

"That's where the Sisters come in. And this is where we leave the road."

"What road?" Christy muttered.

Cain stopped and shifted the Suburban into low range. Then he turned right and headed straight up a sandstone slope.

"Cain!"

"You've been in the city too long. Hang on, honey. It looks a lot worse than it is."

The slope was broken and weathered, a long rough ramp onto the top of another mesa. Cain let the Suburban set its own speed. The truck rocked from side to side unpredictably, for the angle of the ramp was so steep that the hood hid everything but the sky.

Christy held on to the door with one hand and Moki's ruff with the other, bracing both of them until the truck gained the top of the mesa.

"Moki's going to wonder what he ever did without you," Cain said.

There was another faint track out through the scrub forest of piñon and cedar. Though rough, the way was better than the sandstone chute had been.

"Those are the Sisters up ahead," Cain said.

Christy's head whipped around. "What?"

"The Sisters. At least that's what some people call them."

He pointed to two rock spires that rose a hundred feet above the mesa. Like massive stacks jutting out from a piñon sea, the Sisters were the remnants of a long-vanished, much larger rock formation.

"Is that where we're going?" she asked.

"Yeah."

"How far away are they?"

"Several miles."

The columns stood together and had generally similar shapes, but they were distinctly different colors. The smaller was a reddish sandstone that rose in slender elegance above the land. The other was nearly white toward the top, the color of the mesa's cap rock.

"The Sisters are hard to see from the flats, even when it isn't cloudy like today," Cain said. "From most angles, only the white one shows. But once we get over to them, you can see damn near to Arizona and New Mexico."

The intensity of Cain's eyes as he watched the Sisters was almost tangible. He was like a wolf sighting prey.

"Why are the Sisters so important to you?" Christy asked.

"I have a theory about the Anasazi, why they settled in some of the unlikely places they did. If my theory is right, there will be Anasazi sites clear up here, close to the mountains."

"And you want to be the first to find them."

Cain gave Christy a glance.

"You have a problem with that?" he asked.

"I'm old-fashioned," she said after a moment. "I think archaeological sites should be explored by professionals rather than stripped by even the most highly educated pothunter."

"I'd agree with you, if it were that simple."

She raised auburn eyebrows but said nothing.

"There are thousands and thousands of sites that the academic archaeologists won't get to for decades, if then," Cain said evenly. "Some of those sites are on public lands. A lot are on private ground, farms and rangeland."

"Still—"

"What's the local bean farmer supposed to do when he plows his most productive fields in spring and turns up artifacts?"

"Call in the university," she said.

"Then what? He could wait a long time before

the professionals show up to do their research, particularly since neither the state nor the federal government has money enough to properly explore and document the sites that are known already."

Christy grimaced. She might have lived in the city since she was nineteen, but she hadn't forgotten the intractable rhythms of the seasons.

"Planting time doesn't wait," she said.

"Modern farmers and ancient Anasazi have that in common," Cain agreed. "Short growing season. If the farmer knows his discovery means taking that field out of production for years, he'll keep his mouth shut, plow the whole damn thing under, and plant beans."

"So in come the salvage archaeologists."

"Yeah. Not a perfect solution, but not as bad as it could be. We get to look at something new and the farmer gets on with the job of making a living on marginal cropland."

Christy thought about the designs Peter Hutton had derived from the finds on his own land. He had simply gone in and taken what he wanted when it had been found, despite the protests of his hired archaeologists.

Not a perfect solution either. Yet having seen the extraordinary turtle, Christy wondered if she could have taken a chance on leaving it behind in its academically proper place.

And perhaps losing it to unstable walls.

Cain braked the truck at the edge of a five-foot-deep channel in the rocky top of the mesa.

"End of the line for wheels," he said. "We go on foot from here."

The two massive pinnacles Cain called the Sisters were still more than a mile away, but they were close enough to tell that the red sandstone column was straight-sided and clean. The white spire, though taller and thicker at the top, was shot through with cracks and miniature fault lines wherever the white stone appeared. Sections of pale rock had fallen away in several places, leaving the column with an appearance of being hump-backed, twisted, oddly misshapen.

As Christy opened the door, Moki leaped across her seat to freedom. While she climbed down from the truck, the dog dashed off a dozen yards, sniffed around beneath a spreading cedar tree, left his mark, and came trotting back.

There was a wildness in the wind blowing through the stunted junipers and piñon pines. Overhead, the gray clouds seethed and parted. A shaft of golden light flowed across the red pinnacle but soon vanished as the clouds flowed together again.

"You picked a fine morning for a hike," she said as Cain joined her.

"Talk to your friend Hutton. We could have gotten a lot closer than this if he weren't so damned irritable about trespassing. We're close to the edge of his deeded land now. Then it becomes federal land. Of course, he leases that and treats it as though he owned it, but so does every other western rancher."

Cain scrambled down the near side of the runoff channel that had halted the truck. A few moments later he clambered up the other side and headed off through the broken country.

Moki jumped down onto a rock, leaped across to the other side with muscular, four-footed grace, and trotted after his master. Cain disappeared behind a screen of head-high brush without so much as a backward look to see how she was handling the rough land.

"That will teach me to call him a pothunter," Christy said to herself.

She scrambled through the channel with less grace than Moki, but she got the job done. A gust of chill wind combed through her hair as she climbed up the far side. She zipped the windbreaker, pulled the watch cap over her head, and trotted to catch up with Cain.

He strode along easily, his vest unzipped and his hat back on his head. Against the gray clouds, his eyes gleamed like citrine. For all the ease of his stride, there was an intense wariness in him that made Christy uneasy.

"Is something wrong?" she asked.

He shot her a surprised look. "Not yet."

"Are you expecting something to go wrong?"

"No, but I wasn't expecting anything the last time I was here, either."

"When was that?"

"The day I got shot."

Christy felt a chill that had nothing to do with the wind. She waited, but Cain said nothing more.

"Did you get shot right here?" she asked.

"No. Closer to the base of the Sisters."

"What were you doing?"

"Walking along through a stand of piñon pines, just like we are right now."

"And someone just shot you? No warning?"

Cain nodded.

"Why?" Christy asked.

"If you believe Danner, somebody mistook me for a deer."

She looked at Cain. There was nothing the color of deer hide anywhere on him.

"I suppose it's possible," she said. "God knows a lot of range cattle buy it every hunting season."

"This wasn't hunting season."

"Were you out Moki poaching?"

"Red, Moki poaching may be a joke to you, but it's a felony," Cain said in a flat voice. "An ex-con would find himself in jail real quick if he picked up so much as a stinking potsherd without the landowner's signed, notarized permission."

"I'm sorry."

A flashing sideways look was Cain's only answer. Then he said something under his breath, yanked off his watch cap, and raked his long fingers through his hair.

"I'm a bit touchy on that score," Cain said finally. "I don't have permission to dig here. Hutton won't let anyone on his land, and the Bureau of Land Management won't let anyone dig, period."

"Then why are we here?"

"You can hike on BLM land. That's what we're

doing. Hiking. If you pick up so much as a pebble I'll make you put it back."

"Why are we hiking here, if it makes you so uneasy?" Christy asked.

"Because I believe I'll find evidence to support my theory about the extent of the Anasazi empire."

"Like what?"

"Ruins, grinding holes, potsherds, anything," he said.

"Why here?"

"Jesus, you're a regular fountain of questions."

"I'm a—"

"Reporter," he said, interrupting. "Yeah. I've noticed."

They walked quickly for a few minutes. Cain said nothing more.

"Well?" Christy said.

"Well what?"

"Why do you think the Anasazi will be here when nobody else thinks so?"

"I'll give you a copy of my dissertation," he said in a clipped voice.

Christy sighed and tried another tack.

"Is it likely you were shot by some jealous rival archaeologist, either professional or amateur?" she asked.

Cain laughed.

"Well," she retorted, "it makes as much sense as someone thinking you were a deer!"

"Most archaeologists are good at hunting pots and lousy at moving targets."

"So?"

"Whoever shot me was good enough to bring me down at three hundred yards."

Christy's hand wrapped around Cain's arm, stopping him.

"How do you know he was that far away?" she asked.

"I felt the bullet hit me and throw me back. I was on the ground, trying to figure out what the hell had happened, when I heard the report."

A small sound escaped Christy's lips. Without realizing it, her hand moved slowly, almost caressingly, on his arm.

"I'd estimate the time between the shock and the sound at not quite two seconds," he said evenly. "That means a range of three hundred yards."

With that, Cain started walking again.

"It also means," he said, "that whoever shot me had a telescopic sight."

Christy walked beside Cain, thinking hard. She snatched a twig off a cedar tree as she walked past it. The scent of the flat green needles was rich and astringent, like that in Jo-Jo's closet.

With a shudder of memory, Christy threw away the twig.

"Can you see much detail through a telescopic sight at three hundred yards?" she asked.

"You sure as shit can see the difference between a deer and a man, especially when the man is standing out in the open."

"Can you see enough to identify someone?"

Cain thought silently for a moment.

"Maybe," he said finally, "but only if you knew him on sight already."

"Do you know what you're saying?" Christy asked in an appalled voice.

"Yeah. Whoever shot me knew exactly who I was. Not an accident, Red. Murder, plain and simple."

12

Christy stood rock still, unable to move as the reality of what Cain had said broke over her.

Up to that instant she hadn't believed the shooting to be a deliberate act. She had assumed Cain was simply making an accident more understandable, more meaningful, by saying that the shot had been deliberate rather than a random bit of rotten luck.

But it hadn't been random and it hadn't been luck.

Murder, plain and simple.

Even now, Christy had a hard time accepting it. No one commits murder without a motive, and Cain himself had no idea why he had been shot.

Yet there was no doubt the shooting had occurred. Cain had the scar to prove it.

I've been in the city too long, Christy told herself unhappily. I find it easier to accept random violence than the idea of premeditated murder.

"Hello-o-o," Cain said, waving his hand in front of Christy's face.

She gave him a startled look.

"You keep staring at me as though I've just grown a set of antlers," Cain said, smiling.

"It's not every day a man calmly tells me that somebody tried to kill him."

"It's not the first time I've said it," Cain pointed out.

"But it's the first time I've—"

"Believed it?" Cain finished.

Christy nodded.

He turned away.

"Damn it, Cain! How would you feel if a stranger walked up to you with a story that someone was trying to kill him but everyone else thought it was just an accident?"

After a moment of hesitation, Cain ran a big hand through his hair, yanked the watch cap back into place, and looked over his shoulder at Christy.

"Come on," he said. "We've got some rough country to cover before those clouds decide whether they're going to get together and rain."

Moki came dashing in from some piñons with a predatory gleam in his eye and his long pink tongue hanging out. There was no doubt the dog loved the wild land and the even wilder wind. He nudged Cain's hand and danced over to Christy, vibrating with life.

"What does he want?" she asked.

"Not much. Just a little company when he's lonely or has something to share."

Before Christy could say anything, Cain was walking forward with long, lithe strides. Moki yapped excitedly and took off once more. Christy followed.

The sun was warm in protected places. Everywhere else the wind stripped heat from land and flesh alike. Yet Christy found herself enjoying the clean chill of the air and the slow-motion seething of the clouds high overhead.

The mountains that rose behind the mesa were already aflame with aspens turned gold by the frost. She knew that deer and elk at the higher elevations would begin to gather and drift toward the valleys, following summer as it retreated down the mountain slopes.

You thought you had left all this behind, she told herself. Yet it was always here, always waiting for you just a handful of hours from Manhattan.

And it will always be here.

Once that thought would have appalled Christy. Now it comforted her in a way she didn't understand, just as she didn't understand the depth of her attraction to Aaron Cain.

But like the land, the attraction was real.

As Cain and Christy approached a thick stand of piñon, Moki caught a hot scent and bounded into the thick of the trees. The grove exploded with noise and flashes of dark blue as birds flew up in all directions. The birds were bigger than robins and four times as loud. The blue of their feathers had a shiny, misty sheen, like the bloom on a plum.

Smiling, Cain and Christy watched the birds' wild flight, enjoying the bright blue specks of life racing before the wind. The birds jeered and called back and forth while they re-formed into a new flock. A few hundred feet away, they settled into another stand of piñons and attacked the ripe cones, stuffing the bounty of rich, oily seeds down their throats.

"Piñon jays," Cain said.

He bent over and picked up a deep blue feather that one of the birds had dropped. The feather seemed much darker now than any of the birds had been. Absently he held the feather next to Christy's red hair. His eyes said the contrasting colors pleased him.

Then, as though realizing what he had done, Cain opened his fingers and let the wind take the gleaming feather.

"Free and damned glad of it," Cain said. "But they've got a lot of work to do before winter, if they expect to survive. Out here, there's no such thing as a free lunch."

Calling Moki away from the jays, Cain resumed his swift pace. Christy followed, but only after her eye had followed the brief, erratic flight of the single feather. She went to the shrub that had captured the feather, plucked it free, and tucked the fragment of blue into her pocket.

As Cain and Christy approached the Sisters, they could hear the faint whistle of air currents playing around the twisted form of the white spire.

The sounds were eerie, ghostly, flutelike in their purity. They belonged to a world and a time where spirits had walked with mankind in uneasy unity.

Moki reappeared and paced beside Christy. Cain's pace slowed as his eyes scanned the landscape, seeking something only he knew.

"What are you looking for?" Christy asked finally.

"Anything that's out of place."

"Such as?"

"If I knew, I would have found it by now."

Christy looked at the Sisters and the raw, rocky land. Fallen slabs of red and white sandstone lay in heaps at the base of the two spires, but the disorder seemed quite natural. The tumbled rock was the result of untold years of wind and water erosion. Elsewhere, the mesa top was windswept and almost clean, like a well-kept floor.

The more Christy looked, the more she began to understand the rhythms of the land. For all its appearance of permanence to human eyes, the sandstone of the mesa was only temporary. Wind and weather dominated here, dissolving rock grain by grain and creating red sand that blew away on the wind.

The same forces worked on life, as well. In the sheltered spots, the cedars and piñons were straight and healthy. In open spots where the wind blew freely, the trees were knotted and hunched, like old men whose bodies have been twisted by time.

Cain walked to a small rock cornice that was a hundred yards from the base of the white spire.

He checked an angle over his shoulder, then scrambled up.

Silently Christy watched as he inspected the rock.

"This is where the killer shot from," Cain said.

"How do you know?"

"It's where I'd shoot from if I expected to kill a man exploring around the Sisters."

He moved back and forth on the stone ledge until he finally settled for a spot that was sheltered behind two waist-high boulders. He hunkered down behind the rocks, going through the motions of a sharpshooter seeking to rest the barrel of his gun in the notch between the boulders.

After a moment Cain found the best position, raised an imaginary rifle, and mimicked the actions of firing, working the bolt and reloading. His gaze traced the arc a spent cartridge case would make when it was ejected. He scrambled over to that spot and dropped out of sight, searching for something behind the boulders.

Alone with the wind, Christy waited for Cain to reappear. It seemed an unreasonably long time before he emerged from the shadowed spot in the rock and jumped down with a grimly triumphant smile.

"Three-oh-eight, just like I thought," he said.

In his hand was a dark metal cylinder the size of a pencil stub. He dropped it into Christy's palm.

"It's spent brass. A shell casing," he explained.

Christy nodded. She had seen many such bits of metal as a girl, worn and weathered from many seasons out in the elements. But this casing was bright, new, barely touched by the relentless elements that reduced stone to sand.

"Makes you feel good to know the sheriff has done such a thorough job of investigating my shooting," Cain said sarcastically.

He took the casing from Christy and dropped it into his shirt pocket.

"Shouldn't you wrap it up in cloth or something?" she asked. "Can't someone use it as evidence, even if the sheriff doesn't know his rump from a warm rock?"

Cain's smile flashed, then faded.

"Half the deer hunters in southwestern Colorado shoot that caliber Winchester," he said. "Unless I can come up with a weapon—and a motive—it would be like hunting red sand on the Colorado Plateau."

"But somebody tried to kill you!"

"You sound like you believe me now."

"I do," she said simply.

"There was more than one 'somebody,'" Cain said.

"How can you be so sure?"

Cain gave Christy an odd look. "I was there, Red. Remember?"

"At three hundred yards, without binoculars, lying on your back and wondering what hit you— how the hell could you be so sure it was deliberate, much less that Jo was involved?" Christy demanded.

For a moment, Cain was too surprised by her intensity to respond.

"You *said* you weren't ever lovers," Christy continued in a rush, driven by fear and something more, a complex of emotions she couldn't name and didn't want to examine. "What motive would she have for wanting you dead?"

Cain's eyes narrowed. "You sound like you changed your mind about believing me."

"I believe someone tried to kill you," Christy said. "I have a hard time believing any man would turn down a girl like Jo."

"She had a hard time believing it too. But I wasn't nineteen anymore."

"What does that have to do with it?"

"A smart man needs only one Jo-Jo in a lifetime," Cain said bluntly. "I had mine when I was nineteen."

The bleak look in Cain's eyes was a warning against asking any more questions.

Christy ignored it.

"You're not making sense," she said.

"How about trusting me?" he retorted.

"How about trusting *me*?"

For the space of several breaths, the only sound was the spectral fluting of the wind around the Sisters.

"Jo-Jo came on to me just like she did to every other man between the age of eighteen and ninety-eight," Cain said in a clipped voice. "When I didn't send back the right signals, she got curious. We talked."

Christy waited, breath held.

"She was a strange, scared kid, down underneath that beauty," he said. "But you had to dig damned hard to get under the veneer."

"What was she afraid of?"

"Growing old. Getting ugly. Living. Dying." Cain shrugged. "You name it. If she couldn't control it with sex, it scared her."

Christy's ragged sigh was covered by the eerie notes of the wind.

"From time to time she would show up at the cabin," Cain said. "She wanted a place to sleep because Hutton was pissed off at her. At least, that's what she said."

"You didn't believe her?"

"I don't think she knew the difference between truth and lies. Whichever worked was fine with her."

"So you think she came up there because she just couldn't wait to trip you and beat you to the floor?" Christy asked acidly.

Cain's mouth curved in a smile that was as thin as a new moon.

"Jo-Jo would have lain down for me if I'd asked," he said. "But that wasn't what she was after."

"Was she really afraid of Hutton?"

Again, Cain shrugged. "What interested her was my Anasazi stuff."

"Jo?" Christy said, startled.

"Yeah, it surprised me too. But she was really excited about it, kept asking me questions."

"So you let her stay."

Cain nodded curtly.

Christy remembered what Cain had said about what Moki wanted from people. Not much. Just a little company when he's lonely or has something to share.

Cain had wanted to share his love of the Anasazi culture. Jo-Jo had been willing to listen.

"Then," he said, "I came back from a trip last winter and found Jo-Jo had been shacked up in my cabin with Hutton's hotshot jet jockey. I threw both of them out so hard they bounced."

Christy winced.

"Later I discovered some of my Anasazi bowls were missing," Cain said.

"And you think Jo took them?"

He nodded.

"Why would the world's best-paid model need to steal Anasazi artifacts?" Christy asked.

"Jo-Jo's like that," Cain said with a faint grimace. "She sees something she wants and she takes it."

Christy thought about Gramma's necklace. Jo-Jo had taken it, but not for the usual reasons. The money value of the nuggets didn't matter to her. It was the loss to Christy that had mattered. Simple vengeance against someone Jo-Jo couldn't control.

"Were the artifacts especially valuable?" Christy asked curiously.

"Just to me. They were key pieces of evidence supporting my theory of Anasazi settlement patterns. My paper had been accepted, but suddenly the best evidence was gone. If I gave a damn about academic recognition . . ."

"It could have ruined you," Christy finished.

"It sure didn't help. Even with all the in situ photographs, I had a hell of a time getting the dissertation published."

"So that's why you hate Jo."

"No."

"Then why?"

"Leave it alone, Red."

"I can't," she said starkly.

For a long moment, Cain watched Christy out of bleak eyes.

"Jo-Jo liked having men fight over her," Cain said in a flat tone. "After I threw her out, I ran across her in a bar in Montrose. She had Johnny Ten Hats panting after her, but it wasn't enough. She did everything but a hand job to get me interested. Then she tried to get me to fight Johnny over her."

Christy stood so still she ached with tension. "What happened?"

"Johnny was willing. Hell, he'd fight over a bent penny. But I wasn't nineteen anymore. I wasn't going to hammer on a man for the sake of a lying slut again. I walked away."

A chill went over Christy. "Again? The fight in California? It was over a woman?"

Cain didn't answer.

He didn't have to. Christy saw the old rage and pain quite clearly in the instant before he narrowed his eyes, shutting her out.

"I understand now why you hate Jo," Christy said after a moment. "But . . ."

The look on Cain's face was closed and cold. Christy took a deep breath and chose her words carefully.

"But just because Jo tried to get you to fight Johnny," she said in a low voice, "is that any reason to think she tried to kill you?"

"Look around," Cain said.

Christy started to object, then did as he asked. She saw nothing that she hadn't seen before.

"You see any way a man could follow me here and then scramble up into that niche without my spotting him?" Cain asked.

She looked around again before she turned back to Cain and shook her head slowly.

"A few days after I walked out on Johnny in that bar, Jo-Jo called me," Cain said.

An odd stillness settled over Christy. She wanted to tell Cain to stop talking, to stop telling her more than she wanted to know about the beautiful little angel who had grown up into something quite different.

"She apologized for taking the bowl that had a drawing of the Sisters with Kokopelli and his flute," Cain said. "She told me she had found a little ruin up here on the Sisters mesa."

"No."

Cain didn't hear Christy's low, ragged voice. He was caught in his own moment of agony when he had nearly died trying to breathe icy air thorough a bullet hole in his chest.

"She said she wanted to explore the ruin but didn't have—"

"No," Christy whispered again.

"—time, so she thought she'd pass it on to me as a way of telling me how sorry she was."

"There must be a mistake."

"Yeah. It was made by the man who didn't quite murder me."

"Jo is selfish and sometimes cruel but I can't believe she would do that. I just can't."

Christy's words stopped abruptly as she realized that Cain was watching her with predatory intensity.

"You sound like you know her real well," he said.

"I do." Christy heard her own words and added quickly, "I have the same file on her that I have on Hutton."

Black eyebrows lifted.

"Besides," Christy said. "It's . . . hard . . . to believe that beauty isn't more than skin deep. I can't believe that Jo . . ."

There was no comfort in Cain's smile.

"Yeah, I had a hard time myself. But I learned the truth of the old cliché at nineteen. Pretty is as pretty does."

Christy opened her mouth to protest again, then thought better of it.

"As far as I'm concerned," Cain concluded, "women like Jo-Jo are literally as ugly as sin. Any more questions?"

"No," Christy said in a low voice.

"Good. Now let's see if we can't find that ruin."

"You don't think she lied about that too?"

"She might have, but this doesn't lie."

Cain held out his hand. On his palm was a potsherd crossed with black lines.

"Where did you find it?" she asked.

"Over there," he said, gesturing with his hand.

"When?"

"Just before I was shot."

13

"You take that side," Cain said.

He pointed to the column of red rock rising up to the sky. Without a word, Christy turned toward it.

"Look for pictographs or petroglyphs," he said.

"Oh, sure," she muttered. "Unfortunately, I never remember which is which."

"Pictographs are painted on. Petroglyphs are hammered in."

"Got it."

Christy circled out from Cain, following the irregular base of the red spire. There were no drawings of any kind on the blocks of rubble or on the face of the pinnacle itself.

"Anything?" she asked when she met Cain on the other side.

"No. Let's try the white sister next."

Christy circled one way and Cain the other while the wind fluted its eerie music all around. When they met in back, neither had found anything.

"Damn," Cain said. "I was afraid of that. Too exposed."

"What is?"

"The Sisters. The wind has sandblasted them. Any drawings the Anasazi left are long since worn away."

Christy studied the outlines of the two stone Sisters that had spent unimaginable eons standing next to each other.

She wondered if they understood each other any better for all the time together.

"What did they look like a thousand years ago?" she asked.

"About the same as now. A thousand years isn't a long time for rock."

"The drawing in the bowl."

"Yes?"

"How was it oriented?"

Cain glanced at Christy thoughtfully. Abruptly he nodded.

"Good idea, Red."

With that he turned and began walking so fast that Christy had to trot to keep up.

"Where are we going?" she asked.

"To look at things from another angle."

Christy made a frustrated noise. Smiling slightly, Cain touched her cheek. The caress was gentle and so swift it was over before she had time to react.

"The Anasazi's closest surviving relatives are the

Pueblos over in eastern New Mexico," Cain said, as though nothing had happened. "Their shamans have one job—to keep track of the place the sun rises each morning."

He scrambled up a low rock ledge onto another flat stone platform. The mesa top had many of them, as though it had once been a sea that had frozen. Now the tops of its low stone waves had been beveled off by time and wind into random broad steps that came from nowhere and led nowhere.

"Here," Cain said, holding out his hand. "It's steeper than it looks."

No sooner had Christy reached for Cain than his hand closed around her wrist. He pulled her up onto the new level with an easy strength that belied the idea he had ever been shot.

But she knew he had. She had seen the scar. She had seen the pain in his face when he stretched a certain way.

"The most important day on the solar calendar is the solstice," Cain continued.

Christy followed his intent glance. He was examining the stone wall in front of him as though he expected to find a treasure map.

"What are you looking for?" she asked.

"Any indication that this was a place of power and importance for the Anasazi. If it was, it would have to do with solar events."

"Then we're out of luck. The sun is hiding."

Cain's smile flashed briefly. "It will burn through before noon."

She looked up and saw that Cain was right. As the sun climbed, it was slowly subduing the clouds. Even behind the misty cover, the sun was an incandescent circle far too bright to look at for more than an instant.

Slowly Cain walked until he could see the sun disk bracketed by the Sisters. He circled to his left, walked a dozen paces, then stopped and stared back toward the Sisters. The red spire now blocked the sun. He adjusted his position a few feet, then gestured with his hand toward the gap between the rock needles.

"The sun would rise on the morning of the solstice right there," Cain said, gesturing toward the eastern sky. "The first light would be visible back there somewhere."

"How do you know?"

"I'm a shaman," he said dryly. "Come on."

Together, he and Christy headed across the windswept mesa toward a spot a quarter mile away. Behind them the wind swirled around the sandstone needles, wailing like a lost child.

When they came to another of the broad stone steps, Cain levered himself up and offered Christy his hand again. Moki danced around on the lower level and finally leaped up of his own accord. He stood between them, facing the wind and waving his plumed tail proudly. Cain put his hands on Christy's shoulders and turned her until she faced the Sisters.

"On the summer solstice, from here the sun would rise directly between the two spires," he said. "This side of the mesa top would have been a very special place for the Anasazi. There's got to be a kiva around here somewhere."

Christy was keenly aware of the weight and warmth of Cain's hands on her shoulders.

"What is a kiva?" she asked, her voice almost husky.

"The navel of the world."

She looked over her shoulder at Cain. He was so close that she could sense the warmth of his breath on her cheek. He smiled at her.

"A kiva," he said, "is also a circular room dug into the earth and roofed over with cedar beams and plaster."

"Into the earth? Why? Wouldn't it be easier in this country to build above the ground?"

"Probably. But more important to the Anasazi was their belief that all the clans originally emerged from the underworld on their great journey toward the sky. Going to and from the kiva mimics that journey."

Christy frowned. "So a kiva is a kind of church?"

"A church. A social club. A clan headquarters. A symbol of secrecy. The kiva could have been all those things."

"Or none of them?" she suggested.

A smile flashed through Cain's short black beard.

"Or none of them," he agreed. "All we know for sure is that the kiva was very important to the Anasazi. They went to a lot of trouble to build kivas next to their apartment buildings. The Pueblo people do the same today."

Releasing Christy, Cain turned and examined the mesa behind them, looking for any sign that once, long ago, people had built here, lived here, died here.

Nothing showed but the rough mesa top itself, marked with dark evergreen and red rock, swept by the restless wind. The abrupt, rocky platform where he and Christy stood was close to the edge of the mesa. Nearby, a deep slit canyon cut through the sandstone. Beyond the slit canyon, the land fell away into the distance, leaving a sheer stone precipice behind.

"How are you on heights?" Cain asked.

"I live on the forty-third floor."

"How are you when there aren't any elevators to take you down?"

"I'll manage."

"Good. Come on."

Cain leaped down from the small stone platform. When Christy started to follow, he lifted her down as he had done once before, when they had been fleeing from Hutton's guards.

And again, Christy was sharply aware of Cain's palms gliding lightly over the sides of her breasts. She saw an answering flare of awareness in his eyes before he released her and turned away.

Moki barked eagerly from atop the rock platform.

"You got up there yourself," Cain reminded the dog. "You can get down the same way."

Moki barked again, circled the little platform, then dashed to one edge and jumped. He touched a small chuck of rock on the way down. The rock gave way suddenly, dumping the surprised dog to the ground. He scrambled up, shook off the surprise as though it had been a rain shower, and raced off over the mesa once more.

"Cain? Is this something useful?"

He turned in time to see Christy pick a white fragment from the fresh fall of dirt that had come loose when Moki had kicked the rock out of its resting place in a crevice.

"What is it?" he asked.

"Something that doesn't fit," she said.

When Cain held out his hand, Christy dropped the fragment into it. He brushed a thick layer of red slit from the surface and smiled. There was a pattern of black crosshatched over white.

"A potsherd!" Christy said.

Excitement rippled in her voice and gleamed in her eyes.

"Your first?" Cain asked, trying not to smile.

She nodded so quickly that locks of red hair slipped free of their moorings beneath her watch cap.

"How did it get there?" Christy asked. "I don't see any ruins around."

"Some Anasazi probably did what we did—climbed up there for a look around. He might have broken his canteen or a seed pot he was carrying. He walked on, and the pieces stayed behind."

Christy looked back at the windswept little platform with wonder in her eyes.

"It's quite a feeling, isn't it?" Cain asked softly.

"Sharing just for an moment the life of someone who died centuries before you were born."

"Yes," Christy said, and the word was almost a sigh.

"Too bad we didn't find this over on Billy Moore's land," Cain said, handing the sherd back to her. "He wouldn't mind if you kept it."

"But the owner of this land would?"

"Yeah. You keep that and you've committed a felony. The feds will harass your ass into an early grave."

Christy looked around the mesa. "This is all federal land?"

Cain nodded.

"Where's Xanadu?" she asked.

"It starts somewhere over by the edge of the mesa."

"Where?"

"You'd have to be a surveyor to know," Cain said. "Hutton's ranch is a hodgepodge of leased grazing land and deeded land."

"But he doesn't run cattle."

"He'd rather pay the grazing fees and keep other folks' cattle out," Cain said. "Come on. Let's find the rest of the pot."

Christy looked at the damp reddish earth where the stone had fallen away. There was some more dirt in the crease, but not enough to hide a pot.

"Not there," Christy said regretfully, replacing the sherd.

He laughed. "The first rule of potsherds is that they go downhill."

Cain crossed the strip of wind-smoothed sandstone that separated the low stone platform from the edge of the mesa. A nose of rock extended out into the canyon. The wind was stronger at the edge but felt less chilly, as though the ground below the lip of the canyon still held summer's warmth.

When Christy walked out and stood next to Cain, she gasped in surprise. The canyon floor was a long, long way down. Below her feet, the black backs of ravens gleamed as the birds floated on the wind, calling sharply to one another.

She was swept by a feeling of being weightless, of soaring and falling in the same instant. Without realizing it, she took a step closer to the edge.

Cain's hand shot out and closed firmly around Christy's arm, but he didn't pull her back. Instead, he moved to stand just behind her.

"Heady feeling, isn't it?" he asked.

His voice was calm and low, very close to her.

"It's . . . incredible."

"The Anasazi loved the mesa tops too," Cain said after a moment. "They must have been sorry to leave. There's no place in the world like this."

The soft morning air rushed up from the canyon below like a great, fragrant sigh.

Slowly Christy's perceptions adjusted to the vast distances that had just been revealed by the shearing away of the land. What looked like small shrubs at the base of the sandstone wall were really full-sized trees. A narrow path was really a dirt road. The featureless canyon bottom was really rugged and tumbled, filled with boulders the size of Cain's cabin.

Small side canyons occurred wherever runoff channels had carved through the rock. Like everything else in nature, the edge of the mesa was asymmetrical and unexpected, built not by rulers and blueprints but by wind and time and storms.

The small nose of rock Christy and Cain were standing on was little more than an irregularity on the edge of a vast, ragged shawl of stone whose fringe was cliffs, and the spaces between the fringe were deep canyons filled with sun and silence.

"That's a big place to find something as small as a pot," Christy said finally.

"We're not looking way down there. We—or rather I—will look just underneath the rim."

Gently Christy eased forward and craned her neck, trying to see straight down.

"Looks like more of the same to me," she said.

"If there are rooms or storage cysts or anything like that, they will be tucked just under the overhang of the rim, away from the weather."

She turned and searched Cain's face for signs that he was teasing her. She saw only the intensity she had come to associate with him when he was in pursuit of something he loved.

"Are you telling me that the Anasazi chipped out places to live on the face of this cliff?" Christy asked.

"No. Nature took care of the chipping out. The Anasazi just filled it back in with buildings."

"I don't understand."

"Imagine two slabs of stone," Cain said, holding one hand over the other parallel to the ground.

Christy nodded.

"The top slab depends on the bottom to hold it up," he said. "If the bottom slab is softer than the top, it wears away more quickly and an alcove or shallow cave is created."

As Cain spoke, he bent the fingers of his lower hand, making it shorter.

"The roof is solid stone," he said, moving his top hand. "The second layer holds the alcove. All the other layers underneath are still solid."

"Homesites by Mother Nature," she said. "Nifty."

"Yeah, until the weight of the ceiling overhang becomes too great and it falls."

"Does that happen often?"

"In a human lifetime? No. Over the span of a thousand years? Often enough, I suppose."

Christy shuddered. "Not a happy thought."

"Life's a gamble, honey. The only guarantee is that nobody gets out alive."

"Cheerful soul, aren't you?" she muttered. "What will those buildings look like if we find them?"

"Lines of rubble, most likely, but oddly shaped rubble, as though someone piled flagstones around and then gave up and walked away before finishing the patio."

Cain saw the disappointment on Christy's face. Smiling, he tugged lightly at a flyaway lock of red hair.

"That's good news, not bad," he said. "If there were well-preserved ruins up here, somebody would have spotted and mapped them already—right after they looted them down to bedrock and masonry walls."

Slowly, Cain let the lock of Christy's hair slip free of his fingers. He turned back to face the mesa edge where only wind and ravens moved.

"It's too close to noon for the shadows to be any help," Cain said. "So search just beneath the rim of the canyon, where pale rock meets rock the color of your hair."

Christy took in a long breath and forced herself to turn away from the man who became more compelling to her each time she looked at him. It took her a moment to focus on the land rather than on the memory of the gentle tug of his fingers sliding over her hair.

"Look for debris slopes that show gray or black areas," Cain said. "The Anasazi burned wood and threw their ash and garbage over the front porch into the canyon below."

"A long, thin layer of black?" she asked.

He followed her glance.

"That's a thin seam of coal," he said. "Anasazi middens—garbage heaps—occur in patches rather than in long lines."

Suddenly Cain leaned forward. "Like that!"

She followed the line of his finger. Two hundred feet away, and a dizzying drop below the rim, there was a dark stain in the debris slope that fringed a small alcove.

"See it?" Cain asked.

"Yes! There's another one to the left."

"About a hundred feet," he agreed. "See that dark green weed?"

The excitement in Cain's voice riveted Christy.

"The stuff all over that second little slope?" she asked.

"Yeah. That's Moki weed."

"Why do they call it that? Did the Anasazi eat it?"

"No," Cain said. "It only grows in Moki middens."

"Then there are ruins there?"

"Near there. Somewhere. There have to be."

Frowning, Cain studied the canyon walls for a time. Nothing more caught his eye. He shrugged off the small backpack he had been wearing, pulled out a pair of binoculars, and studied the wall above the streak of green Moki weed.

"If there are any ruins, they're damned well hidden," he muttered. "Must have eroded away to nothing at all."

He continued studying the walls but said nothing more.

"What are you looking for now?" Christy asked.

"A way down."

"That?" she demanded. "It's a cliff!"

"I noticed."

Uneasily, Christy fell silent while Cain finished examining the rock face. When he was done, he handed the binoculars and backpack to her.

"There's a network of ledges and creases that go down to the midden from the top of the mesa," he said. "Stay here while I check it out."

"But can't I—"

"No way," Cain interrupted flatly. "You're staying."

The mutinous look on Christy's face made him sigh.

"It's going to be a bastard of a climb," he said. "I'm not sure I can do it myself."

"I wasn't shot last spring. Let me at least try."

"No. You don't recognize the limits of your own strength."

"And you do?" she retorted.

"Yes."

Christy glared at Cain. He simply shook his head.

"Look," he said finally, "if you go, I'll have to watch you like a mother hen because you won't ask for help even if you need it. The trail is too rough for that kind of game. We both could get hurt."

She closed her eyes, knowing she was defeated. She couldn't push Cain into doing something he clearly believed was unsafe for him. Nor could she demand that he let her get herself out of any trouble she got into.

He wouldn't let her hurt herself. She wouldn't expect him to. In fact, she would be counting on him to help her out. He was simply that kind of man.

"Damn!" Christy said, accepting it.

"Sorry."

"If I get bored, I suppose I can throw rocks," she said sweetly.

"Don't get bored, honey."

With that, Cain bent over, kissed Christy hard

and fast, and turned away. Before she caught her breath, he had vanished over the rim.

Cautiously Christy went to the edge of the mesa and watched Cain pick his way along the small ledge he had found. It led to a tongue of steep rock-studded dirt where scrubby cedar and stubborn piñon had taken root. He moved over the rough, uncertain ground with surprising speed, utterly at home.

"What are you," Christy muttered under her breath, "part mountain goat?"

Then her breath wedged as Cain dropped from a rock platform onto the first dark patch, the one where no weeds grew. Immediately he began to slide downhill toward another, much longer drop.

"Cain!"

Even as Christy screamed his name, he caught his balance, threw himself to the side, and found solid ground.

Christy brought up the binoculars with hands that trembled. The slippery slope leaped into focus. It was spread out in front of a small overhang, but the alcove beneath it was empty. She watched while Cain searched for building blocks or potsherds, the remnants of walls, any sign that man had once lived beneath the overhanging rim of the canyon.

"Anything?" Christ called when she could stand the suspense no longer.

"Not yet," he yelled back.

Cain went farther into the alcove. The angle of

the rock hid him from Christy's sight. He emerged a few minutes later.

"This dark patch isn't a midden," he called. "There's a spring at the back and a crack leading up to the mesa top. Runoff water has washed the alcove clean."

Disappointed, Christy watched while Cain scrambled around an outcropping of sandstone and into the next alcove. When he was out of sight, she hurried overland to the rim just above him, hoping to see more from there.

All she saw was air, distant ravens, and fully grown trees that looked the size of thumbtacks.

"Lord," Christy said, stepping backward. "That first step is forever."

She found herself a spot to sit down at the base of an elegantly twisted cedar. From there she could hear Cain's passage from time to time below the rim, even though she couldn't see him.

Moki appeared, panting with pleasure from a recent run. He flopped down on the slick rock beside her.

Christy looked south across the ragged country. The lid of clouds was being scored and thinned by the great burning torch of the sun. As she watched, mountains condensed in the distance. A network of incandescent blue appeared across the sky. Golden heat spilled through the gaps in the clouds.

With a sigh of pleasure, Christy opened her jacket, leaned back against the wind-smoothed tree, and enjoyed the gentle caress of the sun on her face. Cloud shadows dappled the red sandstone, making the mesa country ripple as though alive.

Eyes half closed, Christy let the kaleidoscope of cloud and landscape play across her awareness, sinking past her rational self to the most primitive levels of her mind. Slowly the world of second hands and concrete sidewalks slid away, revealing the underlying elemental rhythms of sun and earth, wind and time.

A shadow eclipsed part of the design. At first Christy thought it was just another passing cloud. When it lingered, she sat up and looked around.

The sun had passed behind the white sandstone Sister. The spire was throwing a long, wide shadow that would not lift for some time.

"And I was just getting comfortable," Christy muttered.

Slowly she got to her feet and looked for a new spot in the sun. Moki scrambled to his feet and waited expectantly while she surveyed the mesa top.

A dozen yards to Christy's left, a slice of white-hot sunlight lay across the sandstone like a giant knife. It took her a moment to realize that the knife blade of light was caused by a shaft of sunlight passing between the two Sisters. The white shaft of light was no more than ten feet wide. It pointed directly across the mesa to the rim above Cain.

The effect was striking. It reminded Christy of what Cain had said about the sun being important to the Anasazi.

What would the Anasazi have made of a slice of sunlight like this? she wondered. Would they have worshiped or feared or celebrated it? Sure as hell they couldn't ignore it.

Christy walked into the blade of light. With Moki at her heels, she followed the shimmering path to the very edge of the mesa. A vague pattern appeared at her feet. The hair on the back of her neck rose as the pattern solidified into an ancient drawing.

On the rim of the canyon, a hunchbacked flute player was calling to the ravens far below.

14

"It's right over there!" Christy said as Cain scrambled over the rim in response to her call. "Hurry! The sun is moving so fast!"

"The rock isn't," he said, breathing hard.

Yet Cain didn't object when Christy took his hand and all but dragged him to the lip of the mesa thirty feet away. The sun had indeed moved. The result was to highlight the petroglyph.

"Son of a bitch!" Cain said reverently.

He sat on his heels next to the drawing, running his fingertips very gently over the rough surface of the rock. Kokopelli's figure was faint, eroded but unmistakable. The universal Pan, bursting with sexuality and life.

And the point of the dagger of sunlight burned only on his magical flute.

Cain looked up at Christy. His eyes, like the flute, burned with light and life.

"You're good luck for me," he said.

"What's luck got to do with it?"

"Everything."

Cain glanced back toward the two Sisters, then checked his watch.

"Noon, exactly," he said.

"So?"

"Do you know what day this is?"

Christy thought for a moment. "September twenty-first?"

Her tone made it clear that she didn't attach any particular significance to the date.

"Yes. The autumnal equinox, the day of balance when the sun is directly over the equator. Day and night are of equal length."

Cain's voice was like his eyes, full of life. He compelled Christy as surely as the blade of sunlight had.

"Look," he said. "The narrowest part of the shaft of sunlight is touching Kokopelli's flute at exactly noon on the equinox."

"The Anasazi knew that?"

"If you had a growing season that was just barely long enough to produce corn or beans, what would you give to know that the days were lengthening or shortening?"

"A tenth of my crop," she said dryly.

Cain smiled. "The standard religious tithe. I suspect the price of Anasazi peace of mind was a lot steeper."

Again he ran his fingertips over the figure of Kokopelli. The combination of strength and delicacy in his touch reminded Christy of how he had held the Anasazi bowl when she had first seen him in the Two-Tier West.

In terms of second hands and concrete blocks—rational terms—it had been only yesterday that she had met Cain. In terms of sun and land, wind and time—elemental terms—it had been a lifetime.

"Honey?" Cain asked.

Christy's breath caught as she realized how often Cain had come to use that endearment with her.

And how natural it seemed.

"What?" she whispered.

"Did you touch this at all?"

"No. As soon as I saw it, I started hollering for you."

A smile gleamed momentarily against Cain's beard. Then his mouth settled into a hard line as he looked from the sandstone dust on his fingertips to Kokopelli.

"What's wrong? Isn't the figure real?" Christy asked.

"Oh, it's real. So real someone tried to blot it out. If it hadn't been in full blazing sunlight, you'd probably never have seen it."

"Why would someone vandalize a piece of ancient art? Sheer meanness?"

"Maybe. But maybe it wasn't Kokopelli they were trying to destroy. Maybe they were trying to hide something else."

As Cain spoke, he looked around slowly, searching

for anything else that might have been overlooked.

Moki's sharp, aggressive barking made both of them turn toward the sound. It came from below the rim.

"Did he fall over?" Christy asked, alarmed.

"Doubt it."

But Cain followed Christy to look over the rim into the canyon below.

Moki stood on a rounded boulder eighty feet below, wagging his tail like a battle flag and looking up at them expectantly. When they didn't move, he barked again, impatient to get going.

Christy looked at Cain in alarm.

"Moki wouldn't be wagging his tail and dancing around if he had fallen there," Cain said. "There must be another way down."

"Was Kokopelli pointing the way?"

"Could be. Maybe that's why someone tried to blot the old boy out. Come on."

Cain quartered the rimrock until he came to a small cleft in the rounded sandstone.

"This is as good as it gets," he said.

He eased into the cleft.

"Cain?" Christy asked hopefully.

"Let me check it out first."

Saying nothing more, Christy watched anxiously as Cain disappeared into the cleft. A curse and the sound of pebbles rolling floated back up to her.

Just when Christy was fearing she would be left behind again, Cain reappeared.

"It's a hell of a lot better than it looks at first," he said. "Still want to play mountain goat?"

A delighted grin was Christy's answer.

"Hand me the backpack, then," Cain said.

After he settled it on his back, he held out his hand once more. She took it as she slid into the cleft.

"I've got you," he said.

He caught Christy, held her until she found her feet, then released her with a slow smile.

"I could get to enjoy hiking rough country with you," he said. "Watch your footing, now. It's not what you expect it to be."

"Neither are you," she retorted.

Cain gave a crack of laughter and turned away to lead her farther beneath the mesa's eroding rim.

The cleft became a gap between two massive sandstone blocks, one of which rested beneath the other. The gap quickly turned into a tunnel that was hidden from above and lit only by sunlight from either end. Despite Cain's warning about the uneven footing, Christy stumbled several times over badly placed rocks.

"Damn it," she muttered.

"Yeah, those stairs are a real bastard for people used to evenly made steps."

"Stairs?" Christy said blankly.

"Look at the surface. See those pockmarks?"

She squinted into the gloom. "Yes."

"Those were left by a hammer stone wielded by some poor son of a bitch who was told to chip steps out of solid rock."

Christy walked slowly, amazed at the work that had gone into making a steep watercourse into a path. As she settled into the rhythm of slope and stairs, she found herself stumbling less.

"Low ceiling," Cain warned.

The ceiling of the tunnel was indeed dropping. He was bent over already. Soon Christy had to bend over too.

"If this keeps up we'll be on all fours," she said.

"Starting real soon," Cain agreed.

Twenty feet ahead, the incandescent blue of the sky and Moki's excited barking promised an end to the tunnel. Cain and Christy had to crawl on all fours for the last ten feet.

Cain's shoulders were too wide to fit cleanly through the exit. He had to twist his torso and slide through sideways, pulling the backpack behind.

"Very neat," he said, grunting as he forced himself past the constriction. "A ten-year-old with a sharp stick could hold off an army."

"When I went to school," Christy said, "I was told the Anasazi were peace-loving subsistence farmers."

"Your professors were left over from the hippie dippy sixties," Cain said, amused. "Nobody builds and lives on the face of a cliff because they like losing toddlers and old folks over the edge."

"You make cliff dwelling sound irresistible."

Cain's hand came back through the opening. "Grab hold."

Christy did. Very quickly she was pulled out of the tunnel and into the sunlight. The first thing she noticed was that there was nothing in front of her but air.

Lots of it.

"Steady," Cain said as he shrugged into the backpack again. "There's not much room on this ledge."

Christy made an odd sound.

"You okay?" he asked.

"Give me a second to get used to the idea of walking on air."

"Stone, actually."

"You could have fooled me."

Breath came out of Christy in a long sigh. She looked up at Cain. He was watching her intently.

"I'm okay," she said. "Really."

She took another deep breath.

"And I take your point about living on cliff faces," she added. "You'd need a damn good reason to do it. Sheer survival comes to mind. Nothing else would be good enough."

Moki came bouncing across the rock face like a rubber ball, urging them on. The dog had the advantage of four sure feet. He was headed straight for Christy.

Cain's hand moved in a short, sharp motion. The gesture had the same effect on the dog that a yank on a leash would have. Moki stopped so fast he skidded. Another brief motion of Cain's hand and the dog stood as though nailed to stone.

"Impressive," Christy said.

"He would have made a good hunting dog," Cain agreed.

"You don't like to hunt?"

"Ex-cons can't own firearms."

Cain's voice was matter-of-fact rather than bitter, for he was absorbed in studying the rock.

"More steps," he said. "Follow me and do what I do. Exactly. Like a child's game, only damned serious. Understand?"

"Yes."

His eyes pinned Christy for a moment, measuring her agreement. Then he smiled.

"I'd kiss you again, Red, but it has a bad effect on my sense of balance."

"It doesn't do much for mine, either," she admitted.

Christy followed Cain across the rock, using steps so faint and weathered she wasn't even sure they were there. It was faith in Cain that drew her, not any evidence of her own senses. She put her feet where Cain's had been.

Exactly.

Slowly, they made their way for fifty feet along the face of the cliff. From the corner of her eye, Christy gradually became aware that their path was leading them out and away from the talus slope and over a steeply slanting section of mesa wall that had sheared away and fallen to the canyon bottom far below.

"Am I the only one who hasn't noticed there's nothing below us but air?" she asked uneasily.

"Don't look at the air. Look at the rock," Cain said. "Especially here."

He stopped and pointed to a place where the steps came at a different interval than they had before.

"Stop and switch feet here," he said. "Most people lead with their right foot on a stairway. Lead with your left from here on or you'll find yourself down in the canyon."

A single look at Cain's face told Christy he was quite serious.

"Left foot, huh?" she said. "Okay. Left foot it is. But why? Did they measure the steps wrong or something?"

"It's an old trick, like a long step thrown in with a bunch of short ones. Causes no end of grief to invaders."

"Peace-loving, huh?" Christy asked, deadpan.

"You bet. Gentle, fruit-eating apes, every last one of them."

She snickered. "I'd love to have seen you in academia."

Cain smiled lazily. "It was fun."

Christy watched and changed leads at the spot he indicated. Walking that way was awkward at first but she quickly caught the new rhythm. They made their way across the rock face for another fifty feet before Cain stopped.

"I'll be damned," he said softly. "No wonder nobody ever found anything up here. Look at the size of that flake."

"Flake?"

Cain gestured.

Belatedly Christy realized that the "flake" he

was talking about was a sandstone slab as big as a basketball floor and nearly as thick as Cain was tall.

"That," she said, "is one hell of a flake."

From a short distance away, the sandstone slab appeared to have broken neatly off the canyon rim and slid thirty or forty feet down the face of the mesa. In geologic time, the event was recent. The edges of the sandstone slab looked newer, brighter, less weathered than the rest of the mesa face.

"Look at the steps," Cain said in a hushed voice.

The faint path of worn steps led directly up to the edge of the fallen slab and vanished.

"End of the line?" Christy asked, disappointed.

"Maybe. Maybe not. Look up there."

Five or six feet above the path, there was a little hollow, as though the sandstone slab had fallen over the front of a small alcove in the face of the mesa. The hollow was in full shade.

Christy stared and then stared again, feeling excitement sweep through her.

"Is it . . . ?" she asked breathlessly.

"It sure as hell is."

Without looking away from the flake, Cain held his hand out. When Christy took it he squeezed hard.

And then he laughed, a sound of pure excitement.

Suddenly Christy was laughing too. In that instant she forgot her uneasiness at being perched on the exposed rock face. There was no need for fear, for she knew what it was to fly like a raven above an ancient, timeless land.

Ahead of them the corner of a man-made wall loomed from the shadows.

"Look at the thickness of those vigas," Cain said.

"I would, if I knew what they were."

"The cedar roof supports."

Moki emerged from the shadows at the edge of the fallen slab. His whole body vibrated with eagerness for them to join him, but he didn't race forward or bark. He was on his best hunting behavior now, watching his master's hands for instructions.

The order was to stay put. Christy nearly laughed at the dog's visible disappointment.

"I don't want him to go through a kiva roof or trash a pot while chasing rats."

"Rats?"

"Not the New York kind. The Moki kind. Pack rats. They move into ruins and fill up the storage cysts and lath walls with nests."

"Rats," Christy concluded. "I hope Moki's part terrier."

"Moki is part everything."

When they reached the tumble of rocks where Moki waited, Cain stopped Christy with a hand hard around her wrist.

"Wait," he said. "Ruins can be dangerous. The walls are often unstable. Kiva roofs can be rotten. And the alcove stone itself—"

Cain measured the massive sandstone flake that had fallen within historic times, shutting off the alcove but for a narrow window or doorway at each end. The standstone slab looked as if it was teetering on the edge of falling again.

When it did, it would take a lot of the rim with it.

"I don't like the looks of that flake," he said bluntly.

"Are you going in anyway?"

"Yes."

"Then so am I."

He turned to argue with Christy and saw she wasn't having any.

"Okay, honey. But be damned careful where you put your feet."

Cain started up the rubble pile to the entrance of the alcove. The sandstone debris seemed to be stable, as though it had been wedged together during the fall.

Halfway up the ramp, a fist-sized chunk of stone came tumbling out of the pile. The rock hit the ledge at Christy's feet and bounced down the steeply sloping stone face until it disappeared soundlessly over the edge.

Cain looked at Christy.

"Whither thou goest and all that," she said through her teeth.

"What happened to the girl who said cluck cluck?"

"She discovered her wings and flew away."

Smiling, shaking his head, Cain stepped onto the little sill of rock that ran across the alcove window. After a moment, he motioned for Christy to follow.

A faint breeze stirred within the shadow-filled alcove. When Christy reached the sill, she saw another wedge of sunlight on the far side.

"Let your eyes adjust," Cain said. "When you can see into the shadows, let me know."

As Christy's eyes slowly adjusted to the low light, she saw what lay behind the huge sandstone curtain.

"My God," she breathed.

"Amen."

The alcove held a well-preserved cliff dwelling, intact except for a fallen wall across the front of the structure. The corner of wall and roof they had seen from below was part of a block of rooms that stretched for almost a hundred feet across the alcove. There were from two to four stories in the building, depending on the slope of the alcove roof.

"Is this as good as I think it is?" she asked softly.

"It's damned good, honey. It's like a time capsule. I don't know of another ruin in the Southwest that's been protected like this."

"How old are the buildings?"

"I can't say for sure, but the doorway style looks a lot like Mesa Verde. Mid-twelfth century. About the height of the Chaco empire. And about the time things started coming apart."

Cain took another look around. His left hand moved slightly. Moki bounded past them and into the ruins.

"Change your mind?" Christy asked.

"Yeah. He's better at sensing bad footing than

we are, and better able to get himself out of trouble if something gives way."

"Is that really a possibility?"

"Hell, yes. In ruins this size, some of the floors will be lucky to support themselves. And no, you're not going with me if I go exploring."

One look at Cain's set expression convinced Christy to wait and argue the matter if and when it came up again.

Moki appeared atop one of the rooms close to their window, tail wagging and coated with what looked like twigs. The breeze from the interior of the alcove suddenly smelled rank.

"Yuk," Christy said.

"He's found a pack rat's nest."

"Wonderful," she said without enthusiasm.

Cain laughed softly. "I hope you don't mind getting dusty and dirty. These ruins haven't been cleaned for nearly a thousand years."

He eased down onto a low wall that once had run along the lip of the alcove. The masonry was thick and strong.

"The kid-catcher is still solid," he said.

"Kid-catcher? Oh, the low wall. Is that what it's called?"

"That's what I call it." He looked around. "This must have been one of the first rooms built."

"How can you tell?"

"It's full of rubbish now. The Anasazi often filled in old rooms and built new ones. Sometimes they buried the dead in the rooms. Sometimes they threw them in the midden with the rest of the garbage."

Christy frowned. "A status thing?"

"Some say yes. More say no."

"What do you say?"

"No one that I know of has ever found grave goods with human bones in a midden. Grave goods have been found in room or crevice burials."

"Status."

"Looks that way to me, but I'm just a Moki-poaching son of a bitch."

Cain ventured a little farther along the wall, testing his footing and the stability of the ruin every bit of the way. When nothing gave, he returned.

"If I tell you to stay here?" he said.

"I will, for a while."

"How long?"

"Until you turn your back."

His eyes narrowed. "About what I figured."

"I'm your good luck charm, remember? You don't want to leave me behind."

Unwillingly Cain smiled.

"Okay, my redheaded rabbit's foot. Move softly, like a ghost. I don't trust that sandstone flake worth a damn. I swear I felt it shiver when I leaned on it."

With that, Cain walked back along the wall, the sandstone flake in question only inches from his shoulder.

Christy followed carefully, steadying herself with one hand on the massive slab of rock. It felt cool and steady, but even without Cain's words she was unwilling to trust the stone.

"This looks like an apartment building," she said.

"Close enough."

The second room they came to was empty except for a huge mound of sticks and debris. The musty smell was thicker here, almost overwhelming.

"Thousands of generations of pack rats have lived there, adding their little bit to the pile," Cain said. "Reminds me of New York. Except it smells better."

"New York does?"

"Not in summer. It stinks."

"You sound like you spend time there," she said.

"Only when I can't help it."

The floor of the third room was flat and relatively clean. Cain ducked in through the low doorway and let his eyes adjust to the near darkness inside. Christy followed, standing close beside him.

Gradually the details of the room's construction became visible as their pupils dilated. The walls had been plastered with red mud. In places the mud had fallen away, revealing a lattice of sticks beneath the plaster.

"Willow," Cain said in response to Christy's unspoken question.

"Look," she said. "The pattern."

Her hand traced a ragged ellipse of tiny white stones that had been set into an unusually thick layer of mortar.

"This didn't add to the wall's strength," she said. "It was done purely to please the eye."

"Like the paint."

Startled, Christy looked up. Sure enough, the upper part of the room had once been painted in designs that reminded her of the pottery she had seen.

"Look closely at the plaster," Cain said. "See the hand prints?"

Christy eased closer to examine the wall. Cain was right. There were many clear hand prints in the plaster surface. She laid her hand over one of them.

The hand that had built the room was smaller than her own, with short, blunt fingers, but her own palm fit easily in the cool depression that had been made almost a thousand years ago. She ran her other hand over the rest of the wall, trying to absorb through sheer touch what the life of those other people must have been like.

"So much time," Christy whispered. "So human."

Cain laid his own hand over hers, measuring the difference in their sizes. The act was curiously intimate.

"Yes," he said simply. "So human."

Delicate tendrils of warmth shivered through Christy. She was caught between the cool plaster surface of the past and the living warmth of the present.

"And nobody's touched this place for a thousand years," she whispered.

Cain was on the point of agreeing when something caught his eyes.

"Shit!" he said in a disgusted voice.

He lifted his hand from Christy's, bent over, and snatched up something from the floor of the room.

He held his fingers in the vague light coming in through the doorway.

"Oh, no," Christy said, disappointed.

"Oh, yes."

Cain had found the burned butt of a very modern, machine-rolled cigarette. He held it to his nose and grimaced.

"No more than six months or a year old," he said.

He turned the butt over and read the small print on it.

"Dunhill," he said in a low voice.

"Dunhill?" Christy asked. "Who is he?"

"Not he. It. Dunhill is a brand of cigarette."

Christy looked blank.

"The Remington Super-Valu doesn't stock them," Cain said. "Westerners like their cigarettes plain and simple. It takes a self-consciously exotic type to smoke Dunhills."

A chill replaced the warmth Christy had felt only a moment ago. Memories came, a beautiful blond fourteen-year-old who had seen a cigarette ad in a fashion magazine and driven the local boys crazy until one of them somehow found a way to get her a pack.

"Do you—" Christy cleared her throat. "Do you know anyone who smokes Dunhills?"

"Guess."

"Jo," Christy whispered.

It wasn't a question, but Cain answered anyway.

"Yeah, the cowboys' walking, talking wet dream."

With a hissed word, Cain flicked the butt into a corner and wiped his fingers on his jeans.

"Well, let's see how badly her boyfriend trashed the place."

"Hutton?"

"Doubt it. Last I saw Jo-Jo, she was flat-backing with the Indians, not the drugstore cowboys."

15

Cain ducked back underneath the lintel and into the alcove. Moving quickly, as though he no longer cared whether he damaged anything, he strode along the low wall at the front of the room block. He stopped at each doorway to stare into the dark recesses.

Only once did he step into the darkness. When he came out a moment later, there were potsherds in his hand. He showed them to Christy.

"They cherry-picked the entire site," Cain said flatly. "I guess they didn't think this was worth taking out."

The sherds joined perfectly, becoming the painted bowl of a ladle. Even with the handle missing, it was a handsome piece.

Cain tipped his palm and let the pieces fall to the ground. Christy started to object, but when she saw him wipe his palms on his jeans as though he had touched something unclean, she bit back her words. There could have been no clearer expression of his contempt for Jo-Jo and all she stood for.

Unhappily Christy watched Cain climb up a short, irregular stairway of rubble to the second story of the building. The rooms were even smaller on this level. Some of the walls were smoke-blackened. All the rooms were bare. Except for a broken clay mug and a few rough, tiny corncobs preserved perfectly in the dry air, the rooms had been looted to their floors.

Operating from instinct and experience honed by the exploration of a hundred ruins, Cain made his way to a block of rooms that formed a right angle to the line of the original building. There he stood staring down at the remnants of a small plaza in the crook of the L-shaped structure.

Christy paced him on the ground level. As she stepped over a low wall onto the floor of the plaza, there was a low, hollow groan, as though she had stepped on a ghost. She jumped back, more in surprise than fear.

"Watch it!" Cain said. "There's probably a kiva under that debris. Don't trust the roof to hold your weight."

Christy skirted the little plaza, peering into half-lighted corners. When a metallic glint caught her eye, she ventured a little closer.

Had Cain not already told Christy about the underworld myths, she might not have recognized the square black hole in the plaza floor as an entrance. A few inches of aluminum ladder stuck up out of the hole.

"There's a ladder here," she said.

"Stay put," Cain called out.

Using one of the thick vigas, he swung down off the roof of the room and walked toward her, skirting the level area that was a kiva roof of uncertain strength.

Moki looked out from one of the upper windows of the building block. He was thoroughly filthy and quite pleased with himself. Resting his chin on the windowsill, he watched his master below.

Cain poked around in a pile of rubble until he found a piece of cedar bark. He pulled a pack of survival matches from the pocket of his shirt and struck one. The bark flared quickly into flame. It cast an eerie, flickering light on the walls of the alcove.

Leaning down into the hole with the makeshift torch, Cain looked around the kiva.

"Cleaned out."

His voice was like the line of his mouth. Flat. Hard.

Christy ducked underneath Cain's arm and looked into her first kiva. The wavering light revealed a dusty, circular chamber beneath a low, roughly plastered ceiling that was supported by four straight log pillars. Niches had been carved into the curving walls of the kiva.

"They look like stations of the cross," Christy said.

"You've got it, Red. You're looking at an Anasazi church whose icons have been looted for sale to the unbelievers."

The bark torch guttered. Its fading light caught something shiny on the kiva floor.

"Hold this," Cain said.

He handed the nub of bark to Christy, showed her where he wanted it to be held, and dropped quickly down the ladder. A moment later he struck another match, touched it to the wick of a kerosene lantern, and lowered the glass chimney in place.

Christy dropped the makeshift torch just as her fingers became uncomfortably hot. The fire winked out before the bark reached the kiva floor.

"Come on down," Cain said. "See what real Moki poaching looks like."

Silently Christy climbed down the ladder into a room that seemed to vibrate with Cain's cold rage. It didn't take her long to understand why he was angry.

The ground beneath the kiva's circular ceiling had been turned over with shovels. One of the log pillars had been hacked at with an ax for no reason Christy could see. Pottery sherds were mixed with dirt and twentieth-century plastic trash.

Kneeling, Cain scooped up a double handful of the sherds and examined them.

"This pot could be salvaged," he said. "They just junked anything that wasn't whole."

Angrily Cain put the sherds back when he had found them. As he straightened, he saw a glimpse of pattern. He became wholly still, utterly intent on the low, curving sill that went around the whole kiva.

Parts of the sill had been cut away. The segment that remained was painted with an unusual design featuring Kokopelli in many incarnations.

"I've never seen anything like that," Cain said in a low voice.

"What?"

"The painted sill. Once it must have gone all the way around the room."

"Is that unusual?" Christy asked.

"The sill? No. But to have the painting preserved . . . yes. It's a miracle. And they hacked it up like firewood and hauled it out of here."

Christy knelt where some of the rubble showed painted surfaces. She fitted several together. Slowly a distinctive black-on-white pattern formed, a flowing abstraction that became a pure distillation of style. Unique, vivid, the design was a painted message sent from one millennium to the next.

Ancient, yet oddly familiar. After a few moments Christy figured out why.

"This looks a lot like one of the motifs Hutton is using in his new collection," she said unhappily.

"You going to write about that in your magazine, Red?" Cain asked bitterly. "You going to tell all the fashionable folks how Hutton raped a priceless Anasazi site to come up with the inspiration for some yuppie threads?"

Christy winced at Cain's tone but said nothing. There was no defense for what had been done to this ancient place.

He snatched the lantern and held it head high, inspecting the shambles of the past with naked yearning.

"God, but I wish I could have seen what it was like," he said in a low, intense voice. "There may not be another kiva this good in the whole world. And now . . ."

Christy closed her eyes, unable to watch Cain's pain.

"Gone," he said. "Just *gone.* All the king's horses and all the king's men couldn't put this mess back together again."

Cain kicked at a pile of rubble. A piece of thin, rough rope sprang free of the dirt. The rope was attached to a small mat of fibers.

"This was a shoe," he said. "A sandal made of yucca fiber. Not as rare as cloth or turkey feathers, but still a miracle of preservation against the odds."

His fists clenched. He drew in a quick, ripping breath.

"And those bastards threw it away like it was trash," Cain said. "God knows what kind of stuff they kept. A king's ransom. Feast for a hundred scholars.

"And it was all sold for a few thousand dollars to keep a lying little slut happy. Christ. If Johnny weren't so stupid I'd feel sorry for him."

"Johnny Ten Hats?"

"Yeah. He's the cigar-store idiot who was banging Jo-Jo when I was shot. Of course, that was six months ago. She's probably had a hundred like him since then."

Cain's contempt resonated in the space within the kiva. He was like a priest enraged at the desecration of a church. Christy tried to find words that might ease his anger but there were none.

Something irreplaceable had been lost for no better reason than greed. In the face of that barbaric act, anger was not only justified, it was necessary.

Silently Christy went from niche to niche in the kiva, hoping to find something of the artifacts that once had been the focus of Anasazi religious tradition. In the fifth niche, she found a small fragment of smooth black stone. It had been worked into a bead, perhaps part of a necklace.

Whatever the bead had once belonged to was gone. The black bead remained, overlooked in the destructive rush to wealth.

She held the rounded stone between her fingers. It had a smooth, cool, soapy feel.

"Is there any way of salvaging the site?" she asked quietly.

"No. They might as well have gone through here with a backhoe," Cain said.

"They might have overlooked something."

He made a curt gesture. "Sure, some of the pots might be put together again. But the potential for knowledge is gone."

Unhappily Christy looked around at the combination of plastic garbage and ancient debris.

"The layers are trashed," Cain said. "Fireplace ash from the early years is mixed in with the later stuff. There's no way anybody could even get a decent date out of the hearth. It's a total write-off. Null. Zero."

Silently Cain ran the lamp around the interior again, hoping to find something the looters had overlooked. There was nothing but blackness receding before the lamp, then flowing back to claim the kiva as the light moved on.

The lantern light cast eerie shadows in the dark niches and irregularities of the curving kiva walls. Shapes glided and vanished, only to reappear as though squeezed out of the stone itself.

Christy's skin prickled with a primal sense of *other*. There were spirits here. Some were benign. Some were as vicious as the ones she had seen in the paintings in Peter Hutton's hallway.

"All those niches," Cain muttered. "I haven't seen that many outside of Pueblo Bonito."

"Where is that?"

"Chaco Canyon."

For a few more breaths Cain studied the kiva in silence. Then he made an inarticulate sound of pain or rage. Or both.

"No ruins have been found this far north," he said. "From the size of this kiva, this was an important place to the Anasazi. A vital place. And now we'll never know why!"

Cain lowered the lantern with a speed that made light and shadows mix dizzyingly.

"I've seen about as much as I can take," he said.

Lantern in one hand, Cain climbed back to the plaza. Christy followed.

The lantern gave new insight into the waste that had been made of the little village that had been hidden behind the sandstone slab. Protected, but not well enough.

Cain walked from room to room. Everywhere he looked there were telltale marks where pots or other artifacts had been dug out and carted off with no thought to their intellectual worth. Only money counts in the world of the Moki poacher.

In a corner close to the sill where Cain and Christy had entered, there was a partially collapsed wall. It seemed to be holding the rest of the block of rooms in place.

"If you have to come in here," Cain said, "don't kick anything. This place is ready to come down."

He walked closer. His breath came in with a harsh sound. Along the back wall of the alcove, there was a framework of modern timbers.

"No closer," he said flatly to Christy.

"Why?"

"From here, it looks like some fool is using toothpicks to hold up the mesa."

Cain turned up the wick of the lantern until it smoked. Then he made his way over a fallen rubble pile to the far wall of the alcove.

Christy didn't follow. She had seen what Cain was talking about.

Hands in her pockets, she watched while he examined the framework with a delicate care that said more than words about the danger. As she watched, she rolled the black bead with her fingertips, taking an odd comfort from its ancient, smooth surface.

A cold nose pressed against Christy's wrist, startling her. Moki had given up on pack rats for the moment. Ignoring the grit and bits of straw clinging to the dog, Christy took her hands from her pockets and thrust her fingers deep into Moki's fur.

After a few minutes, the dog pulled away and went to lie down on a slab of cool sandstone. In the gloom, Moki was all but invisible. Only the occasional flash of his eyes as they caught the lantern light gave away his location.

Finally Cain had seen enough. He trimmed the lantern wick and walked back to Christy. He looked grim.

"Well?" she asked.

"There's a flake about fifteen feet square that looks like it's suspended in midair. There's a crack behind it big enough to crawl into."

Christy's nails dug into her palms as a primitive claustrophobia swept over her. She shoved her hands in her pockets again. This time her fingertips encountered the metal of Jo-Jo's key as well as ancient stone.

Hello, enigma, Christy thought with a humor that wasn't far from stark fear. Meet the mystery bead. May all your secrets be little and safe.

"What about the shoring?" she asked roughly. "Will it hold?"

"Whoever was here before us had mining experience. He built some braces to stabilize the flake."

Breath held, Christy waited.

Cain said nothing more.

"For me," she said tightly, "ignorance is no particular bliss."

"The flake of stone must weigh twenty tons," he said. "You don't handle that kind of weight with four-by-four timbers."

She let out a long breath. "Finish it."

Cain threw her a surprised look.

"If the flake was all you were worried about," Christy said, "you would have dragged me to the lip of the alcove before you said a word."

He smiled. "You know me pretty well, honey."

"Well enough to know you're not telling me all you know."

Christy's hands clenched in her pockets. The bead was smooth. The edges of the key cut into flesh. She wasn't telling Cain all she knew, either.

"The flake is supporting a second slab," Cain said finally. "The crack separating it from the cliff looks like it goes all the way to daylight. The gap is so big the Anasazi built storage cysts in it."

He ran his hands through his hair, displacing the watch cap. Absently he stuffed it into his hip pocket.

"The whole ceiling of the alcove is ready to drop away," he said bluntly. "The second slab is bigger than the one that closed the alcove. When it goes, it will wake the dead in Denver."

Automatically Christy looked at the ceiling of the alcove, where the rock spread above them like the canopy of a dome tent. The sandstone was darkened with the soot of thousands of fires and dampened by seepage from millions of winter melts and summer storms.

"It looks so . . . solid," she said.

"It was, once. But there are always cracks. Water gets in. It dissolves the glue holding sand grains together. In winter the water freezes, pushing the crack deeper into the stone. When the crack is big enough, gravity takes care of the rest."

Silently Christy tried to imagine the subtle forces at work, water that froze and expanded in winter, pressing stone apart. Then the time of melting came and ice became a gentle acid dissolving away stone.

Drop by drop, season by season, stress by stress.

Then one day, one hour, one instant, and the massive flake broke away. When the last crushing echo faded and the fine dust settled, a new balance was achieved.

And the whole cycle was repeated. Drop by drop, season by season, stress by stress.

"Are you saying we should get out?" Christy asked.

"I'm saying I'd hate to be in here in a thunderstorm."

"That bad, huh?"

"It's a matter of luck. The ceiling has held this long. It should hold a while longer."

Christy shuddered.

"If you want to go outside the alcove," Cain said, "I sure as hell won't blame you."

"What about you?"

"I saw something along the edge of the building block. I want to take a closer look at it."

He picked up the lantern again and headed toward the massive slab of sandstone that had fallen sometime after the Anasazis had nearly filled the alcove with their cliff house.

After a moment's hesitation, Christy followed Cain. Moki watched but showed no desire to follow.

"What are we looking for this time?" she asked.

"I think there's another kiva over near the other window at this edge of the alcove. It looks as though the ceiling caved in when that slab fell. Somebody spent a lot of time digging at one side."

The second kiva was situated well beyond the block of rooms. Lantern light revealed a tangle of splintered cedar-log roof timbers. The ceiling was completely collapsed. The upright pillars that had once supported the roof had been broken in half. Dirt and chunks of stone nearly filled the sunken room.

A mound of loose dirt was piled beside a small tunnel at one edge of the kiva. The tunnel dropped down beneath the collapsed dome, then widened out into a small chamber the size of a telephone booth.

Cain and Christy knelt at the mouth of the tunnel and peered into the chamber.

"It's a pile of jackstraws," Cain said, surveying the tangle of broken timbers and tumbled rock. "Whoever did the digging must have had cast-iron balls."

"What were they after?"

Cain ventured a few feet into the tunnel, being careful not to brush against the sides.

"It looks like a cyst of some sort," he said, shining the lantern into the dark corners of the chamber. "They got down below the floor level of the kiva, almost as though they were—"

Abruptly his voice broke off in a soft oath. He reached into the chamber and scratched in the dirt.

At first Christy thought Cain had unearthed another potsherd, but when he handed the fragment back to her, she knew instantly it wasn't pottery. Something about its shape made her uneasy. Or perhaps it was the texture.

When Cain backed out of the opening, Christy handed the fragment to him instantly.

"Here. Take it," she said.

"You don't like it?"

"No."

He brought the lantern to bear on the fragment and grunted.

"Just as I thought," he said. "Bone."

"Human?"

"The head of a femur."

Christy grimaced. "Do you run into them often?"

Cain shook his head. He laid the scrap of bone aside and scratched through the loose dirt.

"I wonder where the rest of the skeleton is. This is the biggest Anasazi grave I've ever seen."

He scooped out several handfuls of soil and set

it aside. Then he scratched some more but failed to turn up anything.

Cain's gentle excavation deepened the hole, triggering a miniature cave-in along the back edge. A flicker of color caught Christy's eye. She snatched up the lantern and held it closer.

"Look!"

"I see it," Cain said.

Very carefully he leaned into the chamber, stretched, and gently retrieved a flat green pebble that was smaller than a postage stamp.

"Jesus," he said softly. "Turquoise. Some pothunter really struck it rich in this grave."

Cain held out the turquoise piece for Christy to see. The size and shape reminded her of Hutton's extraordinary inlaid tortoise.

"If that weren't turquoise, I'd swear it came from Hutton's collection," she said slowly.

"What do you mean?"

"He has an abalone, turquoise, and argillite tortoise that came from somewhere on his ranch," Christy said. "But the turquoise inlay was intact."

Cain's narrowed eyes gleamed in the lantern light as he looked from the turquoise fragment in his hand to Christy.

"Then why does this remind you of his artifact?" Cain asked.

"The shape and size is the same as the inlay on the tortoise's head. An odd kind of partly curved polygon."

Thoughtfully Cain turned the piece of turquoise

over in his hand. The shape of the piece was indeed odd. Despite his previous orders to Christy about not picking up so much as a pebble, Cain put the turquoise into his pocket.

"Can you describe the tortoise?" he asked.

"Sure. My business is describing things. Four legs retracted so that only the clawed feet were visible. Tail barely a nub. Extremities of abalone inlay. Head and neck not retracted, frankly phallic in shape. Eyes made of two tiny turquoise spheres. Turquoise collar. Argillite shell."

"Any more?"

Christy frowned. "As big as my palm, two-dimensional rather than sculptural, sophisticated rather than crude, curvilinear more than angular, meant to be viewed from one side only, like a pendant. The workmanship was very fine. And there was something . . ."

Her voice faded.

"What?" Cain asked.

"It was more than the sum of its parts," she said after a moment. "Whoever created it was an artist. The tortoise was invested with a sense of wisdom and longevity and fertility that was riveting."

Cain let out a long breath. "I'd like to see that. It sounds like a fetish from a very wealthy, very powerful clan."

"That's pretty good guessing, for a white man."

The gravelly voice came from the darkness behind them. Cain spun and held the lantern above his head, sending a wash of light into the shadows.

Johnny Ten Hats stepped into the light. In one big hand was a shotgun with a sawed-off stock and barrel. His finger was over the trigger.

The barrel was pointing right at Cain and Christy.

16

"Hello, Johnny," Cain said. *He gave a* low, curt whistle. "Somebody worked you over pretty good."

"Don't come any closer!" the Indian snarled.

"I'm not going anywhere," Cain said.

Christy stared, unable to believe how casual Cain was.

He flicked a sideways glance at her. The look in his eyes made her cold.

When Johnny turned and looked quickly over his shoulder, Cain made a brief motion with his hand, as though warning Christy not to move.

"Somebody on your trail?" Cain asked.

"Back away from that hole," Johnny said. "Put the lantern down on that rock and keep your hands where I can see them."

Cain set the lantern down carefully and moved

away from it. He watched the big Indian with cold, predatory intent, waiting for an opening.

"Not that I need to worry much about you," Johnny said with faint contempt. "You won't fight me. You proved that before you were shot."

Christy stared, unable to believe that Johnny didn't see the battle readiness in Cain. It fairly shouted to her, scraping her nerves until she felt as if she were bleeding under her skin.

"Some things just aren't worth fighting about," Cain said. "A piece of ass is one of them."

"Shut up," Johnny snarled.

He lifted the shotgun to chest height and pointed it at Cain's head.

Fear froze Christy. The bore of the shotgun looked as big as a railroad tunnel and as black as death itself. Yet Cain's face was expressionless.

Then she glanced back at Johnny. He was staring at her. Cain moved to one side slowly, as though to draw attention back to himself.

"Hold still!" Johnny said roughly.

"Take it easy, man. You on speed or something?" Cain asked.

The Indian shook his head, in denial or in response to some private pain.

"I gave that shit up," he said.

"Good thing," Cain said easily. "Makes you paranoid."

Johnny blinked and swiped sweat and blood off his forehead with the back of his left hand. The muzzle of the shotgun in his right hand didn't waver.

"You the one who looted this place?" Cain asked.

Johnny grunted.

"You sell it all for dope?" Cain asked.

The big Indian glared blackly at Cain.

"Yeah, well," Cain said, shrugging, "I warned you how much Hutton's whore would cost."

The Indian's response was a stifled sound that might have been a laugh. He took a ragged step closer, trying to intimidate Cain by pure bulk.

When Johnny moved, the side of his face that was toward Christy came out of shadow. She made an involuntary sound. He looked like a dead man walking. His face was bruised and covered with the crusted blood from several cuts. Other cuts were bleeding. His left hand was held stiffly, as though injured.

"You don't look real good," Cain said calmly.

"I look better than you will if you don't shut up and stand still."

Johnny gestured curtly with the shotgun.

Cain showed him empty hands. "I'm not dumb enough to go bare-handed against a shotgun."

"Hell, you won't go bare-handed against nothin'," the Indian said scornfully.

"Coming from you, that's funny."

"What's that mean?"

"How does it feel to shoot someone in the back?" Cain asked. "Did it make you forget what a fool you are for paying for a piece of ass every cowboy in Remington County had for free?"

Johnny took a step, stumbled, and caught himself on a waist-high chunk of sandstone. He sagged against it like an old man sinking into a rocking chair. Then he grinned in the lantern light, revealing a mouth full of broken teeth.

"So you think it was me," Johnny said.

He laughed thickly, then spat off to the side, blood and saliva darkly mixed.

Cain watched, measuring his chances.

Christy bit back a scream. Johnny was too far away, the shotgun too dangerous. Cain would be killed before he took one step.

Then she noticed it was Johnny that Cain watched, not the gun. His actions told her that the man was the more dangerous weapon.

"How much did you take out of here, Johnny?"

Cain's voice was matter-of-fact, a man making casual conversation with an acquaintance. Only his eyes weren't casual. He watched Johnny with reptilian intensity.

"Who says I took anything out of this place?" Johnny challenged.

Cain laughed softly. The sound was like a rasp on stone.

"This ruin was a cultural gold mine," Cain said. "Now it's a trash heap. That's your style. You destroy a whole site for a few good pots. I know you, Johnny. I've seen your sign all over the San Juan Basin."

Johnny wiped the back of his hand across the corner of his mouth. His hand came away dark with blood and dirt.

"You got any water?" he asked.

"In my backpack."

"Where is it?" Johnny said, glancing around.

Cain eased forward in the instant before the Indian looked back at him.

"I'm wearing it," Cain said. "I'll just take it off and—"

"No! Don't move, you bastard! I don't trust you!" he said in a rising tone. "I don't trust no one no more!"

"Easy, Johnny," Cain said. "You're fine. You've got control of everything and you're just fine."

The Indian's black glance darted erratically around the alcove. He looked at Christy as though he had never seen her before. Then he looked again, surprised.

"Hey," he said. "Don't I know you? Come here."

"Stay put," Cain said softly. "Not one inch, Red."

Christy didn't move.

Johnny shook his head like a drunk trying to clear the cobwebs. Slowly he focused on Cain.

"Who's the bitch?" Johnny asked.

"Nobody you need to worry about," Cain said gently. "She was just getting ready to take a walk while we talk about old times."

Johnny thought it over, then spat again.

"No," the Indian said harshly. "She stays. Don't trust no one."

"You have to trust someone," Cain said. "You need help."

He took a step forward, then another one, before Johnny reacted.

"Back off or I'll blow a hole through you!"

Cain stopped moving. Only Christy seemed to notice that he was poised to move again, in any direction, at any moment.

"You still need help," Cain said.

"Bastards."

The comment seemed aimed at people in general rather than Cain in particular. The shotgun was much more discriminating. Its unblinking eye never shifted from Cain's chest.

Johnny coughed.

Cain inched forward.

The Indian spat blood into the darkness.

Cain moved again.

"I never shoulda got involved with those eastern assholes with their pretty-boy manners and their fancy dope," Johnny mumbled. "My head ain't been right since."

Johnny coughed.

Cain inched closer.

Christy held herself so tightly she ached in every muscle, screaming silently within her mind.

It's too far, Cain. Don't try it! He'll kill you!

She wanted to scream the warning aloud, even though it would do no good. Cain knew the odds as well as she did.

Better.

The gun was pointed at him.

"Did you do the dig for Hutton?" Cain asked.

"Hell, yes," Johnny said. He made a sweeping gesture with the muzzle of the shotgun. "I found the place," he added savagely. "I dug the pots. I did it all. Pretty good for a no-good redskin Moki poacher, huh?"

"That'll teach you, Cain, you and all your fancy university friends. I found this ruin, me and Jo, and I dug it. Hell of a lot more than you can say."

Christy stiffened at the mention of her sister's name. Johnny didn't notice that any more than he noticed Cain's aching progress toward him, a quarter inch, stop and wait, a half inch, stop, a quarter inch. . . .

Then stop.

And wait.

"Would you have found it if I hadn't told Jo there had to be something around the Sisters?" Cain asked calmly.

Christy's nails dug into her palms.

Johnny glared at Cain and swiped his hand across his mouth again. Then he grinned like a boy.

"No, I wouldn't have found it. I didn't have to. I just let you do all the thinking and Jo do all the screwing. She picked you clean, got all your secrets."

"Did she?"

"She got the Sisters," Johnny said roughly. "After that, who gives a shit what else you know?"

"What happened, Johnny? How did you end up spitting blood?"

"It's all gone to hell," the Indian said heavily. "People dying, gonna die."

Abruptly he began chanting in a low voice. The atonal, alien words made the hair on Christy's nape stir.

"You need help," Cain said.

"Just some dirt, man. Just dirt and then get outta here before they catch me."

"Who's after you?"

"Sheriff. He'll never catch me. I know this country too good. As good as you, Cain."

Johnny laughed, coughed, spat.

Cain inched closer.

"Was I you," the Indian said, "I'd go back in the mesa country and not come out for a time. They're planning on killing me and blaming you."

Christy threw a quick look at Cain. His expression hadn't changed. He looked calm, relaxed. . . .

And he was a foot closer to Johnny.

"They?" Cain asked. "Who?"

"Find out the hard way. I ain't never seeing none of you again."

Abruptly Johnny focused on Cain. The Indian straightened and thrust out the shotgun.

"Back up!"

"I'm just trying to help you," Cain said.

"I don't need you. I got me a plan. I'll take care of that bastard Autry and all the rest. All I need is some dirt, and my little BLM buddies will take care of me."

Johnny drew a ragged breath and laughed like a demon in one of Hutton's paintings.

"You have friends in BLM?" Cain asked. "That's a switch."

"Yeah, ain't it? I been a pothunter all my life, and now my only hope is the Bureau of Land fucking Management."

Johnny reached into his hip pocket with his injured hand and pulled out a small burlap bag of the kind used to sell Anasazi beans to tourists.

"Just dish me up a couple pounds of dirt from that hole over there," Johnny said, gesturing to the kiva. "Then I'll be on my way. Any questions you got, you ask Danner. He's about fifteen minutes behind me."

Johnny tossed the burlap sack toward Cain. "Fill it."

Cain caught the sack with one hand. He seemed to hesitate.

No, he's still too far. Don't do it!

Cain must have reached the same conclusion. Slowly he turned toward the kiva that had been used as a burial place for human bones. He dropped into the small chamber. Using his hands, he began filling the small bag.

"How many skeletons were in here?" Cain asked.

"Two."

Johnny heaved himself away from the rock's support and went to the grave to see what Cain was doing.

"Male, female, or both?" Cain asked.

"Both women. Prettiest grave goods you ever saw, too. Turquoise, jet, abalone. I damn near rusted my zipper."

Motionless, Christy stood at the edge of the heap of broken timbers, trying not to attract any attention to herself. From the corner of her eye, she caught a flicker of movement that was pacing every motion Johnny made.

Moki, belly flat on the ground, was creeping forward out of the shadows. He was gathered like a great, living spring, waiting only for the moment of release.

Christy's heart beat so loudly she was sure Johnny would hear it.

"Did Hutton get everything?" Cain asked.

"Dunno. I took everything in sight, but I didn't have a chance to dig this baby out."

Johnny wiped his eyes. He had trouble lifting his left hand.

"The bitch got him too. She cut off his balls and fed them to him."

Cain stopped throwing of dirt into the sack. "Who, Jo?"

Johnny didn't answer.

"Do you know where Jo is now?" Christy asked before she could stop herself.

He turned to look at her.

"If she's smart," the Indian said, "she's gone. Autry will kill her if he gets his hands on her."

"*No,*" Christy said starkly.

The emotion in her voice caught Johnny's attention. He stared at her a long time.

"Don't I know you?" he asked again.

Christy looked away hastily.

Cain was watching her with dawning understanding. And fury.

"Wait a minute," Johnny said. "You're the sister, the redheaded reporter from New York."

Coolness slid down Christy's spine.

"Autry thinks you were in on this with Jo," Johnny

said. "She set it up to look that way. She's a cunning one. Was I you, I'd disappear."

"I'm not in on anything with anyone," Christy said.

Johnny laughed, coughed, spat blood.

"No skin off my ass," he said. "Hutton's going to beat the truth out of you one way or the other. He likes bathing pretty women and putting baby powder on them and then hurting them where it doesn't show."

Christy could feel the pressure of Cain's stare, but she couldn't force herself to meet his eyes. His expression was a study in stark shadow and hard white light. He was motionless.

"Do you know where Jo is?" Christy asked Johnny again.

"Why? She double-cross you too?"

"Something like that."

"She's a real snake queen, ain't she."

Christy took a step toward the Indian. Reflexively, he turned to cover her with the gun. The movement exposed his weak side to Cain.

Belatedly, Johnny realized that he couldn't cover both Christy and Cain with the gun any longer.

"Back up," he snarled.

Instead of obeying, Christy took another step, opening the distance between herself and Cain, forcing Johnny to choose between them.

"Do you have any idea where Jo might have gone?" Christy pleaded.

She refused to allow herself to look at the gun barrel that was now hovering between her and Cain.

Suddenly the gun was pointing only at her.

"Get over with Cain!"

A savage, snarling shadow leaped from the darkness, going straight for Johnny's throat.

The surprise was so complete that Johnny couldn't bring the shotgun to bear on the dog. It was all he could do to throw up his injured left arm in self-defense.

Cain began scrambling up and out of the burial chamber as soon as he gave Moki the signal to attack. Just as Cain cleared to the rubble pile, Moki's jaws closed on Johnny's wrist.

Johnny screamed and twisted aside, flailing and stumbling under Moki's weight. But even as the Indian staggered, he lifted the shotgun muzzle to the dog who was hanging from his wrist.

Barely three seconds after Moki attacked, the shadowy alcove was filled with the incandescent flash and violent report of a shotgun.

Christy was deafened by the blast, unable to hear her own screams. The concussion seemed to last forever. Even worse, the muzzle flash had blinded her. For a few terrifying instants she could see only dim shapes and hear only the endless echo of the shotgun in her mind.

"Get down!"

Without any more warning than his shout, Cain knocked Christy aside, out of the line of fire. Head ringing, she felt blindly in the dirt for a stone big enough to use against Johnny Ten Hats.

The Indian flung Moki's limp body aside as though the big dog weighed no more than a shadow.

With the same motion, he spun toward Cain. The shotgun came up, pointed right at Cain's chest.

There was no way Cain could reach Johnny before he triggered a shot. There was no cover for Cain and no time to seek any.

Christy screamed in futile denial.

The shotgun's hammer fell on an empty chamber. Johnny hadn't had a chance to reload.

Cain didn't give him one. He attacked with the same snarling ferocity as Moki had.

Johnny used the shotgun as a club. The blow caught Cain on his shoulder, knocking him to the ground. Immediately Johnny tried to work the shotgun's pump action, to reload. His wounded hand didn't respond.

Christy's fingers closed around a rock the size of an apple. While Johnny cursed and tried to work the pump one-handed and Cain struggled to his feet, Christy hurled the rock at Johnny. The range was close and the target was big. The stone hit him in the side of the face with a solid thunk.

Johnny yelled and staggered backward, instinctively trying to get out of range. As he retreated around the ruined kiva, he clamped the shotgun under his left arm and tried to work the pump with his good right hand.

Silently Cain pursued, intent on getting to Johnny before he could reload. Skirting the tangled wreckage of the kiva, Cain caught Johnny in the window left by the slab of sandstone at one end of alcove.

Cain lunged, and both men disappeared in a tangle onto the rocky face outside the alcove.

From deep within the alcove came a spectral vibration that was more sensed than heard, as though masses of stone were slowly, slowly shifting. A timber groaned and splintered.

And then the sounds stopped.

Christy clawed to her feet, another rock in her hand. She reached the edge of the alcove in time to see Cain land a short, chopping blow on the point of Johnny's right shoulder. Abruptly the Indian's arm went limp.

The shotgun clattered on stone, bounced, then skidded down the steep slope to the sheer drop below. Seconds later, the shotgun vanished over the brink.

With an inarticulate cry of rage, Johnny threw himself at Cain and bore him down to the stony ground through sheer weight. Whatever damage had been done to the Indian's right arm was only temporary. Johnny grabbed Cain in a crushing bear hug.

The two men thrashed around on the stone lip of the precipice, coming closer to disaster with each instant. Neither man seemed to notice the drop, which was more dangerous than any human opponent.

Finally Cain butted Johnny's chin hard enough to daze him. Johnny had enough sense left to lower his chin and protect his Adam's apple, but doing that left his face wide open. A short, hammering blow from Cain's forehead broke Johnny's nose.

Another blow in the same place made Johnny scream, yet he didn't let go his crushing hold.

Instinctively Johnny turned his face aside, protecting his ruined nose. Cain wrenched an arm free and chopped across Johnny's throat. Instantly the Indian began choking.

Yet he didn't let go.

"Give it—up," Cain panted harshly. "You can't win—and you know it!"

Finally Johnny let go and rolled to his hands and knees, gagging and fighting for breath. Cain got painfully to his own feet and stood with his hands on his hips, breathing in great gasps.

"Cain!" Christy screamed. "Watch out!"

He turned just as Johnny lunged for him. Cain tried to duck beneath the tackle. He almost succeeded. Johnny's weight landed on the backpack Cain still wore.

For an instant Johnny's momentum threatened to bowl Cain over the edge of the canyon. With a raw cry of effort, he straightened his legs and back, using every bit of his strength literally to throw off the attack.

Johnny sailed out over the cliff like a massive black fledgling launched too soon from the nest. Seconds after he vanished below the stone lip, an eerie chant rose in his wake. It was cut off abruptly.

Christy ran to where Cain knelt, staring over the edge of the rock face. She took his arm and tried to pull him away.

"Get back from the edge," Christy said. "Damn it, Cain! Get back! It's not safe."

Slowly, he turned toward her. His eyes were coldly luminous. The wild exhilaration of survival was mixed with the bleak finality of having caused a man's death.

Then Cain focused on Christy. The look in his eyes became bleak. The contempt in his voice made her flinch.

"I shouldn't have worried about disinfecting those clothes before I gave them to you, should I?"

17

"Are you all right?" Christy asked tightly.

In answer, Cain forced himself to his feet. Without a word he headed back for the alcove.

"I heard a timber break just after the shotgun went off," Christy said.

But as she spoke, she was grabbing the lantern and going into the alcove.

"Moki is back here somewhere," Christy said.

"I know."

"Moki," she called softly. "Where are you, boy?"

A faint whimper came from the darkness beyond the ring of lantern light.

As Christy turned toward the sound, Cain grabbed the lantern from her hand and went swiftly to his dog.

"Easy, boy," Cain said gently as he knelt. "Let's see how bad it is."

Moki lay stretched out full length, seemingly too weak to move. Yet at the sound of Cain's voice, the dog's tail stirred in a feeble wag.

"Hold this," Cain said curtly.

Christy took the lantern and held it up. The dog's front quarters were drenched with dark red blood.

Lantern light wavered, dipped, shivered.

"Hold still, damn it," Cain snarled.

"I'm trying."

Cain looked up. Christy was trembling all over. Her left arm braced her right in an attempt to hold the light steady. Tears ran silently, steadily, down her cheeks. She was as pale as salt.

"If you think you're going to faint," he said, turning back to Moki, "put down the lantern."

Christy hissed something between her teeth.

Very gently Cain probed in the bloody fur. Moki whined once and flinched. Other than that, the dog made no protest while Cain examined him.

"Hold the lantern closer," Cain snapped.

When Christy leaned forward, the lantern light revealed a long furrow through the fur and muscle at the front of Moki's shoulder. White bone gleamed.

Steel clanged on stone as Christy set the lantern down.

"You faint and I'll leave you where you fall," Cain said coldly.

"Go to hell."

Christy's voice was strong and every bit as cold

as Cain's. He looked up in surprise. She peeled off her jacket and handed it to Cain.

"What's that for?" he asked.

"Moki."

Cain picked up the lantern and held it overhead, ignoring the jacket.

"Dogs go into shock just like people do," Christy said tightly. "Put the jacket over him."

Instead, Cain stood up and peeled off the backpack and then his own shirt. The light transformed scrapes and bruises from his brief, brutal fight with Johnny Ten Hats into dark smears across bare skin.

Cain folded his shirt into a broad, flat pad and very gently placed it over Moki's wound. Without looking at Christy, he took the jacket she held out, eased it beneath the dog, and wrapped it around him.

When Cain finally did look at Christy, she wished he hadn't.

"I didn't dare tell you Jo-Jo is my sister," she said.

"Why the hell not? If you had, Johnny might still be alive."

"I doubt it," she said curtly. "He wasn't what I'd call rational."

Cain turned back to Moki. He worked quickly, for the alcove was cold and the dog looked very small against all the stone.

With an effort, Christy took control of her adrenaline-frayed temper.

"Cain, I didn't know you," she said urgently. "I

didn't know what kind of a man you were. Local gossip wasn't very comforting."

"Yeah, yeah, yeah," Cain said in disgust.

"And . . .Jo-Jo had warned me that you were dangerous."

"Shit. Johnny was right. Whatever the scam is, you're in on it with your sister."

"No! She called me, said she needed me, had to see me. I hadn't seen her for a long time. How could I turn her down?"

"Ever tried the word *no?*" he asked sardonically.

As Cain spoke, he took a knife out of the backpack and slashed a slit in the back of Christy's jacket.

"If it had been your brother calling you," she demanded, "what would you have done?"

Silently Cain tied the two new ends of the jacket into a tight little knot and looped the arms around Moki's neck. Then he made another knot to secure the dressing. Finally he looked up at Christy. His eyes were almost opaque.

"I've killed two men," he said flatly. "Both times there was a lying little slut involved."

Christy drew a deep breath and looked around the shadowy alcove. Jo-Jo and Johnny and Hutton had ransacked a thousand years of history, and now they were fighting over the spoils. They didn't care who got hurt in the battle.

"I wish," Christy said distinctly, "that none of this had happened. Had I known what it would cost, I never would have involved you."

"I kept you last night because I thought you

needed help," Cain said as though she hadn't spoken. "What a laugh. Did Jo-Jo send you to finish what Johnny couldn't?"

"You couldn't be more wrong about me."

Cain ignored Christy. He talked softly to Moki, soothing him with voice and gentle touches. Then he eased his hands beneath the dog and lifted him carefully.

Moki whimpered and struggled a little when Cain shifted the dog's weight to his arms. A few words calmed him.

"I saw a canvas tarp in the first kiva, at the bottom of the ladder," Cain said. "Get it. I'll wait on top of the rim for you."

"What right do you have to judge me and—"

"Just get the damn tarp!" Cain interrupted savagely.

Christy grabbed the lantern and headed for the kiva. She scrambled down the ladder, grabbed the tarp, and climbed up to the surface once more.

When she reached the sandstone slab that had nearly sealed off the alcove, Cain was climbing up the mound of rubble. He seemed to be moving effortlessly, finding his footing without a stumble on the uneven slope.

She took a deep breath and wondered what Cain was using for nerves. Her legs no longer shook, but the whiplash of adrenaline still gave her hands a fine trembling.

Forcing herself to breathe deeply and evenly, Christy set down the lantern, stuffed the tarp in the backpack, shouldered it, and started after Cain. He was already walking on the ancient, deceptive steps that had been cut into the sandstone by distrustful Anasazi.

Suddenly the rock in front of Cain exploded in a shower of shrapnel. There was a flat, keening sound, followed by the faint but unmistakable report of a high-powered rifle.

Christy froze in the act of stepping out from behind the cover of the sandstone slab that nearly covered the alcove.

There was no such shield for Cain. He began moving as quickly as the steps allowed. The only safety for him lay in the cleft that came down from the top of the mesa.

A second bullet screamed off the sandstone below Cain's feet. Then a third.

In the shadows of the alcove, Christy held her breath and prayed Cain and Moki across the naked stretch of rock. It seemed like weeks before Cain reached the shelter of the tunnel. It seemed like months while he set Moki down, went feet first into the narrow opening, and rolled over to drag the dog into the tunnel after him.

Shots keened and screamed around the rock as long as either man or dog was in sight.

Christy hugged the rocks of the alcove wall and peered down at the canyon floor, trying to see who was shooting. A thousand feet below, there was a vehicle on the road. A man was bent over the roof, using it to steady his rifle barrel. Sunlight flashed harshly on the telescopic sight. There were three block letters painted on the roof: RSO.

She had seen a truck that size and color in

Remington. Sheriff Danner had been driving it.

Another shot sang off the rocks close to where Cain had disappeared, then another and another, but the quarry was gone. The man stepped back, jerked open the door of the truck, flung the gun inside, and got into the driver's seat. Dust boiled up from the tires as the truck accelerated down the dirt road and disappeared around a bend.

Christy didn't wait for the attacker to change his mind. She crossed the sandstone steps with reckless speed, intent only on reaching the relative safety of the tunnel. She dove into the darkness, barely squeezing through with the extra bulk of the backpack.

Cain was gone.

Christy gathered herself and pushed through the tunnel on all fours at a frantic pace, ignoring the pain to her knees and hands. As soon as she could stand, she rushed forward, only to come up against the final, sheer length of stone that separated her from the rim.

Cain wasn't there, either.

There were streaks of blood on the wall. Christy made a low sound and shook her head, not wanting to know how Cain had managed to carry the injured dog up a wall that was taller than he was.

Christy looked at the bloody wall. She had gotten down it with the help of gravity and Cain's strong arms.

There was no way for her to get up alone.

Despite that, she attacked the stone, scrambling and seeking hand- or footholds. Three times she fell back. Each time she picked herself up and flung herself at the stone once more.

Two bloody hands shot down and grabbed her flailing wrists just as she would have fallen for the fourth time.

"Slow down before you hurt yourself," Cain said roughly. "Danner's an hour away from getting any help."

Christy looked up. There was no comfort in Cain's eyes, but he hadn't abandoned her. She drew in deep, tearing breaths, fighting for oxygen.

"Thank you," she said shakily.

"For what?"

"Not leaving . . . me here."

Cain's eyes narrowed. He looked at Christy's face where the dirt was streaked with tears and blood from a small cut. Her skin was white and her pupils so dilated that barely any color showed around the rim.

"There's a crevice to your left," he said tightly, "and then a knob of rock on the right. See them?"

After a moment or two, Christy cleared the tears enough to see what Cain was talking about.

"I see them."

"Put your boot in the crevice," Cain said.

She did.

"Now step up and find the knob with your right foot."

As soon as Christy stepped up, Cain lifted. She put her right foot out blindly, connected with the knob, and pushed upward. Cain pulled her out of the crevice like a cork out of a bottle.

When he let go of her, she stood with braced feet, trembling, her arms wrapped around her body as though she was cold.

Cain turned away, gathered up Moki, and headed for the truck. After a few deep breaths, Christy started walking. By the time she reached the truck, she felt as though she would never breathe evenly again. She peeled off the backpack and threw it on the ground. The tarp trailed out of the pack like a dirty flag.

The look Cain gave Christy said he was surprised she had bothered with the pack and tarp. He picked up the tarp, shook it out with a snap of his wrist, and laid it on the floor of the truck's cargo area. Gently he put Moki on half the tarp and folded the other half over, keeping the dog as warm as possible.

Moki neither whimpered nor moved.

"Is he dead?" Christy asked starkly.

"Not yet. But getting him through the tunnel and up that last pitch was rough. He passed out. Better that way."

Christy made a ragged sound. Then she climbed into the cargo area and sat next to Moki.

"Get in front," Cain said curtly. "It's going to be a rough ride."

"I know. I can keep Moki from sliding around."

Cain gave Christy an odd look, started to say something, and then simply got in the truck. Moments later the big vehicle was in motion.

"Did you say Danner was the one shooting at you?" Christy asked after a time.

"Yeah. He's the only one I know who wears a white hat and drives a Remington Sheriff's Office truck."

"But why was he shooting at you?"

"I imagine he saw me kill Johnny," Cain said.

"It was self-defense!"

"Danner doesn't know that. Probably doesn't give a damn, either. In the eyes of the local law, I'm what's known as 'bought and paid for.' Danner will kill me where he finds me and consider it a public service."

"Jesus Christ," said Christy in a raw voice. "What kind of place is this?"

"A place just like every other. The local cops know who's important and who isn't. Danner will do whatever he thinks he and Peter Hutton's money can get away with."

"What are we going to do?"

"We've got maybe an hour before Danner gets back to a spot where he can call for help on the radio," Cain said. "If we're not back at the highway by then, we'll be cut off."

Christy stopped asking questions and concentrated on making the ride as easy for the injured dog as possible. The moment they reached the smooth blacktop of the highway, she checked the bandage.

Both Cain's shirt and her jacket were soaked almost through. She had no idea how much blood the dog had lost, or how much more he could afford. She only knew that Moki couldn't last much longer.

"I'll drop you on a little road that runs behind the hotel, so nobody will see you," Cain said.

The sound of his voice startled Christy. He hadn't spoken to her at all during the drive.

"Moki first," she said. "After he's taken care of."

Closing her eyes, Christy fought for self-control. She really didn't know what she should do next. She knew only that she had to find Jo-Jo.

You got me into this damned mess, sister. You're going to get me out again. And Cain with me. Somehow.

No sooner had the thought formed than Christy shuddered. She wondered if her sister was in a position to help anyone, even herself.

Jo-Jo, for the first time in our lives I need you. Stop hiding from me!

"As soon as Moki is safe," Christy said, "I have to make some calls."

Cain glanced at her in the rearview mirror. Whatever he was thinking, he kept to himself.

The veterinary hospital was in a little settlement outside of Remington. The place was no more than a weathered frame building, a gas station, a general store, and a handful of houses scattered along the highway. The windows of the store were blank and dirty. Obviously it had been closed for years. The gas station's two pumps squatted dismally in puddles of rainwater. A muddy black dog was the only sign of life.

Cain pulled the truck around behind the frame building, where the vehicle couldn't be seen from the highway. He gathered up Moki in the blood-stained tarp. When Christy would have followed, he gave her a hard look.

"Stay here," he said curtly. "The vet's office girl is the biggest gossip in Remington County."

Christy got back in the truck, but into the passenger seat rather than the cargo area. . . .

Fifteen minutes later, Cain emerged from the little clinic. He paused only long enough to pull on a borrowed shirt. Afternoon light played across a livid pink scar in the middle of his back and an equally bright one on his chest.

Through and through, Christy thought, horrified at seeing evidence of Cain's injury in bright daylight. My God, how did he survive?

Cain looked exhausted and enraged at the same time. He tucked in the tails of the shirt with short, savage motions. Then he got in the truck and slammed the door behind him.

"How is Moki?" Christy asked instantly.

"About bled dry," Cain said.

He looked at Christy, then looked away as though he couldn't stand the sight of her.

"It took Doc Tucker five minutes just to find a vein he could use," Cain said in a low voice.

Christy looked away also. Being hated at such close range was unexpectedly painful.

"But he's still alive?" she asked huskily.

Cain nodded curtly.

"Is Moki as tough as you are?" she whispered.

Surprised, Cain looked at Christy again. She was staring out the side window.

"Tougher," he said.

"Then he'll make it. You did, didn't you?"

"So far. The divine Jo-Jo will be the death of me yet."

Cain started up the truck and backed out.

"I have to make some calls," Christy said.

"Why?"

"To find Jo-Jo."

"Why?"

"For God's sake, Cain! She's my sister and she's in trouble!"

"So are you."

Christy shrugged impatiently.

"How long since you've seen her?" Cain asked after a moment.

"Years."

"*How long?*" he asked savagely.

"Ten years. No, twelve. Thirteen?"

Christy gestured sharply with a hand that was marked by Moki's blood. She turned toward Cain.

"I don't remember," she said. "What the hell difference does it make? *She's my sister.*"

Cain flicked a glance at Christy and then concentrated on the dirt road he was taking.

"Younger sister," he said.

It wasn't a question. Christy answered anyway.

"Yes."

He let out an explosive breath and shook his head.

"Go back to New York, Red," he said finally. "Jo-Jo has bitten off more than her older sister can chew."

Saying nothing, Christy stared sightlessly out the

side window. She tried to swallow the fear that knotted her throat. She couldn't.

"You heard what Johnny said, didn't you?" Cain asked.

"Johnny said a lot of things."

"Jo-Jo did something to Hutton."

"Jo-Jo has done something to a lot of people," Christy said wearily.

"Hutton may look like a damned angel, but he's not nice."

Christy remembered the demons hanging in his hallway.

"I know," she whispered.

"Go home, Red. Let your little sister clean up after herself."

"She's not very good at that," Christy whispered. "She asked for me. She needs me."

"She wants to use you. There's a difference, honey. All the difference in the world."

The change in Cain's voice made Christy feel as though the steel bands around her lungs had finally been freed. She turned toward him.

"Then you don't really believe I'm in this—whatever it is—with her?" she asked.

Cain sighed and cursed at the same time.

"I believe Jo-Jo wouldn't have sat in the back of the truck," he said, "and helped a bloody dog not to roll around and cried the whole way without making a sound. Jo-Jo wouldn't have given a rat's ass for Moki's pain."

The savage contempt in Cain's voice when he spoke of Jo-Jo hadn't changed. Christy closed her eyes and clenched her fists until her nails dug into her hands.

"You can't know that," she said.

"Can't I? You haven't seen her for ten or twelve or thirteen years. I have. Johnny has."

"You're men."

"Jo-Jo wouldn't walk across the street for you if you were screaming for help," Cain said coldly.

"I don't believe that," she whispered.

"Jesus, Red. Take off those rose-colored glasses and look at what your sister is rather than what you want her to be!"

"I was able reach her," Christy said in a raw voice. "I was able to reach her when no one else could get close. And then I went east. ..."

Cain's hands clenched on the wheel until white showed around his knuckles.

"So you blame yourself for abandoning Jo-Jo," he said grimly.

"Yes."

"You think you're responsible for what she has become."

Christy closed her eyes. Tears slid from beneath her dark eyelashes.

"Yes," she whispered.

"That is a crock of shit," he said, spacing each word. "Jo-Jo is old enough to take responsibility for what she is and what she isn't."

Christy didn't answer.

"Get out of here, Red. Get out while you can. Don't let her pull you down with her."

"I can't just turn my back on my sister," Christy

said in a raw voice, "any more than you could leave Moki to die while you ran for cover!"

"Jesus," Cain hissed. "What if I just dump you by the side of the road?"

"And do what? Look for Jo-Jo?"

The slight flinching of Cain's eyelids told Christy he was planning to do just that.

She didn't want Cain to find Jo-Jo. Not alone.

He hated her too much.

18

"*What are you going to do?*" Christy asked bluntly.

Cain turned the truck onto another, smaller dirt lane before he answered.

"I'm going to see a friend," Cain said.

"Where?"

"Remington."

"That could be dangerous," she said.

"So could being seen with me if Danner has given shoot-on-sight orders."

"I figured that out when the rock chips started flying," Christy retorted.

Despite himself, Cain smiled slightly.

"You're something else, honey."

She gave him a wary glance.

"Don't tell me what," Christy said. "I've had all the excitement I can take for today."

He made a muffled sound and shook his head.

"After you've seen this friend, then what?" she asked.

"I start looking."

"For Jo-Jo."

"Yes."

Cain turned the truck onto another country lane.

"Where are you going to start?" Christy asked.

"I'll think of something."

"I already have."

He said nothing.

"Don't you want to know what it is?" Christy asked after a moment.

"What will it cost me?"

"We work together until we find her."

Cain gave Christy a sharp look.

She held her breath.

"You do realize that Danner is back in radio range by now?" Cain asked sardonically.

Christy nodded.

"I don't know how long I can stay ahead of the local law," he said, "but it's either hunt like a wolf or run like a rabbit."

"Somehow I don't see you as the Easter Bunny."

"And I don't see how a woman like you is sister to a—" Cain stopped speaking abruptly. "God must have a sense of humor, honey."

Christy's mouth curved in something less than a smile.

"Well?" she asked after a moment.

"Well what?"

"Do we have a deal? I give you a lead and we look for Jo-Jo together?"

"You might not like where it takes us."

"I'll . . ." Christy drew a deep breath. "I'll have to chance that."

A slow, cold smile spread across Cain's face.

"How do you know you can trust me not to take your information and then dump you on the side of the road?" he asked.

"I'll have to chance that too."

"Yeah, Red, you sure as hell will."

Narrowing his eyes, Cain stared out the windshield.

"Is it a deal?" Christy asked when she could stand the silence no longer.

Cain nodded curtly.

She let out a long breath. Then she dug around in her jeans pocket until she found the key. She held it up in the bright light coming through the windshield.

"Do you have any idea what this might open?" Christy asked.

Cain glanced at it, looked at Christy in disbelief, then back at the road again.

"Yeah," he said. "I have an idea. Where did you find it?"

"Jo-Jo's room," Christy said.

"Anything she had, Hutton knew about."

"Not this key. It was taped to the bottom of a drawer in her closet."

"How did you know where to look?" Cain asked casually.

"I spent my last six years in Wyoming searching Jo-Jo's room for forbidden fruit of one kind or another."

Cain took a hand off the wheel and reached for the key. At first, Christy didn't let go.

"If you don't trust me, you're better off alone," Cain said evenly.

She opened her fingers, giving him the key. Without a word he reached down for the ring of keys that hung from the Suburban's ignition. Deftly he fished one of the keys out of the cluster on the ring and let it dangle down his palm next to Jo-Jo's key.

They looked identical.

"I don't understand," Christy said.

"You've been in the city too long."

"Fine. I've been in the city too long. What the hell does that have to do with these keys?"

"It means some country folks drive in to get their mail out of little boxes opened by keys just like these."

"You mean Xanadu doesn't get mail delivery?" Christy asked in disbelief.

"Sure it does. Makes you wonder what Jo-Jo was expecting in the mail that she wanted to hide from Hutton."

Cain flipped the key back to Christy.

A few minutes later he turned into a tiny, dusty ranch lane. A weather-beaten house was tucked away behind some big elms.

"Wait here," Cain said.

Christy watched while he walked to the door,

knocked, and was greeted by a woman who was neither young nor old. She had dark brown hair with a dusting of gray and a smile that lit up the old, run-down porch. She kissed Cain soundly, hugged him, and led him into the house.

A few minutes later he emerged with an armful of clothes and a paper bag full of food. He put the food behind the driver's seat, tossed the clothes into Christy's lap, and got in.

"Change into these while we drive," Cain said.

"What about you?"

"I'll do my best not to drive into a ditch watching you."

Christy tried not to laugh but couldn't help it.

"I meant," she said carefully, "what about *your* clothes?"

"Out here, a man with dirty pants is no big deal."

"Where I came from in Wyoming, the women got just as dirty as the men."

"Were they wearing white designer jeans?" Cain asked.

"Point taken."

"Strip," Cain said laconically. "I won't see anything I haven't already seen."

"In your dreams," she retorted.

He laughed and made a point of shading his eyes with one hand so he couldn't see the passenger side.

Christy peeled off her filthy sweater and blouse and pulled on the soft, faded plaid shirt Cain had gotten for her. She kicked out of shoes and socks, pulled off the ruined white jeans, and pulled on a pair of Levi's that were as soft and faded as the shirt.

The clothes, though loose, fit well enough. She transferred the contents of her pockets to her new jeans, put on her socks and shoes, and turned to look at Cain.

"I was wrong about not seeing anything new," Cain said blandly.

"What?"

"Nice underwear, Red."

"Stuff it."

He threw back his head and laughed.

"You're more fun to tease than my little sister ever was," Cain said.

Christy ignored him. She pulled her purse out of the console where she had locked it away before heading out on the hike with Cain.

The purse was small, smart, and hopelessly Manhattan. She stripped out money, ID, and credit cards, and pushed them into her pockets. Then she sorted through the remaining clothes. A bandanna, a frayed quilted vest, and a faded red T-shirt rounded out the collection.

"Who should I thank for these?" Christy asked.

"Angie."

"Friend of yours?"

"Yes."

"She must be, to lend clothes to another—er, friend of yours."

Cain gave Christy a sideways look.

"Angie is like every other human being. She gets

lonely. So she'll cook dinner while I bore her with my latest Anasazi theories."

Christy made a neutral sound.

"Or I'll chop some firewood for her," Cain said "and she'll swap ironing my shirts for some tutoring for her oldest kid. Angie never learned to read books, but she's a fine judge of people."

Christy's cheeks burned. "I didn't mean . . . you know."

"Sure you did. So I'm telling you. She's a friend. They're a hell of a lot harder to find than a piece of ass."

There was silence in the truck until Cain entered Remington from one of the dusty country lanes that crisscrossed the valley. He kept off the main street, working his way through town on the unpaved, unmarked back roads. He stopped in an alley a block and a half off the main square in downtown Remington.

Through a gap between two sagging old frame business buildings, Christy saw the second story of the Remington County Courthouse, as well as the rear side of the buildings that fronted on the square. In the middle of the block, an American flag snapped lightly in the afternoon breeze.

"That's the post office," Cain said, pointing to the flag. "All you have to do is figure out which box is Jo-Jo's."

"Wasn't the number on the—no, of course it wasn't. I would have seen it. Damn. How many boxes are there?"

"About a hundred."

Christy looked at both sides of the key again, as though hoping a number would appear. None did.

"A hundred. God." She shook her head.

"Start at one hundred and work backward," Cain said.

"Any particular reason?"

"The boxes with the low numbers have been in the same families for the last century."

"Oh. Makes sense. Won't people get suspicious if I spend ten or fifteen minutes trying to open boxes?"

"They'd get a hell of a lot more suspicious if I tried it. I've had the same box for the last ten years. Most people in town know it. And me."

"I imagine most people in town know most everyone else. I'll stick out like a boil."

"Lots of summer folks rent boxes, and lots of summer ranch workers are transient. There's quite a bit of coming and going during the fall."

Christy looked uncertain.

Cain reached for the key.

"No," she said, jerking her hand back. "You'd be spotted for sure. Every woman in town looks up when you walk by."

He gave her an odd glance.

"Well, it's true," Christy muttered. "It's something about the way you carry yourself." She reached for the door handle. "Damned arrogant western—"

Her words ended in a startled sound as Cain casually dragged her back into the seat.

"You forgot something," he said.

"What?"

His long fingers slid into her hair.

"This," Cain said. "Blazing red and damned beautiful."

"My hair?" she asked.

"Your hair. Looks like fire, feels cool and silky, and if you don't cover it up and get the hell out of this truck I'm going to kiss you until neither one of us can stand up. That would be a really stupid thing to do."

"I—I don't have a hat," Christy said.

Without looking away from her eyes, Cain pulled the bandanna out of the clothes he had given to her. He folded the cloth diagonally, pulled it over her hair, and tied it at the back of her head. The stroking of his long fingers over her sensitive nape made her shiver.

"Better run, honey. Fast."

Blindly Christy found the door handle, opened it, and slid out.

"I'll meet you in there when you're finished." Cain nodded toward the blank back door of a building. "Don't take long. I've got to ditch the truck damn quick."

Christy read the rude sign over the building's door. "The Dew Drop Inn? I don't believe it. On second thought, I do."

"Head for the booths in back," was all Cain said.

She waved her understanding and walked quickly down the alley to the street.

Remington's sidewalks were busier than they had been the day before. There was a crowd in the parking lot of the supermarket. The Greyhound bus had just unloaded across the street. A troop of trail bike enthusiasts was lounging in the shade of one of the square's huge trees.

The ranchers, townspeople, and tourists didn't give Christy a second look. Part of it was her clothing. A woman in old jeans, plaid shirt, and bandanna was unremarkable and natural in Remington.

Christy realized that she felt natural, too. The town's rhythms and social nuances were as familiar to her as the lettering on the stop sign at the corner. She knew how to meet the passing glance of the cowboy and his wife so that they categorized her as a newcomer rather than as an outsider.

The lobby of the post office building had a musty pipe-tobacco smell to it. Someone was ignoring the rules and smoking in the sorting area. The customer at the counter was a sharp-faced Indian woman with two long, beautiful black braids down her back.

No one gave Christy a look.

She went around the corner to a smaller lobby where the boxes were located and saw that Cain had been right. One hundred postal boxes stared at her like the prisms in the eye of a bee. The area was empty of people. The floor was littered with discarded junk mail.

Without looking around, Christy went straight to Box 100 and went to work. The key slid easily into the lock but refused to turn. Box 99 was the same. So was Box 98.

The key grated softly each time she tried a new

lock. It sounded like a file on a live microphone to her, but nobody else seemed to notice.

Christy tried three more boxes before she heard footsteps approach. Shielding the next box with her body so that no one could see the number, she tried it quickly.

No good.

Straightening up, Christy walked past a pot-bellied store merchant heading for his own box.

There was a pay phone at the other end of the lobby. Christy headed for it, pulling change out of her pocket as she went. Her first call was to the hotel.

"This is Christa McKenna," she said. "Any messages?"

A sharp intake of breath followed by a pause told Christy that she was glad she hadn't gone back to the hotel for her own clothes.

"Er, where are you, Ms. McKenna?"

"Pocatello," she said blandly. "Any messages?"

"Mr. Hutton would most urgently like to see you."

"How sweet. Any other messages?"

"Um . . . er . . ."

Christy hung up. After a moment's hesitation, she used her calling card to pay for a long distance connection.

"*Horizon,* may I help you?"

"Hi, Amy," Christy said. "You're working late."

"So is Myra. Damn good thing you checked in. She's climbing the walls. Peter Hutton wants to see you, and he wants it right away."

"So I've heard," Christy said. "Any other messages?"

"Ask your boyfriend, Nick."

"Nick? Why?"

"Myra told me to give out his number to callers since you weren't checking in at the office."

Anger flashed thorough Christy. "I see."

"What should I tell Myra?" Amy asked.

"The possibilities are limitless."

"What?"

"We must have a bad connection," Christy said. "I can't hear a word you're saying. I'll call back."

Christy hung up and punched in her calling code plus Nick's office number.

"Hi, Nick. I hear you've been nominated as my personal message drop."

"Christa! Where are you?"

"That seems to be everyone's favorite question. Has anyone other than Peter Hutton and Myra been asking for me?"

"Ted Autry."

"He belongs to Hutton."

"Oh. Well, someone who claimed to be a sheriff or something called too. Got my number from Myra, for chrissake. What the hell is going on?"

"Myra's rabies shot must have failed," Christy said curtly. "Who else is after me?"

"Me," Nick said. "Are you thinking about me?"

Cold washed over Christy. "What did you say?"

"Have you been thinking about me, darling? I've been thinking about you."

"Oh, my God. It was you, not Jo-Jo!"

"What?"

"Did you leave a message for me at the hotel?"

"Of course I did."

Christy hung on to the phone and tried to fight the sick fear washing through her as she remembered Johnny's words.

People dying. People gonna die.

"Are you, Christy?"

"What?" she whispered.

"Thinking about me," Nick said impatiently.

"Right now I'm thinking about Jo-Jo."

"Jo-Jo? Your sister?"

"Yes. Has she called asking for me?"

"No. When do I get to meet her?"

Christy grimaced. "I'll be sure to introduce you if the three of us are ever in a room together."

"Dy-na-mite!"

"But don't hold your breath. I'm not likely to be in any rooms with you in the future."

"Huh?"

"It's over, Nick," she said wearily. "Good-bye, *adiós, ciao,* babe. I'm gone. You're free. We're history."

"What?"

"Don't make me repeat it."

"Does this have something to do with a man called Aaron Cain?" Nick asked abruptly.

"How did you—" Christy stopped talking.

"It *is* Cain, isn't it?" Nick said.

"No. It's just that you and I aren't—"

Nick ignored her and kept talking.

"Autry warned me about Cain. Says he's a real hand with the ladies," Nick said bitterly. "Especially the New York kind looking for a souvenir of the Wild West."

Christy said nothing.

"Christa?"

"Most of the time you're a nice man, Nick. Go find a nice woman to love you most of the time."

"Christa, I—"

She hung up before Nick could finish. For a long time she stared at the phone without seeing it. Then she straightened her shoulders and went back to the lobby where post office boxes waited in taunting array.

No one was getting mail or watching other people get mail. Christy tried a dozen more boxes, working the key as quietly as possible so as not to attract the attention of the clerk in the sorting room on the other side of the wall.

Two wind-burned women in rough work clothes like Christy's walked into the lobby chatting with each other. One opened a box while the other gave Christy the kind of casual yet thorough examination only one woman can give another.

Christy felt a momentary rush of uneasiness. She left the lobby, crossed the street to the hardware store, and pretended to window shop while watching the door of the post office.

A minute later the women came out, climbed into a pickup truck, and drove away. Christy started back across the street. She glanced in the direction of the courthouse in time to see a familiar truck pull into the space reserved for the sheriff.

Danner got out from behind the wheel and

headed for his office. He was joined on the side-walk by a man dressed in a business suit that would have been at home on Wilshire Boulevard or Madison Avenue.

At first, Christy didn't recognize Autry. He had shed his drugstore cowboy costume along with the barbecue sauce. Now he looked like what he really was, a highly paid corporate cop, a private police-man in the hire of a Fortune 500 company.

Christy fought an almost uncontrollable urge to break and flee. Danner might not have seen her there on the face of the mesa, but Autry was hunting her for his boss. Watching Autry and Danner together, Christy suspected that the only difference between Autry and the sheriff was that Danner had been elected.

Turning her face away, Christy made certain the bandanna hid every lock of her red hair. She hurried across the street. Just as she reached the sidewalk and was about to duck back into the lobby, a police cruiser with a light bar and state police insignia pulled up beside Danner's truck and parked.

Christy watched from the shelter of the lobby as a state highway patrolman climbed out and joined the other two men. Immediately Danner began talking, waving his arms around to dramatize his words. He pointed back to the mesa where the Sis-ters lay hidden from view. Then he made a falling, twisting, diving gesture with his hand.

Christy had no doubt he was describing the death of Johnny Ten Hats. And Cain's part in that death.

The uniformed patrolman listened, then reached back into his cruiser and picked up the microphone on his two-way radio.

Oh, God, she thought. The word is going out at the speed of light. We have to get out of here. But first I have to find the damned lock that fits Jo-Jo's key.

The lobby was empty again. Christy went to work on the boxes with a grim efficiency. Dropping all pretense, she tried box after box with the key.

When a young mother pushing a stroller came in to collect her mail, Christy looked up and smiled.

"Forgot the darned number," drawled Christy.

The woman laughed sympathetically. "You can skip seventy-nine. It's mine."

"Thanks."

Christy went back to shoving the key in slot after narrow slot, trying to turn the key.

On Post Office Box 73, the key worked.

19

The box was so full Christy had to fight to remove the thick wad of letters that had been bound together with two fat rubber bands.

You don't come here much, do you, Jo-Jo?

Christy smiled to herself rather grimly. She had no doubt Jo-Jo would have been able to pass occasionally as a tourist or a transient ranch cook. She too had been raised in a small western town.

There was also no doubt in Christy's mind that her sister had hated every instant of dressing down so as not to be recognized.

Okay, what were you so eager to hide from the world in this little box?

The top letter was addressed to Christa Jody McKinley.

Thanks a lot, Jo-Jo. Nice of you point the finger at me.

The McKinley was like the rest of Jo-Jo. Half invented. Half real. All trouble.

Footsteps sounded in the main lobby. They were coming toward the post office boxes.

Quickly Christy stuffed the letters under one arm, closed the box, and locked it. No one gave her more than a casual glance as she walked out of the post office, across the street, and in the front door of the Dew Drop Inn.

Inevitably, the jukebox was playing Merle Haggard. Ignoring the irritating nasal music, Christy scanned the long bar for Cain. Several weathered outdoor types stared back with blunt masculine interest. Her clothes were loose, but nothing could disguise the essentially female curves of her body.

Belatedly Christy remembered that Cain had said he would be in a booth in the rear. She started forward.

"Hey, darlin', looking for somebody?"

The cowboy's dusty sweat-stained hat was pushed back on his head, revealing a shock of straw-colored hair. He was good-looking in a raw-boned way, and he knew it. He held a half-full pilsner glass in his hand. There were three pitchers on the bar in front of the men. The pitchers were empty. The cowboys were about half loaded.

Christy gave the blond cowboy a quick glance. Something about him was familiar. She looked at his partner. They reminded her of her past, of men who looked at a woman as one more farm animal to be appraised, discussed, and used when they got around to it.

Once, that look had enraged her, for she was afraid the men might be right. Now she knew just how wrong they were.

She met the cowboy's appraising gaze with an amused female smile.

"You're too late," Christy said. "I've already found him."

The cowboy's intent, predatory expression turned into a smile of simple masculine appreciation.

"You change your mind, ma'am, you know where I am," he said.

"Bet your wife does too," Christy said, still smiling.

The cowboy's buddies hooted, and so did he.

No one else tackled Christy as she walked to the booths in the back of the saloon. As she approached, Cain looked up from a glass of beer that had gone flat while he waited. When his eyes met Christy's, there was a cold, calculating light in them that burned like a laser.

Uneasily, she examined the man who was sitting across the booth from Cain. The stranger was as tall as Cain but hadn't been fined down by injury and rehabilitation. When he glanced toward Christy, he smiled approvingly but without blunt sexual interest.

"This your lady friend?" he asked Cain.

Cain nodded.

The big man stood up, removed his hat, and waited to be introduced. Light glanced off the shiny five-pointed star that was pinned on his shirt.

Christy's mind went blank as she looked from

the lawman's badge to Cain and then back again. For an icy instant, she felt trapped, as though they were back in the alcove again.

"Christy McKenna, this is Larry Moore," Cain said. "He's the Remington town constable and brother of the man who owns a ranch up near the Sisters."

Christy gave Cain a glance that said he had lost his mind. He smiled slightly, knowing what she must be thinking.

Moore swept his hat off his head and bowed with a flourish. His skin was weathered, and he sported a flowing, beautifully sculpted handlebar mustache with tightly waxed ends. He moved with remarkable grace despite a solid gut that struggled to escape over his ornate silver and turquoise belt buckle.

"Pleased to meet you, ma'am," he said. "Cain here is dead particular about who he keeps company with."

She looked away from Cain, swallowed, and said, "Good to meet you, Mr. Moore."

"Larry," he said easily.

"Uh, Larry."

Christy glanced around uneasily. Half the booths at the back of the bar were empty, but there were still too many possible eavesdroppers for her comfort.

Cain slid out of his side of the booth.

"Get in," he said. "Even in Angie's clothes, you put every man in here on red alert."

"Yeah, right," Christy muttered sarcastically.

"Would you believe yellow alert?" he whispered as she slid by him.

"I'd believe you've been doing tequila shooters."

Silently Cain pointed to his single, nearly full glass of beer. As Christy settled into the booth, he tucked a lock of red hair back beneath the bandanna. The motion was frankly intimate, as was the smile he gave her.

Moore's revolver clunked against the side of the booth as he sat down again on the other side.

"Well?" Cain asked Christy.

She looked at him blankly.

"The box," he said.

"I took care of it."

"What was—"

"No," she interrupted. "My turn. May I speak privately with you for a few moments."

It wasn't a question. It was a demand.

"Larry's a friend," Cain said.

"That's nice."

Christy stared at the constable's badge. Moore smiled at her.

"Don't worry about me, ma'am," he said. "I'm on Cain's side."

"Looks more like you and Danner are on the same side," she said flatly.

"I'd sooner side with a polecat," Moore said. "To our lord high sheriff, I'm just a declining door-knob shaker who ought to be fired."

"Danner made a pitch to the town council to take over patrol duties in Remington," Cain explained to Christy.

"Luckily, I had the votes to put him off for the time being," Moore said, "or I'd be a jobless loafer like Cain."

"You're already that," Cain retorted. "If it weren't for stray cats in trees and folks who lock their keys in their cars, you wouldn't have a single thing to do."

"That's why the council passed up Danner's kind offer," Moore drawled. "They couldn't see paying good money for what I do."

Christy glanced from one man to the other in disbelief. The bond of friendship between them was quite real, despite Moore's shiny star and Cain's spotted past.

"Don't worry about Larry," Cain said. "He's the only honest lawman in southwestern Colorado, so far as I'm concerned."

Moore's face lit up at the compliment.

"Yeah," he drawled, "and I'm the lowest-paid, too. There seems to be a direct relationship."

Cain looked at Christy. "Spit it out, honey."

"I hope you know what we're doing."

"I do."

"I'm so relieved," she said acidly. "Because right now Danner is in front of the post office chatting up a Colorado state cop."

"Shit," Cain hissed.

"Was that jackleg cop Autry with them?" Moore asked.

The drawl was gone. His lips were pursed as though he was going to spit on the floor.

"Yes," she said. "Danner and Autry drove up

while I was in front of the post office. A state policeman arrived a few seconds later. I think he got a full briefing about—"

She broke off and glanced quickly at Cain.

"I told him about Johnny," Cain said.

The bleak look was back in his eyes, the look that said he had killed a man.

Christy grabbed Cain's forearm and said urgently, "It wasn't your fault."

"Dead is dead," Cain said bluntly. "What did the state cop do?"

"He got on the radio."

Cain and Moore exchanged looks.

"That'll make it a lot harder to move," Moore said. "The alert will be picked up in all four states. Inside of an hour, you're going to be hotter than a two-dollar pistol."

"Do you have a rental car?" Cain asked Christy.

"Yes, but Autry and Danner are chasing me too. They called my office in New York and my ex-boyfriend."

Cain gave Christy a sharp look. "Ex?"

"Ex," she said flatly.

"Do they know you're with me?"

"Autry suspects it. He warned Nick about you, what a stud you were with the ladies, especially the New York kind 'looking for a souvenir of the Wild West.'"

Moore snickered and shook his head. But an instant later he was serious again.

"If they suspect anything," he said, "they'll pull the tag number of the rental car off Christy's hotel registration."

"Great," Cain said sarcastically.

"You'll be nailed inside of a hundred miles," Moore added "You sure as hell won't make Albuquerque."

"Why Albuquerque?" Christy asked Cain.

"Larry's given me a lead on a Bureau of Land Management investigator."

She frowned. "So?"

"He might be able to explain why Johnny had me filling that bag with grave dirt."

"What good will that do?"

"I'll know when I hear the explanation." Cain tapped the bundle of paper underneath her arm. "Got something to share, Red?"

Christy pulled the bundle of letters out and put it on the table.

"I don't know. I wasn't about to stand around in the lobby and read Jo-Jo's mail."

"Don't start here," Moore said bluntly. "You have a lot of friends in Remington, but Hutton has a lot more money."

"Yeah."

For the space of a long breath, Cain stared at the letters. Then he scooped them up and turned to Christy.

"It's too dangerous to stay with me, Red."

"No."

"Larry will see that you're safe."

"No."

"I could have Constable Moore here throw you in the city tank for a while," Cain said bluntly.

"For my own good, of course," Christy said sweetly.

Cain's mouth thinned. "Yes."

"No. For *your* good. Not mine. You just want to get your hands on Jo-Jo when there aren't any witnesses!"

Cain became very still as he realized what Christy was afraid of.

"Do you really think I'd hurt her?" he asked in a low, savage voice.

"I don't know. All I know is that when you talk about her, I'm afraid."

Moore sighed loudly and took a sip of Cain's beer.

"Flat," Moore said to no one in particular.

"Shit," Cain said.

"More like piss, actually."

Throwing Moore a disgusted look, Cain shot out of the booth, pulling Christy after him.

"Jo-Jo doesn't deserve you," he said savagely. "Let's go."

"Hold it," Moore said. "No use going off half cocked. What are you going to do about a car?"

"There's a rental agency in Durango," Cain said. "That'll buy me a few hours."

Moore dug a silvered key ring out of the watch pocket of his faded jeans. He flipped the ring to Cain.

"Take my truck," Moore said.

"But—"

Moore ignored the interruption. "Camping gear and change of clothes are in the box in back. Sharon is shorter than Christy but wider in the beam. Maybe it will all even out. Where's your truck?"

"Out back," Christy said when Cain didn't speak.

"I'll take care of it," Moore said.

"Dammit, Larry, you can't—" Cain began.

"Bullshit I can't," Moore interrupted. "I didn't carry you on my back off the Sisters mesa just to turn you over to the likes of Danner. Now get your stubborn butt out of here before you make me mad."

Cain hesitated, then accepted. "I owe you."

"Like hell you do."

When Moore turned to Christy, his expression gentled. He tipped his hat and smiled.

"Pleased to have met you," he said. "I do like a woman with sand."

The old western phrase made Christy smile.

"You all be careful now," Moore added.

Cain grabbed Christy's arm and led her out of the saloon. He didn't speak to her again until they were in Moore's truck and safely out of town.

"Okay, Red. Let's have it. What was in Pandora's box?"

Christy pulled off the rubber bands and began sorting envelopes.

"Letters, mostly," she said.

Moore's police scanner connected with a transmission, held for three seconds, then moved on, seeking a new transmission. Cain turned down the volume until it was barely louder than the sound of the tires on the asphalt road.

"Sealed letters?" Cain asked.

"So far they've all been opened."

"Who are they from?"

"No return address," Christy said. "Same handwriting on the envelopes."

"Read one of the letters," Cain said.

"I'd rather not."

"Hell, honey, I'd rather be home in the hot spring with you on my lap, but nobody's offering me a choice."

Christy gave Cain a sideways glance. The smile on his face reminded her of the instant in the saloon when he had tucked her hair into the bandanna and caressed the nape of her neck at the same time.

She pulled the most recent letter out of its envelope and began to unfold the page of notepaper.

"Read aloud," Cain said.

Sighing, Christy began reading without really thinking about the meaning of the words.

"*Hi, babe,*" she read. "*How's my creamy little fur pie?*"

Cain gave a crack of laughter.

Despite the red creeping up Christy's cheeks, she laughed too.

"Good friends, huh?" he offered blandly.

She said nothing.

"Keep reading," he said.

"I will."

"Aloud."

"I won't."

"Chicken."

"Cluck cluck."

"What happened to those wings you flew away on?" he asked, smiling widely.

"I molted." Christy took a deep breath. "Does fur pie mean what I think it means?"

"What do you think it means?" Cain asked innocently.

She gave him a disgusted look.

"Yeah," he said, relenting. "It means pussy."

"Thanks—I think."

"Any time, honey. Any time at all."

Christy began reading the letter rapidly. Silently. Her eyes widened.

"Good God," she muttered.

"Need a translator?" Cain asked dryly.

"I may need one, but I don't want one. Apparently Jo-Jo was head over heels with this Jay character."

"Heels over head, more likely."

Christy grimaced and folded up the letter. Before she could set it aside, Cain plucked the page from her hands. He shook it open, held it near the steering wheel, and scanned the pages with the speed of a man used to reading dense, scholarly textbooks.

His black eyebrows climbed.

"Find a new word?" Christy asked, deadpan.

"Poontang is an old word, honey."

"Same meaning, right?"

"Right."

"That boy—"

"Jay," Cain interrupted, looking at the signature.

"—has a one-track mind," Christy finished.

"Yeah. Tie 'em up, ride 'em hard, put 'em away wet."

Christy laughed. She couldn't help it.

Smiling slightly, Cain handed back the pages.

"So she kept her lust letters under lock and key," he said sardonically. "Big deal. Anything useful in the rest of that pile?"

Christy sorted through the stack, dividing the correspondence into groups. The letters from Jay were the biggest stack.

"Mostly Jay?" Cain asked, glancing over.

"Looks that way. The postmarks span about eight months."

"Not a one-night stand, then."

"If the first letter was any sample," Christy said absently, "standing was the only way they didn't do it."

Cain gave her a startled look, laughed, and reached across the truck. He tugged lightly on the bandanna, letting her red hair free.

"It's a miracle I don't burn my fingers," he said, stroking a soft, flame-colored curl.

"It's a miracle you don't get them smacked," Christy retorted, but there was no heat in her voice.

Smiling, Cain released the lock of hair and concentrated on the road while she finished sorting through the contents of her sister's box.

Once Jay's letters were set aside, the rest of the papers were barely a handful. They were stuffed into small manila envelopes with a word or two written on the outside. One of the envelopes was rather heavy and had no label. It was sealed with wide, clear tape.

Reluctant to intrude on her sister's privacy any more than necessary, Christy put aside the sealed envelope and concentrated on the others.

She pulled up the metal tabs on one of the manila envelopes and shock out the contents. She went through them quickly, giving Cain a running commentary.

"AmEx credit card bills, correspondence with several upscale hotels around the Southwest, gas chits."

Cain grunted.

Christy opened another envelope.

"Same stuff, different envelope," she said.

She opened the third envelope.

"More of the same," she said, reaching for the fourth envelope. "She and Jay must have traveled to every—hello, what's this?"

Cain looked over as Christy fanned out a dozen smaller envelopes and held them at his eye level.

"Recognize anyone?" she asked.

"Scottsdale, Beverly Hills, Santa Fe, Dallas, Taos. Yeah, I recognize them. Galleries and art dealers."

"Fine art?" Christy asked, thinking of the demon paintings.

"Southwestern-style fine art. Except for the Sherberne Gallery in Santa Fe. He's almost exclusively Native art and artifacts."

"Anasazi?"

Cain shrugged. "Navajo. Zuñi. Apache. Moki. Any kind that sells is fine with him."

"Five letters from Sherberne."

"Read 'em aloud. Can't be any worse than Jay's, right?"

Christy organized the postmarks and went to work, opening the most recent first. As she unfolded the paper, a slip of paper fell out. She picked it up, glanced casually at it, and then stared.

"What is it?" Cain asked.

"The voucher half of a cashier's check."

He looked at her oddly. "So?"

Wordlessly she held out the paper.

Cain took one look and whistled softly through his teeth. The check had been made out to Jay Norton and paid by the Sherberne Gallery.

The amount was $537,840.

20

"What's the date?"

"Last week. The day before Jo-Jo started leaving messages for me in New York."

"You better read those letters, Red. We need to know what Hutton's jet jockey had to sell that was worth half a million bucks, wholesale."

"I could make a wild guess," Christy said unhappily, thinking of the alcove.

"So could I. We both could be wrong. Dead wrong. Read the letters."

"Aloud?" Christy asked.

Cain gave her a slanting sideways look and a smile that was very white against the black of his beard.

"I love it when someone talks dirty to me, honey."

"Then turn up the scanner," Christy retorted.

She flipped through the stack of mail again. This time she chose the oldest letter instead of the more recent ones. When she was finished reading it, she put the letter back in its envelope, pulled out a new letter, and began reading again.

She worked her way through five letters before Cain became impatient.

"Anything?" he asked.

"A postgraduate education in slang and ways to screw your employer's 'hot little whisker biscuit.'"

Cain smiled crookedly and said not one word.

Christy folded up the letter she had been reading, put it in its envelope, and pulled out the next letter.

"You know," she said after a minute, "I think Jay really cares for Jo-Jo. His vocabulary is just a bit limited."

Cain gave her a look that said he thought she had lost her tiny little mind.

"He's about as subtle as a baseball bat," Christy agreed, "and has a one-track mind, but—"

She shrugged.

"But what?" Cain asked after a moment.

"There's a sort of primitive energy in what he writes, as well as real affection. Coarse, but real. He worships the ground Jo-Jo walks on."

"More like the ground she sits on," Cain muttered.

Christy ignored him. "He wants her obsessively, and Jo-Jo needs to be wanted that way. I think . . . I think she's always needed it."

A disgusted sound was Cain's only answer.

"Reading between the lines," Christy said, "Jo-Jo's longtime affair with Hutton was pretty well finished eight months ago. Jay caught her on the rebound."

Cain grunted.

"It's a good match," Christy insisted.

"As long as the equipment doesn't wear out."

"Oh, they've got more than sex going for them."

"Yeah? What?"

"Some kind of hauling business."

"Ashes?" Cain suggested dryly.

"What?"

"Never mind," he said. "Just more slang. What was their business?"

"Packing, transportation, and delivery. Using Hutton's airplane, of course. Wonder what he thought about that?"

"You're assuming that he knew. What were they shipping?"

"Something fragile and valuable," Christy said. "They don't mention what."

Christy went back to reading. For a time there was silence except for the hum of tires on pavement and the occasional muttering of the scanner when it connected with a law enforcement radio transmission.

"It's the alcove," Christy said, looking up from a letter. "Jay mentions the Sisters."

"Yeah, I'll just bet he does," Cain said.

She opened another letter. Pieces of paper fluttered out.

"More check stubs," Christy said.

"How much?"

Silence, then, "Almost half a million in this lot. A million, total."

Cain whistled.

"Was the alcove that good?" she asked.

"It was the most promising site I've ever seen," Cain said simply.

"Why?"

"Protected. Hidden. And then there's Kokopelli. I've never heard of a kiva decorated with his symbol. That site was special to the Anasazi. There would be special artifacts in the kivas."

There was a combination of yearning and anger in Cain's voice as he talked about the extraordinary site that had been raped and ruined before it could be understood.

"But a million dollars in artifacts?" Christy asked. "Even at ten or twenty thousand a pot, that's a lot of pots."

"Not these days. The Japanese collect anything the western world collects. And the Germans are absolutely nuts about Anasazi artifacts. They pay hundreds of dollars for a handful of sherds."

"Still, a million bucks—"

"Wholesale."

"—is a lot of money."

"Both the yen and the mark are strong," Cain said. "The dollar isn't. What we think is an outrageous price is a bargain to them, relatively speaking."

Though Christy said nothing, her expression was doubtful.

"Then there's the collector mentality," Cain

added. "You get some rich, aggressive collectors bidding, and the outcome is big bucks for you and to hell with rational prices."

The scanner kicked in with a warning that a dead cow was a road hazard two miles inside the reservation's northern boundary, northbound side of the road.

When the scanner was silent again, Christy let out a long breath. Each time the scanner came to life she was afraid she would hear about a man fleeing a murder charge in a white truck with a redhead by his side.

"The large kiva artifacts could easily have been worth a half million by themselves," Cain said. "If you throw in the grave goods from the second kiva, you've got quite a haul, even at wholesale prices."

"It looks that way," Christy said unhappily.

"That must have been the richest find in the last thirty years." Cain's voice was rough with anger for all that had been lost. "Was there any kind of inventory?"

Quickly Christy scanned the pieces of paper that had fallen from various letters.

"They refer to 'your shipment' and 'the pieces' but never to anything specific," she said. "Odd."

"Damned odd. In legitimate deals, newly dug artifacts are photographed in situ and described millimeter by millimeter. The documentation becomes part of the value."

"Would this many dealers be involved in something illegal?"

"Most dealers don't give a damn about anything but a quick resale. The dealers paid in cashier's checks, right?"

"So far."

"That means they knew they could turn the artifacts around immediately," Cain said. "They didn't have to worry about getting caught with dubious goods."

"Jay went to just one dealer, at first. Sherberne. He offered to take everything off their hands, but Jay didn't like the price."

Cain grunted.

"So Jay went to some other dealers and solicited bids," Christy said.

The scanner crackled to life, muttering about a car upside down in a ditch two miles inside the reservation's northern boundary, southbound side of the road.

"They should try fencing their livestock," Christy said.

"The cow is worth more as road kill than it was alive. Cash is damned hard to come by on the reservation."

Christy skimmed the page of angular printing that was becoming familiar. She flipped the page over and kept going to the bottom before she spoke again.

"They ended up parceling out fifty-seven pots and twelve consignments of other goods," she said.

"What goods?" he demanded instantly.

Christy simply shook her head. "He doesn't say."

"Damn!"

"Everybody paid by cashier's check," she said, "and everybody would have bought five times as much if they could have."

Cain's fist struck the wheel a single sharp blow that made the tough plastic vibrate like a tuning fork.

"Christ, but I wish I could have seen it, photographed it, catalogued it!" he said savagely. "There must have been an entire village preserved behind that flake. And so far north! It would have turned the Moki world upside down!"

"When we catch up with Jo-Jo, maybe we can recover—"

The look on Cain's face made Christy swallow the rest of her words. His quick glance reminded her just how cold his amber eyes could be.

"I'll catch up with Jo-Jo, all right," Cain said, "but the artifacts are long gone. They're in Germany and Japan, New York and Los Angeles, locked up in private collections, hidden beyond anybody's reach."

Christy began reading again, grateful for the excuse not to confront Cain's anger.

After a few minutes she went back to a previous letter, pulled it out, and began glancing back and forth. She set both of them aside, opened a new letter, and read only partway through before she set it aside and opened another letter and yet another.

The quiet frenzy of reading and comparing letters drew Cain out of his angry thoughts. He reached for one of the pages.

"No!" Christy said. "Don't mix them up. I'm try-ing to check something."

"Give me some hints. Maybe I can help."

"When did you tell Jo-Jo about the Sisters?"

"The first time?" he asked.

"Yes."

"Maybe a year ago," he said.

"Don't you remember?"

"Contrary to what you believe, Jo-Jo just wasn't a big blip on my scope. When Hutton got too rough for her, she'd call up and talk to me."

Something in Cain's voice made Christy uneasy.

"What did she want you to do?" Christy asked.

"Kill him, probably."

"You can't be serious."

"Why not?" Cain asked. "She knew my past before she ever met me. Ex-con. Murderer."

"That's crazy. You're no more a murderer than I am."

He gave her a sideways glance.

"Red, you just saw me kill a man."

"Self-defense isn't murder!"

There was a strained silence. Then Cain let out his breath.

"Besides," Christy said. "Hutton was Jo-Jo's meal ticket."

"Hutton was into bondage games. Real ones," Cain said, "not the satin whip kind of romp Jay talks about in those letters."

"I can't see Jo-Jo going in for that."

"You can't see Jo-Jo, period. You keep seeing the past. That little blonde girl is no more."

"She wasn't an angel," Christy said. "But she was—fragile, I guess. I always felt I had to protect her."

"Yeah, Jo-Jo's good at that game. She used it on all the local men. Get two men hot, complain to one that the other was hitting on her, and watch them fight."

"Don't give her all the blame. The men—"

"Have to be stupid enough to play her game," Cain interrupted curtly. "I know. I was, once."

"You were only nineteen."

"The other guy was only twenty. He never got any older."

Christy looked at Cain's closed expression and changed the subject.

"It looks as though Jo-Jo was planning to loot the alcove for at least eight months," Christy said. "Maybe more."

"Ever since I told her about the Sisters, I imagine."

"Yes," Christy said evenly. "I don't know when she and Jay became an item—"

"Probably about the time she needed transportation out of Colorado for the artifacts."

"—but about seven months ago Jo-Jo talked Hutton into hiring Johnny Ten Hats to search the area around the Sisters for ruins."

"Using my information," Cain said.

"And the bowl Jo-Jo took from your cabin."

"How long did it take them to strike pay dirt?"

There was silence while Christy sorted through various letters, reading quickly, her mouth a flat line of unhappiness.

"A few weeks, I guess," she said. "They took

most of the good pieces before Hutton ever saw
them. Lord, what they must have taken! The artifacts I saw in Hutton's house were incredible."

"Did Hutton even know about the alcove?"

"He knew. He didn't get those artifacts he
showed me out of a Christmas stocking. Maybe—"

Cain waited, but Christy didn't say any more.

"Maybe what?" he prodded.

"I read the *Horizon* file on Hutton pretty fast. I
could be wrong."

"About what?" Cain asked impatiently.

"I think Hutton was in trouble financially as
well as artistically. He had started a new line of
perfume and cosmetics. Those kinds of things
require a huge amount of cash to get going."

"How are the lines doing?"

"Too soon to tell," Christy said absently, looking
at another letter. "The costs are all up front. The
payoff is a few years down the line. If it comes at
all."

She frowned and reread a section.

"Listen to this. *He'll go for it. Hutton is so desperate for cash, you're lucky he's not selling your
platinum ass on street corners.*"

"Maybe Hutton was selling artifacts and forgetting to give Uncle Sam his cut," Cain said.

"It would fit. In any case, Jo-Jo planned to
double-cross Hutton from the very beginning."

"Why?" Cain asked. "As you said, he was her
meal ticket."

"She found out he had been secretly interviewing
models."

Cain's black eyebrows shot up.

"The spring line of clothes was going to be her last work for Hutton," Christy said.

"Any reason?"

"He told Jo-Jo she was too old."

Cain whistled through his teeth. "I'd like to have been there."

"So she came up with a scheme to steal artifacts from the alcove."

"Revenge?" Cain asked.

"Partly. Mostly she was broke."

"Broke! She was billed as the Million Dollar Body."

"Jo-Jo spends money as fast as she makes it. The future has always been unreal to her." Christy turned another page over. "Besides, Jay has expensive plans. This sounds like he has already bought one airplane. He wants several to start his own charter service."

"Any man who stays that long in the sack with Jo-Jo has earned it," Cain said ironically.

Christy ignored him and kept reading.

"Somehow Hutton found out that Jo-Jo and Jay were skimming artifacts from the alcove," Christy said. "He threatened them both."

"When?"

Christy looked at the postmark on the envelope.

"It's smudged," she muttered. "Two weeks, max."

"What happened then?"

She read quickly. "He—Jay—thinks the threat is funny. Says Hutton is in it with them up to his ass and can't burn them without burning himself."

Cain grunted. "How did they know which gallery owners to approach?"

"Johnny. He knew the private collectors too."

"Figures," Cain said in disgust. "Jo-Jo had a real twist on Johnny's cock."

"Maybe she wasn't sleeping with him. There was Jay, remember?"

"Honey, Jay wasn't around all the time. Jo-Jo went bar-crawling in Montrose and took her trophies back to Xanadu for Hutton to enjoy. Ah, love. Ain't it grand?"

Christy said nothing.

"But then, maybe Jay was like Hutton," Cain continued coldly. "Maybe he liked watching Jo-Jo do what she did best."

"Jay doesn't say anything about watching her model."

"I wasn't talking about modeling. Hutton liked to watch Jo-Jo in the sack with the local cowboys. It was the talk of the damned county."

Christy's head snapped up and she stared at Cain.

"What?" she asked.

"Don't look so shocked, Red. Jo-Jo liked strutting her stuff. Hutton liked watching." Cain shrugged. "It happens."

A shudder of distaste when through Christy. She set her jaw and went back to the letters.

"I don't believe it," she said.

"Long way from the high plains of Wyoming, huh?" Cain asked.

She looked up. His expression was a mixture of sympathy and impatience.

"A long way from anywhere I want to be," Christy said evenly. "Ever."

Without another word, she went back to the letters. A few minutes later she finished the last one, folded it, put it away, and leaned her head against the window.

"Anything new?" Cain asked.

"No."

The strain in Christy's voice made Cain wince.

There was a long silence, broken only the scanner's occasional mutterings.

Cain drove through a settlement that consisted of five wind-scoured houses, a one-pump gas station, and a store. The buildings were huddled at the base of the mesa. They looked old, beaten, bereft of joy.

Christy felt the same way. . . .

Slowly, after many miles, the clean immensity of the land seeped past the darkness of Christy's thoughts. The air was so clear she felt as though she could see to tomorrow.

She let out a long sigh and leaned back, allowing the spare beauty of the landscape to ease the aching deep within her when she thought of the past, the present, and the secret sister she had always loved and now despaired of ever understanding.

The last of the sunlight threw long shadows from a line of red-rock mesas. Cedar and juniper trees burned along rocky ridges like deep green torches. The steeply slanting light burnished ridges and set fire to slopes, giving a special, almost spectral glow to the land.

The truck came down a winding grade and into a narrow river valley where the leaves of huge black-trunked cottonwoods had already begun to turn a deep yellow. Sunlight made the leaves dance like pieces of beaten gold on the autumn wind.

Looking at the clean, vivid landscape, Christy could understand how the Anasazi had come to worship the sun. It was more than a farmer's understanding that light was needed for corn and beans and squash. Sunlight was also a blessing for the land, giving it a rich, warm beauty that never grew old, never became corrupted, never was less perfect than it seemed.

Reluctantly Christy looked at the stack of letters on the seat. They made her feel old, used up, bleak.

The sealed envelope that had no writing on the outside was buried beneath the others. Christy had no desire to pull it out, open it, and find out more things she didn't want to know.

She turned her head and looked out the side window, watching shadows lengthen and flow together, claiming the land.

The gentle caress of Cain's fingers on Christy's cheek was so unexpected that she flinched. Instead of withdrawing, he simply repeated the slow caress.

"Sorry, honey," Cain said in a low voice. "I was out of line. There are some things about Jo-Jo you really don't have to know. I keep forgetting how much you love your sister, come hell or high water or human frailty."

Christy's breath came out in a long, ragged sigh. "If you had known her as a child. . . . Sometimes she just broke your heart, she was so sweet."

Cain's answer was silent, another gentle stroking of his fingers over her cheek.

After a moment, Christy straightened, smiled wanly at Cain, and reached for the last envelope. It was so heavily taped that she ended up shredding it with her teeth.

Another, smaller envelope fell out. It had been rolled and taped until it looked like a fat pencil. With it came three folded envelopes. One had Jay's familiar, bold handwriting.

Christy's eye was immediately drawn to the two others. Both were in plain white envelopes that had been addressed in big printed letters. They looked as if they had been written by a child.

"A new player?" Cain asked.

"I guess."

She checked the postmarks. One letter was three weeks old. The other had been mailed the same day that the big cashier's check had been drawn. Both envelopes were postmarked Alturas, New Mexico.

The letters inside were written in the same blocky, semiliterate hand as the envelopes. The paper itself had been ripped from the kind of cheap tablets schoolchildren use. The message was simple.

YOU GIVE ME SISTERS OR I GIVE YOU BIG TRUBLE

The note was signed by what looked like a brand consisting of a 10 with an arch over the number.

The second letter was even shorter.

YOU WANT TRUBLE YOU GOT TRUBLE

The same stylized brand was drawn at the bottom of the paper.

"Let me see that," Cain said.

Christy held one of the notes out.

"Looks like Johnny was screwed out of some goods," Cain said after a quick glance.

"Johnny Ten Hats?"

"That's his sign. A number ten with a hat on it." Cain looked at the rolled, taped envelope. "Want my knife?"

As he spoke, he dug around in his pocket for the small jackknife he always carried. When he handed the knife over to her, it felt warm against her palm, infused with the heat of his body.

"Thanks," Christy said.

As her hand curled around the jackknife, she realized how chilled she felt inside, a chill that Cain's masculine warmth somehow eased. She knew she should resist the elemental lure.

She also knew she hadn't the strength.

Carefully Christy slit the tape and unrolled the envelope, which wasn't sealed. When she tipped the envelope, a chain spilled out into her hand, along with a pile of splinters.

Her breath came in with a surprised sound. The gleaming chain was old, handmade, fragile. Delicate gold nuggets no bigger than peas alternated with the worn links.

"Gramma's necklace," Christy said huskily, fighting tears. "Jo-Jo kept it for me after all."

Cain looked at the splinters in Christy's palm, started to speak, and thought better of it.

"Mind if I look at what came with the necklace?" he asked.

She gave him an odd look but tipped the palmful of fragments into his open hand.

"What is it?" she asked.

"Old, old bones."

Christy shivered.

"Open the envelope," Cain said. "I'll put them back for you."

She pulled the edges of the envelope apart. A slim, pale green sheet of paper was hidden inside. She knew even before she pulled it out that she would find Jo-Jo's writing.

> *Hi, Sister.*
> *If you got this far, I'm in more*
> *trouble than I thought.*
> *Help me get out.*
> *And then I'll help you.*
> *I left a trail pointing right at you.*
> *But I'll clear it all up from Rio.*
> *Help me, Christmas.*
> *Please.*

With shaking fingers, Christy showed the note to Cain. He read it in a single sweeping glance.

"What about the other letter?" he asked.

"What?"

"Lover boy's. She thought it was special enough to hide."

Christy looked at the envelope with Jay's handwriting. She reached for it, deciding more of Jay's crude enthusiasm would be easier to deal with than Gramma's necklace wrapped in ancient bone fragments and a plea for help from her secret sister.

Numbly Christy pulled out the letter, expecting the familiar coarse endearments. What she found was a lament from Jay Norton that he hadn't been able to finish Cain off before the Moore brothers showed up.

Christy made a low sound and closed her eyes.

"Honey?"

"You were right," she said raggedly. "Jo-Jo set you up to be killed."

There was nothing Cain could say without adding to Christy's pain.

"But you were wrong about Johnny," she whispered. "It was Jay who tried to murder you."

21

"*What are we going to do?*" Christy asked.

"Find flyboy."

The flatness of Cain's voice made Christy feel cold. That surprised her. She hadn't thought she could feel any worse than she had when she realized what Jo-Jo had done.

"How?" Christy asked.

"We'll start with Sherberne Gallery."

"Santa Fe." She sighed. "How far?"

"Too far."

Christy gave Cain a questioning glance.

"You look done, Red."

"It doesn't take much energy to sit."

"We'll stop up ahead at Ghost Ranch," Cain said, as though Christy had never spoken. "Ever heard of it?"

She smiled wanly. "Anyone interested in design, style, art, and women has heard of Ghost Ranch and Georgia O'Keeffe."

"Then you've heard of the Chama River Valley and Abiquiu."

"Sure."

"Look around you, honey. That's the Chama River shining off to the right."

The names triggered a flood of images in Christy's mind: "The Road to the Black Place" and the "Church at Rancho de Taos," the cottonwood series, and the black raven soaring like death and freedom over the landscape.

Cain pointed toward the hills ahead. "Ghost Ranch is right over there. It's a retreat for church groups now. A friend of mine runs it."

"Is Ghost Ranch as beautiful as I've heard?"

"Tell me tomorrow," he said.

Christy made a questioning sound.

"We're going to sleep there tonight," he explained.

A mile later, Cain turned off the highway and headed up a gravel road toward the clay hills and stone mesas. Little of the establishment had been visible from the paved road, but the buildings weren't far away.

Cain drove into a small parking area and turned off the engine.

"It looks like a classy resort," Christy said.

"If you look harder, you can see the remains of an old working ranch."

He got out. "I'll be back in a bit."

Christy got out, stretched, and sat on the chrome running board of Constable Moore's pickup, watching daylight fade over Ghost Ranch.

Cain was right. Just beneath the new buildings of the retreat lay remnants of the old ranch. There were corrals and loading chutes, the stately, gnarled remains of an orchard, and overgrown irrigation ditches that fed water to fifteen acres of pasture and hay.

All the lines of the old ranch flowed together like a shadowy skeleton just beneath the surface. Then the last of the light drained away, taking the shadows of the past, leaving only the present, where new buildings gleamed with artificial brilliance against the coming night.

After a few minutes, Cain emerged from the long ranch house that served as offices for the resort and crossed the yard to the truck.

"We're in luck," he said. "Mack always keeps one of the old cabins in reserve for family visits and other emergencies."

"Which are we?"

The corner of Cain's mouth turned up. "Both. There's even some food, if we don't mind cooking."

"I don't mind," Christy said, yawning. "Sorry. I don't know why I'm so tired."

"You're finally coming down off your adrenaline jag."

"Oh, God." She groaned. "Don't tell me I'm going to be flattened by the adrenaline express again."

Laughing softly, Cain held out one hand. Christy

took it, allowing him to pull her to her feet. Gently he stuffed her back into the truck and drove toward a cabin that was set apart from the other buildings in the mouth of a small canyon.

Soon the headlights of the truck revealed a small adobe building with weathered vigas showing just beneath the flat roof. French windows looked out across the ranch toward the looming, mysterious mesas. The adobe had been sanded down by sun and wind and storm.

When Cain shut off the engine, the companionable chirping of crickets filled the night.

"Not much by Manhattan standards," Cain said.

"This adobe has its own standards and traditions," Christy said. "It's part of time and the land, like the cliff houses of the Anasazi."

The certainty and approval in Christy's voice were unmistakable.

"You keep surprising me," Cain said after a moment.

"Probably because you keep misjudging me. You look at me and see East Coast, Jo-Jo, trouble. . . ."

Christy's voice faded. She sighed.

"Well, you were right about the trouble," she admitted. "I've been a lot of that."

"Not your fault. It started months before you came here."

"Years before," she said in a strained voice. "It started when I went east and left Jo-Jo rudderless in Wyoming."

"Bullshit, Red."

Wearily Christy shook her head. "I was the

only one who could get through to her. I left anyway."

"Jo-Jo made her own choices," Cain said, getting out of the truck. "Every last stinking one of them!"

The door shut hard. Cain went around to the passenger side in time to help Christy down. She moved stiffly, drawn by the tension that hadn't left her despite her tiredness. Her knees gave slightly when her feet reached the ground.

"No more talking about Jo-Jo for a while," Cain said. "You're nearly finished. If you don't let down, you'll fall down."

Christy didn't argue with his blunt assessment. For the first time in her life she felt fragile. She didn't like the feeling, but she couldn't ignore it any longer.

The cabin wasn't locked. Cain opened the door wide and flipped on a light. The adobe was a western version of an efficiency apartment. The single room still held the warmth of the day and smelled of dried flowers from a vase on the table. There was a kitchen in one corner, bathroom off in a closet, and a sofa that unfolded into a double bed.

Christy turned and looked at Cain, a silent question in her eyes.

"After dinner we'll flip to see who sleeps in the back of the truck," he said.

"On metal?"

"On a mattress. Larry's no fool."

Cain opened the French windows to let in the cool twilight air.

"We'll need a fire before long," he said. "I'll get the wood if you'll see what's in the kitchen cupboards."

"Any requests?"

"As long as it doesn't bite first, I'll take it."

Christy knew how Cain felt. It seemed like days since she had eaten.

No wonder I feel fragile, she told herself. I'm hungry.

It didn't take Christy long to inventory the contents of the cupboards and the tiny refrigerator. Eggs, cheese, butter, and a small package of tortillas came from the refrigerator. A big can of *frijoles refritos,* a bottle of salsa, and a tin of coffee came from the pantry.

The coffeepot and the cast-iron skillet were already on the stove, for cupboard space was at a premium. After a brief hunt, Christy found matches and was ready to go.

By the time Cain laid the fire in the small stone fireplace, Christy had *huevos rancheros* on the table. The corn tortillas were steaming from being warmed in a skillet with just enough butter to glaze the pan.

"Looks great," Cain said as he sat down. "Thanks for cooking."

Surprised, she glanced up from her own plate.

"No thanks needed, Cain. It was nothing."

"Not to me. I love a home-cooked meal."

They ate quietly, watching the last purple light fade from the western horizon. Somewhere between the old adobe and the ranch house, an owl called several times. Another answered from a stand of trees across the narrow little valley.

Closing her eyes, Christy drew in a deep breath and let it out slowly, absorbing the peace of the valley. The sound of coffee being poured into her cup by Cain became a variation on the sound of cottonwood leaves being stirred by a freshening wind.

A chair creaked as he sat down again.

"Why did you break up with your boyfriend?" Cain asked.

Christy shrugged.

"That exciting, huh?" Cain said dryly. "In that case, why was he your boyfriend in the first place?"

She opened her eyes.

Cain was watching her over the rim of his coffee mug. His eyes were the clear gleaming gold of lantern light or scotch whisky.

"Mistaken identity," she said. "I thought he wanted someone to take to concerts and exhibits and—"

"Bed?"

She shrugged again. "Sex isn't a big deal for either one of us. Then he turned forty and wanted home, hearth, and heathens."

Laughing softly, shaking his head, Cain said, "What else?"

She gave him a puzzled look.

"Why did you break it off while I was talking to Larry in the saloon? That's what happened, isn't it? You told What's-his-name—"

"Nick."

"—to get lost."

"What should I have told him? That I'm raving around the Southwest with an ex-con who's wanted for killing an Indian called Johnny Ten Hats, who just happened to be trying to kill us at the time? That I saw a man die and heard a dog whine softly with pain and bleed and bleed and—"

Her voice broke.

"Easy, honey. It's all right."

"No," she said bleakly. "It isn't."

Christy felt her throat tighten and knew she should stop talking, but she couldn't. The enormity of what had happened kept breaking over her in great dark waves, dragging her down in her sister's muddy wake.

"Maybe I should have told Nick that I'm looking for my secret sister," Christy said, "who happens to be the Million Dollar Body that Nick drools over whenever he sees a magazine layout?"

Cain's eyes narrowed. "Nick liked Jo-Jo?"

"He'd never met her. He didn't even know we were sisters until this week."

"Why not?"

"I get damned tired of being the ugly sister, that's why."

"Ugly? Christ, Red, you're not—"

"Compared to Jo-Jo, I am," she said flatly.

"Not to me."

Christy ignored Cain. "Or maybe I should have told Nick about Peter Hutton, who has demons on his walls and gets off by watching my sister screw local cowboys?"

"Somehow I don't think Nick is up to hearing that."

She laughed a little wildly. "Neither am I!"

With surprising gentleness, Cain took the coffee mug from Christy's fingers.

"The last thing you need is caffeine," he said.

He dumped the coffee in the sink, rinsed the cup, and went to the firebox in the living room. A moment later he pulled a bottle of brandy out of a nest of kindling. He poured half a mug and put it on the table in front of her.

"I can't drink all that," she said.

"I'll help."

Christy inhaled the aroma, sipped, and shivered. "It tastes . . . too good."

"Now who's the closet Puritan?" he asked.

She made a sound that could have been a laugh or a stifled sob. He stroked her hair once, then went about clearing the table without any fuss or wasted motions.

"I'll do that," Christy said when she realized what Cain was doing.

"You cooked," he said. "Isn't that the rule? One cooks and the other cleans up?"

Slowly, she nodded. Then she just breathed in aromatic brandy and watched Cain move between table and sink with the unconscious grace of a wild animal.

When the kitchen was in order, he went to the fireplace, dropped a match into the tinder, and stepped back, watching the flames appear. Silently they spread across the hearth, taking tiny, delicate bites out of the wood. Within moments the smell of burning cedar perfumed the air.

Cain went to the table, picked up the mug of brandy, and looked at Christy.

"Come sit over here," he said. "Watching a fire is as relaxing as brandy."

The sofa was soft and worn. Christy sank into its embrace and leaned her head back. The gentle crackling sound of burning cedar and the chirp of crickets were the only sounds for a time. Flames danced and flickered over the fragrant wood.

At first Christy just let the minutes go by as silently as the dance of flames. But finally she drew a deep breath and turned her head toward Cain.

As she had sensed, he was watching her instead of the fire. Silently he held out the mug of brandy. She took it, sipped, and returned the mug. When he took the mug from her, his fingers moved over hers in a light caress that reminded her of the previous night.

"You look like the adrenaline express just ran over you," Cain said.

"When you handed me the brandy, it reminded me of a lifetime ago, when you caught me on the way out of Hutton's house and took me to your cabin."

"A lifetime?" Cain smiled crookedly. "It was only last night, honey."

"It was a lifetime."

Christy's voice was as tight as the lines of strain in her face.

"Take another sip," he said.

"Are you trying to get me drunk?"

"Could I?"

Something in Cain's voice made Christy turn toward him. He was looking at her hair, her face, her mouth, her breasts, her hands. For an instant she was afraid to breathe, afraid to move from this moment into the next.

"It's a little late to be frightened of me," Cain said.

"You haven't looked at me like that before."

He smiled strangely. "I haven't looked at you any other way. You just haven't looked back at me. Until now."

Deliberately Cain set aside the mug of brandy. Just as slowly, he reached for Christy, giving her every chance to turn aside. Instead, she came to him with a soft sigh and a shiver of anticipation she couldn't conceal.

She was too tired to fight the pull toward Cain she had felt from the first time she saw him, an attraction that had increased with every moment she spent with him. She knew him better already than she had ever known any other man.

She knew she could trust him.

Now she wanted to know all of him. She needed it with an urgency that was consuming her as softly and quickly as the fire was consuming dry cedar.

Another shiver rippled through Christy as Cain's hard, warm hands framed her face. He

looked at her for a long moment with hungry eyes.
Then he bent and brushed her mouth with his,
just once.

"Yes or no?" Cain whispered. "Tell me now,
honey."

"Yes," she said simply.

Christy felt sudden tension sweep through him.
She smiled against his lips, enjoying the knowledge
that she affected him as deeply as he did her. When
his hands shifted from her face to her ribs, she
made no objection, for she wanted to be stroked
by him.

But instead of the intimate caresses Christy
expected, she felt herself being lifted, turned, and
resettled across Cain's chest. She opened her
eyes. He was watching her as though curious
whether she would back away from the passion
that bound them together as surely as the opposite shores of a river are bound by the water
between.

"I meant what I said," Christy whispered. "I'm
not a tease."

Cain's head lowered even as she rose up to him,
giving herself to the powerful currents that flowed
between them. There was no hesitation, no subtle
adjusting of bodies as they learned how to hold
and be held. The two of them blended together as
though they had been lovers for years.

The first taste of Cain went through Christy like
fire. With a small sound, she moved even closer to
him, winding her arms around his neck, needing
him as she had never needed another man. When

she gave him her mouth, he took it with stabbing urgency.

As one they twisted down and around until they lay facing each other on the couch. The kiss turned deep and sensual, feeding the heat that was seething deep within Christy. Cain's hands slid down to test the resilience of her waist, then moved up her rib cage with tantalizing delibera- tion until her breath caught in her throat.

When he still didn't touch her, she tore her mouth from his and sank her fingers into the corded strength of his shoulders.

"Cain," she said urgently.

"This?" he whispered.

Christy's breath caught as his thumbs traced the outline of her nipples. Sensation burst through her, shaking her, surprising her. She arched against Cain's caressing hands, feeling her body burn with unfamiliar fire.

Then his hands shifted and the buttons of her blouse slowly began to come undone. With a soft whimper, Christy sought Cain's mouth again. She kissed him with a hunger so new she didn't know how to disguise or control it.

Yet no matter how deeply she kissed Cain, his hands didn't hurry their careful unbuttoning of her blouse. She twisted against him, silently offering him the freedom of her body.

For long seconds he didn't take her gift. He simply deepened the kiss even more, until she was dizzy with his taste and with the slow penetration and retreat of his tongue.

Even after Christy's blouse was finally undone, Cain didn't caress the breasts whose nipples had gathered into tight crowns at his first touch. His fingers stroked her neck, the hollow of her throat, her collarbones, her breastbone, until she moaned and twisted with anticipation and need.

When his long finger finally slid beneath the sheer lace of her bra, she cried out with pleasure.

"God," Cain said hoarsely. "You're going to push me over the edge."

Christy barely heard him. His fingertips were plucking delicately at the tips of her breasts, sending streamers of fire from her throat to her knees. Tiny sounds of pleasure and hunger rippled from her throat. When her bra loosened suddenly, she whispered his name even as she arched her back, giving herself to him.

His hands closed gently, taking the warm weight of her breasts while his thumbs teased her taut nipples. She could feel the subtle textures of his palm and the calluses at the base of his long, elegant fingers as he pleasured her until her breathing was ragged and broken.

Never had a man been so knowing, so careful in his caresses. She arched in sensual reflex against his hands, lifting her breasts to be kissed. The touch of his tongue was agonizing and delicious. When he took the sensitized nipple into his mouth, the heat sank deeply into her. When he drew rhythmically on her, splinters of fire burst through her.

Christy moaned her pleasure and Cain's name and felt the shudder that ripped through his strength. Even as he turned to her other breast, she felt the sudden release of pressure as her borrowed Levi's opened.

Cain's hand slid between cloth and skin. When his fingers eased between Christy's naked legs, she shifted, allowing him to touch her. Asking for him.

The feel of his warmth curling around her, cupping her, dragged a hoarse sound of need from both of them. She melted in his hand, moaning softly and lifting her hips in a sensual reflex that was new to her. She had never offered herself so openly before. She was thoroughly aroused, completely ready to join with him.

Cain knew it. He could feel it, see it, breathe it. He caressed Christy slowly, and the sound he made was that of a man in pain.

She understood, for the pleasure of his touch was so intense it was nearly pain. Blindly she lifted against him. Never had she felt so free and yet so enthralled at the same time. His name broke on her lips as flames coursed wildly through her, a fire started by the sweet friction of his hand between her legs.

Even as pleasure claimed Christy, she drew her nails down Cain's back in a silent demand that he finish the sweet torment he had started. He answered with another slow caress, his hand sultry with her passion. The sleek, gliding touch made her cry out.

"Cain," she said raggedly. "I want you."

His answer was a throttled sound and a deliberate movement of his hand. Before she could draw another quick, shallow breath, she felt a gliding penetration as he probed her with a violent kind of restraint. Her breath came out in a broken moan.

Blindly Christy's hands sought the waistband of Cain's jeans. Her fingers fumbled with the metal button for only an instant before Cain's hand shifted, catching her fingers beneath his, preventing her from undressing him.

At first Christy was too wild with need to understand why she couldn't get the stubborn fastening open. Then she realized that it was Cain himself preventing her.

"Cain?"

There was no answer. Christy tilted back her head so that she could see Cain's face. His eyes were golden slits and his mouth was bracketed with effort. His expression was unreadable.

"What—what's wrong?" she asked. "Did I do something wrong?"

Cain closed his eyes and slowly dragged Christy's hands up to his chest with a grip so harshly restrained it was numbing. He said something savage beneath his breath and opened his eyes.

"No, Red." Cain's voice was rough with frustration and pent emotion. "You did everything right. Too damned right. I've never been so close to losing control with a woman in my life as I am right now."

The bleak reflections of fire in Cain's eyes made Christy look away.

"Isn't that what making love is supposed to be about?" she asked after a moment. "Losing control?"

"Christy—"

Cain swore bitterly and looked away from her flushed, bewildered face.

"You've made it clear how much you love your sister," he said finally. "Most people care shallowly, if at all. You don't. You care all the way to your soul. It's a great strength.

"And it's a great weakness. Jo-Jo figured that out and used it against you. I can't bring myself to do the same thing."

When Christy understood what Cain was saying, she felt as though she had been dumped in ice water.

"You think I'm a whore," Christy said flatly.

Cain's head whipped around. The shock on his face would have been amusing if Christy hadn't been so coldly furious.

"I never said anything like that!" Cain said.

"Really? What else do you call a woman who trades sex for something she wants?"

"Honey, all I meant was that you have a soft spot in your heart—and your head—for your goddam sister!"

Christy wrenched herself free of Cain's touch. Ignoring her undone clothing, she reached in her pocket, dragged out a nickel, and flipped it.

"Heads," she snarled.

As Christy caught the coin, she smacked it down onto the back side of her left hand. Without bothering to look which side was up, she jammed the coin back in her pocket.

"You lose," she told Cain. "Now get the hell off my bed."

22

The crowing of a rooster in the corral came as a relief to Christy. She had been beginning to wonder if she was the only thing alive on Ghost Ranch. The sun had pushed night from the sky hours ago.

The rooster had been a late riser—and proud of it, if the continuous crowing from the corral was any indication.

Christy had spent too much of the night awake, her thoughts chasing around in smaller and smaller circles. When she couldn't bear thinking about Jo-Jo any longer, she thought about Cain. Never had a man taken her up so high. Never had she been dropped so hard.

Even now, in the clear light of dawn, her body seethed with anger and with memories of what it had been like to be fully aroused for the first time in her life.

Unfortunately, the seduction had been strictly one-way.

Christy rolled out of bed. The air in the room was cold enough to show her breath. Outside, in the open truck bed, Cain must have passed a frosty night.

I hope he froze his ass off.

She grabbed the coffeepot, filled it, and banged it down on the burner so hard that water sloshed over. With a hissed word, she moved the pot to another burner, scraped a match against the stove-top, and turned on the gas.

By the time the coffee was perking cheerfully, Christy had a fire going on the hearth. She went back to the stove and began making scrambled eggs. While they cooked slowly, she wrapped the remaining tortillas in a damp cloth and warmed them in the oven.

Sun streamed in the back of the cabin, which had been built to take advantage of the southern exposure. An old wooden glider chair sat on the back porch. Christy opened the door, found the air delightfully warm, and went outside. Balancing breakfast in her lap, she ate and rocked slowly in the glider, letting the warmth of the southwestern sun chase the chill of the night from her body.

Just as Christy was eating the last bite, Cain appeared silently at the corner of the house. He was carrying a towel over his shoulder and his hair was wet. He was dressed in different clothes. The heavily faded chambray shirt might have belonged to Constable Moore, but the jeans had come from another source. They fit like a faithful denim shadow, reminding Christy of just how male Cain was.

Her mouth turned down and she looked away. She didn't need any reminders. She didn't want any, either.

"Good morning," Cain said.

"It's morning," she agreed coolly.

He stopped at the corner of the little porch and looked out at the ranch.

"The shower inside is broken, but—"

She interrupted. "I figured that out last night,"

"—there's a small stream just up the canyon. It's not as warm as the hot springs at my cabin."

"I took a basin bath last night."

"About last night. It—"

"Forget last night," she interrupted curtly.

Cain looked at her. "Impossible."

"Not at all," she shot back. "I'm quite easy. Scared the pants off you, didn't it? Well, not the pants. You hung on to them valiantly. Be sure to stick a gold star on both cheeks, if you can reach around that far."

With a muttered curse, Cain swiped a hand through his wet hair.

"I shouldn't even have kissed you," he said.

"I'll drink to that."

"It's a bad idea for us to get involved. There's too damned many distractions in both our lives at the moment."

"Not to worry," Christy said. "Unlike some people I could mention, I'm not a tease."

Cain's mouth flattened into a grim line.

"And I won't be a distraction in your life," she said. "So far as I'm concerned, last night is a nolo."

"What?"

"Lawyer talk. *Nolo contendere.* It didn't happen, and I promise it won't happen again."

"When this whole mess is cleared up, we—"

"Not in your lifetime," she said, cutting across Cain's words. "Not even in your dreams. I'm not a closet masochist."

Cain said something brutal beneath his breath.

Christy realized she had been holding hers. She let it out slowly. When she spoke again, her voice was nearly normal.

"Your breakfast is in the oven," she said.

"Honey, we can't act as though nothing happened."

"Why not, *honey?* Nothing did!"

With distinct satisfaction, Christy saw that Cain was on the edge of losing his considerable self-control. She smiled like a cat and waited for the explosion.

For a tense minute, Cain stared into the morning sky. Overhead a pair of hawks circled slowly in a rising column of warm air. The wild russet of their tail feathers burned like fire against the cobalt blue of the sky.

Cain turned on his heel and walked away.

"We better get on the road," he said without looking back. "There's a lot of ground to cover between here and Santa Fe."

* * *

The run to Santa Fe was painfully quiet. Cain stared grimly at the highway and drove. Christy sat without relaxing in the least as she watched the countryside unreel beyond the side window. The cab of the truck was filled with a thick, seething tension.

The plaza at Santa Fe and the streets around it were crowded with cars and motor homes. Flat-landers jostled one another for the best view of the Navajo jewelry vendors who had spread their velvet blankets on the shaded sidewalks in front of the Governors' Palace and the Museum of Fine Arts.

Canyon Road did business more sedately. The high-ticket galleries didn't hang out welcome signs or wait with open doors and cash registers. Canyon Road galleries invited only the most dis-criminating to enter and do business.

Or the most wealthy.

Cain cruised past the Sherberne Gallery twice before he circled the block and found a parking spot on a side street.

"They're not going to be happy if you barge in and start asking about stolen artifacts," Christy said.

"As my cellmate used to say, if you can't do the time, don't do the crime."

Christy grimaced.

Cain opened his door. "I'll be back in—"

"No way. I'm coming with you."

A single look told Cain he could have a scream-ing match at the curb or he could shut up and take Christy along.

"Do you have the letters that mention Sherberne?" Cain asked tightly.

Silently Christy lifted a battered manila envelope.

"Are you familiar with the good-cop bad-cop routine?" he asked.

"Yes."

"Guess which you're going to be?"

"The bad cop," she retorted.

"Guess again."

Cain stalked to the gallery door with Christy hurrying along behind. The silver bell over the gallery door was delighted to announce their entry. A slim, tan, and sun-blond male in a white cowboy shirt emerged from the back room.

"Sherberne himself," Cain said very softly to Christy.

Sherberne's bolo tie was held by a chunk of turquoise the size of a hen's egg. His polite smile faded as he took in Cain's clothes. By the time the man catalogued Christy's well-used outfit, his welcoming expression had disappeared completely.

"May I help you with something," he said.

It wasn't a question. The man's expression said he was quite certain he had nothing that they could afford to want.

Cain and Christy looked around the gallery. It was Santa Fe modern, white-on-white adobe walls, polished glass display cases, and intensely focused overhead lights. The cases were full of excellent artifacts, yet Cain cataloged and dismissed them with a single educated glance.

Good, but not unique.

"Mr. Art Sherberne, right?" Cain asked.

Sherberne hesitated, then nodded slightly.

Cain's easy smile turned hard. He went to the front door, snapped the deadbolt into place, and turned the OPEN sign around.

"What *are* you doing?" Sherberne asked in a rising voice.

Automatically, he took a step toward his desk.

"Forget your silent alarm," Cain said calmly. "The last guys you want in your lap right now are cops."

The gallery owner froze in the manner of a man who might know exactly what Cain was talking about.

"What do you have in mind?" Sherberne asked.

"I'm looking for some pots," Cain said. "Good San Juan Basin black-on-whites, ones that use Kokopelli motifs and maybe a tortoise clan symbol."

Sherberne's eyes widened fractionally.

"I'm afraid I can't help you," he said.

"Just like that? You don't even have to consult an inventory sheet?" Cain asked.

"Items such as those you described are quite rare," Sherberne said. "I don't have any."

"You're certain?"

"I personally select every piece that passes through this gallery," Sherberne snapped.

Cain smiled.

"Good," he said. "Then you'd be able to tell me whether you've handled any pieces like that in the past."

"That is none of your business."

"Don't bet on it," Cain said.

Sherberne didn't like whatever he saw in Cain's eyes. The gallery owner looked away.

"Who are you?" He asked.

Cain ignored the question and asked one of his own. "Have you handled goods using symbols of either Kokopelli or a tortoise?"

Sherberne's jaw worked. "No."

"Wrong answer."

Cain turned to Christy. "Show him the letters."

She brought out the envelopes that had Sherberne Gallery in their return address.

Sherberne swallowed.

"Does the name Christa Jody McKinley mean anything to you?" Christy asked.

Sherberne's thin, tanned face turned as pale as his shirt. He looked at Cain with dawning horror.

"You're the—"

Abruptly Sherberne regained control. The sentence remained unfinished.

"I'm the what?" Cain asked.

Sherberne shook his head.

"Don't be a fool," Cain said calmly. "These letters prove you're involved in the buying and selling of stolen property."

"Stolen?"

Sherberne looked genuinely surprised. He went to his desk, picked up a pack of cigarettes, and shook one out. After it was lit he stood and looked at Cain narrowly.

"So you did handle the pieces?" Christy asked.

Blowing a stream of smoke, Sherberne nodded.

"Where are they?" Cain demanded.

"Sold," Sherberne said succinctly.

"Japan or Germany?"

The gallery owner gave Cain a hard look.

"I don't discuss business with strangers," Sherberne said. "Unless, of course, you are the police?"

When Cain and Christy were silent, Sherberne smiled thinly.

"Good-bye," he said. "I wish I could say it has been a pleasure."

"We can get the police, if that's what you want," Cain offered.

"Listen," Sherberne snarled. "I vetted the documentation. It was adequate to the letter of the law."

"You seem to know a lot about criminal law for a guy in the fine art business," Cain said sardonically.

"I've bought and sold artifacts for years. I've been rousted by the Bureau of Land Management, the Navajo Tribal Police, and even the Federal Bureau of Investigation."

"Impressive," Cain murmured.

"Nobody's ever caught me with a stolen pot or one whose provenance is suspect in the eyes of the law," Sherberne concluded. "And nobody ever will."

"Does that mean you got documentation on the items the McKinley woman sold you?" Christy asked.

"Of course."

"And they were legally dug?" she pressed.

"That's what the paper said. It was notarized, by the way."

"Of course," Cain said under his breath. "Christ."

"And you believed her," Christy said.

"Naturally."

"This Christa Jody McKinley," Christy said carefully. "Do you know where she is right now?"

Sherberne's smile was malicious.

"More or less," he said.

"Where?" Christy asked eagerly.

"Hell."

"What?"

"The bitch is dead."

"No," Christy said in a low voice. "Damn it, no!"

Sherberne looked at her oddly.

"Are you sure?" Christy asked raggedly.

The gallery owner took an impatient drag on his cigarette.

"Yes."

"I don't believe it," Christy sai. "She can't be dead."

"Why not?"

Christy couldn't answer.

"Look, if you don't believe me, try the morgue," Sherberne said curtly.

She tried to speak but had no voice.

"Not that you'll be able to identify her," Sherberne said. "She and her half-smart boyfriend were killed in a plane crash. They spread his new plane over half the damned landing strip. Took a day just to pick up the pieces. At first it looked accidental, but now the cops are thinking sabotage."

Abruptly, Christy believed.

A cold wave broke over her, loneliness and regret, guilt and despair.

Sweet child loved by everyone.

Beautiful woman loved by no one.

Color drained from the world first, then black ate from the edges to the center, shutting down her vision.

Cain caught Christy as her knees gave way.

"Breathe, Red. Deep and hard. Breathe!"

Blindly Christy reached for Cain, hanging on to his strength while the world spun dizzily around her. She fought for breath, forcing air into her numb body, breathing deeply until the roaring in her ears stopped and color returned to her vision again.

With it came pain.

She bit back a cry and gathered the shreds of her self-control. Oddly, the pain helped.

It told Christy she was alive.

"At least Jo-Jo doesn't hurt anymore. Does she?"

Christy didn't know she had spoken aloud until she heard Cain's low voice and felt the warmth of his breath against her ear.

"She doesn't hurt anymore," Cain whispered, stroking Christy's hair. "Whatever demon was eating Jo-Jo alive died with her."

With a great effort, Christy lifted her head and looked at Cain. His eyes were watching her with an aching kind of sympathy, as though he would have borne the pain himself if that would have taken the agony from her.

"I'm sorry," he said simply.

"She was my sister," Christy whispered, as though Cain didn't know.

"I understand."

"Do you?"

"She knew you as a child, when the future had no limits. And now . . . she's dead and there are too many limits."

Christy fought against the tears she had never cried for the loss she had never before admitted.

Jo-Jo wasn't within Christy's ability to heal now.

She never had been.

"You can let go," Christy said. "I'm all right now."

"You look pale."

"I always look pale. I'm a redhead."

Reluctantly Cain loosened his hold. But he stood very close, watching Christy intently.

"I'm fine," she said. "Just fine."

When Cain was certain of it, he shifted his attention to Sherberne.

The gallery owner took one look at Cain's face and backed up several steps before being brought to a halt by a glass case.

"What makes you think there was something fishy about the plane crash?" Cain asked.

"The plane was sabotaged. The police assume it was a drug-related killing."

"Why?"

"Because the two of them acted like cocaine dealers," Sherberne said. "No class, lots of cash."

"When was the last time you saw them?"

Sherberne said nothing.

"Start talking," Cain said coldly, "or I'll start doing the kind of damage your insurance doesn't cover."

The gallery owner hadn't gotten where he was by being a bad judge of character. He started talking.

"Day before yesterday. Just before they went to the airport."

"Were they selling stuff to you or just collecting money?" Cain demanded.

"Selling. It surprised me. I didn't think they had anything left."

"Did you buy?"

"Yes."

"Do you still have it?"

Sherberne didn't want to answer, but he did anyway.

"Yes," he said. "It in the basement. They were in a hell of a rush."

"Let's see it," Cain said.

Sherberne stubbed out his cigarette. They followed him through his office into a basement work area that was as messy as the gallery was coldly ordered. Artifacts were scattered over tables and on chairs, heaped on the floor, crowding shelves and cupboards on the walls.

"Frankly," Sherberne said, "it's not the sort of material I usually handle. Not on consignment. Not even on outright sale."

Cain looked around hungrily.

"I didn't want it at all," the owner continued,

"but they were so desperate to sell, I took it for a flat fee on consignment."

"Where is it?" Cain demanded.

Sherberne went to one of the worktables. As he started to lift the lid on a rectangular box that took up most of the table, he looked warily at Christy.

"You're kind of squeamish," Sherberne said. "Maybe you'd do better upstairs."

"Open it," Christy said.

"Suit yourself."

He took off the lid and waited.

The long box was lined with a plastic foam such as was used in packing photographic material. The foam had been hollowed to cushion long, darkly stained pieces of what looked like wood.

But it wasn't wood.

Empty eye sockets looked out from an equally empty skull. Arms, shoulders, and most of the rib cage were intact, as were the pelvic girdle and one leg.

Christy forced herself to look at the remains dispassionately. Death wasn't fresh to these bones. They had lain for a long, long time in their grave before being dragged unwilling into the sunlight once more.

"I told the woman there wasn't a big market for human remains. She really wanted to sell. She said she'd take as little as five thousand."

"Five thousand?" Christy asked in disbelief. "You can get five thousand dollars for a human skeleton?"

"Twice that, probably," Sherberne said. "Maybe three times that."

Christy looked at Cain.

"Collectors are a strange lot," Cain said. "They collect anything, including human bones."

Christy grimaced in distaste.

"But I'm not wired into that end of the artifacts trade," Sherberne said. "She left this on consignment anyway."

Cain glanced around the workroom. "Judging by the goods I see here, I'm surprised anything is beneath you."

Sherberne shot Cain an angry look.

"I draw the line at bones," Sherberne said coolly. "Ghoulish collectors and Moki sorcerers are not my thing."

"Moki sorcerers?" Christy asked quickly. "What are you talking about?"

"Medicine men who practice the black arts," Cain said. "They claim to be descendants of the Anasazi."

"What do they want bones for, accent pieces for their stage shows?" Christy asked dryly.

Sherberne didn't answer.

Cain did. "They use skulls for certain ceremonies. Some of them grind up bones to use for devil powder."

"Devil powder," she said neutrally.

"Soul poison. Some of the Navajo and Pueblo medicine men use powered human bones to strengthen their curses."

A feeling of dread welled up in Christy. She had

THE SECRET SISTERS 365

felt the same kind of thing the first time she saw the bone fragment in the alcove, and again when a gold necklace and bone splinters had tumbled out into her palm. She had felt the clammy sensation in one other place, too—Peter Hutton's private gallery of demons.

The dread was primitive and deep-seated, an acknowledgment that immense darkness exists just beyond the circle of firelight that is civilization.

"Anything else I can do for you?" Sherberne asked with exaggerated courtesy.

"Yeah," Cain said. "When the police backtrack the blonde back to your gallery—and they will— forget we were ever here."

Sherberne shrugged.

"In return," Cain continued, "we'll forget that we know where the blonde stole her stuff."

"My hands are clean," Sherberne said instantly.

"Good for you," Christy said. "I'm sure the reporters will point out how innocent you are."

"Reporters?" Sherberne asked. "What the hell?"

"Right now, only the three of us know who sold off Peter Hutton's stolen artifacts," Christy said. "If you don't tell the police we were here, we won't tell the newspapers who sold the pots."

"And the bones," Cain offered. "Don't forget them."

"Ah, yes. The bones." She grimaced. "Headline stuff. Famous designer double-crossed by famous model. Sex and skeletons. *Hard Copy* will be slobbering. They won't care what kind of documents Mr. Sherberne says he has."

"You have made your point," Sherberne said icily. "I won't say anything to the police."

Christy looked at Cain and asked, "Does that cover it?"

"Almost."

Cain put the lid back on the box, picked it up, and tucked it under his arm.

"Wait a minute!" Sherberne said. "You can't—"

"It was on consignment," Cain said coolly. "We're taking it back. If you don't like it, think how much your customers would like having their names attached to the underground trade in human remains."

"Ridiculous. I've never—"

"Right," Cain interrupted. "And now you never will."

Silently Cain and Christy walked out of the basement, through the gallery, and out onto the sidewalk. As the gallery's door shut behind them, she looked at him.

"Do you think it will work?" Christy asked.

"Probably, until someone uses a better twist on him."

She said nothing else as they walked to the truck. Nor did she say anything while Cain unfastened a corner of the vinyl cover that protected the open bed of the pickup, slid the box underneath, and fastened the cover again.

When they were both sitting inside the truck, Christy let out a long breath.

"Now what?" she asked.

"Albuquerque and the Bureau of Land Management."

"Why?"

"Johnny seemed to think they could save his ass. Maybe they can save ours instead."

23

Albuquerque lay under a dirty blanket of noontime smog. East-west traffic on Interstate 40 melded unevenly with the north-south flow on Interstate 25.

Cain emerged from a telephone booth in a service station for the second time that day and looked at the sky unhappily. He was feeling edgy as a coyote on Main Street. The urban haze did little to calm him.

The fact that Christy was about as much company as the skeleton in the box hadn't helped.

"Larry got the investigator's name for us from some other cops," Cain said as he climbed into the truck.

Christy turned and looked at him. Cain realized it wasn't the silence that was getting to him as much as the pain in Christy's eyes.

"It's all set up," Cain said. "His name is Hoyt Jackson. He has agreed to a deep background interview for *Horizon*."

"We're going to interview a *cop*?"

"Hoyt Jackson is more archaeologist than cop."

"I hope you're right."

"You can go home any time," Cain said.

"You wanted to find out who tried to kill you," Christy said tonelessly. "You found out. Now I want to find out who killed Jo-Jo."

Cain started the engine. "Just as well. I'd rather keep an eye on you until I'm sure you're safe."

"What a hero," Christy muttered under her breath. "First he saves me from myself, then he saves me from the world."

Cain's hands tightened on the steering wheel.

"No one knows about Jay and Jo-Jo," he said in a harsh voice. "Johnny's death hasn't hit the news yet. Danner found my truck where Larry left it in the woods. If anyone has noticed you're gone, they aren't raising a fuss."

"No surprise. No one is left who cares."

"I care."

"Give me a break," she said with weary sarcasm. "We both know just how much you care."

"Last night had nothing to do with caring!"

"Yeah, I figured that out all by myself."

"Honey—"

"Besides," Christy continued, talking right over Cain, "last night never happened, remember?"

"*Shit.*"

"Amen, brother."

Cain set his jaw and headed through the smog. Neither one of them spoke again until they were inside Hoyt Jackson's office.

The BLM investigator's room looked as though it belonged to a badly organized museum curator. The tiny desk was stacked with paperwork. The shelves of freestanding bookcases on three walls were filled with boxes of potsherds and whole artifacts.

Every box and artifact was marked with an official-looking tag that said EVIDENCE. That was the only sign of organization in the whole place.

Hoyt Jackson wore a khaki shirt with BLM shoulder patches, but the rest of his uniform was as haphazard as his office. His work boots were badly scarred and his Levi's hung low beneath a spreading belly. Jackson's face was tanned where it wasn't bearded. He wore metal-rimmed reading glasses. He looked less like a cop than any cop Christy had ever seen.

Jackson cleared boxes of corrugated grayware 'sherds from two office chairs and motioned for Cain and Christy to sit down.

"What can I do for you?" he said.

"I'm writing a piece on southwestern artifacts for *Horizon*," Christy said calmly. "Aaron Cain is acting as my guide."

"As I told Constable Moore after Joe got in touch with me," Jackson said, "I really ought to refer you to our public information office for any press interviews."

"This is strictly for background," Christy said.

"I'm interested in the traffic in illegal artifacts from the Southwest to New York. Larry said you were the best man in the West on that subject."

The compliment pleased Jackson, but he still looked uneasy.

"I won't so much as mention your name in the article unless you specifically want me to," Christy said. "What I need from you is enough background to ask intelligent questions of the people who *will* be named and quoted."

Jackson still looked a little skeptical, but finally he shrugged.

"Joe said Larry was okay," the investigator said. "Larry vouched for you two. I'll do what I can."

"Thank you," Christy said.

"Where do you want to start?"

"I'm particularly interested in the activities of a man named Johnny Ten Hats."

"Ten Hats, huh? Yeah, that ol' boy has a few tales to tell. Have you tried interviewing him?"

"He gave us your name," Cain said when Christy hesitated.

Jackson looked uncomfortable.

"Johnny told me he was working with the Bureau of Land Management," Christy said, hoping her voice didn't show her strain.

"I hope the bastard—'scuse me, ma'am, but Ten Hats and I didn't exactly get along."

Christy smiled reassuringly. "Was Johnny working with you?"

"He's not an employee, and he's certainly not an informant," Jackson said.

"How would you describe him, then?"

Jackson tugged at his chin whiskers and squinted over his glasses, first at Christy and then at Cain.

"You've already talked with him?" Jackson asked.

Cain nodded.

"Did he mention his aunt?" Jackson asked.

"He mentioned a lot of things," Christy said before Cain could speak. "The point is, we don't know how much of what he said is true. What did he tell you about his aunt?"

Cain gave her a look of veiled admiration.

"Smart of you, young lady," Jackson said. "Ten Hats wasn't the most trustworthy sort of man."

"I gathered that," she said. "That's why we came to someone with a reputation for integrity."

Smiling encouragingly, Christy waited for the investigator to continue.

Jackson settled more comfortably in his chair.

"Ten Hats has an aunt in Rio Arriba County, name of Molly," the investigator said. "She got herself in some serious trouble a few months ago, digging where she wasn't supposed to be digging."

"I see," Christy murmured.

"She's really a fine old lady. She just doesn't understand that her people don't hold title to all this land anymore."

"Where was she digging?" Cain asked.

"Some ruin down near Chaco Canyon," Jackson said. "One of our young patrol officers found her."

"Digging, huh?" Cain asked. "That means a felony charge?"

"Yeah," Jackson said with a sigh. "What a stink. A more experienced patrolman would have handled it differently. . . ."

Cain made a sympathetic sound.

"Anyway," Jackson said, "Johnny Ten Hats came in to see me, trying to work out some kind of deal."

"For his aunt?" Christy asked.

Jackson nodded. "He wanted to provide information against someone else in return for his aunt's freedom."

"Is that sort of thing done?" Christy asked.

The BLM investigator looked uncomfortable again.

"All the time," Cain said calmly. "It's called plea bargaining."

Reluctantly Jackson nodded.

"What did Johnny tell you?" Christy asked.

"A lot of bull, apparently. Said he would give me a big case involving lots of pots and famous folks from New York."

"Did he?"

"Not so far." Jackson grinned. "Matter of fact, that's the reason I'm talking to you right now, you being from New York and all. I figured you might be able to do me some good."

"I might," Christy said evenly, "if I knew what Johnny was after. What did he tell you?"

"Not one damn hard fact."

"How many times did you talk to him?"

"Three times," Jackson said. "Ten Hats would make vague statements about New York and then ask me how we connect a pot with one piece of land after the pot has been dug and sold and no one is talking."

Christy sensed the sudden alertness in Cain, but he said nothing.

"I finally decided Ten Hats was just trying to learn how to be a better Moki poacher," Jackson said, "so I told him to get lost unless he had some hard evidence for me to process."

"I see," Christy said. "When was that?"

Frowning, Jackson picked up a smooth, wedge-shaped black stone from his desk and hefted it a few times.

"Not long ago," he said. "Frankly, I didn't like the way Ten Hats was acting. Thought he was crazy."

"Was what he told you that strange?"

Jackson sighed and put the wedge-shaped rock back down.

When the silence lengthened, Cain reached for the smooth black stone.

"Nice gastrolith," Cain said.

Jackson gave a little hoot of delight and approval. "Not many folks recognize a dinosaur gizzard stone."

"I've seen a lot of them in Moki digs," Cain said.

"Why do you think the Anasazi carried these stones around?" Jackson asked eagerly. "I'm collecting theories."

"They probably used them to smooth out the marks on the inside of their pots," Cain said.

As he spoke, his thumb described slow circles

on the stone. Christy watched and remembered just how sensual Cain's touch could be. Color rose in her cheeks.

Cain saw it and smiled.

"Or maybe," he added in a deep voice, "they just liked the satin feel of them."

Smiling, Jackson nodded. "Yeah, I kinda lean toward that theory."

"Are you still pursuing the case against Ten Hats' aunt?" Cain asked.

"Molly is an old lady." Jackson hesitated, then said, "Just between us, I'm going to lose the file."

"Where is Molly now?" Christy asked.

"Don't know, for sure."

"Who might?"

Jackson thought a moment. He pulled open a drawer, found a file folder, and sorted through a dozen scraps of paper and bar napkins that were covered with notes. Finally he found what he was after, a telephone number written on the back of an envelope that looked as though it had once held a utility bill.

"Her full name is Molly Faces-the-Sun," Jackson said.

Again Christy sensed Cain's sudden intense interest.

And again he said nothing.

"Molly lives out beyond Cuba, between there and a spot called Counselors," Jackson said. "There's a little two-pump gas station just after you cross the county line into Rio Arriba County. Ask there. Somebody'll give you directions."

He tore a page off his calendar pad, wrote a telephone number down, and handed it to Christy.

"That's her daughter's phone number," Jackson said. "You might call her first, but I wouldn't do it until you're out there. Molly can make herself real scarce if she doesn't want to talk to you."

Jackson stood, signaling the end of the interview. Reluctantly, Christy and Cain stood up.

"Thank you," Christy said, taking the paper. "We appreciate your time."

"You're welcome," Jackson said. "If you really appreciate it, you'll tell me what Molly was digging for and why."

"She didn't tell you?" Cain asked.

"Not one word. She just clammed up."

"It must have been a religious matter."

"Think so?" Jackson asked.

"She Who Faces the Sun is the name the clan sorceress takes when she is initiated into her duties," Cain said. "If a woman with that name was digging in ancestral grounds, she was doing it for spiritual reasons. Losing her file is a good idea."

"Be damned. Thanks. I get so involved in old pots that I forget the modern tribes are people, too."

Cain nodded and shook the hand Jackson was holding out.

"Was Johnny interested in any particular investigative method?" Cain asked as the handshake ended.

Jackson took the question, inspected it, rolled it

over in his mind like it was a smooth stone. Then he looked at Cain.

"He wanted to know how we proved that an artifact came from a particular dig," Jackson said, "even if the documentation said it came from somewhere else."

"Can you do that?" Christy asked, surprised.

Jackson grinned like a cop. "Yes, ma'am. We sure can."

"How?" Cain asked.

"Ask the lab boys up at Los Alamos—if you can get past the gate. As for me, I just send them the dirt and read the bottom line."

Cain doubted that Jackson was telling the whole truth, but he said nothing. The BLM investigator had told them as much as he was going to.

Neither Cain nor Christy spoke until they were in the privacy of the truck.

"Well," Christy said, "now we know why Johnny was ready to kill for a bag of grave dirt."

"You don't miss much, Red."

"I'm dynamite on the little things. The big things get me every time."

"What big things?"

"Like having a sister who is a murderer and not suspecting a damned thing. Like getting seduced by a man who couldn't hold his nose long enough to finish the job."

"Damn it, that's not—"

"Nolo," Christy interrupted wearily. "My fault. I'm sorry. I'm not as tightly laced as usual. I didn't mean to bring it up, and it won't happen again."

"Last night had nothing to do with how much I wanted you," Cain said in a hard voice.

"Last night had nothing to do with anything." Christy looked at her watch. "Is there time to get to Ruby or wherever before dark?"

"Yes."

"Good. The sooner this is over with, the sooner we can get on with our lives."

"Missing your boyfriend?" Cain asked acidly.

"I don't have a boyfriend."

"Then what are you in such a hurry to get back to? Your job?"

"My job probably won't outlast this assignment," Christy said wearily.

"Then what's the rush?"

"Jo-Jo is dead. There's nothing here for me but the sordid history of a sister I always loved and sometimes hated and never really knew at all."

Cain would rather have heard anger than the bleak acceptance in Christy's voice. He glanced at her, but she wasn't looking toward him. Her head was leaning against the window. Though open, her eyes weren't focused on anything.

"You can't change the past," Cain said. "You can only change the future."

Christy wanted to tell Cain to go to hell, but it was too much effort. She rolled the window down a few inches, letting the cool afternoon air into the truck.

After many miles, the air and the austere beauty of the desert penetrated Christy's stillness. She sat straighter and looked at the man she had known only two days.

Two days. God. How can only two days have passed?

Jo-Jo is dead. I've seen a man killed. Nick is history. My job soon will be history.

And I'm on the run with an ex-con.

"Ready to talk?" Cain asked.

"About what?"

"Whatever you're thinking."

"I'm thinking that time is unreliable," she said.

"Two days seem like two years?"

Startled, Christy looked at Cain.

"How did you know?"

"I've had the same two days," he said dryly.

Her laugh had more sadness than humor in it, but it was still a laugh.

"Yeah, I guess you have," Christy said. "But you don't look like you've been run over by a truck."

"It's a trick I learned in jail. When the big things get you down, think about the little ones."

"Does it work?"

"Most of the time," he said.

"And when it doesn't?"

"I get run over by a truck."

Christy took a deep breath and let it out. "All right. Little things it is. You first."

"Peter Hutton's alcove was packed with so many extraordinary artifacts that he didn't notice when Jo-Jo and Jay skimmed off a million bucks, wholesale," Cain said. "Your turn."

"Johnny knew. He had to. He was doing the digging for Hutton."

"Right. I suspect he was also doing the skimming for Jo-Jo."

Christy frowned. "What went wrong? Why did Jo-Jo and Jay take off running?"

"Maybe Johnny asked for more money. Or maybe they didn't want to pay him at all." Cain hesitated, then added, "Maybe they figured a piece of Jo-Jo's action was all the pay Johnny needed."

"Whatever," Christy said, "they grabbed one last artifact and took off for Santa Fe. And then she . . . died."

"If it was sabotage," Cain said in a matter-of-fact voice, "there are two possibilities."

Christy heard as though at a distance.

"Your turn," Cain said. "Little things, Red. Just the little ones."

She let out a ragged breath and gathered her thoughts.

"Who gained from the sabotage?" Cain prompted.

"Johnny, if he had been double-crossed. And Hutton, who certainly had been double-crossed."

"But Johnny was blackmailing Jo-Jo and Jay," Cain said. "If he kills them, he loses a cash cow."

"That leaves Hutton." She frowned.

"He's my favorite candidate."

"Why?"

"I've discovered that if Johnny wanted to kill someone, he would do it head on."

"The way he was at the alcove?" Christy said.

"Yes. Sabotage isn't his style."

"But . . ." Her voice died.

"But what?"

"Hutton may have been selling artifacts and not

reporting the income, but that's not worth killing someone to keep quiet."

"Jealousy," Cain said.

"From the man who liked watching Jo-Jo in bed with other men?" Christy asked, her voice rough with distaste. "Besides, he was through with her."

"Punishment for stealing from him?" Cain offered.

"Having Jo-Jo arrested for theft, stripping her of her position and her pride—that would have been punishment. Why didn't Hutton do that?"

For several miles there was silence.

"I'll bet Johnny knew the answer," Cain said.

"I wonder if Hutton has any half-literate notes in his file, signed by Johnny? Blackmail is a good reason for murder."

"You're forgetting something, Red."

"What?"

"I'm the one who killed Johnny. If there are any notes in Hutton's files, Jay or Jo-Jo signed them."

A long line of cars appeared on the highway ahead, coming out of the sun toward Christy and Cain. As they drew nearer, the reason for the tightly bunched cars became obvious. A New Mexico Highway Patrol cruiser was driving along at the exact speed limit—55 mph—which forced the civilians to form a slow, involuntary parade just behind him.

Both Christy and Cain held their breath together and watched the truck's mirrors, half expecting to see the cruiser turn around and come after them.

The badlands convoy kept going and disappeared over a rise.

"I hope Molly Faces-the-Sun knows what Johnny knew," Cain said. "We can't keep running forever."

24

The service station at the Rio Arriba county line was besieged by sun and haunted by wind. Cain parked beside one of the two old pumps and opened the door. As he got out, a pair of black ravens flew off the branch of a cedar tree, cawing their displeasure at being disturbed.

Without waiting for the attendant, Cain started filling the tank. He was halfway through the job when a slight middle-aged man in a greasy coverall and a Stetson emerged from the tarpaper shack that served as office and service bay.

The attendant nodded a silent greeting and went to work on the windshield with a wet sponge and squeegee. There was a patch over his breast pocket. It bore the name *Homer*. The man was clearly of southwestern ancestry—Spanish, Indian, Mexican, and Anglo, all intermixed in a weathered whole.

Homer barely noticed Christy when she got out to stretch her legs.

"We're looking for a woman called Molly Faces-the-Sun," Cain said casually. "I understand she lives around here."

For all the response Homer gave, he could have been deaf. He continued working on the truck's window in dogged silence. When he finished one side, he looked at Cain for the first time.

"She lives out there," Homer said.

His chin jerked toward the general area of the desert beyond the tarpaper shack.

As though no more directions were needed, the attendant circled around to the other side of the truck and began cleaning the second section of windshield.

"The desert's a big place," Cain said.

"She likes big places because she don't like visitors."

Cain and Christy exchanged a glance over the back of the truck. He shook his head very slightly, silently telling her to leave it to him. He finished pumping gas and racked the nozzle.

An Indian woman appeared in the doorway of the shack. Dark and thick-bodied, she had hair that was absolutely black except for a few threads of silver at the temples. She wore a western shirt, jeans, and dark glasses that hid her eyes.

A distinct feeling of being watched came over Christy. She turned and nodded to the woman politely.

There was no reaction. Nor was there anything

truly hostile about the woman's stare. It was merely intense, intent, and unreadable.

"It's important that we talk to Molly," Cain said, choosing his words carefully.

"Why?" the attendant asked baldly.

"It has to do with her nephew, Johnny Ten Hats."

The attendant glanced once at the woman in the doorway. She showed no reaction. He laid down the sponge and went to work with his squeegee.

"Molly is too busy," the woman said in a clear voice. "And Johnny is dead."

"I know," Cain said. "I heard his death song."

The woman stepped forward and took off her dark glasses. She looked at Cain, then at Christy.

"How did he die?" she asked quietly.

"Police say he was pushed, Eunice," the attendant said. "Pushed by a white man."

Homer looked at Cain.

When Cain met his glance, Homer went back to cleaning windows. For a few moments there was no sound but that of the squeegee, the ghostly exhalation of the wind, and the two huge ravens settling back into their cedar tree.

"Johnny was acting crazy," Cain said. "He was going to kill both of us."

Eunice and Homer turned to look at Christy, but Cain was still talking.

"We fought. When he tried to knock me over the edge of a cliff, I ducked. Johnny kept going."

The Indian woman's eyes had not left Christy, as though she were using the white woman's face as a lie detector.

"Cain didn't want to kill anyone," Christy said. "He risked his life trying *not* to kill. But Johnny—"

She made a small, futile gesture with her hands, asking for understanding.

Eunice and Homer said nothing. They simply watched Christy's haunted eyes.

"Johnny wouldn't stop," Christy said in a low voice. "He just wouldn't stop."

The ravens rasped at the wind and each other, flaring their wings and walking on stiff, springy legs along a dead branch.

"Johnny was always a little crazy," Homer admitted.

He rubbed his hands on the legs of the coverall and went back to cleaning the window. But his expression was still sour, as though Johnny's craziness didn't excuse what Cain had done.

Eunice looked in Homer's direction. She seemed irritated with him, like a wife who thinks her husband is a fool.

"What can Molly do for the man who killed her nephew?" Eunice asked.

Again, her question was addressed to Cain, but it was Christy's face she watched.

"Johnny was involved in an important dig on a ranch in Colorado," Cain said. "Now Johnny is dead. There were others involved in the dig. Some of them are also dead. We want to know why."

"Why would Molly know anything about a dig so far away?"

"Johnny tried to get Molly out of trouble by selling information about the dig to Hoyt Jackson of the Bureau of Land Management."

The Indian woman continued to study Christy's face for a few moments longer. Then she nodded and replaced her sunglasses.

And said nothing more.

"One of the others who died was my sister," Christy said.

Eunice became very still. She pulled off her sunglasses again and looked into Christy as though she were trying to read the future in a crystal ball.

"Your sister?" Eunice asked.

Christy nodded.

"Did you know her well?" the Indian woman asked.

Cain's eyes narrowed at the odd question. He stared at Eunice as intently as the Indian woman was staring at Christy.

"I thought I did," Christy said. "But I didn't. She was a . . . mystery to me."

"The secret sister," Eunice whispered. Her breath came out in a hissing sigh. "She Who Faces the Sun must know. We have waited a long time. . . ."

The Indian woman turned and walked into the tarpaper shed. Homer straightened, wiped the squeegee on his pantleg, and turned to Cain.

"Wait here," Homer said. "She'll be back."

"What was that about the secret sister?" Cain asked.

Homer acted as if he hadn't heard.

Cain looked at Christy. She was rubbing her palms over her arms.

"Need a jacket?" he asked.

She shook her head. "Just goose bumps."

Without a word, Cain stepped closer and put his arm around Christy, pulling her against his side. She stiffened but didn't fight the intimacy. She was too frayed to turn away from the human closeness she needed right now as much as she needed air.

"Don't be afraid," Cain said. "These people may seem strange to you, but they won't hurt you."

"It's unnerving to be part of something that belongs to a people and a religion I know nothing about."

His hand hesitated, then moved gently over Christy's head.

"The Pueblo people look at the world differently," he said quietly. "They don't separate things into categories. It's all of a piece. It could simply be that Eunice saw something in you that she liked. Therefore, you're her sister."

For an instant Christy closed her eyes. Then she let out breath she hadn't been aware of holding.

"Sorry. I overreacted. I feel like I'm living inside out," she admitted, "every nerve exposed and screaming. No defenses."

Cain's arm tightened as though he would have protected Christy if he could have, but he knew he couldn't.

"It will get better," he said softly.

She let out another breath. "I hope so."

For a time there was no sound but the wind.

"Honey?"

Her head came up sharply. Cain was watching with eyes that were both compassionate and unflinching.

"She Who Faces the Sun may not talk to a man," he said. "You may have to go to her."

"Alone?"

Cain nodded. "Can you do it?"

She smiled uncertainly at him. "I'll get back to you on that."

There was nothing tentative about Cain's smile, or the approval in his eyes. For a few moments he tightened his arm, drawing Christy even closer.

Then he released her and walked toward the cedar trees at the edge of the desert as though called by the wind. Hands in his pockets, he stood and looked out over the wild land.

Restlessly, Christy jammed her own hands in her pockets. Her left hand encountered Jo-Jo's key. Her right hand found the smooth, large bead from the kiva alcove. She wondered if Cain was fingering the oddly shaped piece of turquoise and remembering the hidden alcove where they had nearly died.

And Johnny Ten Hats had certainly died.

"Cash or credit?" Homer asked from behind her.

"Cash," she said.

Christy pulled a twenty out of her pocket. Homer made change from the grubby bills in his own jeans. Then he turned on his heel and went into the shack, leaving Christy alone.

When five minutes had gone by, she stalked over

to Cain. At her approach, the two ravens leaped into the air, scolding and croaking their unhappiness at being disturbed. But it didn't take long for the birds to settle on the cedar again, watching the humans with Kokopelli's shrewd, black eyes.

As the birds quieted, Christy discovered that the wind had a different sound at the edge of the desert. Ancient. Solitary. Whispering of secrets better left unknown.

"Are we waiting for a sign?" Christy asked tensely.

"Patience, Red," Cain said. "These people don't waste words and they don't wear watches if they can avoid it. Relax and listen to the wind."

"I did."

"Listen some more. There's peace in it."

Christy listened.

She heard loneliness, not peace.

High overhead a jet drew a white line across the empty sky, telling of people hurtling toward life in a place far removed from the ancient arid land.

I should be on that plane, Christy told herself. Away from here. Going—

Where? Home? I don't have one.

There's no one in New York tied to me by blood or choice. There's no one anywhere. . . .

The shack's door banged as Eunice emerged from the station. She headed toward them, carrying her dark glasses in her hand. When she approached, she ignored Cain and looked Christy straight in the eye.

"She Who Faces the Sun will see you," Eunice said.

THE SECRET SISTERS 391

"When?" Cain asked.

Eunice said nothing.

"When?" Christy asked quietly.

"Tomorrow at dawn."

"That long?" Christy said, dismayed. "Our business is . . . urgent."

"Tomorrow at dawn," Eunice repeated.

"Where?" Christy asked.

"At the great kiva in Chaco, the one you call Pueblo Bonito."

Christy looked at Cain. He nodded.

"I know it," Cain said softly. "Now ask her why there and why tomorrow at dawn."

For the first time Eunice looked directly at Cain. Whatever she thought didn't show in her expression.

"Why—" began Christy, but Eunice was already speaking.

"Dawn is sacred," the Indian woman said simply. "So is the great kiva. In it, all secrets are known to She Who Faces the Sun."

"We'll be there," Cain said.

Though the Indian's expression didn't change, Christy was certain Eunice was both amused and pleased by Cain.

"Good," Eunice said.

Then she looked past the white people to the desert. Her eyes moved across it easily, as though she were enjoying an old friend's face, remembering old conversations and restful silences. . . .

A light touch on Christy's arm drew her attention back to Cain. Only then did she realize that she had been staring out over the desert as Eunice had.

Christy didn't know how long she had been standing there. She only knew that Eunice was gone and Cain's hand was warm against her arm.

The wind lifted, combing cool fingers through Christy's hair, whispering to her of time and distance, past and future, and life like a rainbow arched between, connecting everything.

"You're right," Christy said softly. "There's peace in a desert wind."

As soon as the truck turned south off the narrow paved highway, the vehicle began rattling mindlessly over the washboard gravel road. The noise startled Christy out of her half sleep. She sat up straighter and looked around.

Nothing familiar looked back at her.

"Where are we?" she asked.

Cain pointed behind them, toward the north.

"See those white peaks way off in the distance?" he asked.

The sky was like a huge inverted bowl of purest blue. It took Christy a minute to be sure she was seeing something more than faint clouds along the horizon.

"You mean those things that look like chips in the rim of the sky?"

"Those chips are the San Juan Mountains, where we started," Cain said. "The northern outliers."

"What are outliers?"

"Outlying Anasazi communities."

"Outlying what?" she asked dryly, looking at the empty land.

Cain smiled. "We're on the road to the center of the ancient Anasazi world."

Christy turned back to the distant peaks. They were outlined in brilliant light, as though they had been dusted with snow during the night.

"How far away are they?" she asked.

"About a hundred and thirty miles."

"So the Ancient Ones lived in a universe that was only a few hundred miles across," Christy said.

"It wasn't small to them. They filled it with spirits and signs and mysteries, more complexity than any man or woman could know in a lifetime."

The farther south the truck went, the more arid the country became. Juniper and cedar were limited to the ridges and a few arroyos. Bare dirt was everywhere. Rocks lay just beneath the thin layer of soil.

"Life must have been precarious," Christy said after a long silence.

"It was. Short growing season. Harsh winds. Numbing cold and killing heat. Summer monsoons that sometimes didn't come."

The road passed over a cattle guard and gave way to a dirt track that wandered off across the scrubland with no apparent destination.

"You're sure you know where you're going?" Christy asked.

"Are you asking in cosmic or pragmatic terms?"

She laughed, surprising both of them.

"Yes, I guess the land does that to you," she said. "Cosmic and pragmatic at once."

Smiling, Cain guided the truck over a particularly wretched piece of road.

"Speaking in cosmic terms, I'm up for grabs," Cain said. "But I do know the way to Pueblo Bonito."

The track wound up a low rise that dropped away steeply toward another rock ridge a half mile ahead. A dusty, faded sign on a steel post beside the road announced that they were entering Chaco Canyon National Monument.

"This must be the back way in," Christy said.

"Yeah, but it's not much worse than the main route."

"Is the government trying to discourage tourism?"

"We've been driving across one of the richest archaeological areas on earth," Cain said. "Too big to fence. Too valuable to ignore. Too expensive to dig. Impossible to protect."

"So you limit access and hope for the best?"

"That's about it. If there's a bulletin out on this truck, they'd catch us at the monument gate or in one of the campgrounds, so I'm keeping off the most-used roads."

"What about right now?" Christy asked uneasily.

"This is the route an old Moki poacher showed me. Hard on man and vehicle but discreet."

"You, of course, have never poached here."

He smiled slightly. "That's right, Red. I've done a lot of exploring, though."

"Huh," she said, but she smiled.

Cain pointed toward a distant ridge of rock.

"See that little stand of willows by the stock

tank?" he asked, pointing to a splash of green perhaps half a mile away.

"Hard to miss. It's the only real green for miles
around."

"Look just to the left. See that notch?"

She leaned forward and shaded her eyes. "Yes."

"That's where the Great North Road came down
from Pueblo Alto," Cain said. "It was the imperial
highway from Chaco to the northern outliers. It
runs back the way we came all the way to the San
Juan River."

Cain slowed as the road dropped down into a
ravine where a stock tank was serviced by a creak-
ing old windmill. The metal blades turned mindlessly in the stiff breeze, drawing water up from an
aquifer below the surface. The overflow from the
tank fed the willows and a small grove of cedars,
which had grown lush with the unusual luxury of
year-round water.

The dirt track circled the grove and ended
against a rock wall. Cain backed the truck into the
cover of the cedars and shut down. The fitful wind
died, bringing silence like invisible light over the
land. Then the wind stirred and the windmill
creaked its complaints to the sky.

Christy got out and followed Cain around to the
back of the truck.

"What do you want me to do?" she asked?

"Count how many times the windmill turns."

For an instant she took Cain seriously. Then she
smiled and shook her head. He smiled in return.

"Rest, honey. You've had a rough couple of days."

"What about you?"

"It's been interesting," he agreed dryly.

Cain wrestled Larry Moore's camp box within reach and began pulling out what they would need. A pair of sleeping bags, self-inflating mattresses, a tarp, jackets, a small ax, cooking gear, and a supply of canned and dried food were soon lined up on the ground.

"Nothing fancy," Cain said.

"Neither is hunger."

He looked over his shoulder at Christy and smiled. "Point taken."

While Cain began setting up camp, Christy went about gathering wood for the fire she knew they would need later.

The sun was sliding down the blue bowl of sky when Cain finished. He shrugged into a jacket that had seen better days and handed another, slightly smaller one to Christy. She put it on gratefully. Without the sun's heat, the dry land quickly cooled.

"Have enough energy for a walk?" Cain asked.

"How far?"

He pointed toward the notch on the ridge.

"Be a shame to be this close and not enjoy the best view in the Chaco empire," he said.

The climb to the ridge was easier than Christy expected. Cain stopped at the notch and stood looking out at the vast sweep of land and sky. She stood next to him, hardly able to believe the clarity of the air and the immense landscape devoid of lights or wires or signs of man.

"What do you see that's different?" Cain asked after a time.

"No streets. No skyscrapers. No hustlers. No gourmet take-outs. No theaters. No bars. No taxis. No street people. No museums. No—"

Cain's laughter drowned out Christy's litany of the differences between the New Mexico desert and Manhattan.

"What do you see that's different for the desert?" he amended.

"Looks pretty normal to me. Empty. Immense. Dry. Rocky. Not very many plants." Christy hesitated. "Except over there."

She pointed to a ragged green swath of unusually lush sagebrush. The strip was about thirty feet wide. It marched up the hillside as though it had been planted by man.

"That's the imperial road," Cain said.

"Looks more like an imperial *roadblock*."

A smile flashed against Cain's dense, short beard.

"Now, yes. The old roadbeds are acting as catchment channels. Plants love that extra water. It's the best way to follow the road across dry ground."

Christy began walking up the hill, following the path of the sage. Cain paced her, saying nothing, caught by the intensity of her eyes as they searched the land.

Near the brow of the hill, wind had scoured away the topsoil, revealing rock.

"Look," Cain said, sitting on his heels. "Sandstone curbs like this run on the sides of the road for a hundred miles."

Christy knelt next to him and traced the cool surface of the stones, seeing the marks left by a stonemason long before Columbus set sail for India and found an unsuspected continent blocking the way.

Awe shivered through her, a sense of touching lives long lost, of dreams unknown, of being part of a whole that was so much larger than she had thought.

"A hundred miles of this?" she asked in a hushed voice.

"A hundred miles in this road, maybe three thousand miles in the entire system," Cain said. "We're just beginning to understand how little we know about the ancient ones."

The sun was low in the sky when they reached the top of the hill. There on a broad bench lay an extensive set of ruins that commanded a view of the entire San Juan Basin. There were no fences, no restorations, no signs, nothing but hand-carved stones slowly melting back down into the land.

"Welcome to the center of the world," Cain said.

The La Plata and San Juan mountains lay straight north, pink in the fading afternoon light. Mesas and shadowed arroyos and red-rock spires lay east and south. Off to the west were more mountains.

The air was clear and clean. The last of the sunlight was warm but there was an invigorating chill just beneath it, like a gentle bite hidden in a kiss.

"You can see four states from up there," Cain said, pointing to a low sandstone wall.

He mounted the ruined wall with an animal grace. Leaning down, he held out his hand to Christy. She took it and learned once again that, for all his restraint, Cain was a powerful man. She went up as though on wings.

The wall was very thick. When she had her balance, he put his hands on her shoulders and faced her toward the distant San Juan Mountains. As he spoke, he turned her until she had made a full circle.

"Colorado," he said. "New Mexico. Arizona. And way off up there you can see the mountains of Utah."

Motionless, Christy absorbed the subtle voices of time and the wind blowing over the clean, wild land.

Only when the last bit of the sun slid beneath the dark horizon did she realize that she was standing so close to Cain that his breath stirred her hair and the warmth of his body radiated into her, replacing the vanished heat of the sun.

"We'd better get back to camp," Cain said. "I didn't bring a flashlight."

He lifted his hands from Christy's shoulders, both freeing her and setting her adrift in the fading colors of the day. She turned and watched as he descended the low wall, landing light and strong on the ground.

When she started down, he reached up and lifted her, pivoting, making her feel as though she could fly. The earth beneath her feet came as a faint shock.

Cain felt the hesitation before Christy regained her balance.

"Okay?" he asked, not releasing her.

"Yes. For a second there, I thought I could fly. Wrong life, I guess."

She turned away, leaving the memory of her bitter-sweet smile to haunt the twilight—and to haunt Cain.

25

Out of reach of the wind, the campsite was calm and scented with cedar. The first stars gleamed in the east, where the sky had shifted from blue to purple.

Christy and Cain prepared a simple dinner, ate, and cleaned up in a silence that was companionable rather than stiff. When they were done with camp chores, Christy took off her walking shoes and sat on one of the sleeping bags Cain had spread near the fire. In her hands was a mug of coffee that had been spiced with brandy.

Cain poured himself a bit more coffee and moved to the fire too. He sat on his heels in front of the flames and added several pieces of fragrant cedar.

From beneath lowered eyelashes, Christy

watched every move Cain made. He had a muscular masculine grace that pleased her. There was something both new and familiar about him, as though she had dreamed him a long time ago in an old house on the high plains of Wyoming and now was remembering the dream in a New Mexico desert that was the center of an ancient world.

The flickering light of the fire bathed Cain's hands in alternating tongues of gold and black velvet. His fingers were long, strong, deft. They fascinated Christy, as did the silky luster of his beard and the thick, straight black hair that he brushed carelessly back from his forehead. The reflected firelight made Cain's eyes gleam.

He was watching Christy while she watched him.

"I want a second chance," Cain said quietly.

Christy's breath hesitated and she looked away.

"I was wrong about you," he said. "You weren't thinking about saving your sister last night. You really wanted me."

Cain waited, but Christy said nothing in return. Nor did she look at him.

"Know when I figured it out?" he asked.

Only silence answered him.

"When you threw me out of the cabin," Cain said.

Looking only at her coffee, Christy held on to the mug to still the trembling of her hands. It didn't work. Tiny rings rippled across the dark surface of the coffee.

She closed her eyes.

"A woman who was looking for leverage over a man wouldn't have done that," Cain said. "And she sure as hell wouldn't have melted and run all over my hand like—"

"Nolo," Christy interrupted harshly.

"Bullshit, Red." Cain came to his feet in a single flowing movement. "It happened. It happened hard and fast and deep."

"For one of us," she said in a flat voice.

"For *both* of us. Just like we were both wrong about each other."

Christy shook her head, making firelight gleam like rubies in her hair.

"I stopped because I wanted you too much, not because I didn't want you enough," Cain said, walking closer.

And then he was so close to her that another step would have put him in Christy's lap.

"I wanted you the way I haven't let myself want a woman since I was nineteen," he said in a rough voice. "I would have fought to have you. Christ, I would have killed—"

"Don't," she said.

"—to have you," Cain continued relentlessly. *"And it scared the hell out of me."*

Shivering, Christy clung to the coffee mug and told herself that the raw hunger she heard in Cain's voice wasn't real.

It couldn't be real.

Men didn't want ordinary women like that. Arousing that kind of passion in men was reserved for women of extraordinary beauty. Women like Jo-Jo.

Christy had never been that desirable.

"No," she whispered, eyes tightly closed.

"Yes! And I still want you," Cain said savagely. "Too damn much!"

There was a hissing of steam as he snapped the dregs of his coffee into the fire.

Christy's eyes opened, then widened in shock.

The view she had of Cain's torso profiled by firelight left no doubt that he was telling the truth.

For the space of several breaths there was no sound but that of the flames licking softly against the body of the night.

"You're staring, Red." Cain's voice was husky, half amused, and wholly hungry.

"You're . . . worth staring at."

He gave a crack of laughter and sank slowly to his knees in front of her.

"You're the only woman I've ever known who could make me laugh and turn me on to the point of pain at the same time," Cain said.

Christy tried to speak, but he was so close she could taste his breath. His eyes were a smoky kind of gold that was as hot as the leap of flames.

"Give me that before you drop it," Cain said softly, taking Christy's coffee mug and setting it aside. "Your hands are shaking."

"So are yours."

"Am I frightening you?" he asked.

"Not . . . quite," she whispered. "Am I frightening you?"

"Yes."

Her eyes widened. "Why?"

"We could just have sex and stay free. I don't think making love will be the same."

"Don't you know?" she asked.

He shook his head. "Do you?"

"No," she whispered.

"Want to find out?"

For an instant she closed her eyes. Then she nodded.

Cain's fingers slid deeply into Christy's hair, caressing and holding her in the same instant. She felt the tremor of emotion that ripped through him, shaking his strong body.

"Cain?" she whispered.

"I don't have any defenses against you," he said simply. "And I don't care anymore."

His teeth closed carefully on her lower lip. When she gasped with surprise and racing pleasure, his tongue shot between her teeth, filling her mouth as he wanted to fill her body. His hands shifted and his arms closed around her, lifting her to him. Heavy, hungry, frankly sensual, his kiss told her more than words could have about his barely leashed hunger.

When Christy struggled in Cain's arms, his mouth lifted just enough so that he could speak against her lips.

"Don't fight me," he said raggedly. "Please, honey. I don't deserve you, but I need you until I'm shaking with it."

The words went through Christy like lightning through a storm. She wanted him the same way, no defenses, needing him as she had never needed another man.

"I wasn't fighting," she said.

"You were trying to get away."

"No." Christy laughed a little wildly. "I was trying to get closer!"

Cain's arms tightened suddenly, pulling her even closer, arching her body against his so that she felt him from her knees to her mouth mated with his in a deep kiss. Her arms went around his neck, holding him with all her strength while he kissed her as though he expected to die in the next instant.

When the kiss finally ended they both were breathing in soft, rushing bursts. Cain unzipped Christy's jacket and his own with two quick motions. The snaps on his shirt and hers came undone in twin ripples of sound. Firelight gleamed on naked skin and licked over black lace.

Cain's breath came hard and fast. Then he eased his index fingers beneath the straps of Christy's bra. Slowly his knuckles slid down over her collarbones.

Her breath broke as his fingers smoothed down the soft slope of her breasts, drawing the lacy cups aside until the cloth was beneath her breasts and they were naked but for the firelight gliding over them. Her nipples tightened in a rush, silently telling him of her own desire unfolding like a hidden, sultry storm.

With a low sound Cain bent and caught one nipple between his lips and then drew it deeply inside, shaping her, making her moan. When she was hard and moist from his tongue, he turned to her other breast.

Her nails dug into his arms as passion spiraled up like flames. The small pain of her nails was a sensual goad, urging him to strip away more of her control and his own until there was nothing between them but unleashed desire.

Cain turned his head from side to side, caressing Christy's sensitized breasts. Their tips were dark, tightly drawn, and they glistened with firelight and the moist heat of his mouth.

"You're beautiful," he said hoarsely. "Just looking at you makes me want to—"

He closed his eyes.

"You're hell on my self-control," Cain said after a moment.

The edge of Christy's teeth on his ear made him bite back a curse of pleasure and eroding restraint.

Cain's hand slid down her body until his fingers curled between her legs. He flexed his hand deeply, savoring and caressing her at the same time, watching waves of pleasure claim her.

Eyes dilated until they were as dark as night, Christy looked at Cain. She felt dizzy, almost weak, yet her body pulsed with a relentless, restless heat.

"Cain?" she whispered.

"Don't be afraid, honey." He let out a rushing,

hissing breath. "I won't hurt you. If you're not ready . . ."

He unfastened her jeans and slid his hand beneath black lace. Long fingers searched, probed, discovered, sank deeply into her sultry heat. The low, husky sound of his name breaking on Christy's lips made him smile.

"Like fire and rain at once," Cain said in a low voice. "Hot, soft, wet . . ."

Christy's hands went from his shoulders to the dark swirls of hair on his chest, dropped to the cool sterling buckle with its turquoise eye.

And stopped.

"Keep going," he said huskily.

As Cain spoke, he dipped into Christy's heat and then withdrew. A thumb slick with her passion circled the satin knot he had drawn from her softness. The broken, hungry sound that came from her lips made him want to tear off her clothes and sink into her.

Instead, he set his teeth and circled the sleek bud again.

Blindly, hands shaking, Christy traced the unfamiliar fastening on Cain's belt, a hook rather than a buckle. She tugged once, but nothing came undone. She tugged harder. Same result.

Reluctantly Cain withdrew his hand from Christy's clothes. His fingers closed over hers. For an instant she went very still, remembering last night when he had refused to be touched. She looked up at him with a question in her eyes.

"Don't you want . . . ?" she asked.

"I want your hands all over me."

Christy's eyelids half lowered and she smiled as though the idea intrigued her.

"Your buckle is in the way," she pointed out.

"Move this hand over here," Cain said, guiding her hands, "and then pull across and up with the other."

"Like this?"

The belt opened.

"Yes, just like that," he said. Then he smiled. "Now you know how to get into my jeans any time you want."

Christy's almost hidden smile was as sexy to Cain as the sound of his zipper sliding down. Her hand eased into his jeans and discovered that he had already escaped the confinement of his briefs. Her fingers hesitated for a moment, then slid down the aching length of his arousal.

The frankly approving, purring sound Christy made as she caressed Cain nearly undid him. A low curse came from between his clenched teeth.

"You going to push me over the edge," he warned.

"Can I really do that?"

"You damn well know you can."

"No, I don't," she whispered. "But I'm going to find out."

His breath hissed between his teeth as the sweet pressure of her fingers gave way to the harder pressure of her naked palm. She measured him once, twice, watching his eyes narrow and his whole body clench. Then she slid her fingers inside his briefs and knew the coarse silk of his hair and the twin spheres that were so tightly drawn with desire.

Cain stiffened and groaned as though Christy had taken a whip to him. With a dismayed sound, she withdrew.

"I'm sorry," Christy said in a low voice. "You'll have to teach me more than how to undo your belt."

His eyes opened. There was little left of gold in them except a glittering circle around a dark, dilated center.

"I never really wanted to touch a man," she said hesitantly, "so I never learned how. But I want to . . . touch you."

The soft confession was more arousing than any caress could have been.

"That did it," Cain said hoarsely.

His hands slid over Christy's back and down inside her jeans. His fingers flexed, sinking hungrily into her hips, drawing a cry of surprise and sensual pleasure from her. Slanting his lips over hers, he sank into the sultry warmth of her mouth, penetrating her hungrily. One powerful arm closed around her back, lifting her.

In the next instant Christy felt her jeans and underwear being stripped away. The sleeping bag felt cold against her back, but the heat of Cain's body covering her more than made up for it.

As she lifted up to meet his kiss, her breasts rubbed tantalizingly against his chest. She twisted against him and shivered at the sensations streaming from her breasts to the pit of her stomach.

Cain pulled away and reached into his pocket.

"Cain?" she whispered. "What . . . ?"

Then Christy saw the gleam of the foil packet in the firelight and understood.

"Let me," she said, taking the packet and opening it with fingers that were trembling. "That's one thing I do know. I've never done this any other way."

"Neither have I. But I came goddam close about two seconds ago. Wait. Let me take off my—"

His breath wedged and his thoughts scattered as slender fingers smoothed over him, caressing and sheathing him at the same time. Then she stroked down his length again, openly enjoying him, feeling just how much he wanted her.

"Honey, unless you want to be flat on your back with a half-dressed man between your legs, you better—"

A groan was torn from Cain when Christy's fingers eased between his thighs, caressing the violently sensitive parts of him that were still naked.

An instant later Christy was flat on her back with Cain's half-dressed body between her legs. He parted her with his fingers, testing her readiness and increasing it at the same time. Her legs twined around his. The rough feel of denim between her naked thighs sent more wild sensations racing through her.

Christy tried to tell Cain how good he felt, but words became a moan as his hips flexed and he pressed into her until she thought she could take no more. Then he moved and a sensual rain swept through her, further softening her. Her legs circled his hips, opening her body completely to him as she unraveled with a shuddering cry.

The heat and scent of Christy's uninhibited response burned away what little restraint Cain still had. His arm went beneath her hips, holding her so hard against him that he could feel the bones beneath her soft flesh.

He took her mouth as he took her body, absorbing her wild cries, driving deeply, repeatedly into her, sparing her none of his heavy arousal. Suddenly she arched like a drawn bow, shivering wildly, crying deep in her throat with every broken breath.

For an instant Cain was afraid that his unrestrained passion had hurt her. Then he felt the rhythmic pulses of her body and knew he had given her ecstasy rather than pain.

He drove into her again, burying himself in her. His head came back and his body went rigid and he knew nothing but the deep, heavy pulses of his own release.

Spent, fighting for breath, Christy and Cain held each other for long minutes. She stroked his sweat-slicked back beneath his shirt, savoring the muscular heat of him while her breathing slowly returned to normal. He turned his head and bit her gently on the curve of her neck. Echoes of ecstasy shook her unexpectedly, making her moan and clench around him.

Laughing softly, he bit her again. Her breathing unraveled even as her body did.

"I didn't know . . . until now," Christy said.

Cain lifted his head and looked down at her with luminous eyes.

"Know what?"

"Why women put up with men."

Very gently Cain kissed Christy's eyelids, the hollow of her cheeks, the corners of her mouth.

"It works both ways," he said against her lips as he slowly withdrew from her. "Pleasure like that is damned rare."

Cain rolled onto his side, taking Christy with him, holding her close, stroking her gently, being held and stroked in return. For a time there was no sound but the whisper of the fire.

Her fingers combed gently down his chest, enjoying the masculine textures of hair, muscle, resilient skin. When her hand drifted below the waistband of his briefs, she discovered that he was no longer sheathed.

He was also fully aroused.

"Don't tempt me, honey."

"Tempt you? It's a little late to be worrying about that, isn't it?"

The husky combination of laughter and sensual

pleasure in Christy's voice made Cain's heartbeat visibly quicken.

"I was afraid it was going to be like this," he said thickly.

"What?"

"You and me. The first time I saw you in the gallery I wanted you."

"And I couldn't stop looking at you."

"I know. It made me feel like I'd grabbed lightning. If it hadn't been for Danner . . ."

Cain closed his eyes and took a long, deep breath, trying to still the hammering urgency of his blood. He pulled off the rest of his clothes and turned to Christy, gathering her against his fully naked body for the first time. They fit one another perfectly.

"Damn, that feels good," he said.

Her answer was half laughter, half the low, purring sound that set his blood on fire. She pulled his mouth down to hers and kissed him slowly, deeply.

"You want me as much as I want you," he said, surprise and pleasure in his voice.

"Of course."

"There's no 'of course' about it," Cain said. "Even people who want each other aren't necessarily suited as lovers. Different needs. Different speeds. Different—"

His thoughts scattered as Christy's hand slid down his body, exploring him gently. He groaned and searched blindly in the pocket of his discarded jeans.

"I like the ways we're different," she said, cupping him.

"So do I. Put this on me, honey. I'll show you the way I like us best of all."

26

Cain awoke an hour before dawn.

The sky overhead was cold and brilliant with stars. He and Christy were warm, lying like nested birds inside the sleeping bags he had zipped together. For a long time he lay motionless, savoring the softness and warmth of the woman curled against him, trying to ignore the rational part of his mind.

That part told him he was still far from cleaning up the mess Jo-Jo had bequeathed her loving older sister.

Cain gathered Christy even closer and gently kissed her bare shoulder, wishing he didn't have to wake her at all. She looked so peaceful sleeping in his arms.

And he was afraid the coming day wouldn't be peaceful at all.

"Good morning," he said as her eyes opened.

"Morning?" Christy said vaguely, rolling over to face Cain. "Looks more like night from here."

She burrowed against his warmth with a sigh and kissed his chest sleepily. Within seconds her breathing changed as she sank back into sleep.

Cain slid his fingers into the silky tangle of Christy's hair, tilting her head back. He nuzzled her lips and kissed her again.

"Morning is on the way," he said. "Listen."

Deep within the willow thicket around the water tank, birds were beginning to rustle, singing soft fragments of song, getting ready for the day.

Christy propped herself on one elbow and looked over Cain to the east. The sky had begun its slow transformation from midnight to the limitless blue-gray that precedes dawn. Shivering, she ducked back down into the sleeping bag and pulled Cain against her like a living blanket.

"She Who Faces the Sun will be waiting for you, honey. Time to get up."

"What about you?"

"I'm already up," he said dryly.

As Christy shifted against Cain, she realized that this was indeed true.

"When did you say dawn was?" she asked, her voice suddenly husky with more than sleep.

"Too soon," he said bluntly.

"Oh." She sighed. "Do I get a rain check?"

"Any time. Do I get one?"

"This is the desert. How about I give you a sun check instead?"

Laughing softly, Cain hugged Christy close, kissed her hard, and then shot out of the sleeping bag as though his heels were on fire. He cursed steadily as he pulled on clothes chilled by a night on the ground.

"You make getting dressed sound irresistible," Christy muttered.

"At the moment, it's right up there with an icy shower."

Without getting out of the sleeping bag, Christy gathered up her clothes, drew them beneath the warm cover, and began dressing.

Five minutes later, shivering, she followed the circle of Cain's flashlight to the ruins of Pueblo Alto. By the time they reached the tumbled stones and low walls of the ancient settlement, the sky in the east was light enough to reveal the outlines of mesas and the ragged rise of mountains behind Santa Fe.

A pair of meadowlarks burst from cover alongside the trail. For a few instants the world was full of the rushing sound of wings. Then one of the birds landed and an intricate, curling song rose into the dawn.

Motionless, Christy listened as the lark called again. It was a sound from her childhood, when life had been limitless. Joy and sorrow twisted through her like a double-edged knife. Tears filled her eyes, blurring the lines between night and dawn.

"I found the path," Cain called softly over his shoulder. "Light is coming on like thunder. We have to hurry."

Christy blinked, releasing the hot tears. As her vision cleared she hurried to Cain.

The path led downhill from the ruins toward the rim of Chaco Canyon. The trail had been cleared and marked for tourists with small piles of stone in strategic places. Even in the half-light, Cain and Christy made good time.

Ten minutes below the remains of Pueblo Alto, the trail dropped over a small sandstone ledge. From there it skimmed along the broad stone lip of the canyon itself.

Putting his arm around Christy, Cain stood with her on the brink. For a few hushed moments they watched the miracle of light emerging from darkness.

Gradually, Pueblo Bonito condensed out of the night. Hand-hewn masonry walls made up a huge apartment block that rose two and three stories high. Countless rooms lay open to the sun and wind. The residential areas were laid out as a new-moon crescent with one curved and one straight side. The straight front was defined by a low wall.

The body of the crescent was a plaza with open spaces the size of basketball courts. Within the crescent were the circular ruins of kiva after kiva, a profusion of sacred places that proclaimed the religious significance of Pueblo Bonito.

In the shadows flowing out into the dawn, the

circles seemed filled with the mystery of centuries. One of the kivas was much larger than the others, first among equals.

As Christy's eyes adjusted to the fluid boundary between dawn and night, she noticed that some of the old masonry walls of the room blocks had begun to slump with the weight of sunlight and time. Those were supported now by braces like the ones she had seen in the alcove.

"Twenty-four kivas," Cain said quietly. "Once, Pueblo Bonito was the most important building in the empire."

"But why so many kivas?" she asked. "Wasn't one church or temple or whatever enough?"

"Maybe each clan had its own kiva, which is the way some of the Pueblo people live now. Or maybe different kivas were used at different seasons," Cain said. "No one knows. Or if they do, they aren't talking to white folks."

Christy leaned forward as though trying to see into the past as well as into the dense shadows that remained like pieces of the vanished night.

"What about the biggest kiva?" she asked. "Why is it different?"

"I don't know. It could be that's where everybody prayed ten hours a day during the long winter for the safe return of the sun in the spring."

Cain glanced at the sky. Polaris was just fading. He turned back to the ruins.

"When that straight wall was built," he said,

pointing, "it was less than a degree off of a true north-south line."

At first Christy didn't understand the ramifications of what Cain was saying. Then she remembered that the Anasazi had no metal, therefore no compasses. In ancient times, the polar star hadn't been the beacon of true north that it was today.

"How did they do it?" Christy whispered.

"Ask She Who Faces the Sun. It's one of the secrets she will pass on to Eunice."

"Eunice?"

Cain gestured toward the ruins of the great kiva. Two human figures had stepped out of the shadows below the kiva's circular rim.

One of the figures lifted a hand in greeting. Cain responded in kind.

"That *is* Eunice," Christy said after a moment. "How did you know?"

"Eunice is Molly's niece."

"Johnny's sister?" Christy asked.

"Yes."

Releasing Christy, Cain stepped away.

"We'd better go," he said. "She Who Faces the Sun wants to see you in the first light of day, when the sun clears the rim of the canyon."

"After a night in the sack with you?" Christy said, smiling but very serious.

Cain's glance roved over her as though remembering and memorizing at the same time. He smiled gently and held out his hand.

"The ancients weren't strangers to the rhythms of life," he said.

Lacing her fingers through Cain's, Christy walked side by side with him as long as the trail permitted. As soon as the path left the canyon rim, they had to walk single file. The trail dropped down into a narrow cleft between two rock faces that became a tunnel, recalling the trail to the Sisters alcove.

Cain and Christy stepped into the shadows of the cleft and began a steep descent down what amounted to a rude stairway. The stairs were faint, uneven, almost nonexistent. Yet in places the walls were smooth with the passage of many, many hands. Cain and Christy were walking along pathways that had been old long before the first Europeans came to the Anasazi lands.

Christy touched the smooth places on the stone walls and sensed time like a vast exhalation moving across the face of the land. Her skin shivered in primal response.

When she looked up, Cain was watching her with eyes as ancient as fire.

Together they emerged from the cleft onto the flat floor of Chaco Canyon. The first faint colors of day had begun to gather low in the eastern sky.

As Cain and Christy walked toward the great kiva, he let her walk apart from him, becoming more guide than mate. She accepted the distance with the same instinctive understanding she had accepted the stones smoothed by and infused with ancient lives.

The eastern sky was a radiant orange as Cain

and Christy approached the long straight wall that ran along the north-south side of Pueblo Bonito.

"The entrance to the great kiva is on the other side of the wall," Cain said. "Eunice will show you."

He turned away, heading toward the ruined apartment block. He didn't look back.

After a moment, Christy walked toward the kiva and a meeting with She Who Faces the Sun, a woman directly descended from the ancients.

Eunice met Christy at a break in the north-south pueblo wall.

"Come," Eunice said.

Christy followed her through the wall to a spot where the kiva wall had collapsed, making the climb down a matter of only a few steps. Eunice gestured for Christy to precede her to the center of the sunken circular room whose roof was the onrushing dawn.

The old woman who waited had the clothes and body of someone who could be Johnny's Aunt Molly. She was an inch or two less than five feet tall. She wore a faded denim riding jacket over a long gray velvet skirt and new white running shoes. Her gray hair was covered with a bandanna that was tied in a knot at the point of her chin. Her face was wrinkled.

Her clear black eyes were those of She Who Faces the Sun.

Eunice said something to the old woman in a language that was utterly alien to Christy.

"This is She Who Faces the Sun," Eunice said to Christy a moment later. "She is the keeper of our clan's spirit."

"Good morning," Christy said, for she knew no other polite way to greet the keeper of a clan's spirit.

She Who Faces the Sun stepped forward, touched Christy's bright hair, and spoke in the language Christy couldn't understand.

"She likes your hair," Eunice translated. "She said she has seen sandstone that color in a small canyon near Mesa Verde."

Christy smiled.

She Who Faces the Sun took Christy's hand and tugged firmly. In response to the silent demand, Christy turned. Just as she faced east, the first direct rays of the sun lanced over the canyon rim, transforming everything in a single, sweeping instant.

A primitive awe shivered through Christy. She felt as though the world had just been newly born, rather than simply the day.

The old woman's hand tightened around Christy's. A low, shifting chant poured from She Who Faces the Sun. Christy couldn't understand the meaning of the words, but she sensed quite clearly that the prayer or incantation centered around her.

When the chant finally came to an end, She Who Faces the Sun reached into a patch pocket on the front of her denim jacket. She brought out a pinch of pale yellow dust and scattered a trace of it over herself and Christy.

"Corn pollen," Eunice said quietly. "It's our way of blessing people. She likes what the dawn showed her in you."

Christy looked at the old woman's clear black eyes. "Thank you."

She Who Faces the Sun smiled. It transformed her face, making her Aunt Molly instead of an ancient holy woman. She said something rapidly in the alien tongue.

Eunice smiled with sly humor as she looked at Christy.

"Aunt Molly likes your man, too. She Who Faces the Sun called him Kokopelli."

Christy laughed and felt heat flushing her cheeks.

Smacking her hands on her thighs with delight, Molly laughed with the vigor a woman half her age. When she looked in the direction of the apartment block, she saw Cain sitting in the sunlight, watching the old kiva as though he had left something valuable there. She spoke rapidly again.

"She says Kokopelli settles when he finds the right woman," Eunice translated. "He looks pretty settled from here."

The old woman grinned, showing a mouth full of sturdy teeth. Then she turned and walked away from the center of the great kiva.

"She will talk with you now," Eunice said.

"Who will speak, Aunt Molly or She Who Faces the Sun?" Christy asked.

Eunice gave her a sharp look, then nodded as

though Christy had just done something right.

"Molly," Eunice said. "Most of the time. Come."

As they moved to join the older woman, Christy spoke quietly. "Please tell your aunt that we regret the death of Johnny Ten Hats."

Christy stopped close to Molly, speaking directly to her.

"The sheriff blames Cain for Johnny's death, but I was there. It was not Cain's fault."

Eunice translated and Molly listened. Finally, the old woman nodded and began speaking. Simultaneously, Eunice translated, as though she had done it often.

"Aunt Molly knows Johnny was a man torn by demons. He drank too much. He stole pots and grave offerings from the ancient ones and sold them to the white man. He spent much of himself trying to be a big man in a white world."

Listening intently while Eunice translated, Christy watched Molly's face. The old woman watched her in turn, nodding occasionally or gesturing fluidly with her hands to make a point.

"One of Johnny's demon's was a yellow-haired witch," Eunice translated. "He stole for her. He spent his money on devil powders that he put up his nose. This made him more crazy, until he was a stranger to us."

"Cocaine?" Christy asked in a low voice.

With a curt nod of agreement, Eunice continued translating while Molly spoke.

"But enough of Johnny survived within the

demon that he knew he was lost. He left the yellow-haired witch and came back to us for a time."

Both Indian women stopped talking and looked at Christy. Her mouth turned down unhappily, but there was no way to avoid the truth.

"The witch was my sister," Christy said simply. "Like Johnny, she lived with demons."

The old woman understood more English than Christy thought. She Who Faces the Sun looked out at Christy, boring into her with eyes as black and bottomless as night.

"She witch all time?" the old woman asked, grappling with the foreign language. "Child. Woman. All time witch?"

Christy shook her head.

"No, not always," she whispered. "Once Jo-Jo was a sweet little girl."

Then Christy shivered, remembering the past with savage clarity.

She Who Faces the Sun narrowed her eyes as she saw the truth dawning in Christy.

"Jo-Jo saw herself much more clearly than she saw other people," Christy said in a low voice. "Always. All the time. Yet she was my sister. Always. That will never change."

The old woman's eyes closed. She nodded once, slowly.

Christy waited.

Nothing more was said.

She turned to Eunice and asked, "When Johnny came back to you, did he break with the people in Colorado?"

Eunice and Molly talked back and forth for a moment, syllables and sounds without meaning to Christy.

"The witch who was your sister gave Johnny a powerful drug," Eunice said after a time. "It took him to a place where rocks had voices and the cedars walked like men."

"Peyote?" Christy asked.

"Powerful. Much more powerful. Afterward, Johnny came to She Who Faces the Sun so that she could get his soul back from the demons. He brought her a gift from an ancient place."

"The alcove," Christy said.

Eunice hesitated. "He never told us. He simply stole it from the yellow-haired witch."

She Who Faces the Sun closed her eyes and began an eerie, sliding chant, ancient words rising and falling in the sunlight and shadow of the great kiva.

"The tortoise soul is very old, one of many such souls. Each made for and worn by a different She Who Faces the Sun," Eunice translated. "They were stolen from this kiva by a sister who wanted to be She Who Faces the Sun and hold the spirit of the clan in her hands. The other sister, the clan's She Who Faces the Sun, followed the thief."

"Where?" Christy asked urgently.

"North to the edge of the desert, where the land rises to a great mesa. Sister and She Who Faces the Sun fought. The sister was killed, but She Who Faces the Sun also was mortally struck. She knew she wouldn't have the strength to return her clan's spirit to the great kiva.

"Nor did she want to. She had seen in a dying vision that the clans were coming apart like kernels stripped from an ear of dried corn. The time of the sun was past.

"The time of the demons was coming."

The chant deepened, taking on a new urgency.

"The clan's spirit must be hidden," Eunice translated. "She Who Faces the Sun sealed her dead sister and herself and the clan's spirit in a kiva hollowed out of solid stone.

"And then She Who Faces the Sun called down the stone of the canyon itself to hide her clan's spirit in sacred silence."

As the eerie duet of Indian chant and modern English died, Christy once more felt the prickling chill of time blowing over her skin.

"The alcove," Christy whispered. "I've been to the grave of the ancient She Who Faces the Sun. Johnny died there."

She Who Faces the Sun spoke again.

"Whoever disturbs the clan's spirit will die," Eunice translated.

"May I . . . is it permitted that an outsider see what Johnny brought to She Who Faces the Sun?"

Without waiting for Eunice's translation, the old woman opened her denim jacket.

Suspended from a thong around her neck was a tortoise pendant identical in shape to the effigy in Peter Hutton's display case. The turquoise inlays were similar in size and shape, but different stones made up different portions of the turtle body.

The matrix that held the turquoise was white abalone shell rather than argillite. One of the turquoise tiles was missing. Instead of eyes made of turquoise spheres, one eye was a polished black sphere.

The other eye was missing.

Abruptly Christy found it hard to breathe. She reached into her pocket. The black bead she had found in the alcove was warm with her body heat and very smooth.

"Cain," she said urgently to Eunice. "Call him."

Eunice gave Christy an odd look, but She Who Faces the Sun was already turning to the place where Cain waited.

"Come," she called.

Moments later Cain was standing in the kiva next to Christy, his eyes luminous, curious, intent.

"The piece of turquoise we found in the alcove," she said. "Do you have it?"

Silently Cain reached into his pocket and brought out the oddly shaped tile. Simultaneously Christy pulled the bead out of her own pocket.

She Who Faces the Sun held out the tortoise on her palm. The tile fitted into place perfectly, completing the turquoise pattern. The bead slid onto a tiny stalk.

The tortoise was complete.

She Who Faces the Sun spoke softly over the pendant, caressed it with a gentle hand, and slipped it into a pocket for safekeeping. Tears of joy glittered in her ancient eyes.

Eunice let out a long sigh.

"We have no way to thank you," Eunice said simply. "The pendant is very important to our clan."

"There is another tortoise," Christy said.

"Where?" Eunice said sharply.

"It's owned by Peter Hutton."

"Who is he?"

"The man who owns the ruin where Johnny found both pendants."

"Not own," She Who Faces the Sun said harshly. "Ours!"

"By your laws, yes," Cain agreed. "White law is different. But you might be able to bring enough political pressure to bear on Hutton so that he'll gives up the bones, if not the grave goods, he found in the alcove."

Eunice translated rapidly, listened, and turned to Cain once more.

"Bones?" she asked curtly. "Were the pendants found in a burial place?"

"There were two skeletons. Female. The two pendants were found with them."

"They were buried in a kiva," Christy added.

"The Sisters," Eunice whispered.

Cain looked intently at the old woman, sensing the turmoil beneath her still surface. She spoke quickly, words tumbling out. Eunice translated just s urgently.

"She dreamed of the two sisters but saw only

one when she looked in the dawn light."

She Who Faces the Sun turned away and walked across the hard-packed floor of the great kiva. Silently she went from niche to niche, staring into the empty places as though seeing a time in the past when each clan's spirit lay safely within.

Finally She Who Faces the Sun turned away from the niches where other people could see only emptiness and walked back toward the three who waited. Her seamed brown face was both serene and radiant with pleasure. As she approached, she did a small two-step dance of joy and laughed like a girl.

She spoke to Eunice.

"Aunt Molly wants you to bring the other tortoise to her," she said to Christy.

Cain and Christy exchanged glances.

"She Who Faces the Sun might not comprehend white property laws," Cain said, "but Molly does. By white law, the other pendant belongs to Peter Hutton. It was found on his property."

"No," the old woman said curtly. She spoke with equal bluntness to Eunice, demanding something.

For the first time, Eunice spoke exclusively to Cain.

"This place where you and Johnny fought," she said. "Was it close to two pillars of stone?"

"Yes."

"Why were you there?"

"Christy found Kokopelli's sign carved into the canyon rim. Below it was a trail leading to the ruins. We followed the trail."

"Was Johnny there?" Eunice asked.

"He came later."

"To steal more?" she asked bluntly.

"No. All he wanted was a bag of dirt."

"You fought over dirt?"

"I fought because he attacked me."

Eunice turned back to the old woman and spoke rapidly. The old woman listened.

And then she laughed.

At first Eunice looked shocked. A moment later she understood. Smiling, she turned back to Cain.

"The ruins you describe aren't owned by anyone," she said.

"What?"

"That's public land. Government land. Johnny was halfway through the dig when Peter Hutton figured it out."

A smile spread across Cain's face.

"No wonder Johnny wanted to know how to identify the origin of artifacts," Cain said.

"He was going to prove that Hutton's collection came from public land," Christy agreed, "and get the government off Molly's back in the bargain."

"Getting dirt from the site won't be a problem. Getting our hands on one of Hutton's pots, though—" Cain shrugged. "We need one that hasn't been cleaned."

"That must be why Johnny was trying to break into the room just off the main gallery," Christy said.

Cain nodded. His eyes narrowed as he thought about what had to be done.

Suddenly Christy wished she hadn't said anything. Johnny had been caught and badly beaten when he tried to steal the evidence he needed from Hutton's house.

This time Peter Hutton and his men would be more dangerous, not less.

27

"*Can't you get Larry Moore to help you?*" Christy asked.

Cain didn't even look away from the road. He was driving fast and hard, holding the white truck to the road with ruthless skill. Ahead of them loomed the San Juan Wall.

"Larry's got to live in that town," Cain said. "He's already put himself way out on a limb for me."

"But—"

"No," Cain said curtly. "Not until I'm sure I can protect Larry from the likes of Danner."

"How can you do that?"

"The same way Johnny was going to," Cain said.

"You're going to steal a pot from Hutton's house." Christy's voice was tight, unhappy.

"You have a better idea?"

435

"Yes. Give it to the government."

Cain's laughter was as harsh as the look on his face.

"You must believe in Santa Claus, too," he said sardonically. "The first time Hutton gets a whiff of any official interest, those pots and grave goods are history, and you know it as well as I do."

"If there's a search warrant—"

"Not a chance," Cain interrupted curtly. "Without probable cause, you'll never get a warrant."

"But if we told what we knew, wouldn't that be probable cause?"

"Assuming the duly constituted authorities believe the word of an ex-con, it might be grounds for a search warrant. Then again, it might not. Either way, word gets to Hutton. You want to take that chance?"

"What about *my* word?"

Cain's hands tightened on the wheel. "You heard what Johnny said. Jo-Jo left a trail of evidence pointing to you as her partner in theft. That's why Hutton and Danner were calling New York, looking for you."

"But—"

"But nothing," Cain said savagely. "If we go to the authorities, Danner will get wind of it. What Danner knows, Hutton knows."

"If—"

Cain kept talking. "The only way we have a hope of clearing our names is by doing it ourselves. I wanted to drop you off in a safe place. You refused. End of argument."

He braked sharply. A moment later the truck was turning onto a dirt road.

"Isn't this the road we took three nights ago, when you grabbed me coming out of Hutton's house?" Christy asked.

"Yeah." Cain smiled oddly.

There was silence for a few minutes. Then Christy sighed and looked at the man who had intrigued and compelled her from the first moment she saw him in the Two-Tier West gallery.

"Did you ever imagine where it would lead when you saw me running down that hill?" she asked.

Cain gave Christy a sideways look and a remembering kind of smile.

"I had hopes," he said. "The very first time I saw you, I knew there was a lot of woman underneath that hundred-dollar haircut."

She laughed. Then her smile turned upside down.

"A lot of trouble, too," she said.

"Last night was worth every bit of it," Cain said. "So was seeing She Who Faces the Sun hold that tortoise in her hand."

Cain shifted into four-wheel drive as they entered the dry wash a mile from the ranch house at Xanadu. He drove the length of the wash and well into the streambed before he stopped.

When they got out of the truck, the sun was high overhead. After the desert at Chaco, the mountain air tasted cool and hinted of winter. There had been a hard frost the night before. The leaves of a black-trunked cottonwood beside the dry stream were golden. They rustled softly in the breeze.

"Stay here," Cain said.

Christy started to object but he cut her off.

"If I'm not back in an hour, I want you to run like hell to Larry."

"I know the layout of the house. You don't."

"You can describe it to me."

Christy said nothing.

"Or I can do it the way Johnny did," Cain said.

Still Christy didn't speak.

Cain studied her face. His mouth flattened.

"Once I walk off, you're going to do what you damn well please, aren't you?" he asked grimly.

"Why shouldn't I? That's what you're doing."

Without another word Cain set out down the streambed. Christy followed, crouching when he crouched, standing still when he stood still, and moving when he moved.

The sand of the streambed still showed their footprints from three nights before. They followed the tracks to the spot where they had slid down the bank to escape Hutton's guards.

Christy touched Cain's hand, stopping him. She didn't want to set off to Hutton's house with anger between them.

"I should have known better than to hang around with you," she said softly, "after the way you lifted me down this bank."

For a moment, Cain didn't understand. Then he did. He circled her waist with both hands. Slowly his fingers reached up to touch her last rib and brush against the sides of her breasts.

"You could have slapped me any time you wanted, honey."

"I still can. But I don't want to."

Christy stepped close and kissed Cain, holding him hard and being held even harder in return.

"Wait in the trees for me?" he asked against her lips. "If we're both caught in the house, we could be as dead as Jo-Jo and Jay."

For a long, taut moment Christy looked at Cain.

"All right. But you have to come back to me," she added fiercely.

"It's a deal."

He kissed her hard and fast.

And then he boosted her up the bank. The spruce trees were not far beyond. Inside the grove it was almost as dark as it had been at night.

They stood side by side in the evergreens, watching and listening. No one was working around the house or the barn. Only one airplane was tied down in the meadow. No one was using the target range. No cars were moving on the road from the gate. The barn and corrals were empty and battened down.

Isolated, alone, its doors and windows shut and draped, the big house stood like a modern sculpture on the brow of the hill.

"It looks deserted," Christy said in a low voice.

"That would be a piece of luck."

"We could use one."

Cain didn't argue.

"Looks like Hutton has already closed up the place for the winter," Cain said. "I hope he didn't empty the display cases, too."

"There was too much for him to move all of it this quickly," Christy said.

Cain nodded. "Especially such fragile stuff. Even if he took the best with him, he had to leave something."

"Besides," she added unhappily, "it's not like the house is unprotected. The security inside is discreet, but it's there."

Together, Cain and Christy circled around to the back side of the hill, where the cedars grew thickly. No one called out to question their right to be on Xanadu.

When they were within twenty yards of the deck Christy had jumped from to escape Hutton's guards, Cain stopped.

"This is far enough for you," he said. "Any closer and you wouldn't have much chance of escaping if something went wrong."

"Wait," Christy said when Cain would have turned away.

Using a stick, she quickly traced a floor plan in the dirt.

"This is the deck," she said, pointing with the stick. "This is how you get to the grand gallery with the display cases."

Cain nodded.

"I don't know how much good those pots will do us," Christy added. "They were scrubbed and polished when I saw them."

"If the cases are empty or the pots look too clean, where's the room Johnny was trying to break into?"

Christy drew quickly.

"Here," she said. "The skeleton of the other sister is probably there too."

"All right. I'll be back as quick as I can."

Cain gave Christy's shoulder a squeeze before he moved to the edge of the cedars, looked around, and ran across the open lawn to the house.

Once there, he plastered himself against the back wall next to a window in what had been Jo's bedroom and listened. Nothing was making noise inside the house. He tried the window.

Locked.

Calmly Cain picked up a rock the size of his fist. He tapped gently on the glass. It broke with a brittle, musical sound. He fished a few long splinters out of the window frame, reached in through the hole delicately, and undid the lock.

The window slid back easily. Pulling the curtain aside, he looked in and listened. Nothing came to him but the sound of his own breathing. He reached up, caught the sill, and began to vault over it into the room.

A shiny chrome steel pistol appeared in the window.

"Gotcha!" Danner said triumphantly.

Cain let his forward momentum carry him

right into the sheriff. As the two of them went down in the room, Cain's hand chopped at the sheriff's wrist. The semiautomatic pistol fired twice, wildly, in the instant before it felt to the floor.

Christy was running before the echoes of the shots faded—but she was running toward the house, not away from it. The fear that Cain might be wounded or even dead wiped all thought of getting away from her mind.

She had just enough sense left not to burst through the window herself. Instead, she did what Cain had done. She flattened out against the house and listened.

"You son of a bitch," Danner said in a strained voice. "I'll get you if it's the last thing I do."

"You'll sure as hell complicate my life," Cain muttered. "Where's Hutton?"

"Fuck you."

"And here I thought you liked little girls."

There was a grunt followed by a thump and more grunts.

Christy took a quick peek through the window.

Sheriff Danner was flat on his stomach. Cain was sitting on top of him. One of Cain's hands was buried in Danner's hair, pulling the sheriff's head back at a sharp angle. Cain's other hand was wrapped around Danner's right wrist, which had been dragged up between his shoulder blades.

Just beyond Danner's right shoulder lay the pistol. At the moment, it was a stalemate. Neither man could reach the pistol. That could change at any instant.

Danner had forty pounds on Cain, and only a few of it was fat.

"Cain?" she called softly. "I'm coming in."

"You don't take orders worth a damn, Red."

"I thought you'd never notice."

Christy scrambled in over the window ledge. Without hesitating, she went to the pistol, picked it up, checked it with a few quick motions, and put the safety on.

Cain raised his black eyebrows. "Not your first pistol, huh?"

"I live alone in Manhattan. I can put ten rounds in the black at thirty feet."

"How are you on live targets?"

"With luck, I'll never know."

"So Hutton was right," Danner said angrily. "She's in this with that sister of hers."

"This?" Cain said sardonically. "Which 'this' are you talking about?"

"Theft," Danner said succinctly.

"I'm a reporter, not a Moki poacher," Christy said.

"I'm talking breaking and entering, not pothunting," Danner said.

"Where?" Cain demanded. "When? What was taken?"

"As if you don't know, you son of a bitch."

Abruptly Danner began to make sounds like a man having trouble breathing.

"You can talk or you can choke," Cain said through his teeth. "Take your pick."

Ann Maxwell

"Two nights ago somebody hit Hutton's house and cleaned him out," Danner said in a strained voice. "Not a damn thing left."

Cain and Christy looked at each other.

"Is that why you're here?" Cain asked. "Looking for evidence?"

"Yeah."

"Find any?"

"No," Danner said grudgingly.

"What was taken?" Christy asked.

"You know better than I do, you little—"

Danner's words ended in a grunt as Cain yanked the sheriff's wrist up to the back of his head.

"Her name is Ms. McKenna," Cain said. "Now answer her."

"Pots," Danner said in a strained voice. "Beads. All that damn Moki stuff Hutton was so proud of."

"There's nothing left here?" Christy asked.

"You should know," Danner retorted. "You cleaned it out down to the dust in the glass cases."

"*Shit!*" Cain said, furious. "The son of a bitch is going to get away with it!"

"What the hell are you talking about?" Danner demanded.

"Murder."

The sheriff made a rough sound.

"My sister and her lover," Christy said.

"Jo?" Danner asked. "Hutton's fancy piece of ass?"

THE SECRET SISTERS 445

"Yeah," Cain said. "She and Hutton's jet jockey died when their plane exploded on take-off down in Santa Fe."

"I don't believe you."

"Jesus, Danner," Cain said in disgust. "Why would I lie about that?"

"Hutton said Jo, Jay, and the two of you were in on it. That you cleaned him out, Jay transported it, and—"

"Jay couldn't have transported a fly," Cain said brutally. "He was spread all over three acres of runway."

Christy drew a sharp breath.

"Besides, if we've already cleaned Hutton out, what the hell are we doing breaking into a empty house?" Cain asked.

Danner said nothing.

"Well?" demanded Cain.

"I don't know."

"That's right, *sheriff*. You don't know enough to come in out of the rain."

"I know I saw you trespassing on Hutton's property. I know I saw you murder Johnny Ten Hats. I know you're a Moki poaching son of—"

"—a bitch," Cain interrupted sarcastically. "Well, one out of four ain't bad, I guess."

"None out of four." Christy's voice was as flat and hard and Cain's. "Self-defense isn't murder."

"What happened?" the sheriff asked. "Did Johnny jump you when he got tired of getting fleeced by the four of you?"

"Sheriff Danner," Christy said, "shut up and listen!"

The sheriff would have objected, but Cain's grip had tightened.

"One," Christy said distinctly. "Until last week, I hadn't seen or communicated with my sister for more than ten years.

"Two. The alcove where Petter Hutton's 'Moki stuff' came from is on public land."

Beneath Cain's hands, the sheriff went very still.

"Three. Jo-Jo, Jay, and Johnny Ten Hats were stealing from the alcove, from Hutton, and from one another."

Slowly the tension began to drain from Sheriff Danner's big body.

"Four," Christy continued. "Cain had nothing to do with any of it.

"Five. Jay shot Cain this spring. And no," she added scornfully, "it wasn't a hunting accident.

"Six. Cain is not a murderer!"

As the fight left Danner, Cain slowly eased his grip. He didn't let go entirely, because he didn't trust the sheriff not to make a lunge for Christy and the pistol.

"Seven," Christy said coldly. "Can you prove that you aren't an accessory to robbery, blackmail and murder?"

"What?" Danner asked, shocked. "Lady, I'm the goddam sheriff of Remington County!"

The outrage in Danner's face was so clear that Christy laughed. And laughed.

And laughed.

"Easy, honey," Cain said, watching Christy closely

"It's almost over. Even a skull as thick as Danner's gets the point eventually."

Christy took a deep, ragged breath.

"I'm okay," she said. "It's just that—you should have seen—his face—"

"Yeah," Cain said, smiling slightly. "I can imagine. You ready to negotiate yet, sheriff?"

"You ready to surrender?" Danner retorted.

It took Cain a moment to realize that the sheriff was serious.

"Uh, yeah," Cain said. "But there's a condition."

"What?"

"Hutton's ass," Cain said succinctly. "Where is the son of a bitch?"

"Are Jo and that pilot really dead?" Danner asked.

"Yeah. You don't believe me, call Santa Fe. They must have identified the scraps by now."

"Let me up."

Cain looked at Christy. She backed up until she and the pistol were well beyond Danner's reach. Cain let go of the sheriff and stood, watching him carefully.

"Damn," Danner groaned, rolling over and working his right arm. "No wonder Johnny was the one that went over the cliff."

Slowly Danner got to his feet.

Christy backed up some more. She had forgotten just how big the sheriff was.

Danner picked up his hat, reshaped it, and put it on. Then he looked at Cain for a long time.

"You really figure Hutton killed his model?"
Danner asked.

"Or had Autry do it," Cain said. "He had the training."

"Why kill them?"

"Blackmail, likely."

"All because of a few ugly Moki pots?" Danner asked. "That's crazy."

"Hutton couldn't afford a scandal," Christy said.

Danner turned toward her.

"It's one thing to be inspired by ancient Anasazi designs found on your own land by experienced archaeologists," Christy said. "It's quite another to rape a unique and important archaeological site on public land."

Danner shook his head slowly, but he wasn't disagreeing with Christy. He simply didn't understand.

"Public land," Danner said. "Be damned."

"Jo-Jo and Jay knew Hutton had been digging on public land," Cain said. "At a guess, I'd say they were blackmailing him as well as skimming from the dig. Or else Hutton feared blackmail in the future."

"Well, you could be right," Danner said, "for all the good it will do you."

"What are you talking about?" Christy demanded. "Cain is innocent!"

"Sure," Danner said, shrugging. "I'll be glad to put it out on the wire. But as for the rest . . ."

Christy waited.

"Even if I believed you," the sheriff said, "an

I'm not sure I do, Hutton has the money and Autry has the brains not to leave any evidence lying around."

"They left a whole goddam alcove," Cain said. "I'll get the evidence I need."

"I don't think so. Hutton and Autry went upcountry about an hour ago. They took a couple of cases of dynamite with them."

Cain began swearing savagely.

With a resigned gesture, Danner tugged his hat into place.

"Win some, lose some, some never had a chance," the sheriff said. "I don't like it, but there's damn-all to do about it."

"I'm not going to lose this one," Cain said in a harsh voice.

"Sure you are," the sheriff said wearily. "Hutton and his like don't ever pay the piper. They just get in their fancy jets and fly off, back to New York or Los Angeles. And we're the little people, the ones they fly over on the way."

A wolflike smile spread across Cain's face.

"But they aren't aboard that private plane yet," he said softly. "They're still down here in the cedar and sandstone.

"And that's my country."

Cain turned and went out the same way he had come in, through the window. As soon as his feet hit the lawn, he was running.

When Christy went out the window after Cain, the sheriff's gun was still in her hand.

28

    By the time Cain parked Moore's truck within fifty yards of the Sisters, the rim of the mesa was already in deep shadow. Cautiously Cain went to the edge and looked over.

Apparently there was an easier trail to the ruins from the valley below. There was a Xanadu ranch truck at the base of the rim far below, but no one was in sight.

He lifted his hand, signaling Christy to come closer. The sound of her approaching footsteps was almost lost in the long sigh of the wind through the cedars.

"They're still inside," Cain said quietly.

Christy let out a long breath. "All right."

"I still think I should take the pistol."

"When was the last time you shot a gun?" she asked.

"Never. When was the last time you killed a man?"

"With a handgun at this range, killing won't be a problem. I'd be lucky to hit the damned alcove."

Cain's smile flashed against his beard.

"But that stretch of open rock is dangerous," Christy said. "If someone is shooting at you, I can at least shoot back."

She was right and Cain knew it. He just didn't like it worth a damn.

"You can come as far as the rock pile below the alcove. No farther, Red. I mean it."

With that, Cain lowered himself into the cleft. Christy shoved the pistol into her waistband and followed.

The air went from cool to chilly as the sunlight vanished. Christy gathered her jacket and zipped it up against the chill. The pistol felt cold and awkward against her stomach.

They made their way slowly down the cleft until they reached the spot where rock steps had been hammered into the sloping front of the mesa. The way across was exposed and dangerous.

"I'll go first," Cain said softly. "Stay put until I find out what's going on. After I raise my hand, come in carefully."

When Christy didn't answer, he turned and took her chin in his hand.

"If someone comes sneaking up behind me," he said flatly, "there won't be any time for questions. There will only be time to reach back and send whoever it is headfirst off the mesa. *Promise me it won't be you.*"

The bleak clarity of Cain's eyes left no doubt that he was serious.

"I promise," she whispered.

He looked at Christy, saw that she meant it, and nodded.

"But I don't like it!" she muttered.

"That makes two of us."

Cain released Christy's chin and turned back toward the alcove. But instead of starting across the rock, he froze.

Hutton and Autry were framed against the alcove's dark entry, facing one another. Autry was carrying a knapsack in one hand. Hutton carried nothing. He was standing nonchalantly, his hands shoved deep into the oversized pockets of one of his own designer jackets.

For a minute longer both men stood atop the rubble pile, talking urgently. Finally Autry reached into the knapsack and jerked out what looked like a two-way radio and began working over it.

A chill that had nothing to do with the cool air went over Cain as he thought of what Danner had said about dynamite.

"How good are you with that pistol?" Cain asked tightly. "Can you pick off Autry?"

Christy's eyelids flinched, but she said nothing as she measured the range.

"From here?" she asked.

"Yes."

"I doubt that I could hit him, but I can sure as hell give him a scare."

"Do it. Fast!"

An instant later a shot echoed. Autry doubled over and staggered backward.

Christy froze in the act of pulling the pistol free of her waistband.

"I didn't—" she began.

Another shot cut off Christy's words. The sound of the report was tinny and flat, almost like the crack of a whip. It echoed into the alcove and out the other side.

Before the sound faded, Autry was on his knees. Peter Hutton stood over him, a gun in his hand.

While Cain and Christy watched in shocked silence, Hutton put the small pistol against the back of Autry's head and pulled the trigger a third time. Autry pitched forward and lay face down on the rubble pile. He didn't move again.

Hutton climbed down to where Autry had fallen. Without hesitation, he put the muzzle of the small pistol against Autry and fired until there were no bullets left.

"Jesus Christ," Cain said under his breath. "I met some cold sons of bitches in prison, but nothing like that."

Closing her eyes, Christy tried to banish the sight from her memory. She clenched her teeth against the nausea rising in her throat.

"Don't ever call yourself a murderer again," she said through her teeth. "Hutton is everything you are *not*."

Hutton looked down at Autry, then shook himself like a man awakening from a dream. He put the pistol back in his pocket, bent down, and grabbed Autry's feet.

Grunting with effort, Hutton began dragging the slack body back to the alcove. After he got to the sill, he wrestled his victim into a sitting position and hauled him up onto the sill.

When Hutton was finished, he rubbed his palms on his trousers with a gesture that said he didn't like getting dirty. He scrambled up onto the sill himself and tried to pitch Autry's body forward into the alcove.

It wasn't an easy process. Hutton had to push and pull and finally half lift and half shove the corpse inside.

The instant Hutton disappeared from sight, Cain straightened up.

"What are you going to do?" Christy asked.

"Catch a murderer before he thinks to reload."

Cain left the cover of the cleft and started over the sandstone in a controlled rush. Halfway across, he switched leads and swiftly covered the rest of the dangerous open space.

Christy was right on his heels. When she reached the rubble pile, Cain's hand shot out and pulled her down. His other hand went over her mouth, forcing her to be silent and very still.

Hutton was talking to someone inside the alcove. His breathing was ragged.

"I told you Jo—would get you. You thought you were so damn smart, fucking her and me at the same time. But I was smarter—than both of you."

There was a grunt and hoarse curses.

"Damn you, Ted. You weigh a ton. Pick up your feet."

Cain put his mouth right against Christy's ear. When he spoke, his voice was a bare thread of sound.

"Hutton's talking to himself."

Christy nodded.

"I want the son of a bitch alive," Cain said. "Just in case Danner has any doubts."

She nodded.

"Stay here."

Christy didn't nod her head.

"Damn it, Red."

She kissed the hand covering her mouth and looked at Cain with steady eyes.

"Then at least stay here long enough to cover my climb," Cain said.

Christy nodded.

Slowly Cain slid his hand away from her mouth.

"Stay safe, love," he whispered.

Then he turned away and began climbing toward the alcove with smooth, powerful motions.

Christy pulled the heavy pistol from her waistband, thumbed the hammer back into the full cocked position, braced her elbows on a boulder, and took up a two-handed shooting stance. The muzzle of the pistol was aimed right at the point where Hutton would appear for his climb back down to the truck far below.

Phrases from Hutton's dialogue with the dead drifted down the rubble slope.

" . . . kill her . . . vicious succubus . . . threaten *me* . . ."

Cain never paused. He moved steadily and carefully, a predator on the stalk, testing each rock to make sure it wouldn't move and make a noise that would betray his presence.

Hutton's voice became fainter and fainter until finally it vanished. Apparently he was dragging Autry all the way to the back of the alcove.

The memory of stone shifting just a bit and a timber snapping echoed in Christy's mind. She wondered if the echoes of Hutton's little pistol had further undermined the strength of whatever bond was holding the massive wedge of sandstone in place.

Cain reached the sill and lay back against the wall, listening intently. He eased his head up, took a fast look, and ducked back down. After a long count of ten, he looked again, more thoroughly, his eyes probing the shadows.

He raised his hand a bit, waving Christy forward.

Slowly, she lowered the hammer on the pistol. She scrambled as quietly as she could up the rocks, following the route Cain had taken. When she reached his side, she was breathing hard.

He pointed to his eyes, to her, and to the sill. Cautiously she raised her head until she could look into the alcove.

Hutton had managed to drag Autry halfway back to the frail supports bracing the sandstone flake. Now he was standing with his hands on his hips, catching his breath and staring down at the dead man.

"There really was no other choice," Hutton said. "I couldn't trust you not to tell. I couldn't trust anyone. If you talked . . ."

Hutton breathed heavily.

"Well, it just couldn't happen. I'm not like other people. I can't go to jail. It wouldn't be fair. It wouldn't make sense. I'm worth a hundred like you."

Hutton's voice was matter-of-fact, the voice of someone pointing out that the sun rises in the east and sets in the west. Nothing unusual. Everyone knows it. A simple fact of life.

Or death.

A chill seeped through Christy. For the first time she truly understood how terribly thin the margin was between complete self-absorption and clinical madness.

Hutton and Jo-Jo had been perfectly matched in more than their physical beauty. Each believed he or she was the center of the universe. Each believed he or she was too special for the rules that governed other lives. Rules were for the little people, the ugly people.

The flyover people in the flyover states.

Bending down, Hutton grabbed Autry's feet again. "Time to go, babe. I've got a plane to catch."

With a grunt and a heave, Hutton resumed dragging Autry far back into the alcove.

Cain touched Christy's shoulder, drawing her

away from the view of the alcove. He held his mouth so close to her ear she could feel his breath.

"He'll be out of sight in about thirty seconds. I'm going in after him."

Frantically Christy shook her head.

"It's all right," Cain said. "I've been watching him. He hasn't had time to reload. In any case, *no shooting.* Back in the alcove, even his little pocket pistol could bring down the works on my head."

Before Christy could say anything, Cain went over the sill and landed soundlessly inside the alcove. Heart hammering frantically, she watched him ghost forward.

"*Ciao,* babe." Hutton's voice echoed eerily inside the alcove. "Say hello to Jo and the Sisters for me."

In the silence that followed, a piece of debris rolled underneath Cain's foot. The sound was shockingly loud.

Hutton spun around just as Cain ducked behind a ruined wall. Hutton saw nothing but a flicker of shadow flowing over darker shadow.

"Jo?" he called uneasily.

There was no answer but the spectral silence of the alcove.

Hutton reached into his pocket. With the automatic motions of a man performing a familiar task, he reloaded the small pistol.

"Jo? That you, babe? You want to play some more naughty games?"

A throttled scream ached in Christy's throat. Every step Hutton took brought him closer to the instant when he would discover Cain crouched and helpless behind the wall.

Christy pulled the heavy pistol from beneath her jacket. She sensed as much as saw the sharp, negative motion of Cain's head. She knew what he was afraid of, stone hanging by a thread, aching to slide.

But it might not.

If Hutton saw Cain, there would be no doubt of the outcome. Cain would be murdered.

Before Christy let that happen, she would pull the trigger and take her chances on the ceiling coming down. Tilting her head back, she spoke to the rock hanging overhead.

"Peter," she called huskily.

The single word bounced off the red sandstone, echoing around the alcove until it was impossible to say which direction the call had come from.

"Peter . . ."

Christy used the second call to disguise the muted, distinctive snick and slide of steel as she cocked Danner's gun and circled to the left, trying to draw Hutton's attention away from the place where Cain crouched.

Hutton looked around wildly. "Jo! How did you find me?"

"I'll always be able to find you," Christy said in a low, throaty voice. "Just like lightning always finds the ground."

The voice came from a different place, for she was still circling to the side, hoping to lure Hutton away from Cain's hiding place.

"But you're dead!" Hutton said in exasperation. "Ted followed you. He watched you walk to my plane. He punched the button, and ten minutes later you were toast!"

"Yes, I'm dead."

Christy's voice came from a different quarter. Hutton turned, tracking the sound.

"But you always liked demons, didn't you?" she asked huskily. "Well, here I am, babe. Your own private demon."

The voice was as elusive as a shadow in darkness. Hutton walked forward only one step, then stopped.

"No good, babe," he said. "What fun is it if I can't see you?"

Slowly Christy's finger tightened on the trigger. She hadn't been able to lure Hutton away from Cain's hiding place. At any moment he could be discovered.

The pistol was still in Hutton's hand.

"I can see *you*," she murmured, sliding off to the side.

But now the pistol was tracking the teasing voice with its familiar, exciting spice of malice.

Hutton turned and took a hesitant step toward the voice.

Relief swept through Christy. If Hutton kept turning, his back would soon be to Cain.

All she had to do was keep moving and pray Hutton didn't start shooting at ghosts.

"Don't be afraid," Christy said huskily, moving farther aside. "I brought the baby powder."

"But there's no bathtub," Hutton complained. "And you haven't just had sex with someone. If I can't wash you afterward and powder you, it's just no good, babe."

His voice was thin, peevish, the voice of a child whose ritual had been disturbed.

Christy opened her mouth, but no words came out. She had no more ideas about how to use the fractures in Hutton's mind against him.

Cain did.

He unwound from his crouch in a long, low tackle that knocked Hutton far back into the alcove. Flailing for balance, Hutton tripped over Autry's corpse and fell backward. His head slammed up against one of the supporting timbers. The crack of skull meeting wood echoed in the alcove.

Hutton fell forward in an oddly graceful, bone-less sprawl.

As Christy ran to Cain, he ripped the little pistol from Hutton's hand.

"Is he—"

"Just unconscious," Cain said, cutting across Christy's question.

"Thank God."

He gave her an odd look. "I didn't know you cared for good old Peter."

Christy shuddered. "He deserves to die. But you don't deserve to be his executioner."

The back of Cain's fingers brushed over Christy's cheek with surprising tenderness.

"What now?" she asked.

"Now we wake Golden Boy up and tell him all about the new designs in his future."

"Gray bars and prison blues?" Christy asked, trying not to laugh.

Because if she laughed, she didn't know if she would be able to stop short of screaming.

"More like white jackets and rubber rooms," Cain said. "The guy is certifiably crackers."

Christy shuddered. "I noticed."

"You see a lantern anywhere?" Cain asked. "I can tell Hutton is breathing, but not much more."

She looked around, spotted a gleam of metal in the middle of the supporting timbers, and started for it. As she bent down to pick up the lantern, a very faint glow from the deep crack in the stone over her head caught her eye. She cocked her head and peered up into the opening.

"Cain!"

The stark fear in Christy's voice brought Cain to his feet.

"What is it?" he asked.

"Oh, God. Autry—the plane—"

He punched the button, and ten minutes later you were toast.

Cain pulled Christy back and looked up into the crack.

It was crammed with dynamite, wires, and an electronic package with faintly glowing digital numbers counting off an unknown amount of time to explosion.

Autry had triggered the bomb before he died.

"Out!" Cain said.

Christy had no choice. Cain's fingers were clamped around her upper arm like iron bands, forcing her through the darkness without regard to the rubble. He propelled her up and over the low wall, dragged her over the pile of rubble, and rushed her across the exposed sandstone steps at a reckless pace.

On hands and knees, Christy scrambled through the tunnel, straightened up, and dashed through the cleft, only to be brought up short by the wall at the head of the mesa.

Cain bent and held out his linked hands. "Put your foot—"

Christy was already doing it. He straightened and lifted his hands at the same time, boosting her up onto the plateau with enough force to send her rolling up and over the lip at the top.

As Christy staggered to her feet, Cain shot up out of the cleft, grabbed her arm, and set off at a dead run away from the mesa edge. The ground flew beneath their feet.

Just before they reached the truck, a sharp, dry thunder rolled through the canyon.

Instants later, the mesa answered.

With a prolonged grinding roar, sandstone pulled away from the mesa's edge. The ceiling of the alcove hung unsupported for a timeless moment. And then the ceiling came down, dragging a piece of the mesa with it.

The alcove was destroyed in one crushing instant, and the remains were buried under a mountain of jumbled stone.

"She Who Faces the Sun was right," Christy whispered as the last rumble of shifting stone faded.

"What?" Cain asked.

"Whoever disturbs the Sisters . . . dies."

Epilogue

The hot spring steamed and seethed gently around Christy and Cain. Overhead the Milky Way burned like a ghostly silver bridge between the undiscovered past and the unknown future.

Moki slept nearby in a nest of blankets that had been carefully arranged to accommodate his healing wound. Christy reached out and eased a corner of cloth over the dog's neck so that the chill night air was shut out. Moki's tail wagged beneath the blankets, and a long pink tongue slid over her hand.

"You're spoiling him," Cain said.

"Yeah. Fun, isn't it?"

He laughed softly and pulled Christy through the water until she was sitting on his lap, facing him, her legs straddling his.

"Want to spoil me too?" he asked.

"What do you think I've been doing for the last two weeks?"

"Spoiling me thoroughly."

"Thoroughly?"

"Addictively."

Whatever Christy had been about to say was lost in a husky sound as Cain's hands slid up to her breasts.

"Have I spoiled you a little bit too?" he asked against her mouth.

"Why do you think I've been hanging around?"

"Moki."

Laughing softly, Christy ran the tip of her tongue around his lips.

"Danner?" Cain offered.

"Wash your mouth out with soap."

He laughed. "Oh, he didn't turn out so bad."

"Was that before or after he started whitewashing Peter Hutton?"

Cain's shrug sent currents of water stirring between Christy's breasts.

"So in the eyes of the world, Hutton becomes a modern *artiste* who gave his all for his design when God blinked and an alcove vanished," Christy said bitterly.

Cain made a neutral sound.

"And Autry becomes a scorned lover who killed Jo-Jo rather than lose her to another man," Christ said.

"Don't forget that She Who Faces the Sun also got something out of the deal."

Christy took a deep breath and let it out slowly.

"Yes," she said. "I'll never forget her eyes when we handed her the second tortoise."

"Like watching the sun come up twice in one day," Cain agreed softly. "A little whitewash isn't such a big price to pay for that, is it?"

A quiver of heat that owed nothing to the pool expanded through Christy as Cain's hands moved beneath the water, slowly stroking her.

"Not a big price at all," she admitted.

"Beats explaining to the sound-bite set that your beautiful famous sister was a thief and a would-be murderer," Cain murmured, "and that Peter Hutton was a kinky killer with the face of a Greek god."

"And that Danner was a fool?"

"So was Jo-Jo. Flyboy spent every last cent of their money." Cain shrugged again, sending currents stirring. "We're all fools, one way or another."

"You aren't," Christy said.

His breath came in with a soft, ripping sound as he felt her hands sliding down his torso, curling round him, savoring his naked strength.

Blindly Cain's right hand searched along the edge of the pool until he found the foil packet he had left on a rock.

"I sure as hell am a fool, though," Cain said. "I'm such a fool that I'm thinking of asking a woman who hates the West to marry me and live here."

"Funny," Christy said, her breath catching. "I was thinking of asking a man who hates the city to marry me and live there."

Cain became utterly still. Then he fitted his mouth to Christy's in a kiss whose hunger was both complex and elemental. When the kiss finally ended, both of them were breathing hard.

Silently Cain held out the tiny packet, a question in his eyes. Christy eased it from his fingers . . .

And threw it away.

Foil gleamed in the instant before it vanished beneath the black water of the hot springs.

Then Christy was fitting herself to Cain in a slow, sleek union that was like nothing either had ever felt before. The intimacy was stunning, perfect, hotter than the seething water.

Cain groaned and fought for self-control.

"Which will it be?" he asked through his teeth. "West or East?"

"Yes."

"What?"

"Both," she said against his lips. "Summer here. Winter there. I don't have a job at the moment but I still want to tell New York a thing or two."

"And when it's not summer or winter?"

Christy moved over Cain with a long, shivering sigh.

"We'll negotiate."

"One of us will lose."

"No. We'll both win."

And they did.

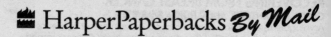

HarperPaperbacks By Mail

HarperPaperback's
"RECOVERING FROM SERIES"
For everyone who shares
in the healing process

RECOVERING FROM A STROKE
JUNG AHN, M.D. AND GARY FERGUSON
A straight-forward guide that offers patients,
friends, and family members insight into the
vital role they play in stroke rehabilitation. A
glossary of terms, answers to commonly asked
questions, and clear explanations provide a
better understanding of what has occurred and
prepares the reader for what lies ahead.

Jung Ahn, M.D., is currently Clinical Associate
Professor of Rehabilitation Medicine at New
York University's School of Medicine.

Gary Ferguson is a science and health writer for
national magazines.

ISBN: 0-06-104137-8 $8.99/$11.99 CANADA

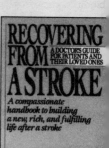

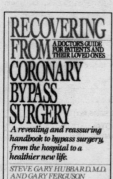

RECOVERING FROM CORONARY
BYPASS SURGERY
STEVE G. HUBBARD, M.D.
AND GARY FERGUSON
A revealing and reassuring handbook for the
thousands of heart disease patients for whom
bypass surgery has given a second chance at
life. Dr. Hubbard clearly explains everything
patients and their families need to know about
the operation, the recovery, and how to
vigorously approach a healthy new life.

Steve G. Hubbard, M.D., is a cardiovascular
surgeon in private practice in Billings, Montana.

Gary Ferguson is a science and health writer for
national magazines.

ISBN: 0-06-104138-6 $8.99/$11.99 CANADA

RECOVERING FROM BREAST CANCER
CAROL FABIAN, M.D. AND ANDREA WARREN

A valuable resource for women diagnosed with breast cancer as well as their friends and family. *Recovering from Breast Cancer* presents an overview of how cancer develops, ways to communicate with health professionals, treatment options, case histories, plus many other important issues. The information provided empowers and encourages the patient living with breast cancer and urges family and friends to take an active role in the patient's recovery.

Carol Fabian, M.D., is Professor of Medicine, Division of Clinical Oncology, at the University of Kansas Medical Center. She is the founder and director of the High Risk Breast Clinic at the university and directs several breast cancer research projects.

Andrea Warren is a freelance writer who specializes in women's health and social issues.

ISBN: 0-06-104135-1 $8.99/$11.99 CANADA

RECOVERING FROM A HYSTERECTOMY
DENA E. HARRIS, M.D. AND HELENE MACLEAN

In this immensely informative guide to hysterectomy recovery, Dr. Harris begins with a tour of the female body and ends with a fearless healing process. Patients and their families come to realize that having a hysterectomy is not the end of femininity, sexuality, or an active life.

Dena E. Harris, M.D., currently runs a private OB/GYN practice in New York City as well as serving as Associate Director of Quality Assurance in the Department of GYN in the infirmary of Beekman Downtown Hospital.

Helene MacLean is a senior writer for *The Child Care Encyclopedia* and a contributor to *Everywoman's Health* and Columbia University's Home Medical Encyclopedia.

ISBN: 0-06-104136-X $8.99/$11.99 CANADA

AVAILABLE WHEREVER YOU BUY BOOKS OR ORDER DIRECT—SIMPLY USE THE COUPON BELOW

MAIL TO: **Harper Collins Publishers**
P. O. Box 588 Dunmore, PA 18512-0588
OR CALL: (800) 331-3761 (Visa/MasterCard)

Yes, please send me the books I have checked:

☐ **RECOVERING FROM A STROKE**
   (0-06-104137-8) $8.99/$11.99 Canada

☐ **RECOVERING FROM CORONARY BYPASS SURGERY**
   (0-06-104138-6) $8.99/$11.99 Canada

☐ **RECOVERING FROM BREAST CANCER**
   (0-06-104135-1) $8.99/$11.99 Canada

☐ **RECOVERING FROM A HYSTERECTOMY**
   (0-06-104136-X) $8.99/$11.99 Canada

SUBTOTAL .... $_____
POSTAGE AND HANDLING .... $ 2.00*
SALES TAX (Add applicable sales tax) .... $_____
                    TOTAL: $_____

* ORDER ALL 4 TITLES AND POSTAGE & HANDLING IS FREE!
Remit in US funds, do not send cash.

Name _____

Address _____

City _____

State _____ Zip _____

Allow up to 6 weeks delivery.
Prices subject to change.
(Valid only in US & Canada)

HO361

HarperPaperbacks *By Mail*

READ THE NOVELS
THE CRITICS ARE RAVING ABOUT!

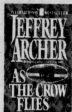

AS THE CROW FLIES
Jeffrey Archer

When Charlie Trumper inherits his grandfather's vegetable barrow, he also inherits his enterprising spirit. But before Charlie can realize his greatest success, he must embark on an epic journey that carries him across three continents and through the triumphs and disasters of the twentieth century.

"Archer is a master entertainer."
— *Time* magazine

FAMILY PICTURES
Sue Miller

Over the course of forty years, the Eberhardt family struggles to survive a flood tide of upheaval and heartbreak, love and betrayal, passion and pain...hoping they can someday heal their hearts and return to the perfect family in the pictures from the past.

"Absolutely flawless." — *Chicago Tribune*

PALINDROME
Stuart Woods

Seeking an escape from her brutal ex-husband, photographer Liz Barwick retreats to an island paradise off Georgia's coast. But when a killer launches a series of gruesome murders, Liz discovers that there is no place to hide—not even in her lover's arms.

"Moves along with hurricane velocity."
— *Los Angeles Times Book Review*

THE CROWN OF COLUMBUS
Louise Erdrich · Michael Dorris

Vivian Twostar—single, very pregnant, Native American anthropologist—has found Columbus' legendary lost diary in the basement of the Dartmouth Library. Together with her teenage son Nash and Roger Williams—consummate academic and father of her baby—Vivian follows the riddle of the diary on a quest for "the greatest treasure of Europe."

"Compelling entertainment."
— *The New York Tim*

BILLY BATHGATE
E.L. Doctorow

In the poverty-stricken Bronx of the Depression era, gangster Dutch Schultz take young Billy Bathgate under his crooked wing. With grace and vivid realism, Bill Bathgate recounts his extraordinary education in crime, love, life, and death in th dazzling and decadent world of a big-time rackets empire about to crumble.

"Spellbinding." — *The Boston Herald*

Harper Paperbacks By Mail

OUTER BANKS
Anne Rivers Siddons

Four sorority sisters bound by friendship spent two idyllic spring breaks at Nag's Head, North Carolina. Now, thirty years later, they are coming back to recapture the magic of those early years and confront the betrayal that shaped four young girls into women and set them all adrift on the Outer Banks.

"A wonderful saga." — *Cosmopolitan*

MAGIC HOUR
Susan Isaacs

A witty mixture of murder, satire, and romance set in the fashionable Hamptons, Long Island's beach resort of choice. Movie producer Sy Spencer has been shot dead beside his pool. Topping the list of suspects is Sy's ex-wife, Bonnie. But it isn't before long that Detective Steve Brady is ignoring all the rules and evidence to save her.

"Vintage Susan Isaacs."
— *The New York Times Book Review*

ANY WOMAN'S BLUES
Erica Jong

Leila Sand's life has left her feeling betrayed and empty. Her efforts to change result in a sensual and spiritual odyssey that takes her from Alcoholics Anonymous meetings to glittering parties to a liaison with a millionaire antiques merchant. Along the way, she learns the rules of love and the secret of happiness.

"A very timely and important book...Jong's greatest heroine." — *Elle*

For Fastest Service—Visa and MasterCard Holders Call

1-800-331-3761 refer to offer HO471

MAIL TO: **Harper Collins Publishers**
P. O. Box 588 Dunmore, PA 18512-0588
OR CALL FOR FASTEST SERVICE: (800) 331-3761

Yes, please send me the books I have checked:
- ☐ AS THE CROW FLIES (0-06-109934-1) $6.50
- ☐ FAMILY PICTURES (0-06-109925-2) $5.95
- ☐ PALINDROME (0-06-109936-8) $5.99
- ☐ THE CROWN OF COLUMBUS (0-06-109957-0) $5.99
- ☐ BILLY BATHGATE (0-06-100007-8) $5.95
- ☐ OUTER BANKS (0-06-109973-2) $5.99
- ☐ MAGIC HOUR (0-06-109948-1) $5.99
- ☐ ANY WOMAN'S BLUES (0-06-109916-3) $5.95

SUBTOTAL .... $_____
POSTAGE AND HANDLING .... $ 2.00*_____
SALES TAX (Add state sales tax) .... $_____
            TOTAL: $_____

(Remit in US funds.
Do not send cash.)

Name _____

Address _____

City _____

State _____ Zip _____

Allow up to 6 weeks delivery.
Prices subject to change.

*FREE postage & handling if you buy four or more books! Valid in U.S/CAN only.   HO471